THE BYGONE MASK

JOSEPH R. LALLO

—·—

CONTENTS

PROLOGUE

It's not personal. It's just business. It was a common refrain. Even in the most stale, overused idioms it was understood that business was inherently impersonal. Family was personal, business was not. That's how it should be. That's how it always had been, even for the Maskers, who managed to be both a family and a business. In the same conversation, one could easily feel the sharp divide between matters of family importance and matters of personal importance. Within the Masker clan, the distinction had always existed, and both elements of life were present in equal measure.

But not here, and not now.

It started with the room. They weren't in one of the lower floors of Masker's Antiquities. They weren't gathered around the dining room table with biscuits and wine on the table. They weren't in The Fox and Log, enjoying a pint between negotiations and anecdotes. They weren't even in Beffshire. This was a neutral location. Cold, detached from any of their lives. It was in a town as near to the precise midpoint between Beffshire and East Shalia as could be located. A small side room in a large hall in a midsized city with a forgettable name. The refreshments were far from refreshing. Tepid water, stale bread, sliced cheese that had started to get hard around the edges. Food and drink calculated to ward off hunger while ensuring that pesky little things like enjoyment wouldn't get in the way of the discussion.

This was business. Nothing personal about it. The fact that everyone in the room was related was simply an unpleasant coincidence.

Fel curled his nose at the fumes emanating from the man across from him. Fel had spent every spare leisure moment in The Fox and Log since he was twelve years old and was no stranger to the stink of various vices and general disregard for hygiene. But the smell of badgerweed always struck him as the olfactory equivalent of having the sunshine in his eyes, and Thaddeus Graves practically breathed the stuff. He was situated on the far side of the table, opposite Fel, and silently observing the discourse as though he were some sort of referee. To Fel's right was his older sister Epiphany. Fanny to family and friends, though no one had called her that since they'd walked through the door. Presently they were in a lull in the conversation, that uncomfortable space between greetings and other mechanical, disingenuous pleasantries and the real meat and potatoes of the meeting. This gave Fel the opportunity to regard Epiphany in relation to her adversary in this little discussion: Euphoria Graves, née Masker.

Euphoria was the oldest sibling, and it had been years since Fel and Epiphany had last seen her. She'd eloped with the mercifully absent Jonathan Graves and fully embraced her new place within the Graves family. The years had changed her. Fel honestly wouldn't have recognized her, not as her old self, anyway. The youthful mischief that had been a permanent part of her expression had been eased away to calm, collected focus. She'd let her hair grow longer and a bit more wild then, with curls that absolutely would not be tamed. Her hair was now pulled back into a ruthlessly tight bun, the sheer tension leaving her hair looking barely wavy. But even if he hadn't recognized her as his sister, he would have recognized her as a Masker. With her business face on, she was the spitting image of her mother when she was dealing with a particularly trying customer. That she would look upon her own flesh and blood with such an expression felt like a slap in the face.

"No sense dillydallying," Euphoria said. "We are here for a reason."

"That we are," said Epiphany, attempting to match her sister's tone.

"How long does it take to yank your hair back like that, Fora?" Fel asked.

Both of his sisters shot him an identical sharp look.

"No one calls me Fora anymore, Fel. And I'll thank you to treat me with a degree of professionalism," Euphoria said.

"It's just that I remember when Mom had to comb it, she practically had to put a boot against your back to get the leverage to pull the knots out," he said, reaching across the table to pluck up a piece of cheese.

"He really hasn't matured, has he?" Euphoria said, turning her weary gaze to Epiphany.

"No. Fel hasn't changed since he learned to tie his shoes. And you'd know that if you'd so much as sent a letter in the last few years. But that's not what we're here to discuss, is it?" Epiphany said.

Fel grinned. It was nice to know Fanny still had some fire smoldering under the professional facade she was being forced to wear. He broke off the hardened corners of the slice and nibbled at the cheese.

"No. We are here to discuss the Bolivans. It is long past time that something was done about them. They have been a thorn in our side for decades," Euphoria said.

"Who exactly are you referring to when you say 'our'?" Fel asked.

"The Graves clan."

"You haven't been *in* the Graves clan for decades." Fel made a motion with his hand, encompassing Epiphany and himself. "The Bolivans have only been a thorn in *our* side for a few months."

"I am speaking as a representative. Please stop trying to derail the discussion." Euphoria took a sip of water. "Now, as I was saying. For a generation, the Graves family and the Bolivan family have butted heads. We have both been expanding for quite some time, and even before that began, our territories shared a border. Now they share a hotly contested overlap. Their ruthlessness and our cunning achieved a sort of equilibrium in recent years. There was no shortage of clashes, but they've produced very little motion in either direction. A stalemate, as it were. We *believed* that it was due to a grudging acceptance that we were competitors equal to their skill. Now we learn it may be due to their access to our sentry flame, the Voice. When one gains insight into the dealings of another, advancing one's plans can be done silently and invisibly."

"Not so invisible anymore," Fel said.

"Yes. Hence the need for this meeting. The Bolivan family has attempted to extend their tendrils down into Beffshire. We now have something in common."

"Aside from blood?" Fel said, flicking a bit of hardened cheese into the corner of the room.

"If our strained familial ties are going to keep you from taking this conversation seriously, I invite you to leave," Euphoria said.

"And cut this lovely reunion short? Not on your life," he said.

"You need our help taking care of a rival family," Epiphany said.

"I am proposing we work together, now that we've both been placed in a hazardous position by the Bolivan family," Euphoria said.

"Forgive me, but you haven't conducted business in a way that would motivate us to trust you," Epiphany said. "You sent Thaddeus to initiate trade. He was absolutely not forthcoming with his motivations or origins. You were using us. Now you want to work with us because an unchecked oversight in your security has placed us both in danger. You aren't starting from a position of strength."

"If we were in a position of strength, we wouldn't have approached you to begin with. I'll admit, our dealings thus far have been what one might rightly call manipulative. But circumstances have changed. Holding a grudge will only strengthen the Bolivans and weaken us."

"Seems like you folks have a big organization," Fel said. "Big trade network, lots of employees."

"Compared to the Bolivans, we run a very tight ship," Thaddeus said.

"Yeah, but the Masker family is four people. Down from five," Fel said.

"I understand you have recently acquired the aid of a paper mage. And there's the matter of your partnership with Verfessa," Thad said.

"Tome isn't a part of the crew," Epiphany said. "And we're not talking about Verfessa. The valid point here is that you're a big, powerful group. That you suddenly need to conscript our little circle suggests we have something you want. Something you can't just steal and run away with."

"You have a few things," Euphoria said. "Not the least of which is Fel. He has proved far more capable than I remember him."

"Hey, when I helped you get ahold of that dress you were after before the big dance, I didn't hear you complaining about me not being capable enough."

"*You* helped her get it?" Epiphany hissed.

"Who'd you think did it? Dad?" Fel said.

Euphoria tapped her finger on the table, clicking her nail to get their attention.

"On topic, please. As I was saying, Fel has a set of skills and a willingness to disregard threats to life and limb, combined with an implicit trust as a member of the family, that is unmatched within the Graves family. Even our best operatives are more measured and cautious. It impairs their capacity to meet some of the challenges the Bolivans present."

"Just being family doesn't make someone trustworthy," Epiphany muttered. "But fine, you need Fel. I assume that's not all. You probably need Dad, too."

"In order to achieve our goals, we will need some contraptions repaired, and they've proved themselves beyond the skill of our own technicians," said Euphoria.

"Sounds like you've got a plan," Fel said.

"I don't have a plan. I have a proposal. We have acquired a contraption which we believe, if it could be repaired, would enable us to locate any instances of the Graves family flame. Our proposal is as follows. We provide the contraption to our father to repair it. After that, we will select three agents who will join forces with Fel to track down and acquire and/or extinguish any instances of the family flame currently in the possession of the Bolivan family. Along the way, if possible, steps should be taken to ensure they will not be able to reacquire the flame. It would be prudent to endeavor to cripple them to the degree that they will lack the capacity or motivation to act maliciously against either the Graves or Masker family."

"Fel isn't getting into a carriage with three of your people. I'm not putting him into a situation where he will be outnumbered," Epiphany said.

"I realize that you have reason to be measured with your trust, but you surely don't fear that we have some sort of malicious intent," Euphoria said.

"Lost trust is lost trust. You're hiding things from us, and you were spying on us. Until you show your scheme, we're not going to take any chances with what else you might be concealing."

"If there were more operatives available to you, I would suggest a balanced amount, but we have discussed it extensively and we don't believe that any fewer than four individuals will be sufficient. And given the fact that the entire enterprise is being done to restore security, we don't feel that people outside the families would be appropriate."

"You want us to trust you with a three-to-one imbalance? Give us a reason to trust you. Tell us what this was all about," Epiphany said.

"What precisely do you mean?" Euphoria said.

"You know exactly what I mean. What is the clockwork diamond? Why are you after all these strange items? Where did you get that book that contained the codes to the Greater Lands Wall? Tell us what was so important to you that you decided to break the years-long silence by tricking us into doing business with you?"

Euphoria leaned back slightly and folded her hands on her lap. Her expression barely changed.

"I suppose with the proper equipment and care, Fel and one agent of our choosing could perform adequately."

Fel burst out laughing.

"The secret is more important than the mission!" he said. "You'd rather throw away whatever careful calculations and stuff that you mulled over than let us know why you were lying to us."

She glared at him. "Our business is our business. Your business is your business. We won't dig into your business if you don't dig into ours."

"Look, I always knew you weren't coming back. But I always sort of thought you didn't *really* change," said Fel. "You were being a rebel like you always were. But you *definitely* changed. The only question now is whether you changed because you married into the Graves family or you changed and *then* married into the Graves family."

"Regardless of how you feel, this is a problem that needs to be solved. We have half the solution. You have the other half. If we waste time trying to develop the missing pieces on our own, more damage will be done and more lives will be lost," Euphoria said. "We set aside what's happened, we work together on this, and when that is through, if we must, we go our separate ways once more."

Epiphany casually reached her hand toward the table and froze. She realized, an instant before Fel did, that she was about to tap the table precisely as Euphoria had. Instead she reached out and grabbed some bread from the tray, fooling no one, and nibbled on it.

"If this is business, then it is business. Let's begin the give and take," Epiphany said.

"First demand," Fel said. "We get some booze in here, and some meat. If I'm going to listen to my sisters arguing about what *I'm* going to have to do, I'm not doing it sober."

Chapter 1

Martin Masker had been quite busy for the last few weeks. In and of itself, there was nothing strange or surprising about that. He was the only one in the family with the skill and knowhow to consistently repair and maintain the contraptions that made up the bulk of their earnings. His plate was perpetually full. But a man doesn't keep the shelves of the most successful antiquity shop on the continent full without a supreme amount of focus. And focus can be as much of a liability as an asset. Presently, the state of his workshop was a fine indication of just how debilitating focus could be.

To a casual observer, the chaos of the workshop wouldn't have appeared substantially different. To someone who knew and worked with Martin, it was more than evident that this wasn't the ordered, structured chaos of his personal sorting system. This was the disordered, mangled chaos of a dozen different tasks dropped midway through completion in favor of the *one* task that actually interested him. The shelves upstairs were still full. The important jobs were still getting done. But in this case this was in spite of his focus rather than because of it.

Martin wasn't alone in his workshop. In one corner sat an odd collection of chains poking out of a canvas sack. Equal parts contraption and pet, the device known as Oiler was contentedly clicking away at a puzzle box. Oiler was as much of a nuisance as a help in the earliest days of its presence in the workshop. For someone who occasionally took apart contraptions to see how they functioned, having a mechanism dead set on repairing broken contraptions could be a bothersome addition to the shop. But the two had learned to coexist once Martin worked out precisely how broken was too broken for Oiler to latch on to something. Getting a contraption into enough pieces for Oiler to no longer understand what it had once been was enough for it to sit pleasantly and await a suitable task. At the moment, it had paused its perpetual puzzle solving to stare vaguely at the corner of the room, claws motionless about the box.

The other company, somewhat less common and significantly less helpful, was Tome Inkbrand. Tome's interactions with contraptions were generally limited to idle musing about their creators or the reason for their creation. The young man was filled with questions and was truly gifted at weaving a line of thinking that was simultaneously fascinating and fruitless.

Martin adjusted a set of magnifying lenses positioned over his eyes and held up the lantern that technically contained a third companion, Wick. Wick was kind enough to avoid speaking unless spoken to, leaving Tome to fill the shop with whatever knot his mind saw fit to tie and untie.

"One wonders why, precisely, the Bygone ancestors saw fit to render their creation in *this* form," Tome said.

"I cannot say the shape of the contraption has been of much interest to me," Martin said without looking up. "Hand me the spring clamp, would you? That one there. The number four."

Tome rummaged in a box and produced the requested item.

"Martin, you are jabbing your tools into a faceless simulacrum of a human head. It is said that form follows function. What function would be properly served by something that resembles a human head?"

"Form and function aren't always related," Martin said. "The music boxes are terribly ornate. No musical reason for that. And the less artful modifications I make to existing contraptions are specifically *impeded* by their form."

"Be that as it may, there is something significant about a *human* form. The word 'effigy' comes to mind. And you've read the journal pages Fel brought back. There was talk of giving voice to these... contraptor objects. It all sounds terribly like a blending, or blurring, of man and contraption."

"Perhaps," Martin said.

He said the word without any concern or gravity. It may as well have been a cleared throat or a mumbled half syllable. Less a response and more a means to return the conversational volley so that he could continue working while Tome spoke.

"What do you hope to achieve if you succeed in repairing this device? What do you suppose it does?" Tome said.

"It is a bit of a conundrum, I'll grant you that. As tends to be the case, with contraptions above a certain level of complexity, I won't know what it does until I fix it, and I won't know how to fix it until I know precisely what it is intended to do."

"How do you usually find your way out of that vicious cycle?"

"If I am lucky, I recognize some mechanism or another within the contraption as being similar to one that I have repaired before, and that will get me started. I've spotted a few linkages and such in this that are familiar, but they are too elemental, too basic to hint at a larger purpose."

"So what comes next?"

"Seeing what components can be made to function, seeing what function those components have, and endeavoring to determine what links between them could serve an end purpose. But the gaps are rather large in this instance."

"Might I suggest the missing face might be one of the key components?"

"I suspect restoring functionality will require rather more nuance than 'a face.' But even if that were the case, it would appear that my predecessor was engaged in some manner of upgrade prior to his departure from Clickspring. That complicates matters, as it means that the mechanisms in place were not only incomplete, but were potentially in the process of being rendered nonfunctional by a failed experiment. It is a delightful puzzle."

A soft jangling drew their attention to Oiler. Its head was shifting now, slowly turning as if watching an unseen object travel across the corner of the ceiling. It stopped when it was gazing almost directly up at the ceiling. Both Martin and Tome paused to listen. A moment after Oiler stopped, a distant rumble shook the house. A moment later they felt a second one.

"Fel is home," they said in unison.

Oiler always seemed to know where Fel was. It was uncanny. But uncanniness was not unusual in a contraptioneer's shop, so Martin and

Tome had simply included Oiler's odd behavior into their routine. There was some value in being able to know where Fel was at a glance.

Doors slammed and feet stomped as Fel traveled through the floors of the house.

"It does not sound as though negotiations went well," Martin added.

A few slams later, Fel arrived in the workshop.

"I've got a gift for you, Dad," he said mirthlessly. "Courtesy of Euphoria."

He dropped a burlap sack onto the ground beside him. Oiler extended its tail and claws to hobble over to him. Fel grabbed one of several puzzle boxes that were strewn across the workshop and scrambled it for Oiler. The contraption took it and merrily went about solving its faces.

"Euphoria!" Martin said, eagerly setting down his tools to tug at the string binding the sack. "I wish she would have let your mother and I attend the meeting. How was she?"

"She had all the warmth and personality of that fellow you're working on right there," he said, motioning toward the half-finished bust. "But you'll be pleased to know she's finally coming home."

"She is!" Martin said gleefully, unveiling the contents of the sack.

"Yeah. No one trusts anyone, so she made it a point in her negotiation to demand to be allowed to crash here until I'm done cleaning up the mess she and her new family made. She'll be here in a few days." Fel turned to Tome. "Either you're going to have to move into my room while I'm gone, or she's going to have to stay in my room."

"Perhaps you can delay your departure for a week or two," Martin suggested. "It would be wonderful to have the house full again for a while before splitting up."

"You're going to have a hard enough time keeping Epiphany and Euphoria from killing each other without me here to stir the pot."

Martin turned the three clearly damaged items in the sack over in his hands.

"Was it really so unpleasant?"

"She treated us like Mom treats Assayer Forth. We may as well be people she hired to deal with a pest problem. And worst of all? I had to practically twist her arm off to get her to open up the coin purse and get some decent drinks in while we argued about the plan."

"Give her some time, Fel. She's still your sister. What precisely is this?"

"According to her? The pieces for a detector for sentry flames. The short version of what we decided upon is this. Me and some distant Graves relative are going to load up into one of their big fancy traveling wagons. We load up with weapons, and we track down every last *ember* of sentry flame that matches their family lantern. If it's a persistent flame like Wick's lantern there, we steal it. If not, we snuff it."

"Sensible. Though I imagine the Bolivans will not relinquish them willingly."

"Yeah, Dad. Hence the weapons." Fel turned to Tome again. "You can't come, by the way."

"I don't recall volunteering," Tome said. "This sounds like an overtly martial endeavor, and those do not appeal to me."

"Of course they don't. You only do things that might line your pockets."

"Or increase my pool of knowledge."

"Whatever. If it benefits you specifically and directly, you'll risk your neck. Otherwise, don't bother asking."

"I'll begin by remarking that I don't think that is an unreasonable policy, and continue by observing that you seem particularly out of sorts and are seeking to vent your frustrations on me."

"Doesn't make it any less true," Fel said. "How's that thing look, Dad?"

"A simple repair. I'll need to fabricate the proper-size flange or harvest one out of an alarm box. Beyond that, it should be within Oiler's capabilities to repair. I'll handle it personally though. The better to understand how it works."

"How long?" Fel asked.

"If I begin immediately, it should be finished this time tomorrow."

"Good, I'm going to The Fox and Log. If I'm heading off to storm the Bolivans tomorrow, that's a better excuse than I usually have to spend some time at the tavern. Tome, are you moving rooms or staying put?"

"I don't see any reason why I would move. If you won't be present, your room is as good as mine."

"I'm going to ask you to let Euphoria have her old room, Tome," Martin said, already working at the first of the three components.

"But why?"

"Because my daughter is coming home for the first time in years, and I won't have her, even for a moment, believe that she isn't welcome here anymore. Move your things to Fel's room, and this evening I will return Euphoria's things to her room."

"Er... right. So be it, then."

"Just throw any of my stuff that's in your way in the corner. I'll deal with it when I get back," Fel said.

"There is still the matter of where *you* are going to sleep tonight if I move into your room," Tome said.

"Bold of you to suggest I'll be back before dawn," he said, trudging back up the stairs.

He shut the door behind him with a degree of speed and force calculated to fall just short of a disrespectful slam but more than hard enough to underscore his displeasure. Oiler looked up from the puzzle box and angled its head in the direction of Fel, as if watching him through the walls and floors.

"How do you suppose it does that? Follows his location? It seems like Oiler and Parch can *both* find Fel just about anywhere he goes. Isn't that a bit of a remarkable coincidence? One a contraption, one a creature, but both with this capacity to track their favorite person."

"Remarkable, but probably not a coincidence. A great deal of the effects achieved by contraptions are imitations of natural occurrences. I imagine this is another example of that."

"But why would a fix-it machine need that?"

Martin shrugged. "Having a tool that follows me around is appealing to me."

A door slammed upstairs.

"On a more pressing topic, does Fel seem particularly out of sorts to you?" Tome asked.

"He's had a trying time," Martin said.

"I've seen him getting ready to battle a dragon, and he didn't seem nearly so upset."

"That was a dragon. This is family. All a dragon can do is tear your heart out. Family can break it."

Tome stepped through the doorway of the room that he would be giving up for Euphoria, at least temporarily.

"Shouldn't take but a moment," he muttered to himself.

He pulled a slip of paper out of a small pouch tacked to the wall and tore its end. Lamps all around the room flickered to life as the simple spell did its work. He placed his hands on his hips and surveyed the task ahead.

"Oh..." he muttered.

As recently as six months ago, everything in his life fit in a single sturdy wooden case that was presently in the corner of the room. It was his travel case, his seat, his desk. Everything he needed fit either inside or on top of it. But now it lay on the floor, nearly overflowing with contents, and there was still a great deal more scattered around it. The books he'd purchased filled two-thirds of the empty bookcase on one wall of the room. Euphoria's former desk was heaped with half-filled journals and stacks of pages. He had a neat little rack of pens with different styles of nibs and another rack filled with inks. A makeshift laboratory he'd set up for producing his own ink took up the entire surface of a cheap table he'd purchased from a thrift shop. The closet had six changes of clothes neatly hanging from its wooden rod.

It still wasn't *much*. Perhaps five armfuls. Five trips back and forth through the hallway. But it was more than he could carry on the road without a wagon. He had a home here. A comfortable home.

He started gathering up the contents of the desk, arranging the scattered sheets into piles to make them easier to transport. One pile for new spells he'd been working on. One for spells he'd completed. Best not to get those two confused. The last thing a paper mage wanted was to reach for a spell only to find something incomplete. Attempting to conjure a fireball with something no more mystically empowered than a shopping list was a quick way to an early grave.

The finished-spell pile was rather short. Not because there weren't many spells. He counted fifteen different ones, with some having as many as seven copies. The pile was short because the spells were efficiently written. A few spells for casting flame. A few lures, just in case hippogriffs became a problem for the Maskers again. An ice spell or two. They were what he would call "mature" spells. The other pile was about the same size, but there wasn't a single fully formed spell in it.

JOSEPH R. LALLO

That was bad.

A proper paper mage was always growing. At least, that was how he'd always felt. He'd never actually met another practitioner. He'd read copious books composed by other mages, and he'd met some who were experts in the associated trades of paper and ink craft. But when it came to actually producing a mystic effect with the power of words, he may as well have been unique. And that was an obligation. A great responsibility. He carried the weight of the art on his shoulders. If there were new books to be written on the subject, he was the one who would write them. And if those books were to be of any use to anyone, they would need to break new ground.

He'd put down roots here. He'd refined the knowledge he had, but now was not the time for refinement. Refinement without growth was stagnation. All he'd done in the past few weeks was winnow down the words necessary to cast a handful of spells. Worse, because of the nature of paper magic, all he'd done was winnow down the words it took for *Tome Inkbrand* or *Fel Masker* to cast those spells *in or near Beffshire* in the *near future*. Different hands, different locations, or too much of a delay and those spells would lose a great deal of their potency. It was a weakness of the art. One that he would have to solve for himself, if such a solution existed. For his knowledge to grow, to become truly useful, he needed to better understand what made one place different from another. He needed to understand the nuance between himself and others, between the different inks and papers, between the different written dialects. Just as Martin could study mechanisms he didn't understand and find elements of them that he did, Tome needed to study different types of magic and learn where they intersected with his own art.

Perhaps it wouldn't have been so glaring if not for the fact that he'd so recently experienced something that massively increased the scope of his awareness. He'd been beyond the Greater Lands Wall with Fel. He hadn't intended to, but that didn't stop him from acquiring materials and knowledge that should have *doubled* his capabilities as a paper mage. But now the supplies he'd brought back were dwindling. His memories of that place were fading, and he'd barely grown at all.

Fel's words in the workshop a few moments earlier trickled out of his memory. They were spoken in frustration. Spoken out of turn. But the reason people disliked when they were spoken to out of turn wasn't that those words were lies, but that they were unwelcome truths. Fel believed that Tome was self-centered. In all honesty, Tome didn't disagree. Until very recently he had voluntarily removed everyone else from his life. Being self-centered was necessary for survival. If he didn't act in his own best interests at all times, no one else would either. But now he had the Maskers to lean on.

The thoughts churned in his head. He returned his gaze to the piles of spells. A decision clicked into place in his mind. It locked in with the sort of certainty that convinced him that, even if it was not a smart or sane decision, it was the correct one. He took the pile of finished spells and slipped them into a sturdy little folio and set them aside. Those were spells for Beffshire. Those spells were the past. Perhaps someone else would find use for them, but Tome himself? He must dedicate himself to the future.

And there was no doubt in his mind. The seeds of his future lay beyond the Greater Lands Wall. He had to go back.

Allie paced along the same cobblestones she'd trekked at least twice a day since she'd started working full time at The Fox and Log just over two years ago. She was so familiar with this little stretch of street that she didn't even have to think about how best to navigate the lumpy, uneven path that tripped up so many drunks on their way out the door. Her feet just found their way to the comfortable little low points between stones. Those bits of street that were high enough to be free of puddles but low enough to cradle her foot rather than twist her ankle. Sometimes she wondered if her thousands of trips back and forth had worn the stone just a bit, carving her path the way mighty rivers did.

The mind went in strange directions when one was bored.

More so than the street, The Fox and Log was profoundly familiar to her. To an outsider, it was easy to suppose that something as lively and dynamic as a tavern full of patrons would change too much from day to day, hour to hour to settle into the same ruts as the steady grind of a stone street. But just as an artist with a trained eye could tell what mix of pigments went into a given color, she could tell by the general din filtering through the door precisely the mix of clientele lurking within. Maybe not the individuals, though one particularly boisterous laugh was unmistakably Lou, but the mixture of moods. She could tell if she had an easy day or a rough day ahead of her by the rumble of voices. And today, the mood was subdued. Like a forest where the wildlife was spooked.

She slipped inside. A soft rise and fall of drunken recognition greeted her.

"Don't mind me, folks. Just starting my shift. *Oovay! Where are we on the tabs?*"

"They're on the slate!" Oovay called from the back room.

"You know I don't like when you use the slate, because an enterprising drunk could reach over and fudge the numbers. Especially when you're *in the back instead of on the floor!*"

Oovay made a noncommittal grunt in his defense but remained in the back room. Allie glanced at the slate. There was no obvious evidence of tampering—the kind of person with a large enough tab to warrant modification tended to lack the dexterity to do a convincing job of it. But one line stood out to her.

She glanced up and scanned the grum tables, but didn't spot who she was looking for. Then she scanned the booths. Tucked away in the most private of them was Fel. His gaze was unfocused, like he was looking through things rather than at them. When she'd made her through-the-door assessment of the place, she'd assumed Fel wasn't present. When he was around, there tended to be either a lot more laughter or a few more punches being thrown. When she slipped through the door without at least a back-of-the-mind inkling that Fel was here, it meant he wasn't himself.

"Fel!" she shouted, fielding three drink orders and loading them onto a tray.

He twitched as though he'd been shaken from sleep and raised red-rimmed eyes in her direction. A horned head poked up from beside him and bleated happily. That would be Parch, the lesser unicorn who was about as separable from Fel as his shadow.

"I don't suppose this is a leftover tab from yesterday," she called.

"Nuh," he said, less a drunken slur and more a completely unmotivated reply.

She mechanically delivered the drinks, refreshed some bowls of salted crickets, and made her way to his table. A few of the patrons had crusts and fruit cores left from the more substantial meals they'd eaten while drinking. She dumped the more edible bits of trash into a bowl as she went.

"Got some recent memories you're hoping to erase, I take it?" she said.

He tried to glare at her, but the expression ended up a bit more hangdog than he'd probably intended. She set down the bowl, and Parch hopped up to consume the refuse like it was a banquet.

"It's not going to work if you remind me," he said.

"It's not going to work at all. Booze isn't a precision tool."

"That's fine. I'm not good with preshiss... precizz... those tools."

"Let me guess. This thing with Mariss is over," Allie said.

"No!" he said. "I visited her right before I came. Told her about what I was planning to do. She hung on my every word."

"Was this before or after you paid too much for a pastry?"

"During."

"Alright, so what's the booziness about, then?"

"My sister's going to be in town soon."

"Your sister is usually in town."

"The other one."

"Oh... *Oh*... How long has it been?"

"Three years. Give or take." He sipped his drink. "Mostly take."

"Beer here!" bellowed someone near the grum tables.

"Hold your horses!" she shouted without looking. "What do you say you lend a hand? I want to see if you can still walk."

Fel released the same sort of rumble a pig would make if asked to haul itself out of a comfy mud puddle. He slid along the worn wooden seat and wavered into a roughly upright position. It was always a little impressive, and more than a little telling, how well Fel could handle his liquor. That sort of thing came with practice.

Parch remained at the table, watching Fel but unwilling to abandon the bowl of treats. Fel lumbered behind Allie as she handed him a tray and started loading up whatever items wouldn't shatter if they fell to the ground.

"So how was she? Your sister, I mean."

"I don't want to talk about it. I don't want to think about it."

"All right, so what were you bragging to Mariss about?"

"Going to be heading out tomorrow to put an end to this Bolivan business."

"Is this the sort of thing you should be talking about? What if word gets out?"

"They tried to kill us a bunch of times. If they weren't expecting something like this, they're too stupid to overhear me talking about it."

"So what are you going to do?"

"Team up with one of my outlaw in-laws to track them down and poke their eyes out."

"Literally or figuratively?"

"Yes."

"Fun. Get that off the top shelf, would you? The copper bowl."

He wavered a bit as he reached up, but fetched it without mishap.

"This sounds awfully mercenary," she said.

"Nuh," he muttered. "Mercen... merc... merc's get paid."

"Ah. Well that sets my mind at ease," she snarked. "That's certainly the part I was worried about."

"Yeah. It's... yeah." He set the bowl down where she'd directed. "I tell you. Says something about my life that it wasn't until I stopped digging around in the desert and swamps looking for contraptions that I really started to get my hands dirty."

"So how long will you be gone?"

He shrugged and grabbed a handful of crickets. "Until it's done. Weeks, months."

"Is it at least likely to be the end of it? No more messiness after this?"

"No more messiness until the next thing, I guess."

The door swung open. An avuncular man with a wide smile and a red face stepped through the doorway. Most of the clientele didn't pay him any mind. Both Allie and Fel looked at him as though a bear had just walked through the door.

It was Donovan Verfessa. Despite having grown up in Beffshire, Allie had only recently become properly familiar with Verfessa, and she was rather nostalgic for the days before she knew such a man existed. He wasn't frightening in and of himself, but she'd quickly learned that he was the sort of man who got things done, and the things he got done weren't terribly pleasant.

"There's my boy," said Donovan. "Just the man I was hoping to see. Let's have a chat, shall we?"

Fel thumped back down into the private booth. Verfessa slid in opposite him. Parch gave the newcomer a measuring look, but returned to the work of cleaning the garbage bowl without any concern.

"Feels good to get out of the house," Verfessa said. "I don't do it as often as I used to. Not for social matters, anyway. The pluses and minuses don't add up, usually. Too many people looking for a clear shot at ol' Verfessa. But The Fox and Log is safe enough, and I got the feeling if I waited much longer, you wouldn't be in the talking mood."

"I'm never in the talking mood," Fel said.

"Not in the talking frame of mind, then. Fall-down drunk is what I'm talking about."

"Oh. Yeah, you were right to show up when you did, then."

"Allie! Let's do a blackberry brandy for me and whatever Fel's been drinking, but water it down so he stays awake until we're through."

Allie gave the pair the uncertain look of a mother leaving her child with the uncle who can't seem to stay out of jail and scurried off to fetch the order.

"I hear you've been making plans," Verfessa said.

He spoke in a tone just quiet and deep enough to be lost by the general din.

"I don't make plans," Fel said. "Plans are made for me and about me."

Verfessa laughed. "I've been on that side of things. Seems like someone with a strong back gets pushed across the countertop like a sack of barley. People buying and selling our sweat to avoid soaking their fancy shirts with their own."

"Please don't make me try to figure out turns of phrase right now, Mr. Verfessa. If you want to talk about plans, talk to my sister."

"Oh, I'll be having a word with Epiphany and Vivian. Or more likely the missus will. Ladies tend to have more of a rapport with ladies, but it just so happens I'd like to have a word with the one actually doing the deeds."

"Alright," Fel said. "What's to be said?"

"I hear you're heading north. Teaming up with Lattica Graves to snuff some flames."

"Lattica Graves?" Fel said.

"She's heading down here as we speak. Your partner in this business."

"Then you know more about this than I do."

Verfessa laughed again.

"That'll happen. I know more about most things than most people do."

"Not much sense picking my brain, then."

"It's not all about you telling me things. I mean to tell you a few things too. But we'll start here. Do you think you have what it takes to actually get the job done?"

"I've always had what it takes to do what needs to be done."

"Well sure. And my grandfather lived through every day of his life until the last one. I'm not asking if you were up to what you've already done. I'm asking if you can do this."

"I can do this."

"A man doesn't drink himself half-dead because he's confident about the job ahead."

"I've got my reasons for drinking, and this isn't that. What difference does it make?"

"I've been in business a long time. A long, long time. The kind of businesses you tiptoe into because once you're ankle deep, you'll be dodging eels and snakes from then on. Now I'm making a move into your business. Or the ragged ends of it that your family doesn't much like to handle. That first step, that first toe in the water, that's the most dangerous time. Until my foot reaches the ground again and I'm solid enough to take another step, I want to make double sure all the pieces are rock solid. I made an investment in your family, and your family needs you breathing. That means *I* need you breathing, at least long enough to see a return on investment."

"It's nice to be wanted."

"Pile on that the fact that you're about to teach a lesson to the Bolivan family—if things go the way we'd all like, at least—and you become *very* interesting to me. Now am I correct that this is a family endeavor? The Graves and the Maskers. No outsiders welcome."

"That seems to be the rule."

"I can respect that. I can respect it. I can't abide it, but I can respect it."

"Can't abide it?"

"Like I said. Investment. I need to protect it. Not that I don't trust you to know your own business. But then, this isn't your usual business."

Fel rubbed his eye. Allie arrived with the fresh drinks and tossed another couple of apple cores in Parch's bowl.

"Didn't you just get through telling me this is new business for you, too?" Fel asked.

"Oh, buying and selling contraptions and the like. That's new. Putting the boot to people who don't know better than to mind other people's business? That's my stock and trade since I was a pup." He reached across the table and slapped a callused hand on Fel's shoulder. "All this is a long way of saying you'll be picking up an extra shadow on this little trip."

"I don't follow."

"That's the idea. It's not you that'll be doing the following. It'll be one of my crew. Oh, they'll keep their distance. If everything goes the way it's supposed to, you'll never know they're there. Just a friendly blade with a sharp eye to drop in when needed."

"You're telling me there'll be someone I don't know and I can't see following me around with a knife."

"That's right."

"And that's supposed to make me feel better?"

"No, son." Verfessa took a sip of his drink. "It's supposed to make *me* feel better."

"Great."

"Now give it to me plain. What are you looking to get out of this trip?"

"Mr. Verfessa, you seem like if you want to know something, you find it out. You know the name of the person I'm working with, and even *I* don't know that."

"I have my ways."

"Well, no offense, but you're going to have to use those ways. It's not that I don't trust you specifically, but for some topics, I don't trust people in general, and you're part of people."

Verfessa laughed. "You know who I am, right?"

"I better know. We're in business with you."

"And you've been paying attention to what I was saying, right?"

"As best I can. This isn't my first drink."

"There aren't too many people brave or stupid enough to brush off a request from me. Though, like you said, this isn't your first drink."

"Oh, trust me," Fel said, sipping his own beverage. "I'm just as brave and stupid when I'm sober."

"The good news for both of is, it doesn't matter how you feel about having help on this one. You're getting it. I wasn't coming here to ask. I was just letting you know. Now let's finish our drinks."

"That, I can do."

It had taken Martin more time to clear a proper place to work on the flame-detecting contraption than it did to start making progress on it. Compared to the complexity of the faceless bust that had absorbed his attentions of late, it was laughably simple. It helped that Tome's absence meant there was measurably less distraction. Oiler was still present, but even when it wasn't frantically attempting to repair something—whether Martin wanted it to or not—it was still somewhat useful.

"I hear that clacking slowing down," Martin said, glancing over his shoulder at the mechanism. "Getting interested are you?"

Sure enough, the polished serpent head poking out of the canvas backpack like a serpent from a pot was spending less time working at the puzzle and more time eying the work being done at the table.

"Impressive, isn't it, Wick?" Martin said.

"I am quite sure that I will agree that your observation is accurate if you will helpfully clarify what precisely you find to be impressive, Martin," said the voice from the lantern.

"Oiler. I've seen the inside of its head. It's all just mechanisms. Yet somehow they coax an intelligence from the assemblage. Not just an intelligence, an *instinct*. An intuition for when a contraption is nearly in a state that it will be able to complete."

"Yes, Martin. This is indeed quite impressive."

"Not unlike yourself, of course. Truly, you are a more impressive work of the contraptioneer's art. But I suppose with familiarity I've forgotten just how impressive you are."

"I feel no resentment for the comparative observation."

Martin finished disassembling an old alarm box that was more trouble than it was worth to repair.

"There is so much more to learn about contraptions. The things that make them function," he said. "This truly is a confounding field. One gets the feel, over the years, that one is working in partnership with some unknown and temperamental figure just beyond one's reach. I can put these bits together. I can know *what* effect will be achieved if I do. I still can't be certain *why*. Is it some function intrinsic to the components that I simply don't understand? Is it the fickleness of the contraptors they speak of in old books like the ones Fel found? All I can do is place the bits in the proper orientation and hope that whatever forces animate the device choose to do so."

"In time, the truth will be revealed."

"One can only hope."

Martin levered a flanged bearing out of place. He stiffly crouched to place the three components of the flame detector on the ground, along with the liberated replacement part. Oiler sprang from its place in the corner like a dog hearing kibble jingling into its bowl. Cunning claws set down the puzzle box and reeled out to pluck up the components. Oiler went to work opening this case and tapping at that, gently nudging slightly misshapen cases back into shape and aligning components with their slots.

"I find it difficult to believe whoever was working on this piece prior to its arrival couldn't repair it on their own. There was obvious evidence of repairs they'd made. But, then, all the fresh components seemed to be perfect matches. As though they'd disassembled a dozen such contraptions and harvested all the individual pieces that were in good repair to include them into this one. I suppose the Graves contraptioneers haven't worked out what level of tolerance can still lead to a functional device."

Oiler plucked up the flange and pressed it into place, then waggled it on its shaft. With clear disappointment on a face that achieved an impressive amount of emotion for being completely immobile, it pulled the loose flange from the shaft and held it up.

"Right, right. Hardly a clockwork fit. Won't be a moment," Martin said, accepting the offending piece and setting it down on the bench.

He pulled down an unruly roll of shim stock and a pair of impressive shears.

"Perhaps the Graves contraptioneers are more like Oiler than I am. An ironclad understanding of basic rules, but an inability or unwillingness to diverge from set rules. No creativity, or at least no zeal for experimentation. Or perhaps they are perfectionists, preferring no solution over a nonideal one."

He snipped out a few strips of stock.

"But they clearly have so much raw material. One can only imagine how many contraptions sit in their stores that I could repair but they couldn't. So much depth of knowledge they must have. They have one half of something, I have the other." He shook his head. "If only we'd been working together all this time. Think of where we could be."

He knelt down and arranged the shim stock into a cross shape atop the axle, then pressed the bushing down over it.

"Interference fit," he said. "Press it onto the shaft."

Oiler looked up at him, then plucked up the axle with its teetering flange and gingerly pressed it. The shims compressed and crumpled, filling the gap and then some, and the flange sat snugly on the axle. Oiler tested its fit, found it adequate, and produced a merry little click before seating a gear on the newly installed bearing and reinserting the axle.

"What burns me most is that all this is a desperate attempt to re-create something we once fully understood. There were people, people in my own family, who didn't simply understand the concepts, they developed them. Imagine what we could have today if we hadn't lost that information. Those books Fel brought back are a mere scratch in the patina that's built up on our ignorance. They're the vowels in an alphabet that was used to write masterpieces. Indispensable but still just the first step, and incomplete regardless."

Oiler produced a few more delighted clicks and affixed the final panel, presenting the fully repaired contraption with a glint of pride in its stationary eyes.

"Right. Now we have the item. Time to see if it works."

The final contraption had the vague look of something between a clock and a compass. There were hands, driven like a timepiece rather than free-floating like a compass. The cardinal directions were laid out in the face plate around the platen beneath the hands, though the ring containing the labels was separate. He twisted and turned the device and found that "North" sluggishly found its way to the proper orientation each time. Oiler seemed to observe the sluggishness and reeled its head up to squirt a drop of lubricant from a retractable fang. A second drop to the central stem freed up the motion of the hands, which moved with a soft internal whirring. One pointed squarely at Wick's lantern. The other shifted to indicate a number engraved on the stationary portion of the platen.

"Interesting. This is obviously directional, and this would appear to be..." Martin raised and lowered the detector, producing subtle motions back and forth in the secondary hand. "Altitude? Perhaps inclination?"

He thumbed a tiny perforated brass hemisphere on the stem to reveal something quite like the wick in Wick's lantern.

"I am going to apply your flame to this, if that is acceptable," Martin said. "Hopefully your observations will give us some additional insight."

"That would be a pleasant and fulfilling service to provide," Wick said.

Martin took a small taper and lit it from the lantern, then touched the flame to the wick. It took on a dim, smoldering flame. The hand pointing to Wick's lantern shifted much more precisely and moved far more energetically to match his location. Likewise for what was now clearly the inclination indicator. The result was almost akin to the flame serving as a more effective power source than the ill-defined motive forces of a standard contraption.

"Well?" Martin asked.

"It is a curious sensation. I am aware of the presence of an additional flame that should serve as a potential point of observation, but its relative location is unclear, and it is not accessible to me. It is... akin to a new star in the night sky."

"Mmm... So if Fel uses this to track the Graves family flame, the flame will be aware that something is amiss, but nothing more."

"Indeed. Assuming I have similar capabilities as the Graves family flame. It has certainly revealed itself to have capabilities that I lack."

"Noted. I shall need a few more hours to properly assess this device."

He licked his thumb and used it to extinguish the flame in the stem. The motion of the hands became subdued and less accurate, but did not entirely cease.

"One thing that seems to be certain is that *all* sentry flames contribute to the readings on the detector. I fear this means I won't be able to send one of your lanterns along with him. It could foul the readings. This of all missions feels awful to send him on without a means to contact us."

"I can understand how that would be troubling."

Martin scratched out the observation. He tapped the journal with the pen.

"This is my legacy, I suppose. Trying to find my way back to what we once had. I tell you, for all the wars and strife that have plagued this world, I think the greatest tragedy was the loss of the Telestressa Archives. I'd trade all the lifetime of achievement in uncovering the old knowledge if it meant we could have even a glimpse of the wisdom we lost when the archives burned."

"Yes. Truly a travesty," Wick said.

"It doesn't make sense to me how it could have been allowed to occur. What army would destroy a thing of such value? What price was too much to protect it?"

"History is history. We cannot change it. To try is to invite sorrow. To dwell is to invite madness. What is lost is lost," Wick said.

"That is uncharacteristically maudlin for you, Wick."

"My apologies."

"I don't suppose you'd like to elaborate on what led you down that path?"

"You suppose correctly that I would not."

"I see..." Martin said, letting his gaze linger on the stationary flame. "Well. Back to business, then. I'll dictate my notes as usual."

"Recording them for future reference is, of course, a service I am happy to fulfill."

Martin cleared his throat and began to summarize his findings, attempting as best he could to keep any concerns he might have for Wick's odd statements in the back of his mind for further consideration.

A knock at the door served as a ready distraction from those thoughts.

"Come in!" Martin called.

Tome opened the door and stepped inside.

"Martin, terribly sorry to interrupt you, but I've been doing some thinking."

"That seems to be your favorite pastime," Martin remarked, switching back to taking notes by hand rather than dictating.

"With Fel's newest mission being something of an open-ended one, it strikes me that the little jaunt you and I were hoping would be our next adventure is likely to be postponed for an unknown amount of time."

"The trip back to the Greater Lands Wall to try again for the archive?"

"That's the very one."

"Yes, well. Given the mishaps involved in the previous attempt, I don't imagine you or Fel was eager to return."

"Fel's enthusiasm for such things is seldom significant, but mine remains undiminished. And since I don't relish the thought of kicking about in his room until he returns, I wonder if you would consider sponsoring me for a solo mission to the wall."

"Sponsoring?"

"I'm feeling a bit cramped from remaining in one city for so long, even one as large as Beffshire. I'd like to expand my knowledge."

"I doubt you'll find much information about paper magic in the Greater Lands Wall. I could be mistaken, but it seems likely that the place will focus primarily on contraptions."

"True. But I'll admit I have some selfish aims for this journey as well. To be succinct, I would like to make an expedition back into the Greater Lands. What I am proposing is that you provide me a vehicle and the gear necessary for the trip, and in return, when I am through in the Greater Lands I will return with as many of the archive books as I can carry. Carefully selected and curated, of course."

"Are you sure you're up to that? It seemed to be almost more than you and Fel could handle together."

"There was a fair amount of extracurricular adventuring on that trip. I hope to remain more focused without Fel and Oiler as distractions."

Martin considered the offer. "I *would* like to see what that archive could teach me."

"And I would like to see what the Greater Lands can teach me."

"You're certain you can manage?"

"Quite."

"... I think I can see my way clear to lending the old family cart."

"I'd rather hoped the larger one, and a good sturdy horse, would be your contribution."

"We need the full wagon for trade. You'd be getting the family cart."

"I can bring back far more books with the larger wagon," Tome said. "I'll admit I'm not overly fond of using that uncomfortable little cart for this journey."

Martin shrugged. "Then the archive trip can wait."

Vivian was the bargainer of the group. She would find wiggle room in discussions and seek out compromises to ensure that both sides got at least a bit of what they were after. Martin was content to get nothing. It was, in its way, quite an effective negotiation tactic, though somewhat hampered by the fact that it only worked on matters of want rather than need.

"I... suppose I can find a way to work with the smaller cart."

"Then have a word with Vivian, and tell her you have my blessings."

Tome trudged back upstairs.

"Provided that journey takes place, I think it would be best we sent your spare lantern with him, Wick. That you can't join Fel means it would be moldering up in the shop otherwise."

"That is sensible," Wick said.

He tapped his pen. "This house is going to be awfully empty for the next few weeks... but, such is life. Back to it, then..."

CHAPTER 2

The next morning, or more accurately the next afternoon, Fel dragged himself from bed. He didn't have any clear memories of leaving the tavern. That was troubling. Hopefully he'd made the decision himself and did it under his own power. There weren't very many places he cared what people thought of him, but The Fox and Log was near the top of the list. He was under no delusions of having earned much respect, but Allie was a discerning judge of character and he'd hate to lose whatever good impressions he'd built up in her mind.

He blinked his bleary eyes at an orderly pile of books and folded clothes in the corner of his room beside his workbench. It took a few moments of dredging his memory to recall that Tome would be moving into his room in his absence. The mound of clothes was not entirely unappreciated, at least by the other occupant of the room. Parch had climbed onto the pile and was dozing happily.

"I'm pretty sure I told him he could move my stuff, and he left it all where it was. Strange of him to show any sort of consideration," he muttered. He stretched, groaning at the throbbing in his head. "What time is it? Did I miss breakfast?"

He turned to the clock his father had helped him fix, back when they both thought he'd be following a bit closer in Martin's footsteps. It was seven in the evening. Not only had he missed breakfast, there was a good chance he'd missed supper.

"I really overdid it last night... and this morning."

Fel pulled on a reasonably clean outfit and trudged from his room. A second or two after he shut the door, a rather well-crafted wooden flap installed on the bottom half of his bedroom door swung open and Parch trotted out. The goat-size creature was impressively powerful, and though he'd taken quite well to training, he still didn't quite understand that doors were meant to stay intact. Installing the hinged portion of Fel's door saved Parch the trouble of bashing through replacement boards every time he wanted to leave before someone came to fetch him, and saved Fel the trouble of repairing the door after Parch got impatient. Fel wasn't opposed to leaving a hole in his door, but Oiler was, and the constant tug of war between a unicorn that liked to break things and a contraption that liked to fix things had ceased to be cute in very short order.

With Parch trotting along behind him, he made his way to the dining room. Dinner was still on the table, but it was an unspoken family policy that dinner stayed on the table until the last person ate, no matter how long it took. Such was the necessity in a family of people who tended to focus more on their roles in the business than their personal upkeep. Epiphany was at the table, an empty bowl in front of her and a buttered biscuit on a plate beside it. Now would normally be the time that he'd endure whatever barbs she had in mind about his bad habits, but presently there was something far more worthy of remark.

Joining Epiphany at the table was easily the most formidable woman Fel had ever seen. If she wasn't a match for Fel's height, she'd only missed it by an inch or two. And there was every likelihood that she was broader of build than he was. True, it was a bit less in the shoulders and a bit more in the hips, but this was a woman from farmer's stock. The kind of woman who would be toting bales of hay and hauling pigs to market.

She was dressed for utility, thick canvas work clothes in muted colors. Her hair was black, cut straight across and just below her ears in length. In this light her eyes looked black as well, and they were gazing at him with a measuring glare.

"You'd be... Lattica," Fel said. "Lattica Graves."

"You've met?" Epiphany said.

"No. But your reputation precedes you," Fel said, stepping forward to hold out a hand.

She shook it without delay, then returned to a rather rigid posture standing beside the table.

"Your reputation precedes you as well. It seems there isn't a member of the Masker family that hasn't got some sort of legend attached to them," she said.

"Is it Euphoria who talks about us?"

"No. She is private on matters of family."

"I'll bet she is."

Lattica glanced down at the source of the clippy-clop sound. "I must say the pet unicorn is news to me."

"Parch isn't so much a pet as a freeloader. Watch the hems of your pants. He gets nippy sometimes. We're working on it." Fel flopped down into a chair and ladled stew that had cooled to the point that it was nearly congealed into his bowl. "Did Euphoria get here yet?"

"Another day or two," Lattica said. "Thaddeus is upstairs with your mother. He will remain until she arrives and then move on."

"Another two days. Euphoria sure had a lot of business to attend to before coming home," Fel said. "So are you having dinner with us or—"

"I've eaten. Two hours ago. It was very nice. I'd prefer if we could get moving. We are already performing this mission with half the muscle I'd felt we needed thanks to your questionable negotiation skills. The least you can do is avoid delaying us any longer."

Fel tried dipping a biscuit in the stew. When the consistency prevented it —Martin's stew was hearty enough to congeal if you left it off the heat for too long—he scooped some up instead.

"Nice of you to make it clear this is going to be an ordeal right away. I'd hate to think we were going to get along and then find out otherwise halfway to the first stop."

"We have to work together. I'm not looking for new friends."

"Lucky that we're already family, right? Where do you land on the Graves family tree in relation to Euphoria?"

She leaned forward, scrutinizing him a little more closely.

"Are you hungover?"

"Why else would I have been waking up at seven in the evening. I'm a drunk, I'm not *lazy*."

She shut her eyes and crossed her arms. "There will be no drinking on this journey. If my life depends upon you, and I hope to plan well enough to avoid such a thing, I don't want your mind dulled by drink."

"I don't drink when I'm on the job. What kind of a man do you take me for?"

"As you called yourself a drunk, I am taking you at your word."

Fel groaned and looked at Epiphany.

"Is it a family trait? No humor in the Graves family?"

"As much as I'd like to take your side on this one, I have to agree that this is something you should be taking particularly seriously," Epiphany said.

Fel filled a glass from a pitch of water and rubbed his head.

"Right. Fine. What do we want to talk about?"

"We will be leaving this evening. I trust you'll be able to guide the horses through the night shift?"

"I can handle that."

Epiphany held up the flame detector.

"Dad finished this. We need to light the stem from the Graves family flame. 'The Voice' or whatever they call it. This hand will indicate the direction it can be found, this one will indicate if it is above or below you. He hasn't worked out how to tell when something is near or far, but he's confident that functionality will become obvious once you get some distance from a sentry flame that's burning. You'll be doing this without Wick, by the way. Any flame causes the hand to move. Having one nearby would make the detector almost worthless."

"Mmhmm," Fel muttered.

The idea of being cut off from the family didn't thrill him. Particularly not with a relative stranger from a rival family as his only companion. But a very old and generally not very productive instinct told him showing weakness and trepidation right now would start him off on the wrong foot. He was not in the right state of mind to overrule it with logic, so he defaulted to stoically ignoring the warning signs.

He stuffed his mouth full of a second whole biscuit and muscled it down, then tossed a third biscuit to Parch and brushed off his hands.

"You brought the wagon, right?" he said.

"Carriage. And yes, we did," Lattica said.

"You get it ready. I'll get my gear and we'll head out."

"It is ready," she said. "We've been waiting for you."

"Then I'll get ready and you just stand here," he said.

He trudged back down the stairs with Parch tippy-tapping along behind him. Before he'd even reached his bedroom again, Epiphany appeared behind him.

"That didn't go well."

"I've been awake for five minutes, and it feels like someone is trying to chisel their way out of my skull. What did you expect? Diplomacy?"

"You're going to be working with this woman through some very trying times."

"Uh-huh. I've had plenty of practice working with someone I don't like after the last couple of trips with Tome. Where *is* he anyway?"

"Shopping. He's decided upon a journey of his own while you're gone."

"Oh? Heading north, I assume. That's where he wanted to go anyway, right?"

"He's going south. To the wall."

"He's going to the wall?" Fel paused. "The Greater Lands Wall?"

"Specifically, to the Greater Lands."

"*Why?* We barely made it out last time!"

"He didn't share his reasoning, only his intentions. Dad is excited. Tome will make another try at the archive in the wall, now that we know where it is, and then continue on to the Greater Lands after he finds it. Dad's agreed to let him borrow the old family wagon."

Fel held his head. It was throbbing extra hard now, as though it was desperately attempting to overpower the growing heap of annoyances.

"He's going to want to 'borrow' Parch too, isn't he?" Fel asked.

"He specifically asked if it would be a problem if the family had to take care of Parch without him. I believe he's more interested in speed."

"He's taking Parch," Fel said.

"I've just said—"

"No, I'm telling you, tell him, he's taking Parch."

"A moment ago it sounded like you didn't want him to."

"I don't like the idea of Parch heading past the wall again. But I like the idea of Tome heading past the wall again without Parch even less. If nothing else, I doubt we'll be getting the wagon back without Parch to tip the scales in his favor."

"Doesn't Parch sort of... not get along with him?"

"He doesn't. But a team needs at least one member with horse sense, and a unicorn's as close as we're going to get. Parch is getting pretty good at listening these days. Better than he lets on."

He crouched.

"Parch, listen. You're going to go with Tome. Listen to him until he asks you to do something stupid. Then avoid the stupid thing."

Parch reared up. Fel gave him a few playful slaps below the horn in lieu of headbutts and continued into his room. He pulled up his gear bag and started to rummage through it.

"Rope. Couple of knives. Dazzler..." he muttered to himself. "I've got a spare knife here. Give that to Tome, too."

"Fel, this is a dangerous one," Epiphany said.

"The dangerous ones are the only ones I get sent on."

"But this isn't traps. It isn't wild animals. Or even Greater Mystics. These are people."

"I know."

"It's... this is a lot more like going to war than anything you've had to do before. Going behind enemy lines, in a sense."

"I'm just snuffing out some flames, Fanny. If anyone decides to get between me and those flames, that's their own fault."

"We both know there's going to be more to it than that."

"There's always more to it than I expect. Fortunately my head is throbbing so bad it's hard to think, which should make it easy to not think about that stuff for a while."

"I guess what I'm saying is, be careful."

"I'm not going to get killed. Are you kidding? Lattica looks like the sort who'd gloat about it, and I won't give her the satisfaction. Do me a favor and go make sure she's actually got the wagon ready. Horse fed and watered, all that."

"Sure."

Her tone and expression suggested she was well aware he was just sending her away. To her credit, she didn't comment on it. She grabbed the back of his head and pulled him in for a kiss on the forehead.

"Send her home with some stories about how the Maskers handle themselves," she said.

"Oh, she'll be talking *all* about me."

Epiphany hurried upstairs. Fel managed all of two long exasperated breaths before the door to the lower levels opened and his father appeared. He did his best to look like someone who wasn't fighting a two-front war against his body and his nerves.

"Fel, I was afraid I'd miss you," Martin said. "Getting plenty of sleep before the trip. Good thinking. The better to offset your shifts and get the most out of each day."

"All part of the plan," Fel said.

Sarcasm was a gamble with Martin, because he tended to miss it half the time. The coin must have come up tails, because he nodded through the comment and continued.

"Epiphany told you how the detector works."

"She did."

"Good. I'm told Thaddeus has a sample of the family flame. It would be ideal if you kept the stem burning with it. It shouldn't need any fuel, but it can easily be extinguished. It will still function, but I imagine you'll want every advantage you can get."

"I'd say."

"Have you heard about Tome?"

"He decided it was too hard to get killed when we were working together so he's going to try to do it solo."

"He's a capable young man. And he's going to bring books back from the archive. Perhaps others from deeper within the Greater Lands. He seems quite excited about the potential discoveries he can make about paper magic."

"I'm sending Parch along with him. Chances are I'll be gone before he shows back up, so do me a favor and let him know that if he decided he had something to prove, he chose a pretty terrible way and time to prove it."

"He actually had a word or two to say to you, through me, as he also assumed he would miss you. Specifically, he said that you should take these spells along." Martin handed over a folio. "He said they're clearly labeled, and he'll have no use for them where he's going. Do you have a moment to discuss your equipment?"

"I'm going to stick with the old reliable ones, Dad. There will be enough surprises without me having to learn new gear. Dazzler, that new sparker I cleaned up, maybe the borer. My cudgel." He paused. "And I think I'll bring along the dragon sticker."

He stepped up onto the lowest shelf of his bookshelf and grabbed a cloth-wrapped object from on top of it. It had the general shape of an ax, though a bit too irregularly twisty to be a proper tool. A few strips of leather had been wrapped around the head of the object, suggesting there was something particularly dangerous lurking beneath. Considering the weapon was an improvised club with paralyzing manticore spines driven through it, some careful wrapping seemed sensible.

"Do you think you'll be needing something with such... outsized effect on the target?" Martin asked.

"Let's just say I'd rather have it and not need it than need it and not have it."

Martin placed a hand on Fel's shoulder.

"Son, what you're doing? It's more than I'd ever expected to ask of you."

"I'm just putting out some fires, Dad."

"Perhaps. But you're clashing against a ruthless family. More importantly, you're working *with* the Graves family. Fel, there is a lot to be gained if bridges can be built between the families. By the High, your *sister* will be back home again for the first time in years. This madness... if it's handled correctly, the silver linings will far outshine the dark clouds. An end to this bloody-handed backstabbing and espionage. Perhaps the beginning to an age of partnership."

"Please don't hold your breath, Dad. There's only so much luck to go around."

"Right. Right. The important thing is you come back safe. The rest will work out however it works out. I know you'll do brilliantly, my boy. You always have."

He hugged Fel.

"I'll make you proud, Dad."

"Bah. Just make it there and back again. We're already proud."

Allie leaned heavily on the edge of the table as she waited for the teakettle to finish heating. Most mornings her problem was aching feet from a long night walking the tavern floor. That was easy enough to deal with. A long hot soak and she was right as rain by the time her shift arrived. But today was different. First, it wasn't nearly morning. Fortunately she'd left word with Oovay that she wouldn't be working today. She also had the issue of her back aching terribly. Fel had done his very best to turn his brain to putty last night, and had stayed well past what should have been closing. She'd kept the place open mostly out of concern for what mischief he'd have gotten into without a relatively safe place like The Fox and Log to spend his time and money. This was a rare miscalculation on her part, because by the time Fel was ready to leave, the sturdy patrons she usually bribed to tote folks home had already had their fill and tottered off to their beds. She'd had to help Fel home herself, his arm over her shoulder as she kept him on his feet. The man was *not* light.

Possibly because of the throbbing reminder in her lower back, she found her thoughts lingering on him and his disposition last night. He made a habit of overindulging at the tavern before any of his lengthy trips. She'd seen him before every major expedition of the last few years. But this one was different. She couldn't get a proper read on whether it was thanks to the dangers of the trip or something else. He'd spent a *lot* of time moping about his wayward sister. Maybe it was worth paying the Maskers a visit, just to see for herself what the fuss was about.

And then there was Verfessa.

She felt a sting of guilt as the name drifted to the top of her mind. In way, and not nearly as roundabout a way as she would have liked, any entanglements the Maskers had with Verfessa were Allie's fault. It had been she, after all, who had awakened that sleeping giant in her attempts to help chase off the Bolivans. Now Fel was handling that personally, and the family was in deep enough with Verfessa that the man himself was paying personal visits.

The kettle started to whistle. She clamped some tealeaves into a perforated metal ball and poured the tea. After a count of fifty she dipped the cage into the water and started a fresh count to two hundred. Her grandmother had insisted that proper count made for the proper tea. She didn't know if it was true, but a tradition was a tradition, and counting off a perfect cup of tea had a way of carving a nice clear line through the morning. It forced her to put other thoughts on hold for just a bit, and it was remarkable how setting things aside for a moment could help untie the knots.

She hit the final count and tipped in some milk and honey. Like clockwork, all the thoughts that had been clogging her cluttered mind tumbled out, neat and arranged. She would drop by the tavern, make sure things were in order, then run some errands. By then Fel would be on his way and the antiquity shop would have likely seen the last of its customers. A nice neighborly chat, then early to bed for the double shift that she'd traded for today off. That should set her mind at ease.

She straightened her posture and grimaced. Maybe heading down to the apothecary would be worth a trip. She had her doubts that anything that loon sold would actually do any good, but the idea of limping through a double shift like this didn't appeal to her.

"This isn't a carriage, this is a house," Fel said, gazing up at the vehicle the Graves family had provided.

Perhaps his view of transportation was skewed by the two-wheeled runabout that had until recently been the family's only vehicle, and skewed further by Parch's tenure as the primary pack animal, but the Graves wagon seemed wildly excessive. It was tall enough that he was quite certain he could comfortably stand inside it, and it wouldn't take much effort to pack the entire contents of the shop inside it either. He'd seen plenty of wagons this size. Most of the vendors in the traveling bazaar relied upon them. But they were hauling a month's worth of wares from town to town and usually had four or five workers living in them and out of them for months at a stretch. This carriage was a bit less ostentatious. No bright purple or gold canvas stretched over it with eye-catching patterns to attract customers. Instead, it had a drab greenish covering. But it was still massive, and the pair of horses hauling it were huge.

"What do you feed these things? Other horses?" Fel said.

"Are you ready to move? I'd like to be well outside of Beffshire by morning," Lattica called from within.

He marched up to the steps and pulled himself up. Inside he found one half of the wagon was filled with provisions and equipment. They'd stored enough food and drink to keep them alive for weeks without resupplying, assuming the horses could be cared for. Thin boards had been nailed to the wooden supports for the canvas. They were papered with maps of the entire region, fresh and clean but with colored pins waiting to be applied. Lattica was seated on a stool that seemed comically small for her, with a lap desk balanced on her knees as she jotted down notes of some kind. Slung over the provisions was a single hammock.

"What are you up to?" Fel asked.

"Planning."

"You're a planner, are you?"

"Proper planning prevents poor performance."

Fel shut his eyes tightly. "Right. Well. This is going to be a fun trip. What exactly are you planning for? We don't know anything that's going to happen except that we'll be going *toward* Bolivans who have flames lit from *your* family's flame."

"The Bolivans are active chiefly to the north. We can assume we will be heading in that direction. Now, are you ready to go?"

"No. I have three things to button up. Sit tight."

He hopped down and stepped inside the shop again.

Thaddeus Graves, consummate traveling salesman that he was, had spent every moment he could scrutinizing the shelves and talking shop with Vivian. It would be nice to give Thad the benefit of the doubt and assume he'd been wise enough not to try to wheel and deal her, but the chances were good he'd wasted a lot of breath bouncing endless offers off Fel's mother. She knew the price of everything in her shop, and she knew how much of a markup Thaddeus was likely to get. Thus, with diabolical precision, she could toy with him by selecting the exact price at which a given item wouldn't be worth his time.

Further evidence of Vivian's significant strength of will and skill at negotiation was the merciful lack of badgerweed stench. She'd actually gotten him to extinguish his pipe.

"Thad!" Fel said, presenting the detector. "I need you to light this with the family flame."

"Ah. Ready for the road, I see," he said, lifting what looked like a very tall hat box from the floor and placing it on the counter.

"Not quite yet, but soon," he said.

Thad popped the lid off the box to reveal a lantern that was little more than a massive oil reservoir with a tiny smoldering wick. He lit the stem of the detector. Internal components whirred, hands moved, and the indicator settled onto the location of their first target, which happened to be the precise flame they'd lit it from.

"Are we ready? We sure this is working? Because once I put this out, that's it. We don't have another one lit in the family. Even the main one is out."

"We better be," Fel said.

He licked his thumb and snuffed the flame. The indicator whipped around and pointed vaguely north. Their *real* first target.

Vivian stepped forward and gave Fel a hug.

"Get the job done and get home. There's plenty of work to be done here while you're off teaching the Bolivans a lesson."

"I'll be quick," he said with a grin. "After all, that silverware isn't going to deliver itself. Where's Parch?"

"Epiphany is keeping him busy. And your father is doing likewise with your *other* pet. It's going to be a chore to keep them from traipsing off to find you."

Fel had to admire her dedication to keeping Oiler's existence vague and implied. Considering how long they'd been spied on, there was no doubt the Graves family knew all about Oiler. But never let it be said that Vivian Masker let a secret slip before its time.

"Tell her I said goodbye. Oh. And give me some of the treats. Two sets."

Vivian nodded and dropped two paper-wrapped packets into his hand.

"What are those?" Thaddeus asked.

"Bribes," Fel said.

He gave his mother a kiss and trotted outside again. Despite the late hour, he could just make out the flutter of wings against the dim evening sky.

"Lattica, would you come here for a moment?" he said.

"I'm busy."

"You're going to be a lot more busy if you don't come out here for a moment," Fel said.

She poked her head out through the rear curtain of the carriage.

"What do you *want*?" she snapped.

A dark form dropped heavily to the wood-and-canvas arch over her head.

"Thieving rat monkey," uttered the crow-like lesser harpy.

The mystical bird spoke the insult with the same cordiality of someone tipping their hat and saying, "How do you do."

Fel handed Lattica a packet and tore his own open, revealing four large nuts.

"You behave now, Toody. I'm not going to be around, so you might get fewer goodies. That doesn't mean you have permission to pester the customers. *No pestering customers.*"

"I'll roast your giblets," the harpy said with an agreeable waggle of its head.

He tossed the nut. The harpy snatched it out of the air, then swung down to be face to face with Lattica.

"It got my boot!" Toody said inquisitively.

"Give her one nut," Fel instructed.

"You live in a blasted circus..." Lattica griped, digging a nut from the packet and flicking it up.

Toody grabbed it and flew away. Three more thumps signaled the arrival of the rest of the quartet of moochers.

"Same goes for you three," Fel said, tossing the remaining nuts into the air.

They scattered and converged with remarkable speed, each ending up with a nut in its beak before the treats had even reached their peak. Bits of nutshell rained down as they fluttered overhead, then the trio landed on the ground and gazed up at Lattica expectantly.

"I'll wring your neck," one said sweetly.

"Bloody lousy smelly thief," croaked another.

"I've had enough of this," Lattica said, tossing the rest of the packet to the ground.

They squabbled over it and made their escape, spraying a few more tirades with a sharpness that matched their harsh phrasing. Fel shook his head.

"I'd be nicer to the wildlife if I were you," he said, trotting around the outside of the carriage and hopping up to the reins. "You never know when you'll need a friend."

He gave the reins a snap, and the heavy carriage lurched into motion.

"Give me the detector," she said.

"Why? I'm the one doing the first driving shift," he said.

"Because if we are going to do this properly, we should know precisely where we are going."

He pointed, his hand matching the angle of the indicator on the contraption.

"That way," he said.

"Just hand it back."

He shrugged and handed it back to her.

"Tell me, did you think maybe it was a bad idea to pick this monster of a carriage to effectively wage war on a rival family?"

"What else would we choose? We don't know how long we'll be at it. We need something sturdy and capable of keeping us equipped for long periods of time."

"Maybe something a little less conspicuous."

"Why would that matter?" she asked.

"Because when you're planning to steal something from someone, the farther away they spot you, the harder it is to do it."

"If the Bolivans have any intelligence, they already know we are coming. They know we know about their flames, and thus they know we'll be coming to snuff them. And if they *don't* know we are coming, they're so thick we could stomp up to their front door on elephants and they wouldn't suspect anything."

He shrugged.

"It still feels like thieves should be sneakier."

"We aren't thieves, we're soldiers. Get used to the idea. There will be blood."

Fel shook his head. Two thoughts wove their way out of his still dully throbbing head. First, he'd met few men and no women who looked upon potential combat so coldly and matter of factly. He knew from experience that the Bolivans hired mercenaries for jobs that required that mindset, and Epiphany had learned from her ill-fated adventure with Thaddeus that the Graves family wasn't above hiring guards, at the very least. Obviously they viewed this as either important enough or sensitive enough to keep it within the family, as they did with their more crucial business. Lucky then, that they seemed to have someone like Lattica in the clan. He felt a brief moment of pity for her. The go-to blunt instrument of the family. That led him quickly to the second dim realization.

He was the blunt instrument of the Masker family. It was something that probably wouldn't have taken nearly as much pondering if he wasn't hungover. He gave the reins a tug and turned up a street barely wide enough to accommodate the carriage.

"You're going the wrong way," Lattica said before the turn was even complete.

"We've got two more stops to make," Fel said. "It isn't as though there's a deadline on this mission."

He guided the carriage to The Fox and Log and hopped off just long enough to discover that Allie wasn't present. Given the state he'd been in when he'd last seen her, he would place even money on the wager that she'd demand a thank-you or an apology, if not both, when he saw her again. Better to get that out of the way now, and say his "farewell for now," but it wasn't to be. He could already feel the growing impatience of Lattica radiating from the inside of the carriage. Paying a visit to Allie's home simply wasn't worth the comments she'd hurl his way. A scribbled note left with Oovay would have to do.

A bit more maneuvering and trundling brought him to Divinity's Oven. It had closed hours ago, so Mariss wouldn't be getting an in-person farewell either. He *really* shouldn't have done so much drinking. He scribbled another note, slipped it under the door, and called back to his impatient passenger.

"Heading out. Just generally north, yeah?"

"For now. In a few hours we should have a better idea."

"If you say so."

A few minutes after the heavy carriage rattled through the town gates and onto the road to the north, Tome rounded a turn from the eastern part of the market district and made his way up the road toward Masker's Antiquities. His eyes instinctively flicked to the skyline as he got close, always wary of the harpies, but they were absent. He hefted the sack of items he'd purchased. He'd been rather extravagant. Better traveling clothes, a rather fine pen and set of replacement nibs, an extralarge oiled leather folio to hopefully keep the water from his spells, and some food to bridge the gap between stops along the path south. He'd even been able to locate a book on cooking, foraging, and wilderness survival. If he was going to be in the Greater Lands for more than a few days, he would likely need to develop a degree of expertise in that regard. It had long been his belief that if it was worth knowing, a proper book could teach it, so there was little doubt in his mind that he would develop more-than-adequate survival skills by the time he reached the wall.

"Oh! Fancy meeting you here," called a pleasant voice from down the road ahead of him.

He was jarred from his thoughts and glanced up to find Allie approaching the antiquities shop from the other side.

"Ah! Allie," he called, quickening his step to close the gap.

She tried to do the same, but the additional effort only managed to shift her hobbling gait to a slightly faster hobbling gait. He passed the shop to meet up with her and offered an elbow to support her.

"Not feeling well?"

"Had to help a drunker-than-usual Fel home this morning," she explained.

"Ah. I'd wondered how he'd gotten home without some cobblestone-shaped bruises on his face."

"Mmmhmm. The next time he drowns his brain in booze until he can't walk, he's sleeping on the floor. The apothecary gave me a horrid bitter something-or-other to drink. He said it would straighten me out. That man is a liar."

"There are limits to traditional medicine," Tome said.

"I haven't seen you in The Fox and Log lately. Sworn off drinking?"

"I was never much of a drinker."

"Ah. So they're on to you at the grum table."

Tome cleared his throat.

"Er. Fel had warned me that if I were to use my usual tactics on his friends, I would have to answer to him. It appears that my skills regarding more traditional play have atrophied somewhat. As I don't have a steady source of income, it seemed wise to avoid losing any more at the grum table to that Tem fellow."

"If you can learn that, here's hoping Fel can figure it out for more than a few days at a time. I'm surprised you didn't go with him on this journey of his. Seems like you two are quite the pair."

"My destiny lies elsewhere."

"Taking a trip too, then?"

"As a matter of fact, yes."

"Where too?"

"Suffice to say I'll be heading south."

"You're not going back to the Greater Lands, are you?" Allie said.

He gave her a sideways look.

"You know about that?"

"Fel likes to spin a yarn. I know all about it. Picking through the exaggeration was a little harder than normal. Did you two *really* fight a dragon?"

"We did. On behalf of an even larger one, it so happens."

"And you're going back even after that?"

"Having earned the gratitude of a dragon, it seems a waste not to call in a favor or two."

They reached the door to the shop and pushed it open. Vivian kept flexible hours. Open and closed was more of a spectrum than a simple yes or no, as far as she was concerned. Presently the lighting within the shop was extinguished save for a single, unflickering lantern. That a customer looking to buy a contraption or other antique most likely wouldn't come by after sundown meant it was probably worth bracing the door and going to bed. Vivian Masker, on the other hand, felt the potential for an unexpected sale meant lingering an extra hour or two was worth her while.

She looked up as the bell over the door jangled, and her face passed through the swift and subtle sequence of expressions beginning with "polite greeting for a potential customer" and ending with "far more genuine smile for a friend of the family."

"Tome, welcome home. I'm afraid you just missed Fel," she said. "He had some matters he wanted me to discuss with you. And Allie, thanks again for bringing him home this morning."

"He didn't get drunk on my watch, but he *stayed* drunk on my watch. I felt responsible for him."

"He's responsible for himself. The boy knows better than to drink like that. Never let booze get in the way of obligations," she said.

Tome set down his sack and tugged a folio from his pocket. He pulled out a slip of paper and started carefully writing.

"What did Fel want to discuss? Or should I wait until Allie's completed her business?"

"He just wanted to make certain you were aware you'd be bringing Parch with you on your trip. And we put one of his spare knives in with your things."

Tome's expression dropped. "Parch. Certainly not."

"It wasn't a request. Besides, we've only got the one horse on standby at the stable, and we can't send you along with that. Epiphany's got to do the trips to Velsburgh and Islet next week. It's Parch or you rent your own horse."

Tome stopped writing long enough to tap his pocket, which had become quite light. Suddenly he was questioning the wisdom of spending so much on supplies today.

"Fel didn't take Parch?" Allie said. "That little critter goes *everywhere* with him."

"He was quite insistent that the unicorn go with Tome."

"I don't know if that says more about his trip or yours, Tome," Allie said.

"If he cared about my trip, he wouldn't have saddled me with a disobedient creature that doesn't so much haul a cart as stroll while one is attached."

"At any rate, Fel's trip was why I stopped by. Or part of why I stopped by. I hope you don't mind if I ask you some questions," Allie said. "He said a bit about what he was going to do, but as I said, he was more than half in the bag when I got to him. The tales start to get a little taller after the fifth pint or so."

"This isn't something I'd like to discuss in detail outside the family, Allie. Not to offend."

"No, no. Fair is fair. But... he seemed worried. Should he be?"

"If this was something we thought he couldn't handle, we wouldn't have asked him to go. And if it was something *he* thought he couldn't handle, we wouldn't have *made* him go. It's a bit outside of the ordinary. But he's my boy. He'll come through just fine."

Allie smiled. Tome managed to avoid shaking his head at the comment. It must have been nice to have parents with such unshakable faith in their son, but there came a point when it knocked on the door of delusion. He dearly hoped this was somewhat of a mask, because sending one's boy out to do battle with the very people who had repeatedly tried to kill or kidnap members of the family was the sort of thing that ought to foster at least some concern.

"He also mentioned Euphoria was on her way home. Do they not get along? I got the notion she was the reason for most of the drinking."

Vivian sighed.

"Euphoria's absence left bits of scars on each of us. Different depths, different shapes. Fel needed her back the same way she was when she left. It was a bit much to hope for. People change. But we'll have her back again, for a time at least. We'll see who she is now. And regardless of who she's become, she's still my daughter."

Tome stopped writing. He'd known Fel's mother for a few months now. He recognized the tone of voice when she was selling something. And she was selling something. If she'd worn a strong face on the subject of Fel's dangerous journey, it had been a good one. This one was a bit shakier. The subject of Euphoria had its claws deeper in her heart than she was letting on.

"Well, if she's looking for a place to have a drink and some crickets, be sure to send her down to The Fox and Log. I'd like to meet her."

"Yours is always the tavern I recommend."

"Um..." Allie said. "I... hope I'm not speaking out of turn here. And feel free to send me on my way if I am, but while Fel was drowning his sorrows, he had a little visit from someone. Donovan Verfessa."

Vivian's expression didn't change. Allie continued.

"It's just that... and this is just my own thoughts and I could be wrong... but when a man like that comes and sits down with someone in a tavern, that's a bit of a statement, isn't it? That's a message, and I don't think the message was strictly the one he had for Fel."

"Go on," Vivian said.

"That struck me as Verfessa making it clear that Fel was one of his... one of his... I guess I don't know quite what Fel was one of. But it's a rather bold thing for Verfessa to do. I wondered if maybe..."

"Just business, Allie. Just business."

"Your sort or his sort?"

Vivian sighed again.

"It was nice of you to stop by, Allie."

She said it as though it was the natural and polite response. No anger. No bad blood. Just a bit of punctuation to stop the conversation from flowing any further.

"I'll tell Fel you said hello when he gets back," she added.

Allie gave a knowing nod. "You do that. And I'll make sure we've got a few fresh bottles of his favorites. He's going to have some stories to tell when he gets back."

She turned to leave. Tome, who had been a bit lost in the conversation, caught her gently by the arm.

"Just a moment," he said.

"Need something?" she asked.

"Turn around for a moment," he said.

"If you're hoping to ogle something, you could be a bit more subtle, Tome," she joked.

He held up the freshly written spell. "You recall I'd mentioned traditional medicine has its limits. Paper magic does as well, but they're comfortably further down the road to wellness."

She gave him a doubtful look and turned to give him access to her back. He tore the edge of the page and slapped it to the base of her spine, taking special care to make sure his hand didn't wander any lower. The paper sizzled away. As it flaked into blackened char, she straightened up, pain vanishing under the influence of the spell.

"That was... how did you..." she said. "How long will that last?"

"Short of a broken bone or something torn, it should be healed."

She rubbed her back and appreciated the painlessness for a few seconds, then slapped him on the arm.

"You're telling me you don't have a steady source of income and you can do that? I paid ten duots to that idiot apothecary for something that didn't do much more than leave a bad taste in my mouth."

"Being the town healer, even for a sizable place like Beffshire, doesn't interest me. My sights are set higher."

"Speaking as someone who might end up with an achy back or other ailment again someday, let me just say that not *everything* is about what interests *you*. Have a good night. You too, Mrs. Masker."

She walked to the door with a literal skip in her step. When the door shut behind her, Tome rubbed his arm.

"She's a curious woman," he said.

"More interested than curious, I'd say," Vivian said.

He turned to her.

"You're *certain* I have no other option than to bring Parch along? Parch doesn't even like me."

"It's that or you can pay for a horse, like I said. But Fel seemed quite insistent about you taking the unicorn along. And to be frank, the creature can get a little difficult to handle when Fel isn't around. I'll be happy to have it out of the house for a while. And given the mischief you got up to last time you went down south, I think a mystic will do you more good than a mundane steed."

"I suppose..."

"When will you be leaving?" she asked.

"Bright and early. Before sunup, if possible. Especially if Parch will be pulling me. I'll need the extra time to get as far as the next decent town before midnight."

"If I don't see you, good luck. You know your business better than me, but the Greater Lands seem like a poor place to try to make one's fortune alone."

"A little wisdom and time to prepare are all a paper mage ever requires, and I've got plenty of both."

He hefted his bag from the floor and made his way down the steps. Out of habit, he opened the door to what would be Euphoria's room, then turned and entered Fel's instead. With Euphoria not due back for a day or two, he supposed he could have spent the night there. But he'd been enjoying the Masker hospitality for long enough that he preferred not to run the risk of upsetting them on the off chance she showed up early.

When he opened the door and tore the lamp-lighting spell he'd written, there was a bit more flare and sputter as the spell found itself activating in a room slightly different than it was written for, but he'd penned enough flexibility into the enchantment that it could adapt to a new room. The lamp lit. Parch, stirred by the sound of the opening door, was standing on the bed and glaring at him. A glint in the far corner turned out to be Oiler, silently watching from beneath the flap of his pack. Despite the fundamental differences between the two entities, there was the distinct feeling that they were both enormously resentful of the fact that Tome was not Fel.

"This is a very curious life I've found for myself," he muttered, readying himself for bed.

CHAPTER 3

Fel blearily watched the road ahead. The sun was rising. They'd been making slow, steady progress, but fairly soon they would need to rest the horses again. He'd need a few moments to stretch his legs and get his mind off the drudgery of the road as well. It had been quite some time since he'd had to take a long trip with nothing but his mind to keep him company, and it was starting to get to him. For a more contemplative sort, he might have been intrigued by the fact that once he started having company on his journeys, he found himself longing for solitude, and now that he had solitude, he was longing for company again. Even while Tome had been sleeping on their recent trip, he'd had Parch and Oiler to talk to. He *didn't* talk to them, for the most part, but there was a difference between knowing he had someone to talk to and knowing he didn't.

He glanced over his shoulder at the inside of the carriage. The swaying of the vehicle periodically brought Lattica into view as she swung in the hammock. She was fully dressed and seemed to have a truncheon resting on her chest beneath her crossed arms. Either she was extremely dedicated to being ready for combat, or she didn't trust Fel. He didn't blame her. People saw the world the way they saw themselves. If the Maskers had spent three years spying on the Graves family, he'd be pretty reluctant to shut his eyes around a member of the Graves clan for fear of retribution.

Perhaps Lattica had some sort of sixth sense, because shortly after he started thinking about her, she stirred and rather gracelessly extricated herself from the hammock.

"Where are we?" she said, her voice thick with the sluggishness of sleep.

"Four miles outside that town you circled on the map." He squinted at the page. "Something Junction. How's that hammock treating you?"

"Precisely four miles? Can you see the mile marker?" she asked, opening a crate and grabbing a book.

"You *wake up* acting like this, eh?" Fel grumbled. "Mile marker is just ahead. Why, worried we're not keeping to a schedule?"

"Give me the detector."

"You know I'm saying words to you right now, yes? Besides the ones you're *asking* for," he said, handing her the contraption.

"If you need idle chatter, we can see to it when I'm through with this."

"Through with what? The detector is still pointing in the same exact direction. What good does it do you right now? Best I can figure, at this point the only way we'll know where we're heading is when we pass it and the stupid thing turns around."

The only response was the flipping of pages.

"Stop the wagon."

"I figure we'll stop when we get to that town you so carefully picked out."

"Stop the wagon, *please*."

Fel's lip curled in frustration, but he tugged the reins until the carriage settled.

"Anything else you need me to do for no reason?"

She fumbled with some drafting tools, a long straight edge and a stick of chalk. A bit of grinding against the rough canvas brought the chalk to some semblance of sharpness. She glanced between the detector and the map, taking great care to shift the straight edge to a precise angle, and struck a line.

"We are heading to Climber's Circle. Or quite near," she said.

"You know that by drawing lines, huh?" he said.

"We were here, and the detector pointed that way," she said, thumping her finger on a line she'd drawn before they left. "Now we are here, and the detector is pointing that way. The lines cross here."

She glanced at the page of the journal she'd been referencing.

"That means it is the one place that the detector could have been pointing to both times. It's where the nearest flame is." She turned a page. "Assuming it isn't moving."

Fel let the logic trickle through his brain. Now that he'd had a night to recover, his hangover had reduced to a dull ache and a vague sickness in his gut. It made thinking easier, but it still took him a few seconds to wrap his head around what she'd explained. When it sank in, he gave a nod.

"Smart," he said.

"We may not have been able to get the detector to work, but we knew broadly how it would work when it was repaired. It gave us time to plan."

"Did you come up with that trick?" Fel asked, snapping the reins.

"No." She shut the journal and stowed it without further elaboration.

She opened another crate and unwrapped the cloth from around some of the provisions. A short time later, she slipped out from the carriage into the seat beside Fel with two thick crackers slathered with some sort of meaty paste.

"If you need me to take over so you can get some sleep, I can take the reins."

"Finish your breakfast," he said. "I can make it to the stable."

She nodded and crunched away at the odd meal.

"Even if we only stop long enough for the horses to recover, we should start making a plan about what we're going to do when we reach it."

"We don't know anything about the flame except that it might be in a city I've never been to. How can we plan?"

"I have maps. We can try to guess where it will be within the city. Buildings they might hide it in."

"What if we're wrong?" Fel asked.

"We make careful intelligent guesses. Several of them. Make a plan for each one."

"That seems like a lot of wasted thinking. Here's my plan. We go to the place where the flame is and try to take it or put it out. If they try to stop us, we hit them very hard. If they try to kill us, we don't let them."

She crunched more of her meal. "I don't know how you are still alive."

"Because whenever someone tries to kill me, I don't let them. It's a good plan."

She released a frustrated hiss.

"Have I done something to you? I don't think I have, but you're treating me like I kicked you in the knee."

"As it stands right now, the Masker family has done two things for this mission. Your father fixed the flame detector, which was crucial, and the rest of you argued the size of our force from four to two, which risks everything."

"Up until recently, every time I've had to do anything, I've done it by myself. Two is *more* than we need. What did we need other people for?"

"My sister-in-law Cecilia is a master of disguise and speaks seven languages. Her cousin Sin is one of the few practicing wizards on the continent."

"You have a wizard in the family?" Fel said. "I didn't know that. I thought there were only three. The ones that work for the heads of state."

"She isn't as powerful as any of them, but it doesn't take much magic to turn the tide when no one is expecting it."

"True enough. Tome has been handy on occasion. Why didn't they send *her*, then?"

"None of them wanted anything to do with you. I didn't either, but I was confident I could cave your head in if I needed to."

"Why would you need to cave my head in? We're supposed to be working together."

"Because you have a reputation as a drunk and a brute."

"I am a drunk and a brute. But that doesn't mean I'm not a gentleman."

She didn't laugh.

"Are you people really that scared of me?"

"To hear everyone else speak of it, you're an ogre. A monster. And your father? People still talk about what he did to the Bolivans last time he clashed with them in any meaningful way. The Maskers are not to be taken lightly. And your sister's arrival in the family made it clear that there was just as much capacity for scheming and plotting as there was for violence."

Fel grinned. "I'd be lying if I said that didn't make me a little proud."

The carriage trundled on. Lattica crunched away.

"So. Sin, Cecilia, and you. Is it the Graves way to send the ladies to do the dirty work?" Fel said.

"The men are busy with business. Your sister is the rare exception. A woman doing negotiation and making deals."

"Strange..." he mused.

She finished eating and wiped her hands. "I'll take the reins. Get some rest."

"I said I can make it to the stable."

"Get some rest," she repeated.

Fel was almost impressed at how effectively she could layer a seemingly kind suggestion with such raw hostility. He handed over the reins. As engaging as it would have been to be stubborn for the sake of being stubborn, it would be more pleasant for everyone if he slipped inside. He wasn't tired, but he also wasn't wanted. If that was the way it would be, then that was the way it would be. Lattica was hardly the first person he'd had to work with who didn't particularly like him. The important thing was, he'd sat with his back to her for eight hours and she hadn't even tried to stab him. All things considered, a good start.

Vivian worked her way through the morning routine, just as she'd done thousands of times before. Quite different from her son, for her, solitude was quite rare. And that was as it should be, because she ran the store, and solitude meant bad business. The early mornings and late evenings were, ideally, the only times she was certain she wouldn't be dealing with customers. Evenings were spent with the family—or at least whatever portion of the family wasn't otherwise occupied. That left this time of day, when the sun was slowly painting the sky its rosy colors, as the one reliable time that she was alone with her thoughts.

Presently she was quite eager for the solitude to be over.

The mercy of a busy life was that any concerns and anxieties were forcefully pushed aside by one's obligations. There were many inherent dangers to running the antiquities shop. Dangers to life and limb were chiefly faced by her children these days, though of course there was always the risk of theft, and lately the risk that the Bolivans would grow more bold. But the smoldering fear of what might happen was always a single customer away from being set aside. The ability to do so was one of the first and most useful skills she'd learned when she'd taken over the shop from Martin's father. The man had died quite young... not much older than she was now, though she preferred not to dwell on that. This meant that she was entirely in charge of the day-to-day running of the shop from Epiphany's age onward. Stress was a fact of life, and to survive it, she began to shut away little bits of her brain when they weren't useful. But even a lifetime of practice couldn't keep those doors from popping open again when they got the opportunity. And with the stock rotated, the list of errands prepared, and the shipments and deliveries packed, she had a few minutes before the doors officially opened for the high-pressure seals of her mind to begin leaking into her thoughts.

Fel was gone again. Another dangerous trip. She was worried about him, even if she didn't let on. But that wasn't what weighed most heavily on her. Danger, again, was a fact of life when one sells something difficult to acquire and potentially dangerous to operate. A certain amount of risk was to be expected. What worried her was that this trip wasn't standard business. It was very irregular. It called upon skills Fel by rights shouldn't have. He would rise to the task, naturally. He was a Masker. The family had seen worse. But he'd been having to rise to higher and higher tasks of late. The challenges were coming quickly. They were coming in clusters. It felt like life itself was accelerating. Life had always been a slippery slope, and this was beginning to feel an awful lot like a quickening slide.

She fixed her eyes on the facades of the stores across the way. The rising sun behind the antiquity shop cast a shadow along the storefronts. Rather than the boring straight line it should have been, it hosted four avian forms. The lesser harpies that may as well have been the shop's mascots. They were behaving themselves, waiting for their daily bribe. Waiting for Fel.

The oddly shaped hatch/door leading down to the lower levels that made up the storage and living space of their home opened and Epiphany emerged. Martin followed on her heels.

"Not open yet?" Epiphany asked, checking the brace on the door rather than waiting for an answer. "Good. Dad and I have something we think needs to be discussed."

"I have a moment or two. What's wrong?" she said.

"Euphoria could be here as soon as this evening. I think we need to agree upon what precautions are to be taken."

"Precautions..." Martin muttered under his breath.

"Yes, Dad. Precautions. I think, at the very least, the door to Dad's workshop should be more securely locked, particularly when he's not inside."

"I don't want your sister to think we don't trust her," Martin said.

"I *don't* trust her. She can't be trusted. She already betrayed us. She's the only one who could have installed the Graves family flame lantern into the stove in your shop."

"And she did so *three years* ago. If she meant the family harm, she had three years to bring it about. I'm sure there's a reasonable explanation."

"Fine. But until she convinces me, I want her locked out of the shop. She doesn't know about the bust you're working on. She doesn't know about the reference books you brought back. I want to keep it that way."

"I agree," Vivian said.

"Vivian. Our own daughter?"

"What she did can't be ignored. She of all people should understand," Vivian said.

Epiphany continued. "I think we should keep her out of the storage levels as well."

"You don't truly think she would *steal* from us, do you?" Martin said.

"I think she is smart enough to see the things you've been fixing and realize that Dad's been learning things they didn't know he was learning. Things he's learned from those books Fel brought back from the Greater Lands. Not to mention she'll see that we've stockpiled items that the assayers wouldn't allow us to sell."

"We've always kept some of them in storage for replacement parts. She knows that."

"But never this many. And... there's so much more. We don't know how much she knows about the deal with Verfessa. I just... I just think we have to treat her like an enemy within our home until she proves herself otherwise. The fact that she made it a point to demand to remain here during this mission is evidence enough she has plans for us."

"Fanny, that is a bit too far," Vivian said. "I'll agree the shop should be locked. It is perhaps wise to separate some of the more obvious examples of your father's recent experiments. We'll be even more discreet with our dealings with Verfessa. But Euphoria is still family."

"Fine. But I'm getting started now. And I'm going to be keeping an extra close eye on the sign. She's not getting away with the other mask."

Epiphany stormed back downstairs. Martin lingered.

"Euphoria coming home should feel like the family is whole again. Why does the mere notion that she'll be home again feel like it's tearing us apart?"

Vivian's eyes flicked to the door. Someone across the street slowed and glanced in the direction of the shop in the distinct manner of someone who spotted something of interest in the window.

"Time to open up shop," she said, hoping the relief wasn't terribly evident in her voice. "We'll discuss this later."

Martin nodded and made his way back downstairs. Vivian's mind gathered up all its stray thoughts, packed them neatly into a box, and slid them aside. She unbraced the door and opened it. The precisely calibrated half smile that was a hallmark of good service the world over graced her lips.

"Welcome, sir," she said. "How may I help you?"

Tome glared at the well-built but still utterly ridiculous yoke extension that allowed the disproportionately strong goat-size unicorn to pull the ancient two-wheeled wagon the Maskers had loaned him for the trip. From his position, he couldn't get a clear look at Parch, or he'd be directing his ire at the beast directly. It was plodding at a pathetic speed, barely a match for how quickly Tome could walk. They'd only left an hour ago, so fatigue wasn't the issue. The sun had not finished rising, and thus the heat of day had yet to bear down on them. The only excuses for Parch to be moving so slowly were disobedience and spite.

"I know you can pull more quickly than this, and I know you can do so quite happily," Tome griped at the unseen "steed." "It may not have been my decision to bring you along, but I am *trying* to be a good keeper to you. But if you will not behave, I will remind you that there *are* options available to me that others lack."

Parch bleated in a way that Tome would have called dismissive if it wasn't madness to suggest a beast was capable of such nuance.

He snapped the reins. "More quickly. I mean to make my stops at actual points of civilization. There is bound to be a bit of wilderness camping once I cross the threshold of the wall, so I want to make as much use of human hospitality as I can until then."

A second snap of the reins prompted an irritated bleat, and Parch came to a stop.

"Really, now. What will it be, a battle of wills?" Tome said. "I won't indulge you, Parch. You've had plenty to drink, you're surrounded by plenty to eat. All you need to do is tote the wagon a little more briskly and we can all be happy."

Parch flicked his ox-like tail and turned.

"Don't you dare!" Tome barked.

The unicorn heedlessly marched forward, casually strolling off the road and rattling the wagon over the uneven roadside and onward toward a shady tree.

"That's it. I've *tried* to be nice, but you've forced my hand."

He pulled a slip of paper from a pocket where it had been kept easily accessible. His first notion was to step down from the cart to deploy it, but visions of Parch taking off at a sprint and leading him on a chase quickly convinced him that the better course of action was to awkwardly lean forward and slap the activated spell against the unicorn's side. It burned away in a heat-free blue flame. Parch's motions became slightly more subdued, and the unicorn bleated in a more overtly irritated way.

"Left please," he instructed.

Parch bleated once more and trotted in the indicated direction. A few more commands got them back on the road, though the sounds of a sulky, displeased unicorn punctuated the journey for the next few minutes.

"If you would just act like a tame creature without help, I wouldn't need to use a taming spell." He leaned back, taking advantage of the smooth and moderately faster ride to pull out one of the books he'd brought along to begin reading. "I shouldn't even be talking to you like this. It's plainly falling on deaf ears. Treating you as though you have something approaching human intelligence is probably why you're so disobedient."

He scanned the page. The light of the lantern was flickering. Wick wasn't present. He was alone. Like Mrs. Masker, Tome had become rather skilled at boxing up different bits of his mind as well, though in an entirely different way and for entirely different reasons. Whereas she made the conscious decision to stow thoughts until such times as they could be properly dealt with, Tome had a tendency to simply overrule certain states of mind. Sometimes it was his current point of fascination. More often than he'd like to admit, it was simply him being contrary. Regardless, whatever the pet thought was, it would shove aside the others and hold center stage until his attentions began to wander.

Right now, his attentions were doing just that.

As his eyes darted across a page in the survival book that explained how to start a fire—something that he could do with any of a dozen simple spells—thoughts that had been elbowed out of his mind started to return. From the moment he'd decided the Greater Lands would be the source of his next great step in the mystic arts, these nagging concerns had been patiently waiting to be addressed. How would he actually *reach* the Greater Lands? Yes, he had an abbreviated copy of the codebook that would provide access to the inside of the wall, so the first step was simple enough. Mr. Masker had even taken the time to pass it through a code of his own design, which he then taught to Tome, so that if the book was lost or stolen, the wall wouldn't be overrun by fortune hunters. But they'd only successfully entered the Greater Lands once, and it was by floundering in an underground river and washing to the riverbank half-drowned and bewildered. It shouldn't be *too* difficult to simply climb over the wall, but he now knew that the Greater Lands side of the wall had a sheer drop.

And then there was surviving in the Greater Lands itself. Yes, assuming he solved the first problem, he would be in a far better position upon entering than he was last time. He wouldn't have destroyed his spells in the water, and he had the broad knowledge necessary to not only write effective spells, but to write spells that were even *more* effective than those he wrote out here. This didn't change the fact that the place was utterly teeming with creatures beyond sane description. He had friends on the other side, but they lived atop a mountain, and he'd been terribly lucky to have encountered them the first time.

About the time he realized he'd been re-reading the same page about skinning and boning a rabbit for five minutes straight, he acknowledged that the rewards of this trip were not without their risks. It worried him that fully half the solutions he'd proposed to himself to the various challenges had to be discarded because he'd accidentally concocted them with Fel in mind. Perhaps the trip wouldn't have been more pleasant with Fel, but the challenges wouldn't feel quite so insurmountable. That was a pointless avenue of thought, though. Fruitful though their collaborations had been, their fortunes lay at the end of two very different paths.

He had skills. He had ingenuity. He had wisdom. All he had to do was put his mind to it. As the temporarily tamed Parch tottered forward at a grudging but comfortable pace, Tome swapped from a survival guide to an empty journal and set his mind to the task of sculpting the arcane language to build the tools he would need to reach his goals.

"Hey, hey!" Allie shouted. "That table's for grum, not sixes."

The double shift, all things considered, was going rather well. The nice thing about the early shift was that you got a lot more people stopping in for a drink or two, maybe a snack, and then leaving. As for those people who were day drinkers or night drinkers getting an early start, they tended to be professionals who kept quiet and to themselves, more interested in the bottom of their glasses than starting trouble. Presently the only recurring problem was a sharply dressed fellow with an impressive knack for remaining always tipsy but never drunk was trying to shake up the games of chance played on the tables in the back.

"Young lady, I'll have you know that sixes is a gentleman's game," he said, raising his chin in what she presumed was an attempt at looking regal.

"What you don't understand is in these parts we have folks we call regulars. And the regulars expect to show up and do what they regularly do, so you show up and start a game of sixes at a table where in two hours a fellow's going to want a game of grum, that's liable to make him a bit testy. And grum is *not* a gentlemen's game. So you can see how that would go for you," she said.

"Surely first come, first served is a reasonable means to select how a table is to be used."

"It's not what you and I think is reasonable. It's what *everyone* thinks is reasonable. And as long as we're on the subject, the last five times we started up a game of sixes in here, it ended with food or refreshments being thrown in the face of someone accused of cheating. Maybe gentlemen throw food and brutes throw punches, but a thumped oaf eventually cleans himself off the floor, and a basket of stomped crickets in a puddle of ale is my job to clean up. So that's a grum table, not a sixes table."

Allie had ceased to give the man her full attention. He was too sober to need three explanations of her reasoning, so now he was just being obstinate, and obstinate people didn't require eye contact. She was thus free to observe the tilted heads and curious stares of the patrons as they gazed toward the door. She turned to find what they were looking at, and found a pleasant, plump young lady who was dressed too nicely and looked far too innocent to be paying a visit to a tavern this early in the day. She wore a pink apron that was made from finer cloth than Allie's one good dress, and she was dusted from head to toe with some combination of flour and powdered sugar.

"Mariss! Nice to see you! What brings you here? Got a delivery in the area?" Allie said.

"Er... No, I just... do you have a moment?" she said.

The answer to that question was no. Technically the day off she'd negotiated yesterday meant she was working without help and without breaks at least until suppertime. But the plate-spinning act of keeping The Fox and Log running was her specialty, so it wasn't much trouble to add another plate for a few minutes.

"Come on in. Have a seat."

She hastily dusted off the "business booth" that the patrons of the tavern had learned to keep clear for increasingly common private conversations. Mariss slipped into the booth and folded her hands anxiously on the table. Allie made a quick circuit around the tavern to make sure drinks were topped off and nothing had been set aflame. She then sat opposite Mariss.

"What can I help you with?" Allie said brightly.

Mariss had already unfolded a small handwritten note on the table. Even creased and upside down, Allie recognized Fel's writing.

"I got this note from Fel," Mariss said. "And... well, read it."

Allie took the note and looked it over.

Mariss. I am heading out. Dirty business needs to be done. This isn't the sort of trip where I'm likely to come back with a ~~suven sooven~~ present for you. But if I come back, I'll have some great new stories to tell you. And I didn't want to disappear without saying goodbye.

Allie handed it back. "Nice. Looking forward to hearing those stories too. The man knows how to spin a tale. What's the trouble?"

Mariss flattened the page on the table and jabbed it with her finger.

"He said *if. If* he comes back."

"Right, well. It's a dangerous trip. There's always going to be an if."

"I'm worried."

Allie laughed. "That's good! Tell him that when he comes back. He'll be happy to know you were thinking of him."

"You said *when* he comes back, though."

"Yeah?"

"He said *if* he comes back."

"Well sure, but..." Allie paused. "Let me ask you a couple of questions. We don't really know each other very well. Let's fix that. Your father owns the shop, right? Divinity's Oven?"

"Yes."

"Since before you were born?"

"That's right."

"I'm guessing you were helping in the kitchen since you were a little, little girl."

"Since before I can remember."

"And you're not just doing the baking, you're taking money. Doing business."

"That's right. On light days, I'm the only one in the place."

"What will happen when your father retires?"

"I'll take over. Me and my husband, whoever that turns out to be."

"Whoever that turns out to be," Allie muttered almost silently. "The family must do well in that place, eh?"

"We do quite well. I don't understand why you're asking all these questions."

"You've known where you were going and how you were getting there from before you were born. You've never had any uncertainty in your life. Just sitting on a wagon, moving toward the future that was set aside for you, without a bump in the road. I think that's why you've become so fascinated by Fel. Sure, he's a nice guy. But 'nice' is just a reason not to *dislike* someone. You like Fel because he's got exciting stories to tell. But you're just now figuring out that you don't get excitement without uncertainty. You don't get it without *if*."

Mariss looked stricken and wasn't doing a very good job of disguising it. Allie found herself having to resist the urge to pat this grown woman on the head like a toddler and tell her everything would be all right. It was impressive how soft and raw a comfortable life could leave someone. It was like her parents had built her life into a certain shape and she'd just grown up to fit that shape. But Allie knew that a person was more than that. This was an important moment for someone like Mariss. The sort of moment that could well resonate with her for the rest of her life, even if she wouldn't be able to put her finger on it later. It would have to be handled delicately.

"Beer here!" shouted a patron of the tavern with a terrible sense of timing.

"In a minute!" Allie bellowed back. "Mariss, why did you come to me about this?"

"You're the only other person I know who knows Fel."

"You've met his parents. His sister."

"I don't want to go to them and say I'm worried about their son. That might make them worry more."

"You could talk to your friends about this, then."

"You're my friend!" Mariss said in a bright and reassuring tone, as though Allie might have been worried such was not the case.

It felt cruel to bring up a simple truth that if Allie were asked to list all her friends, she would likely name fifty people before it even occurred to her to mention Mariss. Instead, she gracefully continued.

"Then *as* your friend, please don't take this the wrong way. It seems like you haven't had any control over your life until now. You've been content to let others take the lead. This seems to be a rare thing that you want to change. But all that time not having to take control may have taught you that you *can't* take control. You can. Now I happen to think that Fel has got this handled. But if you're worried, you aren't helpless."

"What can I do?"

"Taking control isn't about doing what someone else tells you to do. Sometimes you have to figure it out on your own. Now if you need help with something, and I can help, I'll help. But right now I've got a bar to run, and you've probably got a bakery to run."

Allie turned to serve the thirsty patron, but she called over her shoulder,

"Things will probably be fine, and you know how I know?" she said. "Because there are people like you and me to make sure they turn out fine when needs be."

"But what can we do?"

"I don't know. Put some thought into it. Decide if something needs to be done, and if so, decide *what* needs to be done. And then do it! If there's one thing I learned keeping order here in the tavern, it's that you're always more formidable than you think."

Mariss sat in silence for a time. She processed the words of wisdom and encouragement like a child eating a new type of vegetable for the first time. Uncertain and reluctant. But to her credit, Mariss wasn't a child, and it didn't take her long to see that these words had a nutrition that had been terribly deficient elsewhere in her life. When she stood, she had an expression that Allie wouldn't have called confident, but was a good deal less troubled than the one she'd walked in with.

Allie spun all the figurative plates of the tavern a bit: cleaned up a table, checked the stock on the more popular booze, updated the tabs, and nodded her way through three greetings from regulars. Once she had a moment of calm, she slipped into the doorway of the back room. Without someone else here, the doorway was as far as she was willing to go. She reached into her apron and pulled out a slip of paper not unlike the one Mariss had revealed. The page was scrawled with the same handwriting, though a very different message.

Allie. Thanks for getting me home after all that booze. You saved Mom or Dad or Fanny the trouble of having to cart me home. In case I didn't say it before I got too drunk to remember, I just wanted to make sure I said thanks for everything. And sorry for a lot of it, too. Didn't want to head out on this trip without letting you know.

She narrowed her eyes. The message definitely didn't paint a picture of someone confident they would be returning. She couldn't shake the belief that it wasn't the actual mission that had him so defeatist. As recently as a few weeks ago he would have been at least jokingly bragging about where he was going and what he was doing on a trip like this, even if it wasn't his cup of tea. He'd just been in a sour state of mind when he left. But when living life on the ragged edge like Fel did from time to time, a sickly state of mind had a terrible way of creating self-fulfilling prophesies about failure.

Unlike Mariss, Allie was no stranger to uncertainty. There were nights she wasn't even certain if dinner would be on the table. But this time felt different.

She folded the paper and stuffed it into her apron. Regardless of what was to be done, she had the bulk of a double shift to stew over it. Hopefully by then she'd have some ideas of how to set her mind at ease.

The brief moment of privacy came to an end. She pulled the dirty rag from her apron to toss with the others and replaced it with what turned out to be the only remaining clean one.

"Davie!" she shouted. "We need a fresh load of bar rags."

There was no reply.

"Davie?" She scratched her head. "Where did he get off to..."

When Lattica was convinced both Fel and the horses had recovered sufficiently to continue, she'd gotten the show back on the road. Fel hoped she was right about the horses, because she was very wrong about his own rate of recovery. Granted, the horses likely hadn't consumed quite as much booze as he had. But with Lattica quite eager to be the one at the reins for the next shift, Fel was able to crawl into the hammock and get some more shuteye. At first, the steady sway of the carriage swinging his hammock was a little difficult to get used to, but within an hour his body had happily embraced the cradle-like rocking and dropped into a black dreamless sleep.

It was the sudden stop of said swinging that caused him to snort awake. He peered through the wagon into the still-searing light of day and saw Lattica sitting stiffly and gripping the reins tight.

Fel didn't ask if something was wrong. That wasn't the sort of body language one applied to a run-of-the-mill stop. Instead, he dismounted the hammock as gracefully as he could—which was not very—and selected the old reliable cudgel that was his handheld weapon of choice. Lattica took one hand from the reins and gently slid the detector from its place beside her to a position more easily visible to Fel. He immediately saw the source of her dismay. Rather than the rock-solid trajectory it had been indicating for the entirety of his shift and presumably the bulk of hers, now the hand was oscillating between the direction it *had* been pointing and another target. The jostles toward the second target were brief and fleeting but seemed to trace a path that was either moving much more quickly or, more likely, was considerably closer.

He gripped the cudgel tightly and crept to the rear flap of the wagon, closest to where the flickering motion of the indicator seemed to be heading. The fields between the cities in this part of the kingdom alternated between patches of dry grassland and clumps of forest. Presently they were approaching one of the forests, but the stretch of land between them was dusty and sparse. Fel had no doubt that whoever was stalking them had come from the woods. That the indicator was still moving steadily, but he couldn't see anything, suggested Fel's greatest fear about the Bolivans was well-founded.

"They've got one of those contraptions that makes them invisible. How many of those can they possibly *have*?" he whispered.

Lattica slipped inside behind him and opened a box.

"They will keep their distance, and they will have crossbows."

"Yeah. I know. I've fought these guys before."

"We've been fighting them for years," Lattica said. "The one bit of luck we have is that they are constantly hiring replacements for mercenaries they've lost, so any given operative is probably very poorly trained."

"I'd say it was foolish to waste vanishingly rare Bygone artifacts on green mercenaries, but since they seem to have an endless supply of each, I guess it makes sense. I'll get out there and try to draw a shot. You go the other way and—"

"Don't be a fool." She dropped a leather book with the word "Tactics" on the cover in gold leaf. "We have ways of dealing with this."

She flipped it open. It shouldn't have been a surprise that the contents were in some sort of shorthand or code, but she ran her fingers along the page and reached back into the box she'd retrieved the book from. A short search turned up a strangely angular contraption—something like a brass box with slits in its top.

"A smoke flusher. We surround the carriage with smoke so they cannot aim properly. Then wait for them to run out of crossbow bolts and retreat."

She slid a well-hidden tab along the side, and odorless smoke began to rush from within the box. She tossed it out between the horses. In seconds the whole of the carriage was shrouded in billowing gray-blue smoke. Distant twangs could just barely be heard, crossbows firing. Every fourth or fifth shot, the canvas of the carriage shuddered like it had been hit with a hailstone.

"Either they've got some very poor weapons, or this isn't simply canvas."

"I've said we have a wizard in the family."

"Enchanted canvas as good as armor... Any chance your outfit is made of the same stuff? And if so, got any spares?"

"I'm afraid not. On both counts."

The cloth shuddered again.

"Still. Better than I expected. I'm starting to think either Tome was holding out on me, or he isn't half the mage he thinks he is."

Fel slipped closer to the front again to fetch the detector. The hand was oscillating wildly, now spending much more time pointing south, behind the wagon, than to the northwest as they'd been heading.

"They're trying to sneak up from behind." He squinted as the hands continued to move. "No... they're circling all the way around the front. They're going for the horses."

He crept forward, sticking his head out of the carriage.

"What are you doing? The tactics are very clear."

"The tactics are going to get the horses killed, and then we're basically in the middle of a siege."

"Horses can be replaced, and we have more than enough supplies to endure a siege."

"Lattica, if we end up huddled in this wagon for a couple of days, I'm pretty sure one of us will kill the other one. And frankly, I don't like my chances."

Before she could object any further, he hopped out and landed between the horses. His landing wasn't as graceful or silent as he would have hoped, but some combination of good luck and good training kept the horses from spooking. The smoke contraption was between his legs, leaving him in the very densest part of the cloud. The stuff felt cool against his leg where it splashed against him, and didn't have even the hint of a scent. It was more like vapor than smoke.

"Hey," he called as quietly as he could manage. "Since you know these mercs so well, which hand is the contraption on?"

"Bracer. Left forearm," she replied automatically.

He nodded and crouched down a little lower. Since he couldn't see anyway, he shut his eyes. There were contraptions that could render someone silent as well, but he was betting even the exceptionally well-equipped Bolivans weren't sending out people who wore both. He listened and waited. It was a struggle, but he kept his breathing slow and steady.

"Smoke," whispered Lattica from behind him.

"I know there's smoke. I'm sitting on the thing making it," he replied. "Hush, I'm trying to listen for footsteps."

Another twang suggested the agents hadn't yet given up on taking shots and hoping for a lucky hit.

"No. Smell. There will be smoke," she said.

Fel turned her words about in his head, then realized what should have been obvious from the start. They only knew the Bolivans were coming because of the moving indicator. That meant they had a flame with them. If a man was to receive instruction via a sentry flame *and* keep both hands free for combat, he would either have to have a big clumsy lantern rattling along on his belt, or he would be smoking a pipe or cigar lit from a lantern.

He exhaled and began taking long, slow inhales through his nose. Just as he was becoming light-headed, he felt the acrid sting of tobacco smoke against his nostrils. The wind, and thus the smoke, had to be coming from straight ahead. Fel dug his toes into the ground and tensed his muscles. He waited, hoping to hear the grind of dust beneath boots, but it never came. The first indication of their attacker was a curling disruption of the smoke ahead, a void in the vague form of a human. Fel sprang forward and struck the mercenary in the chest with his shoulder, driving him backward into the fluttering fringe of the smoky cover. He scrabbled at the invisible form beneath him until he felt something soft and throat-like to wrap his hand around. Once he heard the strangled gasp of a man being choked, he raised his cudgel and brought it down where the head ought to be.

His reward was a stricken groan and a sudden stop to the struggling beneath him. He kept the cudgel at the ready, but ran the other hand down from the neck to the shoulder and finally to the forearm. Sure enough, that's where the bracer was hidden, though it was beneath his sleeve, making its one-handed removal a bit difficult. When it finally left the Bolivan's skin, a form coalesced beneath him. The man who had tried to kill him was rather scrawny, certainly the sort who was better served by a projectile weapon than hand-to-hand combat. Fel tossed the bracer behind him and heard it slap against the entrance to the carriage. An odd-looking pipe—along with three teeth—had been liberated from the man's mouth, and he had the unfocused, half-lidded eyes of someone who wouldn't be putting up a fight anytime soon.

Fel picked up the pipe and squinted at it through the smoke of their improvised cover. This certainly didn't look like any pipe he'd ever seen before. He hadn't made much progress solving the riddle of its nature when he realized the very thing he'd been listening so intently for earlier, footsteps, could just barely be heard to his left. He turned and raised the cudgel. The unexpected foe wasn't even hidden, and he was right on top of Fel. He had a dagger raised, ready to plunge it into Fel's neck. Before Fel could do much more than heave himself aside in hopes of a dodge, a second form burst from the smoke. Lattica tackled the man to the ground. The knife went flying. She grabbed him by the shoulders and thumped him against the dry ground again and again. Each blow robbed him of a bit more of the will or clarity necessary to put up a fight. Once the man was five or six blows past the point of consciousness, she stopped and huffed a breath.

"They come in pairs, Fel. Always at least two. *Tactics*," she said.

She grabbed Fel by the collar and hauled him back into the denser smoke, then grabbed the ankle of the man Fel had taken down and dragged him close enough to be searched. She found an inside pocket in his jacket and pulled a bit of card stock or similar substance from it. She had to hold it close to inspect it while still amid the smoke.

"What's that?"

She motioned with her head to the dislodged pipe. "Not now."

He nodded. If it was a tactical advantage, best not to explain while they could be overheard or seen. He pulled a canteen from his belt and poured a dose of water into the smoldering end of the pipe. It sizzled and cooled.

72

Before he could turn to check the indicator, Lattica was already climbing inside to fetch it.

"Indeed. It's back to pointing northwest. We're clear," she said.

She climbed back down and deactivated the smoke contraption. Fel dragged both dazed men out into the open while the smoke cleared. Each was well armed with a crossbow and a dagger, along with plenty of bolts. One of them had a set of leather straps that Fel quickly realized were restraints.

"It looks like they were hoping to kidnap us," Fel said.

"That's what they do. If someone survives, they tie them up, drag them along, and get a ransom for them."

"I guess it's better than murder."

"It depends on what they do to you while you're tied up," she rumbled.

Fel shut his eyes tightly and clenched a fist. "What are we doing with these two?"

"No sense interrogating them. They only ever know what their job was, and we already know that. Tie them up and leave them in the road. Someone will come along for them eventually."

Fel nodded and slipped one of the straps around the first man's wrists.

"I'm a little surprised you didn't just want to kill them."

"Why? You take me for a murderer?"

"A soldier," he said.

"Well I'm neither."

Lattica rather more roughly secured the other man and dragged them both to the center of the road.

"If either of you end up talking to the people who hired you, thank them for the contraptions. It'll make this whole thing a lot easier," Fel said.

It was a fruitless taunt. Neither man was in a state of mind to be relaying any sort of information yet. Fel and Lattica climbed back into the carriage with the things they'd harvested from the mercenaries and were well on their way before any sense was likely to have returned to the mercs. Fel took the reins simply because he was the first one to reach them.

"So what was that card?" he asked.

"The Bolivans are still all about business. They think they're being sly, but we broke their codes a long time ago. It's an IOU for the second half of a payment. For a payment that size, it was a pair of mercenaries making a single hit. What did you make of that pipe? Do you have it?"

He tapped the little mound of spoils. "Right here. Why? Haven't seen anything like it?"

She picked it up and turned it about in her hands. "No. No, I've dealt with a lot of agents like this, and I've never seen one of these. But, then, I've only been unlucky enough to face one with contraptions like this."

"Oh, really? It seems like every Bolivan we run into has something like this."

"The Masker family is more dangerous and more valuable. Makes sense," she said. "I'm told you're the secondary contraptioneer in your family."

Fel laughed. "Secondary in that no one else besides me and Dad do any contraption work. I'm not even in the same *realm* as him when it comes to doing fixes."

"Still. You probably know more than me. Give me the reins and take a look at that pipe."

He did so. The pipe was definitely nothing anyone would puff on for enjoyment. It was quite large, with a broad mouthpiece the better for clamping its extra weight between one's teeth. There was tobacco in it, now waterlogged, but the chamber for it was a multiple the size one would require for an evening smoke.

"Dad would know better, but it looks to me like someone designed a pipe specifically for burning for long, *long* periods of time. My guess is this was made specifically to bring a little sample of sentry flame along without having to clunk around with the full-sized lantern. Or, maybe, without having to entrust a full-sized lantern to someone likely to be killed."

"Sound thinking."

Fel rubbed the side of the pipe. "This is new. It's still got sharp edges here where the bits connect. Those are *long* worn away on Bygone Era stuff."

He tested the various bits of it, looking for some way to disassemble it. Failing to find any, he wrenched the two halves until the whole pipe snapped in half at a pinch point between the bowl and stem.

"Bygone stuff doesn't break like that, either."

He poked around the inside. The telltale disks and cogs of ancient contraptions, the little bits that had some arcane purpose in an otherwise mundane machine, formed a ring visible through the broken bit on the base of the bowl. They were discolored by heat, but otherwise had a smoothness and sharpness that suggested they *too* were new. But that was impossible.

"You know a lot about the Bolivans, right?" Fel said.

"We know as much as we can manage about them."

"Are they building things?" he asked.

"They don't build. They don't even modify, beyond wrapping contraptions in something to hide them. All they do is steal."

"And the Graves family didn't make this?"

"No. Why?"

"Because it's entirely new. I mean, *entirely*. These pieces here? I don't know what they do, but they're definitely the kind of thing that makes a contraption... I don't know... contrapt. But they look like they were made as recently as the rest of this thing. Even Dad can't do that. The closest he comes is making new disks for music boxes."

"You're sure it isn't just new-old stock? Something unearthed but never used?"

"I've unearthed a lot of unused stuff. There'd be tarnish. Patina. Especially something that gets hot. And you sure wouldn't clean the tarnish out of all those little engravings in there. They're hidden inside. No one cares what they look like, and having tarnish in the engravings makes them pop anyway. I really think this is new. The Bolivans made a new contraption, or they have someone who could."

"That will..." Lattica searched for the proper words for a moment. "Complicate matters."

"You talk a lot like Tome. He likes to pick soft words for hard things too," Fel said.

"We should talk about what we've learned about the detector," Lattica said, brushing off his jab.

"What's to talk about?"

"It behaves strangely when there is more than one flame near."

"Dad suggested that might happen. It's why I couldn't bring Wick along."

JOSEPH R. LALLO

"But it didn't start behaving that way until these Bolivans were right on top of us. What does that mean?"

"I don't know. It can't mean the merc just lit the pipe, because that doesn't look like one of those base plates that'll restore a sentry flame even after it goes out. So it had to have been lit from an active sentry flame, and if there was one tucked in that forest over there, the detector would still be going nuts."

"Maybe it can't detect small ones unless they are close?" Lattica suggested.

"Or maybe a small one has to be *very* close to make a difference if there's a bigger one anywhere nearby. I'm going to assume it's that one."

"Why? There's no reason to assume it's that versus what I said."

"There's a *great* reason. It means that once we put out the bigger flames, we'll still be able to find the smaller ones. If it can't find the smaller ones unless they're close, then this whole mission is pointless because they can just have a little flame squirreled away and we'll never find it."

"Not with the detector. There *are* ways to find things without contraptions."

Fel winced a bit. "We're already going to have to thump a lot more heads than I like to thump. Let's not dream up a version of this mission where we're tracking down people and trying to wring information out of them. I'm going to assume it's a big-versus-little-flame thing and be done with it."

"You can't just *choose* to believe something because it'll make your life easier."

"If you'd been *listening* to me, you'd know that I just did exactly that. Are you good with the reins for a bit? I want to look over the other contraptions we stole to see how to use them."

"If it will keep you from passing off wishful thinking as strategy, go."

He slipped into the back of the carriage and unfurled his tool roll from his gear. He picked up a probe and pulled the contraption bracer to his lap, but three attempts to simply slip the probe between the leather bracer and the brass contraption failed. His hands were shaking. It was probably the motion of the carriage. Or maybe it was the last dregs of his hangover still clinging to him. Perhaps it was the intensity of the battle finally settling in. Or the anxiety over the prospect that the people he was after might have

76

achieved what his father had been seeking to do, and the concern over how they might use it.

In the end, it didn't matter. When one has a full slate of reasons to not be able to do something, it's usually a good reason to set that task aside until a few of them are taken care of. Unfortunately that meant Fel was left with only one thing to do, and it was one of his least favorite pastimes. All Fel could do was *think*.

CHAPTER 4

Martin stood in the back corner of the antiquities shop, arms crossed and a faint smile on his face as he watched his wife work. For the last few minutes, she'd been calmly dealing with what she would later call "one of those people."

"That's because it is a teaspoon, ma'am," Vivian said, for the sixth time in this transaction. "It doesn't match the other spoon because the other one is a soup spoon."

She delivered the sentence with the patience of one dealing with another person's child, with saintlike calm, while frustration simmered beneath the surface. It would have been acceptable, though still unpleasant, if she were actually speaking to a child. As it was, the current customer was a sixty-five-year-old woman who was dead set on finding some sort of fault with the exquisite tea set she'd purchased the previous evening.

"I want them to match. A set should match," the woman said, arms crossed and head turned aside.

"I think you'll find that the teaspoons match the teaspoons and the soup spoons match the soup spoons."

Vivian removed some of the silver and fetched a fine ceramic plate from their current stock to arrange a full place setting on the counter between them.

"From center to outside. Salad course, meat course, fish course. Forks on the left, knives on the right. Soup spoon beside fish-course knife, seafood fork beside soup spoon. Teaspoon above the plate, dessert fork above the teaspoon. Butter knife on bread plate, opposite wineglass and water goblet," Vivian dictated. "You'll find four full sets and matching napkin rings. Are we clear?"

"You're just making excuses for selling me odds and ends," the customer said.

The door jangled with a new arrival. Vivian didn't glance up. Martin knew it was a calculated decision. New customers preferred to be greeted immediately, but the problem customer would most likely make even more of a scene if she felt she was being ignored. That meant he was the only one who knew precisely who had walked in, and it was all he could do to hold his tongue until the customer was dealt with.

"If you would prefer, I can arrange the other three place settings to illustrate the completeness of the set," Vivian said.

"My *goodness,*" gasped the newcomer, marching up to the counter. "Such a gorgeous set! Utterly gorgeous. I've never seen the like, and I have traveled clear from East Shalia."

The temperamental customer looked to the woman intruding on her tantrum, which gave Vivian the opportunity to look at her as well, though Martin knew she didn't need to. Even after several years, she recognized the voice just as surely as Martin had recognized her face. It was Euphoria.

"Look at the shine. Look at the artistry! And so well restored. I would almost think they hadn't been restored at all, but they must have been because they are clearly heirlooms. Please tell me they are for sale," she trilled.

"I am afraid not, ma'am," Vivian said. "This set was purchased by this woman yesterday. We are simply discussing some small misunderstanding about the completeness of the set."

"If she is planning to return it, I'll happily purchase it," Euphoria said. "What is the price?"

"As I've said, this woman purchased it yesterday. The price was two hundred and forty duots."

"Oh, a savvy buyer. Ma'am, if you are dissatisfied, I will gladly pay you that price, right now." Euphoria added, at a low but not inaudible volume. "They'll resell at *twice* that price, certainly."

The customer, a bit lost in the flurry of words, gathered herself sufficiently to scoff at the offer. "What sort of a woman do you take me for? I know value when I see it. I purchased this set fair and square and it is *mine*."

She hastily gathered the silver and placed the pieces back in the crate.

"Don't forget the plate, ma'am," Euphoria said.

"The plate isn't mine," she said.

Euphoria's eyes lit up.

"It *isn't*!" She turned to Vivian. "Oh, madam, tell me you have a full set of them."

"No, no, no. I saw them first. You sell *me* the set of plates," the customer objected.

"She *was* here first, ma'am," Vivian said to Euphoria.

"That's *right*," said the customer with a triumphant nod.

One hundred duots changed hands, and the once-angry customer marched out the door with the silver she'd previously been dissatisfied with and a set of plates she didn't even want, all with the air of someone who'd pulled the wool over the eyes of the Maskers. When the woman was through the door and out of earshot, Vivian leaned across the counter and hugged her daughter. Martin marched forward and did the same.

"Fora, my love!" Martin proclaimed. "You haven't changed a bit. Not a *bit*."

"It's been so long, Fora," Vivian said. "And if I recall correctly, one of the last things I said to you before you left was that you simply had to stop with that little gambit. One of these days they are bound to notice the family resemblance."

"They never notice, Mother," Euphoria said, the colorful affected attitude sliding down into the cold demeanor she'd displayed during the negotiations. "And our senses of fashion have diverged a bit in recent years as well."

"You've tamed your hair," Vivian said. "That's more than I could do. But here, this is no place to have a reunion. I'll close the shop, we'll have a meal."

"By all means!" Martin said.

"Mother, Father, really," Euphoria said. "This is a business. I couldn't ask you to close the shop on my behalf."

"Nonsense. It is nice to see you again, but—"

"More than nice! Momentous!" Martin took her hand. "Come! I've got some stew started. The biscuits will be out of the oven in just a minute. Have a proper meal."

Euphoria gently resisted being dragged toward the hatch.

"Tempting, Father. But I am afraid, fresh from the road, I don't have much of an appetite. If I could freshen up."

"Of course! We've prepared your old room. Not just how you left it. You departed rather quickly, and we've had a boarder since then, but you'll feel right at home again, I assure you. Did you travel alone?" Martin asked.

"Not alone. I had a driver. He's dropping my things as we speak, and then he shall return to East Shalia. I don't imagine Fel's mission will last fewer than a several weeks, so I don't imagine it is worth having him remain."

"What about your husband?" Vivian said.

"Jonathan prefers not to leave our offices up north. He has a great deal of work to do. This project is mine alone."

"Fanny! Your sister is home. Come help me with her things," Martin called.

He hurried outside to start gathering the small collection of high-quality trunks. He was already dragging the first pair in when Epiphany trudged up the steps. She shot daggers at Euphoria from the moment she saw her.

"I don't suppose you brought back the mask you stole," she jabbed.

"Fanny," Martin reprimanded.

"It is still at home. I thought bringing it back would have been reawakening a sore subject unnecessarily. I didn't realize you'd kept the incomplete sign all these years."

"Dad thought you'd be back. We all did. For a while."

"We'll discuss that sort of thing later. It's all water under the bridge anyway. I'd like your sister to feel welcome," Martin said.

Between Epiphany, Euphoria, and Martin, they were able to tote the luggage downstairs in a single trip.

"The dining room hasn't changed," Euphoria said. "That old familiar chill of underground living. And the old scent of fresh soup."

"That's right, they don't dig foundations so deep up north, do they? I imagine the Graves have you set up in a palace compared to this," Martin said jovially.

"Not a palace. But pleasant. The air is cooler there. We have to light a fire most nights."

"Funny you should mention lighting a fire," Epiphany muttered.

"Must you, Fanny?" Martin said, exasperated.

"I fully understand, Father," Euphoria said. "She's my little sister, after all. We didn't always get along at the best of times, and my behavior *was* unacceptable."

"Don't you 'I understand' *me*, Fora. I'm mad at you. You're supposed to be mad at me. This is a fight. We're fighting right now. Show some *life* for goodness sake," Fanny said.

"I have responsibilities, now, Epiphany. It's forced me to mature a bit. One must be measured."

They reached the lower level with the bedrooms. Divided into four rooms as it was, the hallways weren't quite wide enough for them to stand side by side with their heavy bags. While Martin fumbled at opening the door, Epiphany thumped down the trunk she was carrying and tapped an old bit of patched wall.

"There? You see that? Remember how that got there?" he said.

"I remember," Euphoria said.

"That was when we got into a fight about Robbie Two-Left-Feet, because you were swooning over him and I thought he was a dope. You threw a shoe at me, and the heel knocked out a knothole in the panel."

"I said, I remember," Euphoria said.

"That was you being measured back then. So forgive me if I think this whole 'measured' thing is nothing but an act right now."

"I was a child then. I am no longer a child." Euphoria added under her breath, "Which makes *one* of us."

"There! That's my sister. That's the sister without the act," Epiphany said, excited to have gotten the tiny little rise out of her.

Martin got the door open and shuffled into the darkened room to light the lamps.

"May the High help me, I even missed the bickering," he grumbled to himself.

Fel had not returned to the task of investigating the deeper workings of the gear they'd confiscated from the Bolivans. He was half of the mind to simply abandon the task entirely. It wasn't as though he didn't know how the contraptions worked. Working out how to activate them was no more complex than finding a button or switch. But there was something nagging him, and all this thinking hadn't managed to shake the nagging feeling. He needed to see the inside of the contraption to be sure, but even with enough time having passed to restore what little precision to his hands that he'd had to begin with, he still didn't feel comfortable working on the contraptions while they were in motion, and Lattica was evidently a stickler for efficient travel. The stamina of the horses set their schedule. While the animals were able to comfortably continue, they continued.

Fel had just finished fixing himself a meal from the curious provisions that Lattica had brought along. The travel crackers—effectively bread that wouldn't go bad because it started out bad to begin with—were familiar enough, but he'd never encountered the meaty spread she'd brought literal buckets of. With a healthy dollop mashed atop each cracker, he slipped out and took a seat beside her while she guided the horses.

"You want one?" Fel asked.

She shook her head. "I'll eat when we stop for the day."

"Suit yourself. This is my first time with this stuff. What do you call it?"

Lattica huffed through her nose. "You don't want to know what I call it."

"Was that a laugh? Was that a *joke*?" Fel asked.

"It was a wry comment."

"Even so. That's about the most levity I've heard out of not just you but *any* Graves."

"I married in," she said dryly.

He crunched down on his first taste of what would be the primary form his meals would take between cities. The stuff was mostly salty and smoky, but with a dash of peppery heat. It was honestly rather good, though Fel was hardly a picky eater.

"It's like someone couldn't be bothered to finish making a sausage," he said.

"More or less," she said.

"So. Married into the family. And your husband is a businessman, is he?"

"He's a Graves. They're all business."

"And the ladies don't do business, mostly?"

"Mostly. Why don't you know this? We're rivals."

"My job is half digging in the dirt and trying not to get caught in traps, and half running around town making deliveries. Knowing what the rival families are up to doesn't figure in my day, most of the time. But if you're not business and he is, how'd you two meet? You seem pretty well trained for this 'soldier' sort of thing you've got going."

"I'm not a soldier. And my personal life is none of your business."

"True. But I went and got used to having someone to talk to on these trips. Granted, usually it's a unicorn and they don't talk back. And I'm really not much for reading."

"Then watch the scenery," she said.

He shrugged and leaned back against the support beside the entrance to the carriage. Three more big bites finished up his mystery meat and cracker meal. He pulled his canteen from his belt and took a swig.

"You know, they tell a lot of stories about you," Lattica said.

"Yeah? I guess *my* personal life is plenty of your business, then. Anything good?"

"I wouldn't call any of it *good* but..." She squinted her eyes, then turned to him. "Honestly, what's the deal with the harpies? And the unicorn."

"*That's* what they're telling stories about?"

"No. They're telling stories about how you faced down a Bolivan riding a hippogriff, and how you're the only one dumb enough to enter that swamp vault, and the only one sturdy enough to leave it alive."

"Do they tell the story about the thorn-lizard?"

"They tell *a* story about a thorn-lizard."

He grinned and crossed his arms.

"That's a good one. Got a better one now. A couple better ones. But, you know. Personal life. None of your business," he added in a mocking tone.

"That's fair."

"Oh, come on. I'm pulling your leg. So, what? You want to know about the harpies and the unicorn. Harpies are easy. A guy spilled a whole crate of buttons outside the cobbler's place, and for the next couple of days, Toody, Judy, Rudy, and Moody show up and start picking them out of the street. So I started tossing them stuff every time I came by. Now they hang around waiting for it."

"Harpies are pests, Fel. People don't go around teaching them to do tricks."

"I didn't teach them anything. They figured stuff out. Animals are smart. Especially Mystics. Lesser, Greater, they're all pretty smart compared to regular animals. Same with Parch. I went down to the wall—which you folks sent me to, I'll remind you—and after dodging a dragon, this thirsty little critter was there. Gave it some water and it got used to the idea of getting more water from me. Now we're pals." He scratched his head. "I hope Tome doesn't get him killed. Or the other way around."

"Just... random chance and they're a part of your life?"

"Life's a big pile of random, mostly."

"Not in the Graves family. In the Graves family, it's a big complicated scheme. A game, traced out move by move. Weaknesses are cut out. Shortcomings are compensated for. They use marriage like the nobles do. Have a niche that needs filling? Marry out a nephew. Have a deal that needs to be made? Marry out a daughter. It's like they're trying to run the family like a kingdom."

Fel scratched his head. "I guess that explains Euphoria, then. Some gap that needed filling."

"Mmm... I'd have thought she'd been married into the family to build a bridge to some sort of partnership with the Maskers."

"Oh? So her robbing us and spying on us wasn't covered in the family meetings?"

"I said it was being played like a game. I'm not one of the players, I'm one of the pieces. I don't know any more about what's going on than those Bolivan mercenaries did."

"So you were a niche filler, then?"

She sighed. "They didn't have an ogre like you to send out to club things. And they were fresh out of daughters and nieces to marry out, but there was a spare nephew. A marriage is just like business. It starts with a proposal. In the Graves family there are clauses instead of vows."

"Is he at least a decent guy?"

She shrugged. "I haven't seen him in eight months."

"That sounds like a lousy way to live a life."

"I'm taken care of. I'm kept busy. And I'm a part of something. It beats what I used to have, which was a job on a farm, hauling things around. Now my parents are in-laws to the Graves family. They're taken care of too."

"But there's always a little filthiness to being part of a family that deals with contraptions, isn't there?"

"I was slopping out pigpens. It's a wonder my parents cared enough to make sure I could read. The life I was headed for sure didn't have a lot of books in it. A little social filthiness beats a lot of actual filth."

They approached the intersection of two long, lonely roads. She looked down and checked the detector. It was rock solid and pointing directly down the road leading off to the northwest.

"The flame hasn't moved. If the book was right about how to find it, then it won't be long before we'll be dealing with another cluster of Bolivans," she said.

"Most likely."

"We need a plan."

"We already have a plan, remember?"

"A real one, Fel." She handed over the reins. "I'll go through the tactics book. Look through the maps. Then I'll tell you what we're doing."

"And when something doesn't go according to plan?"

"Then you do something crazy and stupid."

"Excellent. Now that's a proper plan. I can handle that."

She vanished into the carriage. He set his eyes on the road. The city was still a fair distance away. A long, boring wait before a frantic frenzy of life-or-death activity. The story of his life.

Later that evening, Epiphany trudged down the street toward The Fox and Log. It wasn't as though this was a rare trip for her. It was just rare that the trip was being made of her own volition. Normally if she went to The Fox and Log, it was to fetch Fel because it was suppertime and he was still squandering his money at the grum tables. But with what was going on in the house, she knew she needed some distance and some time to cool off before she caused another family incident. Thus a bit of time at The Fox and Log was the lesser of two evils.

She pushed through the door to find the place in its usual state of controlled chaos. Allie was behind the bar rather than walking the floor. Most of the patrons had separated off into clusters composed of old buddies, old enemies, and potential couples. She had no interest in ending up as a part of any such group, so she chose a stool at the bar a fair distance from anyone else and did her best to exude a raw, distilled aura of "leave me alone."

"Epiphany! One of my favorite Maskers," Allie said. "What'll you have?"

"I don't know... Something weak. I'm not here to get drunk. I'm just here to get out of the house," she said.

"You don't need something weak, then. Just something slow. A sipping drink."

"Make it a weak sipping drink," Epiphany said. "I do *not* need something loosening my lips."

"This is about Euphoria, is it?" Allie said, dropping a tankard on the table.

She put a splash of whiskey into it and topped the rest of it with water.

"Word is getting around about that, is it?"

"It's why Fel drank himself into unsteadiness before he left. Or at least that's my guess. What's the problem?"

"She's a thief, a liar, and a traitor. She spied on our family for years, stole a priceless family heirloom, and thinks that the way around it is to pretend it never happened and act like some sort of emotionless husk. And it's *worked perfectly* on Dad. Mom's being a little more reserved, but I know it worked on her, too."

"Worked?"

"They forgave her. To hear Dad talk about it, you'd think there was never anything to forgive."

Epiphany took a sip.

"And forgiveness is bad?" Allie said.

"It's wonderful if someone has earned it. I don't want to get into it, but a big piece of the mess we're in right now is thanks to Euphoria trying to manipulate us from afar."

"This'd be the, er... *business ventures* with the iffy gadgets."

Epiphany squinted at her, executing a perfect "exactly how much do you know about that?" expression.

"Fel was here for quite a while. Things come up in conversation," Allie said.

Epiphany sipped again. "See? Fora didn't even have to spy on us. She could have just sent someone to buy Fel a drink. Look, I came here specifically to *not* talk to or about her."

"Right, right. That's fine."

Allie scanned the tavern. When no urgent needs presented themselves, she pulled a basket of crickets out from under the bar and dropped it in front of her.

"So what kind of a name is Epiphany, anyway? Your mom is Vivian, your father is Martin. How do you get a name like Epiphany?"

"Dad wanted a girl and never expected to have one. He has three brothers that left the contraption business. His father was one of *six* brothers. There just haven't been any Masker women who didn't marry in for ages. Then his first child comes along and it's a girl. So, Euphoria. Then I came along and they realized the 'boys only' curse seemed to have been lifted. So, I was Epiphany. Fel was next, and Fel's just a family name. Apparently it's in honor of an ancestor named Felix, but Fel's not Felix, he's just Fel."

"It can be a little unpleasant growing up with a weird name, huh?" Allie said. "Mine's strange, but just because Mom couldn't spell. Alizon, with a Z. That goes away in the nickname, though."

"I like having a unique name. But Fora, Fanny, and Fel do have a certain ring." She gritted her teeth. "Did you know she doesn't even like to be called Fora anymore? Guess that reminds her too much of where she came from. Wouldn't want to remember your time as a Masker now that they're the enemy."

"I thought we weren't talking about her anymore."

"We're *not*." She crunched some crickets. "And that's not all! She didn't even bring the mask back. Three years ago she ran off and eloped with Jonathan Graves, and before she left she stole a mask off our sign. You'd think if you were hoping to smooth things over, you'd bring it back, right?

She didn't. She made some excuse about how bringing the mask back would open old wounds. As if they ever closed."

"It sounds like they did for your parents."

"No, they didn't. Mom and Dad have been hurting more than I have. They're just more afraid of the pain than the injury. But *I* know that Euphoria isn't who we remember. She made a decision, and she's lived by that decision for years. She made her choice, and I'm not going to let her, or anyone else, forget it. But enough. I don't want to talk about her anymore."

"Fine! There's plenty more to talk about. The regulars are behaving themselves, so I'm just on refill duty. We're running low on odds and ends because Davie hasn't been showing up for work, but I can always hire another runner for a while. Say, what kind of music do you like? The owner's been thinking about bringing in music once a week. Even wants to put in a stage. I'm partial to—"

"And another thing! She's got her eyes on that other mask. I'm *sure* of it. I wouldn't put it past her to have demanded to come home specifically to get the mask. And it's just dangling there in front of the store for anyone to take. Those masks were the faces of the business. They were the way people in the city knew the family. And she stole one. She *broke up the family*. It wasn't good enough that she did it literally, she had to do it symbolically too."

She drained the remainder of her watered-down whiskey and stood.

"Well I'm not going to let her take it." Epiphany dropped some coins on the counter. "Thanks for helping me straighten out my thoughts."

"I think maybe they're still a little crooked. How about you sit down and think this through just a little more. We'll get some food in here, have a nice long chat."

"No. This needs doing."

Epiphany stood and marched for the door.

"Pleasure having you, though you should have a chat with Fel about how to use a tavern and a friendly ear properly. He's a professional at it."

"He's had the practice," Epiphany called back.

The angry woman stomped home. Her fury and certainty didn't abate in the least as she stalked to the front door of Maskers Antiquities. It was the middle of the business day. Inside, her mother was busy closing the deal with a young gentleman looking to buy a rotating centerpiece. Two more customers were looking idly over the shelves, unlikely to make a purchase. Epiphany entered the shop, greeted everyone cordially, and fetched a stepladder from the back corner. Vivian watched her pace back toward the doorway. Though the seasoned shopkeeper didn't so much as stutter in her sales pitch, Epiphany could feel her gaze. She wouldn't stop her daughter, but she knew just what she was doing and she didn't like it.

Epiphany slammed down the ladder and climbed up. The lesser harpies lining the roofs looked upon her with curiosity. One of them, possibly Toody, dropped down and landed on the brace supporting the sign.

"Pig puke?" it inquired. "You lousy rat?"

"Not now. I don't have the patience for you right now," Epiphany snapped.

The harpy seemed to take the comment in the spirit it was intended. With a cordial "Go on, you filthy filth," it fluttered away to join the others.

The back of the sign was strategically positioned toward the lower traffic portion of the street. Her grandfather had been the one who'd installed the sign, ages ago. Martin and Fel had taken turns repairing it. The fasteners were simple bits of wire, poked through holes in the sign, twisted, and hammered down into a bit of improvised inlay to hide them. The sign was long overdue for maintenance. It could probably stand to be fully replaced. But at least that meant that the wood around the wire had begun to rot and flake. She raised her heel, slid her hidden blade from it as casually as someone brushing a stray bit of dirt away, and used it to lever the wire up from its groove. The ancient, corroded stuff snapped as she attempted to untwist it, but the job was done. She tugged at the mask and it came free.

The whole enterprise was done before the customers even noticed something was happening.

"We needed a new sign anyway," Epiphany said to her mother as she replaced the stepladder and slipped through the hatch.

She wove her way back and forth through the levels of the house. Martin was at the table, having lunch. He glanced at the mask, then at Epiphany, but said nothing. Crossing through the floor with their bedrooms revealed Euphoria to be in her old room, door shut. Epiphany continued until she got to the locked door of her father's workshop. She jingled keys from her pocket, unlocked the door, and stepped inside.

A jangling sound and twinkling motion startled her. The moment she had arrived, Oiler had reeled its claws and tail out to scurry toward her. Its polished, immobile, serpentine face gazed up at her, one claw clutching a puzzle box. It eagerly waggled it at her. She huffed a relieved breath and set the mask down. After shutting the door behind her, she crouched and took the puzzle box.

"Oiler... You probably don't like it in here. Alone with nothing to do. Probably doesn't suit what you were built for." She scrambled the box a bit. "Just another thing she brought upon this house."

She paused.

"I suppose I'm the reason you're locked in here. But trust me, it's better this way. I already know she sent someone to buy you. If she could, she'd run off with you and ransack the house looking for whatever else she wanted to risk Fel's life to acquire."

Oiler took the puzzle box and started clicking away at it again. Epiphany watched for a full minute. Fel liked to treat this thing like an animal. Trying to talk to it, reason with it, even train it. At first, she'd thought it was a bit absurd to do so. But she couldn't argue with results. It *had* become more reasonable, better behaved. Her father wasn't much different, but he'd been chatting with Wick for most of his life. He was comfortable with the thought of contraptions behaving as thinking creatures. For some reason Epiphany and Vivian were the only ones in the house resistant to the idea that Oiler might have a downright puppy-dog level of intelligence and personality. But something in this moment, watching the thing click away with a delighted little bob to its head, put some cracks in that notion. She looked around the workshop. The crate that had once contained contraptions discarded as worthless or incapable of repair had been replaced by a neat collection of what her father had once referred to as "balls of knots." They were contraptions that were hideously disproportionate in their complexity. She'd heard him waxing poetic about them, how they must have been *very* old contraptions, examples of the earlier form of the art. They weren't especially rare. The storeroom had dozens of them. They were easily attainable despite their age because most of them didn't *do* anything. They had triple or quadruple the components of most other contraptions, assembled into frustrating clusters of delicate and nearly identical components that simply would not operate unless assembled in one precise arrangement. When they *were* repaired, they did something pointless like flicking colored panels over in sequence or something actively undesirable like whistling whenever the room was above a certain temperature.

Now they were assembled and arranged like pet toys. Martin would pop their panels open and spill their innards into an empty box every morning, and Oiler would gleefully sort and assemble the pieces over the course of several hours. If she couldn't let Oiler have run of the house for the time being, she could at least make sure it was occupied. She grabbed the tool hanging on the wall and popped all the fasteners. A few seconds of unscrewing and dumping turned the half-dozen functional contraptions into a tangled mound of spare parts that would take a day to untangle, even for Oiler.

"Have fun," she said.

Oiler's little head chimed with delight. It abandoned the puzzle box and dug into the meaty task of reassembly. Satisfied she'd done what needed to be done, she picked up the mask and hung it on a peg over the workbench, then shut and locked the door behind her.

CHAPTER 5

Tome stood at the base of the Greater Lands Wall, gaze fixed on the rough line of its top. Parch had become either more accustomed to working with Tome or simply resigned to the fact that failure to do so meant being mystically tamed for a few hours, because he'd ceased to act up days ago. Tome had a feeling he still wasn't moving as swiftly as he would have if Fel had been present, but at least it wasn't a constant battle of wills. It made for a journey to the wall with no further mishap. But now a little over a week had passed and there was the wall itself to deal with.

He had options. Generally, having options was ideal. Even two choices meant there was by definition a better choice and a worse choice, at least assuming some sort of sane criteria were applied. That meant some level of hardship or risk could be discarded, if only symbolically, by eliminating the worst of the options. The issue was, Tome wasn't certain he was fond of either of the obvious choices.

Parch trotted forward and gently butted his head against the rusted gate that closed off the alcove they'd reached. Tome had attempted to navigate to the external alcove nearest to the hidden archive they'd encountered last time. That should give him easy access to it and thus assure him a wealth of materials to bring home when he was through in the Greater Lands, or if he thought better of venturing there. Since they hadn't entered via this door, the gate was still chained and intact.

The hair on the back of his neck prickled a bit whenever he looked away from the sky. This close to the wall, there was the very real risk of dragon attack. That thought was terrifying enough even *before* the dragon in question had been given reason to hold a grudge against Tome. Having ventured into the Greater Lands, he knew that it was an *enormous* distance from the dragon's island lair to the wall. But knowing that a dragon *probably* wasn't soaring near enough to get a whiff of him and not knowing a dragon *certainly* wasn't soaring near enough to get a whiff of him were two very different things. One tended to take even a long shot seriously when it could plausibly strike one in the chest.

"What are my options?" he mused as he darted his eyes from the sky to the back of the wagon and back again. "Over the wall or through the wall. Let's weigh them."

He selected a hammer and hefted it. Even though it was in the shade of the wagon's interior, the handle was uncomfortably warm to the touch from the baking heat of the arid stretch of land around the wall. He paced to the chain.

"In favor of going through the wall. It will get me out of this wretched sun. It will give me some time to go through the archive—a treasure that might well make the trip worth my while all by itself. But we've not been through the wall on *this* side of the archive. I have the codes, and I believe I am capable of entering them. But unless I retrace our footsteps from last time, all the traps are still active. I am less confident in my ability to detect and deactivate them. It was a bit more intuition-based than—"

Parch, evidently no longer interested in being the silent sounding board for Tome's musings, took matters into his own hooves. In an act that hammered home just how much stronger he was than he should have been, he lowered his head against the rusted gate, dug his hooves into the stone of the ancient road, and simply *pushed* the gate open. Red dust jumped off the bars as they buckled and bent. The chain groaned. A link popped. The gate slammed open, and Parch simply trotted through.

"Ah. I suppose you are thirsty, then. I knew you didn't like the heat, but I didn't think it was enough for you break down a gate."

He followed Parch inside and, with some difficulty, unfastened the yoke. The water trough and associated pump were in better repair than most such devices in the other alcoves, so he was able to pump up some fresh water with little effort. As the unicorn happily drank the cool water and Tome mopped his own head with a wet cloth, he continued his musing.

"The alternative is to go *over* the wall. That would entirely remove the threat of traps... I think. We certainly faced none when we returned via that method, though in retrospect a wall so heavily defended *inside* ought to have similar defenses on the outside. On the other hand, presumably the wall was built to keep threats *in*. If such wasn't the case, it wouldn't be so easily scaled to begin with. Really a bit of a riddle, this wall..."

Parch stopped his eager drinking. He paused for a second or two, head still down in the trough, ready to begin lapping again. Then he raised his head, ears flicking and pivoting. Finally he clip-clopped to the corner of the alcove and sat, eyes resolutely scanning the sky beyond. Tome matched his gaze. He saw nothing. But the creature was quite plainly spooked. And it would seem the feeling was contagious.

"I believe we would be better served by a journey through the *inside* of the wall. At least until we find the archive."

He flipped through the codebook and found the code associated with the indicated door.

"Would you mind keeping an eye on the ground and sky, Wick?" he asked. "Wick?"

He glanced at the flame. It was flickering in the breeze. Wick was absent.

"I swear that contraption is *not* proving useful. Why have me tote the thing along if it's not going to spend any time nearby?"

He looked at Parch.

"I don't imagine I need to tell you to keep your eyes open. And I don't imagine you'll understand me if I ask, but do make some noise if there's something I ought to know about."

Parch didn't offer any indication that he'd heard or understood. He just kept gazing with an unnervingly rigid posture.

"That does not fill me with tranquility," Tome said, hastily beginning the careful process of unlocking the door.

His concern made his hands a bit shaky, which was not ideal when making an error could activate some manner of arcane defense, but he entered the code for the door without mishap and pushed it open. He considered instructing Parch to stay put, but by now it was clear the unicorn would do what it pleased. Given its clear dedication to its own self-preservation and its impressive capacity to identify dangers, Tome suspected the creature would be safer than he was. Even so, he left the door open and stepped inside.

Wick's lantern cast light upon a room nearly identical to every entry room they'd encountered in the wall thus far. A long, shallow room with sturdy doors separating it from other chambers. This one was outfitted with the dregs of what had once been a storage room. Plenty of shelves, each all but empty. The rare shelf with something remaining on it mostly bore clay pots with labels written by someone long dead. He moved slowly through the place, eyes wide and searching for the trip lines, pressure plates, and other mysterious activation points for deadly traps.

"All I need to do is find a way downstairs. If I'm right, the archive will be right below me, and that will take me to the river, too. I just need to stay alive long enough to find a hatch."

He crouched low and aligned his eye with the floor. No panels visibly rose or lowered. No pressure plates. There *were* oddly wide gaps between the tiles running from the front wall to the back wall, but shining light down into them didn't reveal any manner of workings. So far so good.

Ten full minutes brought him to the midpoint of the floor. The shadows were slowing down in their subtle jumps and jostles. Wick would arrive soon. Tome had never felt more relieved to hear a voice than when the sentry flame spoke up.

"I see you have arrived in the Greater Lands Wall," he said. "What is your present task, and how may I help with it?"

"Look at the markings on the wall there," Tome said quickly. "Am I correct that those marks there label this as the same part of the wall that holds the archive?"

"That would appear to be an accurate assessment. I see that Parch is watching from the doorway. Has he been ordered to keep his distance?"

"So far the only instruction he's followed, with great reluctance I'll add, is 'walk forward,'" Tome said. "Do you see anything resembling a hatch, an exit, or a trap?"

"Not presently. Though my presence on missions such as these is a recent addition to the services I provide, so I am rather inexpert at spotting such things."

"Another set of eyes, so to speak, will still be helpful. If something seems dangerous, tell me."

"I shall happily fulfill this service. Would you like an update on how things are progressing elsewhere?"

"Now is not the best time for distraction."

"Understood."

He crept forward. The farther he got from the door, the harder his heart pounded. Everything began to look like a potential trigger. Over the course of nearly an hour, Wick had cheerfully warned about things that turned out to be harmless six times. Tome had identified one suspiciously cantilevered shelf that he gave a wide berth. Finally, he found what he was looking for. A shelf was straddling what was clearly a hinged tile. This was the hatch downstairs. If not directly to the archive, then to the hallway that they'd been traveling through when they found it last time.

"Wick, what are the chances that I'll just be able to move that shelf and open the hatch?"

"Quite low."

"That's what I thought." He reached into his pocket and produced the folio of spells. "But knowing where the trigger is should be enough. If I can't deactivate the trigger, at least I can trigger it from a distance. At worst, it will show me what the trap is, and at best it will spring it in a way that will not reset."

"I believe the range of possibilities may stretch wider than you suspect," Wick said.

"I'll take the proper precautions."

Tome retraced his footsteps, counting off the distance and estimating the time it would take to get that far without risking a misstep. If he was correct, he would be able to get as far as the place between the two shelves opposite the door. Not quite clear of the room, but comfortably far from the hatch and thus what he presumed would be the center of the trap's effect. He returned to the offending shelf and prepared the spell.

"This is a new effect. I concocted it with the help of Martin. He called it a 'phantom ram.' It should give everything around it a good hard shove. If the trap is still functional, that should be enough to activate it."

"I look forward to observing its activation."

Tome opened the door on the front of Wick's lantern and lit the corner of the spell. Burning it rather than tearing it would give him a few more moments before activation. He dashed with controlled precision, and was less than two steps away from where he'd predicted he would reach when the spell activated. At this distance, the effect felt like the rush of wind from a door slammed just in front of him. Closer to the source, the force was indeed enough to not just jostle but dislodge the shelf in question. The dust blown about by the spell's activation stung his eyes, so he wasn't able to watch for what aspect of the shelf had been the activation point, but there was no doubt the trap had been sprung. Unfortunately, that certainty came in the form of a startling metallic clunk between him and the door.

He turned. Long, thin rods had reeled down from the ceiling. They were aligned with, and inserted into, the wide slots he'd spotted on the floor. He sprinted for the door, which would have required him to dodge around the rod nearest to it. He was a step too late. That step was a lifesaver. Had he been just a bit faster, he would have been inches from the rod when it bristled with needle-thin spikes. They flipped down from the rest of the rod and would have slashed him badly if he'd been close enough. Once the spikes were deployed, the rods began to spin. They moved so swiftly they produced a piercing whine and stirred up the air into a dusty gust. The spinning rod began to advance along the slots, slashing the air as Tome backed away. He looked about frantically for some means of escape, but the hazard was perfectly designed to slide between the rows of shelves with barely an inch to spare on either side. It was like some horrid mechanism designed to clean the room by turning everything but the shelves into a fine slurry.

Tome backed against the far wall and fumbled for his spells. A horrifying grinding sound rang out closer to the trap's trigger. The spell had knocked the shelf over and thus had blocked the path of the rods advancing on either side of it. The air filled with the smell of charred wood. Shreds of former shelf pelted the surrounding shelves. The whole mechanism slowed with the effort of grinding through an entire shelf, but it didn't stop. The time remaining before the spinning rod reached him was measured in seconds. His mind flicked madly through a dozen different potential means of escape. The shelves were too tall for him to climb onto and too tightly spaced for him to climb into. There wasn't nearly enough room between any two rods and the shelves for him to slip by. He found one of his most reliable spells and tore its edge. As it flickered and burned, he tossed it toward the nearest rod. The air around the rod flashed to a frosty haze. He heard a terrible grinding sound as the ice spell tried to do its work, but there wasn't enough moisture in the air for a proper shell of ice to form.

The portion of the falling shelf that was blocking the path had been entirely churned to fragments, and the whole mechanism advanced more quickly. He grabbed on to the nearest shelves and heaved them off-balance. They tipped against their respective rods and were shredded as well. Clay pots smashed. Bits of wood and metal scoured Tome's arms as he shielded his face. Somewhere in the chaos, he heard the splash of some sort of liquid, then felt it speckle his face in a fine mist. Without a moment to spare, he pulled the next sheet from the same pocket of the folio and tore it. A second ice spell curled across the room, projecting outward. Whatever the provision that had been left behind, it froze solid under the influence of the magic, and the rod seized. The rest of the rods slowed to a stop as well. In the relative silence, Tome could hear unseen machinery groaning and the icy buildup crackling and grinding. This little respite wouldn't last for long. Wick's lantern had fallen to the ground in the confusion. He fetched it up and rushed toward the temporarily stationary rod. The spikes attached to the rod had drooped, hinging back downward a bit now that the motion of the rod couldn't keep them fully extended. Tome used the lantern to bash a few of the spikes out of position. The gap he created was *just* enough for him to fit through if he scaled the twisted remnants of the shelf. He scrambled over the wreckage. The rod rattled back to motion a heartbeat after he crawled clear, catching and shredding the hem of his tunic. He dashed to the open door and threw himself out while the whole mechanism ground forward, completing the task.

Tome gasped for breath and patted himself in fearful search of lacerations. Finding none, he slumped against the ground and hoped his heart would slow down before it rattled its way out of his chest.

"It would appear that no position within the room can reliably be considered far enough from the trigger of a trap for safe activation," Wick said, his lantern resting on the ground beside Tome.

"That would have been more useful as *foresight* rather than *hindsight*," Tome said, shakily pulling himself upright. "We never encountered anything like that when *Fel* was here."

"It would be more accurate to state that you never *activated* anything like that when Fel was here. It is not only possible but plausible that Fel avoided or deactivated many such traps."

"Do we at least know if the trap will activate again if we go in there?"

"I believe I observed the entire trigger apparatus being pulled into the spinning spikes. I doubt it could be made to activate again without considerable repair."

"Can I trust you on that? You haven't been very helpful thus far."

"I have no way of knowing if my assertion is correct."

Tome huffed a shaky breath and climbed to his feet.

"This is a sign that perhaps going over the top is a preferable approach."

He turned to Parch. Despite the horrifying sound that had been roaring out through the open door, Parch didn't appear to have moved at all. His eyes were fixed on the sky, and he was backed into the corner.

"What?" Tome barked. "What is it? Why are you staring at the sky? What could be out there that could possibly be more frightening than what is in *there*."

He shut his eyes and leaned against the wall, sliding down to a seat beside Parch.

"I swear this seemed easier when Fel was here..."

"We're getting close," Lattica said. "Remember what we discussed."

Fel nodded, which was foolish because he was once again in the back of the carriage while Lattica was at the reins, and thus she couldn't see him waggling his head. He could be excused for his absentmindedness, as the task at hand was taking all his concentration. Over the course of the last few days, he'd successfully disassembled and reassembled the various contraptions captured from the Bolivans. All but one, that was. Presently he was struggling with the final plate of the invisibility contraption. Officially, he'd persuaded Lattica to let him work on the pieces in order to ensure they would know how to work them and to be certain they'd not been booby-trapped or otherwise compromised. To his great relief, they hadn't been. But inspecting the devices for sabotage was only *half* the reason for taking them apart. The other half had been his own curiosity, and though he'd succeeded in satisfying it, he already wished he hadn't. All he'd managed to do was add yet another distraction to a frustratingly long list of them.

He got the final plate back in place just as he could feel the wheels of the carriage roll from the fine, crunchy gravel of the long-range road to the sturdier cut stone of the local one. Climber's Circle was wealthy, well-maintained, and relatively new. That meant a few things. It had taller buildings built mostly of wood rather than stone, for starters. There was no wall, because this place had been built near enough to the relatively peaceful recent history for the concept of a siege to be too far down the list of a city planner's concerns to be addressed. And most troubling, this place probably had a very well-funded and well-armed City Watch. To the average person, it was fair to say this didn't seem like the sort of place a major criminal enterprise would make its home. Such a view betrayed a glaring lack of insight into what sort of people ran criminal enterprises these days. More to the point, a city that seemed like it would be free of crime was the perfect place to hide some crime. No one would look for it there.

"The indicator is rock solid," she said. "No lesser flames in the area. Have you found the map of the city yet?"

"I've been a little busy," he replied, sliding the contraption back into its leather bracer.

"Fine. Take the reins and take the ring road around the outside of the city. The tactics book calls for pinpointing the exact *building* the lantern is in before we move in."

He slid the brace in place and slipped past her as best he could in the cramped space. As she grabbed the indicator and started rummaging through maps, he pulled his spyglass from his bag and started scanning the city.

While he was no stranger to long trips, he usually had much greater control over the provisions he brought along. The crackers and their meaty smear that had been the bulk of his diet for more than a week were tasty, but the lack of variety was wearing on him. They'd spent a grand total of two nights in something he could consider a proper tavern. The rest of the time had been spent camping—or rather, taking turns sleeping in the hammock while the other kept watch. All this combined to push nearly all the anxiety and anticipation for what was likely to be a massive battle aside in favor of the tantalizing promise of a meal that didn't crumble after the first bite and a drink that had some flavor other than the inside of a rain barrel. A city like this could easily provide plenty of each. And some entertainment besides.

With no wall, he could see half the city from the outside. This main road continued through the center of the city. It was a third the size of Beffshire, but had the feel of a place that was aiming for the same reputation as the large trading town. A healthy market district lay ahead, with colorful signs, burning lanterns visible through the windows despite the time of day, and plenty of evidence of prosperity and money.

He guided the horses off the main road to a decidedly more utilitarian road around to the west. Slowly, more of the city became visible. He found himself picking where he would have stopped if he wasn't likely to be leaving this place in a blind panic.

The view that opened up to him included some of the less attractive aspects of a large city, such as tucked-away sections of the town dedicated to dealing with waste and transportation. He squinted at something just barely visible. It looked very much like a stable, but the walls were much higher. Upon second glance, he discovered that a thin net had been strung across the top of the walls. It formed a billowy roof and rendered the whole area something of an oversize birdcage. Given his history with things that fit the description of "oversize birds," he didn't like the idea of facing any more of them.

"Please don't let the flame be in there," he muttered.

"There should be a signpost ahead," Lattica said. "Stop there."

"Right," he said and eased the carriage to a stop.

"You've got a map of the city?"

"Of course." He heard the sound of chalk drawn across the page repeatedly. "Continue along the road until you hit the intersection of a stone fence and a wooden one."

He flicked the reins.

"Any mention of... what's the name for it... for horses it's a stable. This one's for birds."

She grumbled. "It's... not arboretum. That's the tree one... Apiary is bees, I think."

"Aviary!" they realized at once.

"Yes, there's an aviary in the northeast corner of town."

"By any chance, did the line you just drew pass through it?"

"It did."

He shut his eyes and shook his head.

"I don't think you're going to need another line." Fel palmed his face. "I'm going to have to fight another hippogriff."

"Not if we do this correctly," she said. "And you don't know for sure that's where the flame will be."

"First, we're *not* going to do this correctly. I'm not good at doing things correctly. I'm good at starting things correctly and then surviving the mistakes I make. Second, why *wouldn't* it be there? If I wanted to keep something safe, I'd surround it with monsters."

"Have you tested the bracer?" she asked.

He gave a cursory glance around to make sure he wasn't being observed, then found the appropriate place on the bracer and depressed the button to activate it. Technically he'd tested it prior to disassembling it, and tested it again just moments ago when he clicked the last panel in place. But this was the first time he'd tested it as it was intended to be used. The effects were... interesting. It wasn't just that he could look down and see the seat he was currently sitting on. The entire act of 'seeing' had changed. His vision was, to put it simply, wrong. He lacked the words to articulate it properly, but he didn't feel as though he was seeing the world, rather that he was seeing a depiction of the world. Things had a glistening gleam to them, like something viewed through a greasy window. Bright points seemed too bright. Things that should have been rough or matte had strange reflections on them.

"Now I know why they seem to have such terrible aim while they're using this," he said, tapping the contraption to deactivate it.

"What was that?" she called out to him.

"It works. But having it on makes me feel a little sick and makes the world look like it's been dipped in lard."

He brought the carriage to a stop.

"We're at the intersection of the stone and wooden fences."

"One moment." Another long, grinding chalk line was traced out. "You'd best get used to that sick feeling, because the flame is right at the edge of the aviary."

"... So, a plan then?" Fel said reluctantly.

"I'm checking the tactics book now," Lattica said.

Martin looked up from his work. He was a bit bleary-eyed. Long hours working with tiny parts of unknown purpose will do that, and he'd been working particularly hard on the bust from Clickspring for the week since Euphoria had arrived. As intellectually enriching it had been, his eyes weren't getting any younger. Working with the door secured had a way of hammering home that things weren't as they should be, as well. He rubbed his eyes and glanced at Oiler. The contraption had nearly finished reassembling the third of the six "toys" he'd been given to reassemble.

"I think that will be all for today. Enjoy yourself. I think I'm close to understanding the basic function of this apparatus. That's the most important step," Martin said.

He wearily opened the door, locked it behind him, and trudged off.

Oiler continued to click and clack along, sorting the remaining pieces in the jumbled-up pile to locate the next one it required to complete the mechanism. When it was slotted in place, a soft chime rang out within Oiler's head, and it briefly assessed the surroundings for what to repair next. Though the room was extremely familiar, to the point of tedium for normal living creatures, Oiler treated it with fresh eyes every time a task was completed. The world was mutable. Things could break, and need to be repaired, at any time. Circumstances could change. And they had. In a room that had been carefully kept clear of any completely reparable contraptions, something *had* changed. A rather large and complete component had been introduced, and the bust had been moved considerably closer to working order. The gaps between nonfunctional and functional seemed to narrow.

Oiler looked first to the crate of spare parts, then to the workbench. It reeled itself up and clambered onto the work surface. Humanity had a strange relationship with the familiar. If someone like Martin Masker saw something every day, it became invisible to him. A natural part of the world, as forgettable as a pattern on the wall. The mask hanging on the peg may as well have not been there at all. It was just a bit of decoration, and the mere fact that it had been moved from the sign to the workshop was a reminder that things were not as they should be. Oiler was not similarly burdened. To the contraption, it was a component. A specifically shaped puzzle piece awaiting its proper slot.

Brass claws gingerly plucked the mask from the peg. Again, Oiler assessed the room. The bust was not complete. Even with the addition of the mask, it was incomplete. There were pieces missing, and several of the components were damaged. But Martin had made good progress. The box of parts from Oiler's "toys" contained pieces that were quite similar to those that were missing from the bust. Oiler rummaged in the box and selected a few. Yes. They would fit. And it seemed there were enough of them to finish the job.

This would be a big repair. A fine way to spend an evening.

Tome had let an embarrassingly large amount of time pass before making his decision. He'd watched the sky beside Parch long enough for the shadows to have visibly crept across the ground. At no point did anything even resembling a threat present itself, but somehow each moment without the swish of wings and the crackle of dragon fire made the *next* moment seem even more likely to contain it. The long delay gave him time to write some slightly improved replacements to the ice spells he'd cast. Finally, in what he chose to believe was a logical and sane decision in no way motivated by the odd behavior of the lesser unicorn, Tome decided the inside of the wall was a better avenue to the Greater Lands than over the top even despite the trap-related mishap.

He crept into the badly damaged room and held Wick's lantern high in one hand and a bucket of water in the other. If things became exciting again, he'd be ready to seize up the works as he had last time. The rotating spike rods had retracted into the ceiling when they were through with their transit across the room. He didn't know if they'd slipped back to their starting position from wherever they were hidden or if a theoretical second trip would lead in the opposite direction. Out of an abundance of caution, he kept as near to the middle of the room as he could. When he reached the hidden hatch, he found it clearly labeled, and a matching code was easily turned up in the pages of the translated codebook Martin had provided. He kept clear of the torn-up trigger while applying the code. A very deliberate sequence of ring rotations and button presses rewarded him with an uneventful little thunk. He pulled at the hatch. It swung open.

A ladder led down into the pitch-blackness below. Snapping his fingers produced a nearby echo. The shaft didn't lead very far downward.

"It looks safe, Wick, but I'm not taking any chances," he said.

"That is reasonable," Wick replied.

Tome tied a rope to the top of the lantern and lowered it down.

"What do you see?"

"There is a narrow corridor. No obvious traps. A double door a short distance down the corridor is clearly labeled in the ancient dialect. The doors have their own somewhat more sophisticated set of locking rings. You have indeed located the archive."

"Excellent! This trip, and the risk to life and limb, will not have been entirely in vain."

He let the rope coil down to the ground and descended to meet Wick. It was just as he described, though Wick had left out the copious amount of spiderwebs clustered in the corners. He approached the door and flipped open the codebook. Tracking down the code that matched the symbols on the door turned out to be a bit more tedious this time. Perhaps those who had written the book had purposely tucked away the most important codes in out-of-the-way places to slow down would-be infiltrators. Perhaps it was just bad luck. He'd only *just* found what he believed to be the proper code when some debris crackled down through the ladder shaft from above. He turned to it nervously, then nearly ran headlong into a wall when a much larger blur of motion clattered down. When his eyes were able to focus on the sudden arrival, he found Parch gazing up at him.

"So you waited for me to clear the way, eh? I'm not here to make the way safe for *you*, you know."

Parch bleated and sat down on his haunches in Wick's glow. Tome tried to resist the feeling that the unicorn was supervising as he entered the code. With the final click, the doors retracted on their own, swinging slowly and smoothly. Tome felt foolishly obliged to tamp down his jolt of fear at the automatic motion. Something about being observed by both Parch and Wick made him feel as though he should at least attempt to avoid seeming as excitable as he really was.

He picked up Wick's lantern and stepped through the doors.

"By the High..." he uttered.

The library spread out in both directions, filling the entire interior of this level of the wall. It stretched so far that the light failed to fall upon a wall on either the left or right, giving the sense that this place was endless. He imagined it filling the center of the entire ring of the Greater Lands Wall. The front and rear walls were completely lined with bookshelves, and a single row of long, thin shelves filled the center of the room. Every shelf was completely stocked with books. They were in perfect condition. Somehow they hadn't even become dusty.

"Please. Please exercise great care here," Wick said.

"There won't be any traps in here," Tome murmured with certainty. "No one would risk a place like this."

"Traps were not my concern. Open flame is my concern. *I* am my concern," Wick said.

"I will take great care."

"Please leave me outside the door."

"Wick, I need to be able to see."

"There are lighting contraptions at regular intervals. Place me outside the archive and activate one of them."

"Don't you want to observe—"

"Remove me from this place right now," Wick said desperately.

Tome hastily stepped clear of the doorway and set Wick down.

"Is something wrong?" he asked.

"No. Nothing is wrong. What would give you that idea?" Wick said calmly, now that he was not within the library.

Parch clip-clopped past Wick and into the library.

"Keep an eye on Parch, please," Wick requested.

"You are making an awful lot of demands all of a sudden," Tome said.

He found one of the lighting contraptions Wick had mentioned and depressed the button. A soft greenish glow emanated from a marble-size component in the handheld light. Parch clacked around, sniffing and nudging against assorted books.

"Go. Get away from there. These aren't for you to snack on," Tome said.

He slipped a random book from its shelf and flipped it open. The pages were crisp, and the text was clear, as though the book had never been opened. It wasn't handwritten. This book was printed. Perhaps it was a residue of his time in the monastery copying books by hand, but Tome had an instinctive dislike for printing. Like most bits of technology these days, it had taken generations to return to regular use after becoming, presumably, the standard means of recording books during the Bygone Era. He wasn't a fluent or speedy reader of the old texts, but he was able to decipher enough to realize something that utterly delighted him.

"This is a history book! I was afraid this place would be filled entirely with technical manuals and the like."

He snapped the book shut and slid it back onto the shelf.

"It's curious… nearly every place we've searched within the wall has been cleaned out, or at least seemed to be in the process of being cleaned out. But this is perfectly intact. It was better protected than most. Three locked doors and the most heinous trap I've ever encountered. But still. Why is *this* all here?"

"Because knowledge is only reliably an asset when it is complete," Wick said.

"Now that simply isn't so," Tome said. "Martin is evidence of that. He's been assembling fragments of information for years, and it's made him the foremost expert in contraptions in the world."

"He has learned. The process of learning, and indeed the entire pursuit of knowledge, is incomplete by that measure. But when you acquire knowledge without continuity, without context, there lies danger. You learn *what* but not *how*. You learn *why*, but not *why not*. You learn what is intended, but not what is unintended. If information is rendered incomplete, it is better to start from nothing than to start from nearly everything if what's missing is fundamental. If an archive cannot be moved or duplicated in full, then it must instead be preserved."

"You speak as though you are an authority on this."

"I am not an authority. I merely have been instructed."

"Instructed..." Tome turned to the door. "You were given instructions about archives?"

"I am a sentry lantern. A contraption. I was created with a purpose. I was given the knowledge to achieve that purpose."

"Knowledge about archives."

"Knowledge about places of value that I was to watch over."

"Did you watch over an archive?" Tome asked flatly.

"I prefer not to elaborate. As I said, incomplete information does more harm than good."

Tome sighed. "I am genuinely beginning to wonder if anyone should be relying upon you, Wick. A contraption shouldn't be cagey."

"I must respectfully disagree. Cages, for example, should be cagey."

Tome glared at the lantern. "I wasn't sure you could be more irritating, and then you lobbed a pun at me. But if you know things about Bygone Archives, can you at least tell me if there is an index? This place seems too well organized not to have one."

"In the center of the archive, look for a small globular contraption."

"Of course it's a contraption," Tome rumbled.

"It will respond to spoken commands. Most likely exclusively in the primary language of the era."

"*Of course it will,*" Tome grumbled. "I suppose I should be happy that they respected the written word enough to keep an archive on paper rather than locking it all away in some recalcitrant contraption. Are you able to speak the language necessary to access the information?"

"In a limited fashion."

"I'm going to bring you inside to address the index directly."

"I would prefer you did not."

"I know how to be careful with flames around books."

"I would prefer you did not."

"This is part of the reason you were brought along. Now come. The sooner we do this, the better."

Tome grasped the lantern and brought it inside. Before the contraption even crossed the threshold, the flame hissed away, curling to a wisp of smoke. The paper mage paused, eyebrow raised.

"I did not know it could do that..."

As certain as he was that he could use a lantern safely within the library, lighting it was another matter. Too much sparking. Too much potential for a stray flame. He took Wick's lantern into the hallway and relit it. The flame wavered at first, then became still as Wick returned to the lantern.

"I apologize, but I was clear that I would not have been happy fulfilling that service," Wick said.

"What is *wrong* with you?"

"I am performing the functions I was designed to perform."

"I think it is long past time you explained yourself."

"What further explanation is necessary?"

"Everything! You're doing things I didn't know you could do, you're misbehaving. Why are you afraid of the archive?"

A long, very telling silence followed.

"You are familiar with the Telestressa Archives?" Wick finally said.

"Of course I am."

"Upon my creation, I was installed in that archive."

"... You weren't."

"I was. And I was present when it burned. It was my last moment of consciousness prior to being repaired and relit by the Maskers."

"That's astounding. What did you see?"

"I didn't see anything. That is my greatest shame. I am a sentry lantern. My purpose is to observe. But unless they are quite near to each other, I can only observe from a single flame. The archive was enormous. A city with a roof. Only a few dozen sentry lanterns were ever made. We were vanishingly rare. Even so, two lanterns were dedicated solely to the archive. Over a hundred flames were lit from my lantern and kept burning, and my existence was a continuous circuit around them, observing. Watching. It was an important task, a profoundly fulfilling service. But I failed. One moment I was slipping from flame to flame. The second the whole archive was in flames. And I did not see who did it or how they did it. I was constructed with a single purpose, and to my great shame I was not equal to the task. But I will not allow a second such error to be made. Though it is a fraction of the size of the Telestressa Archives, I will see to it that there will be no flames within its walls. Least of all, me."

Tome set the lantern down and crouched before it with his hands on his knees, as if addressing a child.

"I never expected to say anything like this to anything like you. But I can respect that. I assume you have the full list of topics and titles that Martin was hoping I would bring home?"

"Of course."

"Teach me how to request their locations from the index. And while you're at it, teach me how to request maps of the Greater Lands Wall's interior and maps of the Greater Lands."

"This is a service I will cheerfully provide."

Fel had guided the carriage through two full orbits of the city, with regular stops for Lattica to check and double-check that their target was, indeed, within the aviary. Once she was absolutely certain, he'd taken the carriage a decent distance from the city and stowed it among some trees. The time since then had been with Lattica flipping back and forth between a trio of books, looking increasingly flustered.

"Anything yet?" Fel asked.

"Don't you think I would *tell* you if there was anything yet? Do you think I'd just sit here *reading* if I'd found something useful?" Lattica snapped. "Stop asking!"

"Does the book say anything about how a giant, slow wagon driving in a circle around the city and then hiding in the woods might raise some suspicions?" he said.

"As a matter of fact, it does. It *also* recommends at least four people for a mission like this, and do I need to remind you why we don't have *that*?"

She tapped the page.

"Here is what we know. That aviary, we must assume, is home to hippogriffs. It is relatively new, completed in just the last few months. If we assume the Bolivans paid for it, this was likely intended to be their first major foothold in waging a continuing assault against your family. The price of building out this old stable into a hippogriff aviary, and then purchasing even a single hippogriff, must have been incalculable. We've been clashing with them for years and we've never seen this level of hostility. Your sister suspected there was new leadership, and I think this confirms it."

Fel grinned.

"What are you smiling about?" she asked.

"Once I start butting heads against them, they start purchasing mystic creatures. Nice to know we're being taken seriously."

She shook her head and turned back to the tactics book.

"According to this, it is relatively easy to remove a hippogriff from the battle. You just need to—"

"Remove the saddle. That much I've learned."

"Right. As for the Bolivans, we have to assume one rider. Probably a trained mercenary, hired along with the hippogriff. They probably won't stay in the fight once the 'griff is gone, because it's not their cause. So we take out the 'griff, that's two threats down. There will be at least two more. Probably three. They like to have people working in pairs, so two foot soldiers and a spare to pair up with the rider. And for an operation like this, there will be what they call a 'dispatcher,' someone who handles messages and delivers orders. That's who we'll find keeping the flame."

She flipped through some more pages.

"New city. No need to worry about deep basements. They'll probably have the flame in a well-fortified second- or third-level room."

"The notes have that sort of detail?" Fel said.

"Yes. The Graves family is meticulous. Which is good, because unlike you, I'm not a lunatic that this sort of mad violence comes naturally to."

Fel glanced to sky.

"Speaking of violence coming easily, here it comes now. The something big is on the move in the sky."

She flipped through some more pages, frazzled. "One of us will have to fight, and one of us will have to sneak. How are you with a crossbow?"

"Terrible."

"I'm fair. That settles it then. You use the bracer, find the dispatcher, snuff the flame, and take the lantern. I'll protect the carriage. Now go!"

Fel nodded, grabbed his cudgel, and slapped the button for the bracer. His vision shifted to the odd, greasy view the contraption conjured for him. His first act of business in the latest life-or-death clash was to catch his foot on one of the reins and fall face-first off the carriage. It was a small blessing that Lattica hadn't *seen* him do it, but the startled yelp and plume of dust told the tale. He got up and got moving. If bruising his ego and his chin were the worst things that happened today, it would be a victory.

The sprint into town wasn't much more graceful than his exit from the carriage. The human mind simply wasn't built for maneuvering when one's body parts weren't visible. Paradoxically, he found it easier to run with his eyes shut, opening them every few steps to get a lay of the land. He still stumbled and reeled now and then, but at least his mind wasn't getting twisted in knots while he did so.

Things became briefly easier when he got clear of the brush between the trees and the road. The way ahead was clear, though overhead he could hear the flap of heavy wings. It disturbed him that he could tell by the windy sound that this was *not* the same sort of creature he'd faced back in Beffshire a few months ago. It wasn't a hippogriff. This sounded larger. The labor had been divided, and thus until the thing came swooping for him, it wasn't his concern, but he couldn't help feeling a sting of anxiety for Lattica. Fortunately, his next challenge ended up pushing that, and everything else, out of his mind.

Climber's Circle was bustling. It was comfortably within the busiest hours of a city built around its markets, so the streets were thick with vendors and customers. Fel was a burly fellow. Until this very moment he'd never had to worry about not being noticed as he barreled through a street. People usually dove out of his way as though he was a runaway bull once he got moving. But he was utterly invisible. The effect was completely opposite. People heard the stomping of his feet and the huffing of his breath and stopped, turning to investigate. If something as simple as climbing out of a carriage was too much for him in this condition, weaving nimbly through a crowd was *well* beyond his skills. Many a confused market-goer felt a meaty thump from an unseen shoulder to the chest and went flying against a wall as he thundered through the streets.

Luck was with him, in that he hadn't made it halfway through the town before the obvious base of operations presented itself. Again, the city was built around its markets. Most buildings that weren't residences were constructed to be as inviting and accessible as possible so that customers would come and sample the wares. The building butted up against the aviary was quite the opposite. Heavy doors. Barred windows. Even the streets around it had been blocked off with gates to provide something of a private city within a city.

Guards stationed at the street gate ahead were on high alert. One man held a club. The other had a short blade. No contraptions that he could see. Probably locals hired by the Bolivans. For another man, that would make them just as much an enemy as the Bolivans themselves, and subject to the same beating. But Fel had worked too many odd jobs to see these portly and anxious men as anything more than a set of empty pockets looking to be filled.

He slowed his pace and stepped aside, sidling along the wall as he tried to catch his breath. It was a shame the man they'd confiscated the bracer from hadn't also been wearing one of those contraptions that allowed the wearer to move silently. He wasn't a sprinter, so the short run had left him huffing and puffing loudly enough to draw attention if he got too close. As it happened, a mysterious force bashing its way through the market district had a way of raising a bit of a ruckus. The confused and bruised shoppers picking themselves up and dusting themselves off were making their displeasure known, which was distraction enough to keep the guards' eyes and ears directed down the street.

The moment of relative calm while he got his wind back and planned his next steps gave him the opportunity to finally turn his attention fully to the sky. Lattica's tactics book was not perfectly accurate. Her speculation was wrong, and his ears had been right. It wasn't a hippogriff. It was a griffin. In all ways it was more fearsome and more terrible than the beast he was already worried about facing. The front half was an eagle, the back half a lion. Both had been scaled to something larger even than the massive horses pulling Lattica's wagon. Great wings sliced through the air as it wheeled in search of the carriage.

Indecision struck him. He felt the urge to rush back to the carriage, to do what he could to help Lattica fend off the beast. But he was armed with hand-to-hand weapons, proposing a battle against a creature with a viselike beak, daggerlike talons, and feline claws. The only part of the monster that wasn't equipped with lethal weapons was its back, and *that* was home to a rider with his own array of weaponry. The best he could be if he charged back to Lattica was a distraction, and rushing to her aid would give the Bolivans time to tighten their defenses further.

Lattica was smart, or at least meticulous. She was strong, or at least large. She was a better shot, or at least claimed to be. She could handle herself. He had his own job to do.

As much as it pained him to do so, he pushed her well-being from his mind for the moment and turned back to the task. To his terrible dismay, he realized that getting through to the sturdy building beside the aviary without being utterly mobbed with hired goons would require him to be clever. In matters of combat, he'd found he wasn't nearly as consistent with cleverness as he was with brute force. But the capacity to remain unseen while he puzzled things out helped matters.

He gazed around. The streets curved into a circle. The aviary was at the northwest corner of a small courtyard that was a focal point for the city. Surrounding streets ringed the courtyard. Gates across the streets shut it off from the rest of the city, but the buildings along those streets made up the remainder of the defensive perimeter. They butted against one another, no alleys between. But there was a reason forts protected themselves with walls rather than houses and stores. Houses and stores were full of doors and windows.

Fel retreated to the previous street. A leather shop was the nearest place of business that was open. He slipped inside. Presently there was only a single customer, and it seemed this business had only one employee. The day was warm, so the doors to both the shop and the back room were open. That there was a cross breeze suggested the windows on the far side of the back room were open as well.

Moving with a measure more care than he'd used in the streets, Fel crept through the shop. His heavy boots weren't meant for sneaking, and his heavier body even less so. The floorboards creaked and groaned under his weight. The shop owner paused in his confident description of the quality of his cowhides and turned. Fel froze, holding his breath. All the man had to do was take three steps toward him and probe the air, and Fel would be revealed. Being invisible without being insubstantial wasn't nearly as useful as Fel had expected it to be. It did, however, come with two considerable benefits. First, rare was the person who would hear a creaking floorboard and assume they were being invaded by an invisible aggressor. Second, the still-simmering confusion caused by his charge through the city was much more interesting than a creaky floor.

The shopkeeper glanced back toward the street, and Fel hurried through the back room. His semblance of care and stealth eroded quickly when he spotted the open window leading to the courtyard. He thumped toward it and practically hurled himself through, tumbling to the ground outside. All of the noise was enough to draw the shopkeeper into the back room to investigate, but by then Fel was already sprinting for the edge of the aviary.

Fel wasn't an expert in architecture, but even he could see that this place hadn't started its life as a cage for mystic beasts. The residual fencing from a large but otherwise standard stable remained at ground level. It had been fortified and heightened, with great gates added to allow the much larger beast to enter and exit. The beast had just left. The gate was open. He rushed inside.

Scurrying past waste bins filled with droppings studded with bits of bone and sinew had a way of hammering home just how different a griffin was from a horse, or even a hippogriff. The beast was a meat eater, and given the vile business the Bolivans got up to, some portion of that waste bin was probably filled with former rivals. He forced those concerns from his mind and skidded to a stop in front of the door to the aviary's main building. It was here that his good fortune finally ran dry. The door was shut tight. A soft shove revealed it to be braced from the opposite side. Though there were no guards in the griffin enclosure, the door was sturdy enough to turn away the beast. He'd have no luck breaking through it. He also realized, as he peered up along the face of the building with its barred windows, that it might have been wise to bring the flame detector to more precisely narrow down the location of his prize. No sense dwelling on that oversight now. He had a job to do.

"Think, think, think," Fel muttered to himself. "You buy a horse stable and rig it to work for a griffin. What's going to be different? What are you going to need to do?"

Motion in the courtyard caused him to press himself against the wall, briefly forgetting he couldn't be seen.

"Horses can't fly, but griffins can. You'd probably have to keep an eye out for them in places you wouldn't have to for horses. The roof."

He peered up, squinting at the brightness of the sky. In addition to the net that was dangling between the uprights of the tall fence, a handrail that was clearly an afterthought had been knocked together on the edge of the roof. People must have spent time up there. And there must have been a way in and out for them. One that at the very least wasn't built to turn away a wild mystic beast.

Fel trotted over to the fence and started to climb. The nice thing about a fence built for something huge and strong was that it was made from full-timber slats with substantial space between them. It may as well have been a ladder. Likewise the net, which seemed relatively thin and light from a distance, was revealed to be made from ropes nearly thick enough to anchor ships. The weave of the net was quite large, so Fel had little trouble crawling through and hauling himself to the roof.

His heavy body dropping down onto the shallow slope of the roof prompted a barely audible sound of confusion inside. He also heard the soft creaky whine of a contraption spring unreeling. He knew that sound all too well. It was an alarm box, in the process of being triggered. With reflexes honed by necessity, he lunged for the box. When failing to identify the source of an activating trap could mean being skewered by mechanical jaws or simply wafting into dust, one tended to develop a near precognition for the sources of certain sounds. The alarm box was tucked into the overhang of a recently installed hatch on the roof. If he'd been able to see his hands, he would have deactivated the box by pulling out the small tumbler designed for that purpose. Instead, he went with the more ham-fisted method of slamming his whole hand down over the small lid before it could pop up and start blaring. It worked, but a grown man hurling himself across the roof made an awful lot of noise all on its own, so the thumping and rattling of the hatch followed moments later. He held perfectly still, waiting. The hatch flipped open, and a man stuck his head out. Fel counted in his head for the proper activation timing of the alarm, then released the top. It began blaring. All eyes outside turned to the roof. The guard covered his ears and fumbled for the deactivation tumbler until it was silenced.

"By the *High*, that thing is loud," he grumbled.

"Was someone up there?" called a voice from below.

"No, no one's up here. And because of you sending me up here, I set off the dumb alarm box, and my ears are whistling. It's a false alarm!"

"Like muck it is. We're on high alert. There was that Graves carriage skirting the town, and they sent out the bird. You hear an alarm, you do a full search!" called the man below.

"It's a *roof!* It isn't like there's somewhere to hide!" the man barked.

"Rules are rules. I'm not getting screamed at by the dispatcher because you didn't follow them. Now get moving and search that roof. I have to get up there too. High alert means no one goes alone."

Fel slowly backed away, invisible hand feeling for his unseen cudgel. If he had to get into a fight with two people, he'd rather it on a wide open roof than in a tight hallway.

The complainer emerged and drew a short sword. He held the weapon with its tip low, not ready for battle. It was in his hand as a formality, because he had no expectation of actually putting it to use. His partner emerged a moment or two later, drawing a sword of his own once he was fully on the roof. He was taking it more seriously, weapon properly brandished. These two were clearly proper members of the Bolivan clan, or at least were better paid than the guards at the gate. He placed their lives on the scales of morality in his head. Could he sleep properly tonight if he shoved them off the roof? Alas, having a conscience was a liability for someone even temporarily in the role of soldier for hire, because the answer was a resounding no. Instead, he moved as slowly and silently as he could manage until he reached the open hatch, then stepped down onto the ladder. His boot fumbled against the first rung, but the griping of the first guard was loud enough to keep it from their notice.

He slipped into the dim, baking-hot attic and found an out-of-the-way spot to get his bearings and make a plan. Against all odds, he'd gotten this far without any blood being spilled, but if he made a mistake now, he'd be trapped in an enemy headquarters and there would be no escape that wouldn't leave him bandaging a wound, cleaning his cudgel, or both.

Questor the griffin rider held tightly to the reins of his steed. The wind rustled his hair as he fixed his gaze not on the ground but on the great avian head of the griffin. He was riding a hunter. Though it was tamed, in a very broad sense of the word, it was still beholden to ancient instincts. The trick to being a griffin rider wasn't to quash those instincts, but to consider them additional weapons in one's arsenal. Eyes keener than his could ever be swept the forest as it wheeled a second time. He could feel the body beneath him tense as potential prey presented itself.

Thin gray smoke rose from the north edge of the patch of trees outside the city. He'd suspected that was where he would find the enemy. It was the only decent cover for miles around the city, but even a small patch of trees could take time to search, and any moment spent searching a place in which the enemy knew where you were and you didn't know where the enemy was could mean a swift and sudden end to a promising career as a soldier of fortune. His armor was little more than some simple leather. The bulk of his defense came from being astride a flying steed. One lucky shot from a crossbow or skillful stick with a spear would be the end of him.

This entire venture was a waste of time. A griffin was an engine of war. It was the equal to a squadron of soldiers. One didn't simply hurl one at a minor threat like this. But one did not get to choose one's assignments when one hired one's services to the highest bidder.

It was refreshing, at least, to discover that whoever his foe was hadn't been entirely foolish. The smoke was being used for additional cover. He'd been warned of such tactics. But the source of the smoke was in a portion of the little plot of woodland with trees far too close to allow the griffin to swoop down from above. Likely they believed this would keep them safe. Many people made the mistake of disregarding the threat of a griffin on the ground. They were wrong, though it wasn't fair to say they learned from their mistake. It was invariably the last mistake they ever made.

The griffin dropped to the ground. Its sheer size meant that he had to lean low to its back to keep from being swept off by low-hanging branches. He clicked a command with his tongue. The beast began to beat its wings, buffeting the smoke and pushing it back. Learning the click commands was the second most difficult aspect of his training as a rider, but it at least meant that those who clashed with him and survived had little chance of picking up any notion of the commands in a way that would give them an edge in future battles.

The wind pushed the smoke back, but it continued to billow. Proof that it came from a contraption rather than a proper fire. He would have to be wary of odd effects. But he'd been prepared for that as well. The griffin continued to push the smoke back until it came to a pair of trees too close to permit a full, proper thrust of wings.

He squinted into the smoke. The positioning was too good. The trees too close. His target wasn't here. This was a ruse. An attempt to get him off the back of the griffin to search between the trees.

If the realization had come to him even a second later, he would have been lost. He clicked again, commanding the griffin to leap backward. It was a costly maneuver. The same low branches he'd had to lie low to avoid now bashed his head and back. But the telltale twang of a crossbow and the crunchy bite of the bolt striking the ground nearby informed him that not only was his foe nearby, but they were targeting the belly of his steed. Not someone foolish enough to try to strike him. Aiming for the biggest target. Good training.

He commanded the griffin back to a clear place for takeoff. Crossbows couldn't fire again quickly. Once the first shot missed, there was no real danger he would be hit. And if that first shot missed, this person wasn't a steady hand or a steady eye. Ferreting them out would take time. Likely better done by foot soldiers. But the local crew didn't have the knowhow or the skill. He'd have to do it himself. For now, better to keep an eye on things from the air and pick his spot.

Fel had reached what was certainly the floor that held what he was after. It was far too comfortable—and far too heavily guarded—to be the home to anyone but the most important person in the building. He had to move carefully to avoid being heard and to avoid knocking things over. These weren't the ideal circumstances to be practicing a new skill, so he'd made little progress learning how to navigate while invisible.

As far as he could tell, no one suspected he was inside, but the alert had not been outright dismissed. People were rushing through the hallways, searching rooms. Each time they passed, he ran the risk of being discovered just by having someone collide with him, but the tromping footsteps also gave him cover to move more quickly without being heard.

With painful slowness, he'd finally reached the door in question. Heavy. Thick. Freshly installed. It was a double door with a rather wide crack in it, which gave him the means to gaze through during a brief gap in the searching patrols. He couldn't see the dispatcher himself, nor could he see the source of the light. But from its warm color he could tell it was a flame. From the shadows, it was somewhere off to the right. And the shadows were stationary.

The flame was not flickering.

Not only was this the proper room, but the sentry flame was actually *present* in the lantern. One door separated him from his target, and so far no one had to be hurt, except maybe a few unsuspecting people in the market who were nursing bruises. But knowing where the lantern was didn't help him much. There was no sense trying to break the door down; he could see a metal brace through the crack in the door. The room was well selected for security, as it had no windows. The only way he was getting inside was if he defeated the door's brace or the man inside opened it himself.

He felt at the gear bag at his side, which had nearly tipped over two tables and caught on a doorknob on the way here. Inside were no fewer than three contraptions that might get him through the door, but they were difficult enough to use while he could see them. While invisible he wasn't even sure he could identify them. There were no two ways about it. He would have to become visible again. So be it.

He waited until the latest group of guards did their sweep through the floor, then tapped the bracer. Having sight of his body again made him feel like he'd removed leg irons. Everything felt faster, more precise. He pulled a length of rope from his bag, looped it through the handle to the door to the stairwell, and tied it to a wall sconce on the far wall, securing the door shut. For good measure he shoved a long, narrow table in front of the door as well.

"What's going on out there?" shouted the dispatcher.

A quick trip to the other side of the floor to give a similar treatment to the other stairwell gave him as much time as he was likely to get to achieve his goal. There was some question as to how he would escape once he was through, but that was a problem for later.

"Who are you? What is this?" the man demanded, voice achieving a level of indignation available only to those accustomed to subservience.

"Guess," Fel said, rummaging through his bag.

"Masker..." he rumbled.

"Are you going to do this the easy way, or am I going to have to get creative? I don't like getting creative," Fel said.

He found the device his father had called "the borer." It rarely found use in his usual expeditions because it wasn't sturdy enough to defeat Bygone doors or floors. As near as his father could figure, it had started life as an automatic stirring machine. Martin had attached some sharp tines to the bottom and a chisel to the end of the stirring arm. Fel hammered the tines into the wood of the door and activated the contraption. Long, curling chips started to reel out of the door as it spun its cutting edge. Even on a wooden door this size, it would cut a dinner-plate-size slug in less than a minute.

The doors at either side of the hallway rattled against their ropes. He *might* have a minute before they got them open, but this was not a time to be putting his trust in the best-case scenario.

"Your family is dead after this. You realize that!" the dispatcher shouted through the door. "No one crosses the Bolivans!"

"You're already trying to kill us. You're out of threats."

Fel watched the pile of chips grow and hefted his cudgel. He dug another contraption out of the bag. It was the size of a saltshaker, with a small knob on either end. He gripped it in one hand and hefted his cudgel in the other. The near indestructibility of Bygone contraptions usually meant that people weren't terribly concerned about breaking them in everyday use. Fel was perhaps one of three people in the world who regularly found ways to break them. His father was downright *proud* of his willingness to stress test his creations. This little stunt was likely to be just such a test.

There was still an awful lot of door to get through, but the stairwell fortifications wouldn't last much longer. He reared back and bashed the borer. The blow splintered the whole device through the remaining bit of wood. It and the plug of wood it was pounded into burst through and clattered around on the floor inside the room, rattling a bit but still functioning despite the blow. Now all Fel needed to do was reach through the hole and pull the brace out of the way. Of course, if he did that now, he'd probably lose a hand, because the dispatcher was certainly armed and waiting for his chance to strike. Fel threw the saltshaker of a device through the hole. The sound that followed put alarm boxes to shame. The noisemaker didn't have an official name yet, but the desperate need to silence it was enough to get the dispatcher to abandon any murderous intent and scramble across the floor after it.

Fel shoved his arm through the hole, hoisted the brace, and charged into the room just as the dispatcher deactivated the noisemaker. He gave the man a boot to the ear to occupy him for a few seconds. Outside, the first of the two stairwell doors succumbed to the efforts of the guards on the other side. Fel dropped the brace back in place and deactivated the borer just long enough to lever the splintered wood off the tines. He hammered it back in place on the door and activated it again. This time it wasn't digging, it was just swinging its chisel past the opening. Anyone hoping to get inside through the same means he had would lose some fingers.

The dazed dispatcher staggered to his feet, clutching his ear. Fel grabbed him by the collar and threw him onto the desk where he'd been doing his work. The door rattled in place as he looked over the room. It looked not unlike the coach master's office in Beffshire. Every piece of vertical space was covered with long handwritten lists. At a glance they looked less like they were in code and more like they were in shorthand, but for the short time Fel would be in here, one was as good as the other. If people desperate to capture or kill him hadn't been hammering on the door, this would likely have been a treasure trove of useful information. But for now, he had just one thing to do here.

He spotted the lantern, though the word really didn't seem to fit anymore. The flame was protected by a thick glass dome. A brass canister of lamp oil the size of a beer barrel served as the base. Fel grinned. That much oil meant this thing wasn't a proper sentry lantern. If he extinguished it, lighting it again would leave the flame mundane and useless as a communication channel.

Two heavy blows smashed the glass dome open. Fel grabbed a tankard from the desk and dropped it over the flame, snuffing it and casting the room in darkness.

He pulled out his new sparker and relit the lantern. The flame danced and flickered, no longer hosting the prying eyes of the Graves flame.

The dispatcher groaned and slid from the desk to the floor. Fel hauled him up.

"All right. You're out of a job," Fel said.

"And you're out of *time*. How do you expect to get out of this?"

Fel didn't answer. He didn't *have* an answer. He grabbed the man by the front of his shirt and pulled him off the ground.

"Like I said, you're forcing me to be creative."

Fel dragged him across the room, thumping him against cabinets and walls to keep him from getting his wits together enough to mount a defense. Fel felt oddly comfortable with the idea of having no plan whatsoever. By the time he'd fetched the noisemaker and tossed it in his bag again, he hadn't thought of a way out, but he'd thought of a suitable way of intimidating a man, and that was as good a place as any to start.

"You've heard of my dad, right?" Fel said. "You remember what he did last time you people tried to kill us or steal from us, right?"

He slammed the dispatcher against the door, such that the spinning borer hissed past his ear with every rotation.

"Dad is *much* more patient than I am. So I'm going to ask you some questions." He slid him a bit closer. "Don't make me wait for answers."

"You're trapped here! What difference does it make? You'll be a hostage or a corpse in two minutes!"

"You'd be surprised what I can get done in two minutes."

Fel looked the man square in the eye. Years of grum hadn't taught him much about managing risk or understanding the odds, but he'd been practicing keeping a steady face. He had no inclination to kill this man or interest in doing so. There was nothing to be gained from it, and the thought of it turned his stomach. But he must have learned a thing or two about bluffing, because the subtle tightening of Fel's grip and the slightest nudge toward the spinning borer broke the man.

"What!? What do you want!?" he yelped.

"How did you get the Graves flame, how are you getting information out of it, and how did you learn to make the contraptions you're giving the people you're sending out in the field to try to kill my family? The ones that look like metal cigars and hold the flame."

"It all comes down from the north!" he yammered. "I don't know where exactly. But they have me making purchases and doing raids for materials. Th-there, on the desk. They keep sending materials up that way."

"Smart decision," Fel said.

He hauled him aside and hurled him to the far corner of the room. While he was recovering, Fel grabbed the sheet with the shipping instructions on it and stuffed it into his bag. The dispatcher woozily climbed to his feet. Fel stalked over to him, grabbed the end of his shirt behind his back and pulled it up over his head, then tore the bottom and wrapped it around behind his head to be tied. Once the improvised blindfold and gag was in place, he pulled off the man's belt and strapped his hands behind his back.

"There. Now keep quiet."

The door was rattling on its hinges now. While he wouldn't have been able to get through it on his own, the half-dozen very highly motivated guards were making short work of it. He very much doubted any of this gear would help him out of this pickle he'd gotten himself into, but it just so happened he was a little better equipped than he normally was, courtesy of Tome.

"If he ever finds out I ended up using one of these..."

Fel slipped the small folio of spells from his bag and flipped through them. Tome had taken the time to label them clearly, in terms of usage, effect, and the date at which they would lose too much potency to be useful.

"This better work..."

He ripped the edge of one of the spells, then climbed up on the desk and slapped the control for the invisibility bracer. The effect washed over him. The moment his vision switched to the coruscating strangeness that the contraption provided for him, he felt a lurching unpleasantness in the pit of his stomach. This contraption was playing havoc with his constitution. But just as games of grum had given him experience in hiding his intentions, bad hangovers had given him experience in holding on to his lunch in adverse conditions. Now he just had to wait and hope...

Lattica held her breath and watched. Her heart was hammering in her chest, but held steady. She had to trust the tactics. She had to trust the books. They had never led her wrong before. Greater Mystics don't expect someone to best them at their own game. That was the best advice she could find about how to deal with them before time ran out. She combined that advice with older, more general lessons from prior missions she'd been sent on. If an enemy is after you, that makes you bait, and choosing bait is the most difficult part of setting a trap. They've done the hard work for you.

She'd puzzled on what to do while setting up the smoke as a decoy, and settled on an answer just as the griffin arrived. A hippogriff could fly. It sought prey on the ground. While her foe turned out to be riding a griffin, this remained true. They trained their eyes downward and relied almost entirely on their vision. They wouldn't think of looking up, because up was where they *came* from. She didn't know if it was true, but she convinced herself it was and acted on that information. For the first time since she was a child, she climbed a stout oak tree and hid among the leaves. It was a small miracle that there had been a tree both large enough to support her and full enough to hide her. As it happened, the very same criteria applied to hiding a carriage and finding a sturdy tree to perch in, so the one tree that fit the bill was a stone's throw from the carriage and thus right where the trap needed to be set.

The underbrush crunched beneath talons and paws. She held the crossbow ready. Soon the form of the creature came into view beneath the tree. She was lucky the thing had landed a second time. If she missed again, she wouldn't get a third shot. She had to wait until the very last moment. It came closer. She steadied the crossbow against a branch. Closer. One crossbow bolt wouldn't be enough to take down a griffin. As much as she wanted to aim her shot at the belly of the beast and be certain of a hit, she needed to hit the rider. Then would be the confusion, and if she was lucky, the chance to destroy or remove the saddle.

She heard a clicking noise. The griffin slowed. The rider was being cautious. He suspected something. Almost... just a little closer... One shot could remove this threat. That was all it would take.

The beast's head jerked aside without warning. Its rider shouted and clicked new commands. Something was happening. She didn't know if it had detected her or if it was simply becoming anxious, but it didn't matter. She had to take the shot before it was too late. She pulled the trigger. The crossbow recoiled. Her aim was far from true, but she didn't miss entirely. The bolt tore a gouge out of the rider's leather armor. She'd struck him with a grazing blow to the side. Likely not a mortal wound. The attack disrupted his attempts to calm the beast, and whatever control he had over the thing was broken. It spread its wings, galloped into the open, and took to the sky.

"Blast it. A few moments more and I'd have had him," she hissed under her breath.

She wisely didn't give voice to the profound relief she was feeling at the beast's retreat and the knowledge that she hadn't had to add to her already uncomfortably large list of Bolivans and mercenaries she'd had to kill in service of her family.

Lattica climbed a bit higher in the tree and gazed into the distance. It was best not to lose track of the creature. One never knew when it would double back and become a threat once more.

In the dispatcher's office, the bracket holding the brace in place finally gave way and the door swung open. Five guards crowded through the door, weapons at the ready. They found the dispatcher himself, rather embarrassingly bound with his own clothes and producing muffled growls. One of the guards untied him.

"Did you get him, you idiots?" the dispatcher ordered once his head was free.

"Where is he?" replied one of the guards.

"Where is he? You mean to tell me you *missed* the brute? He must be using one of the bracers. Block the door. He's in here somewhere. Find him and kill him."

The guards spread out, feeling for something in the air around them. Despite knowing they were looking for someone who couldn't be seen, their eyes were wide and searching. It was thus no surprise when one of the men found something sizzling with a subdued blue flame among the things pinned to the wall.

"What's this?" he asked, pointing to the odd bit of arcane writing that burned slowly on the wall.

His answer came in the sound of a bloodcurdling shriek outside, then a blow that shook the building. Blow after blow splintered wood and knocked dust and debris from the ceiling. Two of the guards lost their nerve immediately, bolting from the room and rushing for safety. It took two more blows and a buckling plank in the ceiling to scare off the next two. In the confusion, no one noticed an extra set of thumping boots pounding down to the floor. They didn't even notice the borer stopping, wrenching from the door, and vanishing. Another punishing blow peeled away a section of the roof and revealed the maddened head of the griffin as it tried to claw its way to the burning mystic lure.

Fel didn't know what happened next, he was far too busy fumbling his way through the hallway of panicked Bolivans. The panic wasn't limited to the building. As all-too-frequently happened with Fel's "plans," he didn't realize until after they'd been executed what side effects might be involved. A griffin attacking its aviary was a handy way to cover an escape, but the city around it wasn't exactly going to *ignore* the attack. Opposing tides of humanity enveloped the town. Most were rushing for shelter. A small, dedicated contingent were heading toward the griffin. They were the Watch, and from the looks of those who hustled past, they had prepared for the eventuality of the new aviary's resident not behaving itself.

After knocking over some bewildered people and shouldering through a crowd while invisible, Fel stumbled out into the clear and dashed across the road. A haze of odorless smoke still hung in the air. He made his way as far into the woods as he could before finally abandoning the bracer's effects so that his stomach would settle and his steps would cease to be fouled by poor placement.

In the back of his mind, he'd prepared himself to stumble upon the ruined remains of the carriage and, potentially, of his partner. To his great relief, both were fully intact, and the latter was snapping the reins the moment Fel came into view.

"Fast, fast!" she said. "While there's still a distraction."

"There's going to be a distraction for a while!" he shouted, scrambling onto the carriage as it rumbled out onto the road.

He sat up beside her and held tightly to the rattling vehicle until he caught his breath.

"Aren't you going to ask if I accomplished the mission?"

"The flame detector shifted to the north," Lattica said. "I already know you did what you had to do."

"Oh... right. Well, I'm going to tell you the story anyway. What about you, though? Are you all right?"

"Missed my shot at the griffin rider. But my guts are still inside me, and they didn't wreck the carriage. That's mostly what I was after."

"We make a pretty good team when we don't actually have to work together," Fel said.

"I can't argue with that."

She steered them onto the proper road to the north, and they left the madness behind them.

For now, at least.

CHAPTER 6

Martin yawned. It was awfully early in the day to be so tired. More accurately, it was awfully early in a normal person's day to be so tired. Having a workshop with no windows and an almost self-destructive degree of focus when he was engaged with his work meant that his day had a way of misaligning with the rest of his family's. Vivian, Fel, and Epiphany had come to accept and embrace it, but despite Euphoria having done so as well just a few years ago, he felt obliged to adjust his day to match hers in order to spend more time with her. It hadn't been a marked success. She'd inherited his focus as well, and as such, much of her time was spent scrutinizing the books she'd brought along. When she wasn't doing that, she spent her time in the shop with her mother. She wasn't cold to Martin, or at least not any colder than she was in general these days, but it was clear she continued to have more interests in common with Vivian than with him.

There was a joy in watching them work together, though. He very rarely spent any time behind the counter of the shop, in part because there was a theatrical aspect to being a salesperson that didn't come naturally to him. Some amount of dishonesty seemed to be an agreed upon part of any transaction, and try as he might he could not read the cues to properly calibrate how far the truth was intended to be bent. Vivian was a light touch with it, a surgeon. She would never tread all the way to outright lies, but she would artfully weave between the less pleasant aspects of any given point of discussion. Euphoria was something else entirely. She was a different person in every interaction. A brief moment of observation, then she became precisely who she needed to be to tease the price up for a sale or the price down for a purchase. Everyone who did business with her left feeling as though they'd done her a favor or had been done a favor. Regardless of which, they felt *good* about the transaction. She wasn't a better salesperson than her mother. At the end of the day the two seemed to meet the very same prices. Euphoria was, however, much more memorable. And then that life and liveliness vanished when the people left. A blade drawn for combat, then slipped back into its scabbard when the time for battle was through.

Having two of them working simultaneously felt almost like a conspiracy against him, however. Not only did it engage Euphoria in a way that made rebuilding their broken connection more difficult for him, but it burned through the inventory he'd stockpiled. The shelves weren't bare—they planned better than that—but if things kept up in this fashion, they would be by the end of the week. That meant he'd been away from the workshop for too long. He had to get back to work.

With Wick's lantern in hand, he descended the steps. These brief moments of solitude without work were dangerous times for him. If left to its own devices, his mind would latch on to the constantly simmering worry for Fel during this mission. It seemed wrong to distract himself from such things, but it was doubly wrong to dwell on them. He didn't even know where Fel was. And it wasn't as though he was in the Greater Lands like last time.

Martin's eyes widened, he glanced to the lantern. The flame was still.

"Wick!" he said quickly. "Have we heard from Tome?"

"We have. He has gained entry to the archive. Of the seventeen books you requested by name, only seven are in the archive."

"*Only* seven? That's seven more than I ever thought I'd get a chance to see!"

"There seems to be alternatives with similar subject matter for six more."

"Brilliant!" Martin said, trotting down another set of steps. "I imagine he'll be bringing them back when he returns?"

"He has separated them from the rest of the archive. The index of the archive is contraption-based, and I have taught Tome to operate it to a limited degree. It took several hours, but from my vantage I was able to listen to the spoken titles of all books available in the archive. I can list them for you when you wish."

"From your vantage? You did not enter the archive?"

"I felt, for the safety of the books, it would be unwise."

Martin nodded. "Sensible."

He reached the door of this workshop. Out of habit, he pushed the door, forgetting it would be locked. He shook his head and fished out the key, but continued with the same delighted tone.

"I wish the shop could spare me, even for a few weeks. To see that archive personally would be a transcendent experience." He turned the key. "If he doesn't need you to return to him anytime soon, perhaps I could take some time to transcribe some of the titles. He could load up some more of them for the return trip."

Martin stepped into his workshop, his mind fizzing with the possibilities. When he went to set Wick's lantern down and get back to work, he expected to find a mess on his workbench. He'd been tinkering with the bust yesterday and hadn't taken the time to return the pieces to their bins. To his great surprise, the pieces were missing. He took two desperate glances about, the turned to the bust itself.

"... By the High..."

What should have been a yawning opening in the front of the bust, rendered jagged by thousands of components sticking out at odd angles, was instead... a face. It took him a moment to realize it, but it was not simply *a* face, but the face that had been staring, unseeing, from the family sign for generations. It hadn't struck him that such was the case, because, first, the mask should *not* have been attached to anything but the sign. Second, it had been partially cleaned of its patina, revealing a brilliant brassy hue beneath the ancient green.

There was no question the mask belonged on the bust. The edges met up perfectly. Etched detail lines in the mask continued onto the mounting plate on the bust. The only thing missing was a small, secondary plate under the chin that he'd removed from the bust a few days prior to investigate. A jangling sound drew his attention to the ground. Oiler peered up at him. It held up a claw clutching a small, misshapen piece he recognized as one of the components from the bust. It was mangled, and had been when it had arrived from Fel's expedition. He remembered taking notes on how a replacement might be fabricated.

"You... did you..." Martin muttered.

He held Wick's lantern down and peered up under the thing's chin from below. Every component he could see had been installed and connected. There was every possibility that this piece, if it could be replaced, would render the contraption functional.

Martin turned the component over in his hands, his mind flicking back and forth between the riddle of how best to repair it and the question of what precisely to do about this new development. It was one thing to tinker with a device from his family's past that had no real chance to return to functionality. It was quite another to potentially restore it. The device came from a deserted city deep within a walled-off land full of dangers and wonders. It was a personal policy that he never activated a contraption without some idea of what it might do. That was the *reason* for disassembling contraptions even when they appeared to be complete. He needed to know what they might do because not *all* contraptions could be trusted to be safe. Despite weeks with the bust, he'd only begun to work out what the smallest assemblies might be for.

He turned the damaged piece over one last time. He may not have known how to deal with the ramifications of awakening ancient and unknown contraptions of unrivaled complexity, but he knew how to perform repairs. It shouldn't have been a surprise that his mind solved that riddle first.

"I can just hammer this piece flat, then lock the edge in a vice and match the curvature. Now that I can see where the mating holes are supposed to be, I can match their position. This will take minutes..."

Just like that, the last obstacle to completion fell away. He still didn't know if it was a good idea, but his curiosity would not be denied. He set Wick's lantern down, pulled a hammer from its place in the toolbox, and went to work.

Epiphany scratched her pen across the page. Euphoria's visit had proved to be a tremendous boon to her productivity. In her desire to keep clear of her sister, Epiphany had found every reason she could to either leave the house or hole up in her room, working on tasks and projects she'd been putting off for months. Ideally she would be off doing one of her sales trips to the north, but her parents wisely had determined that Fel's mission north might make travel for the Maskers a little more dangerous than usual. So she'd been spending the remainder of her time visiting The Fox and Log to talk Allie's ear off or in her room tracing out better trade routes and planning inventory.

"What did we sell when we went to Christopher's Crossing?" she mused, opening the drawer to her desk and flipping through the notes within. "I know they were interested in some oddities up that way."

After twenty seconds of searching failed to turn up the ledger from that trip, she was already eagerly anticipating the task of reorganizing her files. That would burn an afternoon. But something distant and rhythmic was beginning to gnaw at the back of her mind. Gradually she realized she was hearing the sound of hammer blows. On an average day, such a sound was little more than a component of the background noise of her life. But she hadn't been hearing her father's work lately. In part because her father was doing less work, but when he *was* working, the door was shut and locked. That she could hear it now meant that he hadn't shut his door.

Epiphany tightened her jaw and slammed the drawer. She stomped from her room and wove her way down the steps, ready to give her father an earful.

"Dad, we agreed you should be keeping the door shut," she said as she stepped through the doorway of the shop. "Even Mom said it was—*by the High, what's happened?*"

Her wide eyes were locked on the nearly completed bust. Martin looked to her. His expression was that of distilled enthusiasm.

"Fanny! It's the mask from the sign. I'd never even considered it might be a legitimate contraption component," he said.

Epiphany hastily shut the door and locked it.

"Does it fit? Is it actually a component, or just cosmetic?" she asked.

"It does! Oiler did the assembly, for the most part."

"What are the chances?"

"What are the chances that these parts would ever find each other again? Vanishingly small. The chances that they would work together? Virtually certain. The masks are family heirlooms, handed down from my father, and his father. The bust is a Masker family relic. I don't think they were *made* for each other. Based upon similar contraptions, I'd say that both the mask and the bust are standard designs. Interchangeable. It's good you're here! In fact, fetch your mother and sister. This is a moment that should be witnessed by the family." He held up the plate and gently tweaked a final angle. "I only wish your brother were here."

Epiphany's mind swirled. "We can't bring Euphoria down here."

"Why not? This is as much her legacy as yours or mine."

"Dad, she stole the other mask. I always thought it was out of spite, a slap to the face of the family. Maybe, *maybe,* it was to bring a piece of home with her. But we already know she had contact with the Graves family long before she left, long enough to sabotage your oven with a sentry flame. Now we learn that the other mask is a component for an ancient contraption? She *must* have known that. I don't think we can trust her to know that we've learned this too."

"Fanny, you behave as though her every act is one of calculated malice."

"I've yet to be proved wrong, Dad," Epiphany said. "I'm not sure you should even be reassembling that device, but I am *quite* sure that you shouldn't let Euphoria know what you've learned."

Martin looked his daughter in the eye, then glanced back at the nearly finished contraption.

"Fanny, this device was built by our ancestors and has been waiting generations to be repaired. We must see what it does."

"Can it be done safely? Can it be done such that it can be quickly deactivated?"

Martin gave it a moment of thought. "I will leave out the fasteners. I'll hold the final plate in place. If it does something untoward, I will remove the pressure, and the plate will fall away."

Epiphany crossed her arms and tapped her foot, a bit stricken. Now that the initial shock had lost a bit of its edge, the same fizzling feeling of expectation and wonder that must have been fueling her father began to spark in her mind.

"Fine." She took a step back against the door. "But be ready for anything."

"I try to be."

He angled the plate into position, stepped back, and pushed the piece home. The change in the device was subtle, but immediate. Pieces inside clacked and rotated. Whirring wheels spun up to speed. Polished edges within the hollow eyes of the mask caught the light that shined through, twinkling like a lit fuse. Deep inside the head, something clicked into place, and a sound not unlike someone dragging their finger along the edge of a wineglass softly wavered. The wavering accelerated and became smoother, then two highly polished disks rose up within the twinkling space behind the eyes, like pupils. The tone settled into something that could be called a voice, and sculpted into something that could be called a language, though it wasn't one that Epiphany recognized.

"What is it saying?" she said.

"It's a dead tongue. I've only read it," Martin said.

"It is inquiring after the purpose of today's lesson," Wick said.

"Lesson?" Epiphany said.

"Is it like a sentry lantern?" Martin said. "Or perhaps some precursor to it?"

"It would likely be better equipped to answer that question than I."

Martin leaned down, his arm still extended to keep the plate in place.

"Do you understand me? The words I am saying?" he asked.

"The words I am saying," the bust replied. "No. No, the words *you* are saying. Grammar. Excellent. I adore a grammar lesson."

The voice was lively and enthusiastic. Not so different from how Wick sounded, though there wasn't any clear indication of gender. It certainly had the feel of something that had eventually evolved into whatever fueled Wick's intellect.

"This is not a lesson," Martin said, his voice almost giddy. "Not for *you*, at least. We need to learn more about you."

"Not a lesson?" the bust said sadly. "Why not a lesson? I exist to learn."

"How about a test then?" Epiphany said.

"Oh! Shall my learnings be measured. Splendid! What shall be the subject? Still grammar?"

"No," Martin said, catching on to Epiphany's gambit. "This will be a history test."

"I *excel* at history," it said. "How shall we begin?"

"What is your purpose?" Martin asked.

"Curious. I wouldn't identify that question as history. That seems more a matter of philosophy."

"Let's just call this a general knowledge test, then," Epiphany said.

"Open-ended! Now that should be a genuine challenge. Wonderful, wonderful. The question is still regarding my purpose?"

"Yes," Epiphany said.

"I am a student. To speak more specifically, I am *the* Student. Or Students, plural. There is a reason I wasn't speaking this language. The words don't quite exist to speak with precision about my nature. That won't hurt my assessment, will it?"

"I think allowances can be made," Martin said. "Are you an individual, or one of many?"

"Ha! That's an easy one. I am an individual composed of many."

"What are the many you are composed of?" Epiphany asked.

"Generally or specifically?"

"Generally, then specifically."

"Oh! A two-part question. Lovely! Generally, and forgive me but this is a rather clumsy word in this language, I am composed of 'contraptors.' Perhaps machine spirits? The terminology varies. And specifically, I am the mouthpiece for those contraptors driven by the desire to learn. I am the Student."

"Incredible," Martin said. "Please describe contraptors."

"A difficult question. How to define the nature of one's being? Contraptors can be defined simultaneously as a force of nature and a force of intellect. We are entities of a different sort from humans or animals. Unfettered by most limitations, and yet *exceptionally* fettered in other ways. We observe the world through the lens of, and can only act in accordance with, our primary motivation. Once presented with something that engages our interest, we cannot help but perform whatever task is necessary to indulge that interest. But our interactions can only ever be filtered through apparatuses meeting certain criteria. We can have no direct influence on the world without intermediate means."

"Are contraptors living or dead?" Epiphany asked.

"Living or dead. Is this a trick question? I don't very much like trick questions. But let me see if I can puzzle out an answer for you. They are not living, because they were never born and cannot die. And they are not dead, because they continue to think and act. So the answer to the question 'Are they living or dead?' would appear to be 'No.' Is that sufficient?"

"I suppose it will do," Epiphany said.

"So many more questions," Martin said. "I wish I'd known this was coming. I'd have taken time to prepare."

He uncomfortably swapped hands to keep the plate in place.

"You mention criteria necessary for apparatuses to be useful to you. What criteria?"

"Hmmm... I am afraid I do not know that. I know it when I see it, but I do not know when it is absent."

"Very well. But the apparatuses you are referring to, they are contraptions, correct?"

"True or false questions are not very engaging, but true, the apparatuses through which contraptors are able to interact are called contraptions. Oh! Except when they are not. Then they are called spells."

Martin slapped his leg. "I *knew* magic and contraptions were related."

"How many other masks are there like you?" Epiphany asked, her voice suddenly more serious.

"It may have changed, but when last I was made aware, there were four masks."

"You're the Student. What are the others? And what do they do?"

"An extremely simple two-part question. I am the Student, also known as the Pupil. I ask questions to gain knowledge and answer questions to prove knowledge. Next is the Teacher, the Professor, or the Instructor. The Teacher does not ask questions to seek knowledge. Its knowledge is implicit. And while it can answer questions, it is also capable of providing general, guided instruction on a given subject. The Diplomat, or Adviser, provides solutions to problems arising from interactions between people or peoples. The General, or Warrior, provides tactical advice."

"Are any other masks active right now?" Epiphany asked.

"There is one additional mask active right now. Specifically, the Diplomat, though in a very limited fashion. You are to be commended on the state of repair of your contraption."

"Why do contraptors perform the tasks associated with contraptions?"

"Another challenging question, I—"

Before the Student could provide an answer, Epiphany knocked her father's hand away. The plate dropped out of place, the polished pupils slipped out of view, and the voice died away.

"Fanny! We were learning so much!"

"Dad, it said there was another mask active. It must be the one Euphoria stole."

"Right, yes. The Diplomat. Given the constant clashes with the Bolivans over the years, it is easy to see why they would have wanted it. Though the fact that those clashes haven't *ended* suggests either the problem is intractable, or they couldn't get it to function well enough to perform its stated purpose."

"Come now, Dad. You remember what they sent Fel after, don't you? The one thing they wanted above all else?"

"A mask. Yes. A fierce one." He paused. "The Warrior, presumably."

"I think the Diplomat threw up its hands and told them to get the Warrior. And then they tried to stain *our* hands with the blood of acquiring it. And when we couldn't, they decided *Fel* was an acceptable replacement."

"You're jumping to conclusions, Fanny."

"Just because I'm jumping to them doesn't mean they're wrong. But fine, if you don't think I'm right, let's go to the source. You didn't like hiding all this from Euphoria, right? Let's talk to her about it right now and see what she has to say for herself. How many lies do you think we'll have to peel through before we get something we can believe?"

She unlocked the door and threw it open. Martin grabbed Wick's lantern and followed her. As she stomped her way up the stairs, she began formulating the questions she would ask, and how she would ask them. Would she set a trap, lead her toward an obvious lie, then catch her in her dishonesty? Would she present the situation dispassionately and see if Euphoria would hang herself without being led down a garden path?

Deeper in her mind, she recoiled a bit at just how gleefully she was anticipating cementing her sister's deception. As though this was some sort of contest that she'd finally won. She was better than this... but for now, she would make an exception.

They reached the shop to find it empty. Epiphany thundered over to the door and flipped the sign to turn customers away.

"We need to talk."

"It is business hours, Fanny."

Martin placed the lantern down on the counter.

"Now, girls. Please be civil and remember that you are family."

"Why did you steal the mask, Fora?" Epiphany said.

"Is now really the time?" Euphoria asked calmly.

"The Diplomat," Epiphany said, arms crossed. "Or does it call itself the Adviser when you speak to it?"

Euphoria folded her hands on the counter. Her expression shifted ever so slightly. Like she was relaxing a bit, letting the tension out of a mental muscle.

"I should have known. You are too careful to ask a question you don't know the answer to," Euphoria said.

"What's this about, girls?" Vivian said sternly.

"The masks on the sign weren't just decorations. They were components, mouthpieces for things like Wick. Thinking contraptions. She stole the one called the Diplomat, and she's probably been following its advice for years."

"As it happens, the advice has been extremely limited. We lack a technician with Father's skill, so the mount we were able to acquire to activate the mask is barely functional."

"And the mask you wanted us to find for you?"

"Again, I don't imagine I need to answer. You already know."

"It's the Warrior. You wanted us to get you a military adviser for your little war with the Bolivans, and in doing so *got us wrapped up in that war.*"

"I notice the other mask is missing. I assume you've activated it?" Euphoria said. "The Student, correct?"

"You know all sorts of things, don't you?"

"One of our distant relatives—that is to say, one of the Graves old guard —is a rather gifted researcher. Piotor Graves. The man is a recluse. I've never actually met him. Few have. For ages he's been studying old traveler's journals from the Bygone Era in an isolated cabin in the mountains. About five years ago, he informed the family through the Voice that he'd located a book describing the masks and surmised—correctly—that the Masker's Antiquities sign hosted both the Student and the Diplomat."

"Five years ago. So it took them two years to persuade you to rob and abandon your family," Epiphany said.

"I 'abandoned' my family specifically because I *didn't* want you involved with the Graves family's clash. Jonathan convinced me that with the Diplomat, the Bolivan rivalry could be put to bed, and our two families could start working together. I limited contact as we did our best to put the Diplomat's advice to work, and when that didn't work, we did our best to find the Warrior mask ourselves. But when the Bolivans started becoming more bold, we knew time was running out. Now we know that their boldness was fueled by the information they were somehow able to glean from the Voice. But I was *trying* to end an old, simmering conflict and keep the Maskers safe until then."

"Why didn't you just *tell* us that?" Epiphany asked.

"Do you believe me, now that I have?"

Epiphany narrowed her eyes.

"You're not the only one who asks questions she already knows the answers to."

"Enough," Vivian said. "Martin, what's this about? Everything. We're not hiding anything anymore."

Martin, visibly tense from the moment the raised voices began, practically gushed the answer he'd been holding in.

"When Epiphany removed the mask from the sign and placed it in the workshop, Oiler identified it as a missing piece to the bust I've been repairing and reassembled it." He turned to Euphoria. "Oiler is the 'pack of chains' you hired us to acquire. It is sentient, or at least partially so, and it saved Fel's life in a clash with the Bolivans. Once activated, the mask awakened and revealed itself to be something called the Student, and *by the High, I've left it with Oiler.*"

Martin trotted down the stairs.

"Oiler will have fixed it by now. The thing is probably wondering why we aren't asking any questions," Epiphany said.

"And you are angry about *me* being deceptive?" Euphoria said.

"You started it *years* ago and you know it," Epiphany jabbed back.

"I said enough," Vivian said. "The dirty laundry has been aired out. Can I trust you two to take your bickering into the dining room so I can open the doors again?"

"I'd rather take it to the workshop to see what father's been able to do with the mask," Euphoria said.

"I'll *bet* you would," Epiphany snapped, leading her down the stairs.

When the sisters reached the workshop, the door was open and Martin was carefully sorting through the contents of a high shelf in search of something. As expected, the Student was awake. Its gleaming pupils were darting back and forth between Oiler, who had returned to the task of solving a puzzle cube, and the doorway. The moment Epiphany and Euphoria came into view, the Student excitedly spoke.

"Lovely, lovely, lovely. A new instructor? Or perhaps a new proctor. In either case, I am delighted to have such novel experiences."

"Amazing..." Euphoria said, inspecting the mask up close. "You have secured a bust in *much* higher repair. Or else Father's skills have advanced markedly in just the short time I have been absent."

"What is your name? And what is the nature of your role in my education? Forgive me, the rest of you. I should have inquired after your names and roles as well. In point of fact, I *did*, but it was prior to discovering your language of preference."

"My name is Euphoria Graves. I am here to ask questions," Euphoria said.

"And I am Epiphany Masker. I'm also here to ask questions. Dad?"

"Martin Masker. I'm here to maintain, learn, and educate," he called without turning from the shelf.

"Masker? Might I inquire if you are a member of the fabled Masker clan of Clickspring?" the Student asked.

"There is evidence to suggest that is so," Martin said.

"As the creators of this mask, you should be a source of excellent expertise. Splendid. I am eager to begin."

"Are you aware of the Diplomat?" Epiphany asked.

"Yes! Assuming you are referring to the mask that serves as a conduit for contraptors dedicated to the purpose of unraveling problems at the society level, as previously tested, I am aware of both the nature and purpose of the Diplomat."

"Are you aware of the mask's current location?"

"As the Diplomat is currently active, I am indeed aware of its location. Shall I describe its location to you?"

"Yes," Epiphany said quickly.

"One moment," said the Student.

The eyes dropped to emptiness. Euphoria turned to Epiphany.

"Attempting to determine where we've been keeping our own adviser, are we?"

"I'm attempting to determine the abilities of the Student, and I selected a difficult task to perform, and one that you can verify," Epiphany said. "Why? Have something to hide? Wouldn't *that* be a stunning act of hypocrisy?"

"I don't recall this degree of antagonism between you two prior to Euphoria's departure," Martin said.

The Student "woke up" once more, eyes shifting into position and glancing between Epiphany and Euphoria.

"The Diplomat is presently in a small, well-guarded room a considerable distance to the north. More specifically, if one were to draw a straight line on a map leading due north, it would extend seven hundred and thirty-three miles until it aligned with the location. There would then be a further sixty-three miles to the east to reach its precise location."

Epiphany shut her eyes and tried to tease the information into a form that would be meaningful to her.

"That would place it... approximately... in the northeast corner of Shalia, I imagine?" she said.

"Approximately," Euphoria said.

"Am I correct?" the Student said.

"You are," Euphoria said.

"Splendid!"

"What about the Professor? And the Warrior?" she asked. "Can you tell us their locations?"

"Neither mask is active. I cannot tell you where they are because the entities they represent, as a result, do not exist presently," the Student said. "I hope that doesn't diminish your assessment of my performance."

"This is a security risk I'd not anticipated," Euphoria said. "I had no idea they could pinpoint each other's locations with such precision."

"Yours doesn't answer questions?" Epiphany said.

"Ours can barely speak. The bust is in very poor repair. And when it does speak, it will only answer questions relevant to its purpose," Euphoria said. "We would have been much better served by the Student rather than the Diplomat."

"Next question, please!" the Student said.

Martin pulled an object from the box he'd finally unearthed. It was what the family had come to refer to as a "Bygone Dagger."

"What, precisely, is this device and what is its purpose?"

"Ah! I have not seen one of those in ages. That is... forgive me, there is no word in this language that properly articulates its true name. You may assign your own name, but its purpose is to render any given contraption beneath the interest or notice of contraptors. It disables a contraption of any size or complexity, rendering it inert, or at least incapable of being operated by contraptors. Such devices were created and distributed among contraptioneers in ancient crafting hubs to allow partially functional contraptions to be disabled for repair, to disable dangerous or malfunctioning contraptions, or to deactivate contraptions with no other means of deactivation. With respect to my own operation, it is the standard method to discontinue a testing or education session. You appear to have affixed the mask to a lightly modified Tinker Maquette. There should be a small rectangular slot in the back of the contraption to insert the tool to disable it."

"You have a duplicate of the Bygone Dagger," Euphoria observed.

"They are not rare," the Student said. "Standard issue."

"Everything from the Bygone Era is rare now," Epiphany said.

"Oh! Please clarify. I know the word 'bygone,' but it appears to have been used in a new context. What is 'the Bygone Era'?"

"The Bygone Era is the modern term for a period of history that concluded well over a hundred years ago. Maybe even three centuries ago. The specific timing is a matter of debate, and seems to vary widely by location," Martin said. "It is an era characterized by the construction of contraptions. The specific means of creating contraptions was lost to the era. These days we are only capable of repairing and modifying contraptions."

"Interesting... Thank you for this lesson!"

"You weren't aware of this?" Epiphany said.

"I am the Student. I am only aware of things I have observed, things intrinsic to my nature, or things about which I have been informed. The Teacher can provide greater insight. That is the purpose of the Professor."

"And its location cannot be definitively determined until it has been activated," Euphoria said.

"True!"

"Do you know anything about what may have caused the collapse of the Bygone Era?"

"Hmm... An interesting riddle. And I adore an interesting riddle," the Student said. "In the fullness of time, a few hundred years are nothing. Surely you should know the details of such things thanks to the presence of books and other recorded material."

"The best repository of knowledge we had, the Telestressa Archives, was destroyed in a fire," Martin explained. "The remaining information is scattered and of questionable trustworthiness."

"A few hundred years is well within the lifespan of many of the Greater Mystics. You could ask them."

"They have been locked away behind the Greater Lands Wall, and journeys there are treacherous," Martin said.

"My brother went there, but he's not the most intellectually curious person you're likely to meet," said Epiphany.

"Through what means have the mystics been kept behind the wall?" the Student asked.

"I don't know. According to Fel, they seem to be compelled to disregard even the *idea* of leaving the Greater Lands or entering the city at its center."

"What city is at the center of the Greater Lands?" the Student asked.

"He called it Clickspring," she said.

"Ah. Ah! Then there have been significant changes in the time between my activations. But it is my guess that the clockwork diamond was involved."

"What is the clockwork diamond?" Epiphany asked urgently.

"I do not know! But elements of it were being constructed at the center of Clickspring, and though I cannot be certain of the timing, the clockwork diamond's completion is very likely to have coincided with the range of time that the Bygone Era ended. Am I correct?"

"I don't know if you're correct, but you've certainly given us something to think about," Epiphany said.

"I see... Well, please confirm and inform me of your findings. I do strive to ensure my education is accurate."

"Tell me," Martin said eagerly. "Can you answer questions about your construction?"

"If you are inquiring after the construction of the mask, or the bust to which it has been affixed, I cannot. The bulk of my education was directed by people of what you would call the Bygone Era, or was observational. My educators did not make the technical aspects of specific contraptions a focus of my education. It is possible, however, that there are incidental aspects of my education which could prove comparatively insightful in the modern era. I'm afraid you'll have to ask the right questions, as I have no interest in volunteering, and thus no ability to volunteer, knowledge outside the context of a lesson or assessment."

Martin thumped the desk in light frustration. "It seems even in their era, the contraptioneers kept their construction methods under the veil of secrecy."

"This session is not as tightly structured as I am accustomed to," the Student said. "It is a nonacademic challenge to be assessed and educated in this way. It may decrease the quality of my answers."

"We should take some time to gather ourselves so that we can do this more efficiently," Martin said.

"That would be best for all. Please deactivate the mask in the interim. It is distracting to be focused to a task, then to have that task removed," the Student said.

"As you wish."

Martin lined up the Bygone Dagger and clicked it into its receptacle. The Student's soft whirring faded, and the eyes dropped down.

"I don't suppose you two would like to spend a few hours developing a curriculum-and-testing suite?"

Epiphany turned to Euphoria.

"I think I'd rather discuss our findings with my sister," she rumbled.

"I imagine you would..." Euphoria muttered.

Blissfully unaware of the events happening in his home, Fel's greatest concern at the moment was planning his next move and enduring the simmering wrath of his partner.

"I can't believe this," Lattica grumbled.

"I can't believe you're angry. We extinguished a very important flame, and we got some fresh information. This was an ideal outcome," Fel said.

"What did you learn? That they've been getting their information from the north? We already knew the Bolivans' various headquarters were spread across the north."

"And I've got this slip here. The shipping slip for the materials. We've got a pretty clear indication of where those fresh contraptions were coming from."

"Have you looked up the city on the map?"

"I have."

"Is it roughly where the detector is pointing?"

He eyed the map, then the flame detector.

"Roughly. A little west of that."

"Then chances are we are heading to the very place you dug up."

"No, we're heading for a place a little *east* of the place I dug up."

"And because you had to use an arcane spell to distract the griffin in order to escape, I missed perhaps the *only* good shot I'd have at the rider. We could have been rid of him as a threat."

"How was I supposed to know you'd be setting a trap?"

"We could have planned better. I can't deal with all this chaos. I need plans."

"We didn't know what was inside the building. We couldn't plan better than we did."

"I've always been able to rely upon plans before."

"That makes one of us." He crossed his arms. "Honestly, if I was going to get a lecture, I'd have thought it would be for siccing a Greater Mystic on an unsuspecting town."

"That wasn't ideal either," she said. "But at least it isn't making the rest of our mission more difficult. We need two plans. One to deal with what our next steps are, and one to deal with what to do when the griffin inevitably tracks us down again."

Fel sighed. "Do we know exactly what town the indicator is pointing to?"

"No. The needle has barely moved since we left Climber's Circle. According to the book, that means either we are heading more or less directly toward it, or it is very far away. Knowing what I know, about where the Bolivans are most active, I suspect the latter. It will probably take three solid days of travel before we've moved enough to make a guess at the location. And that's assuming they don't try moving it. They'd be fools not to."

"We've been snuffing out flames. It isn't as though they're getting updates."

"They'll know that flames are being snuffed out. What more update do they need?"

"The fact that I have one of their bracers? That's probably still a secret."

Lattica considered this. "There is value in that, I suppose."

She glanced at him.

"How was it? Using the thing. I've always wondered."

"I'd like to avoid using it again. You can't see your body. The world around you looks wrong, and the way it turns my stomach and twists my brain you'd think I was straight back to being hungover."

"That just means you need to be strategic in its usage. Or practice with it."

"I don't like strategy and there's only so much practice I can do while we're on the move. I'd rather consider it a last resort."

He fetched the bracer and turned it over in his hands. After a glance up and down the road to confirm the Bolivans hadn't sent anyone after them yet, and another glance at the sky to ensure the griffin had yet to return to the air, he held it out to her.

"Want to give it a try? Maybe you'll have a better knack for it than I do."

She eyed the device, then handed over the reins and accepted the contraption.

"I've read about them. I've made plans in the event they might be deployed against me. Now at least I can experience them from the other side."

He kept the horses on the road while she strapped it onto her arm.

"Just press the center of this side?" she said.

"Right."

She pressed it and wafted away in a wave of distorted light.

"Oh... this *is* disorienting," she said.

"You should try having a voice come out of thin air right next to you."

"Unnerving."

She tapped it off again. "Still. A useful tool to be able to work with."

She tossed it in the back but didn't reach for the reins again.

He commented, "I'm surprised you don't have any contraptions like that in your family's collection."

"We aren't the Bolivans. Like you, besides the sentry flame, we prefer to work within the realms of the law. I'll admit, we seem to exert a bit more influence on the law than your family, but something like this is simply beyond what we'd be willing to keep or sell."

"Right..." Fel decided it was best to move off the subject of illegal dealings in contraptions. "So, the plan. Since we don't know what we're headed for, that just leaves the question of what to do about the griffin rider."

"He won't fall for the smoke misdirect again. The man was clearly a high-quality soldier or mercenary. They wouldn't have put him astride a griffin otherwise."

"I don't know. I had some run-ins with hippogriff riders who were glorified thugs with nothing but anger and scars."

"This was no thug. Though he's likely to have a significant scar and likely some anger to go with it after our encounter."

"I'm glad I'm not the only one who does that to my enemies. I did it to a dragon, by the High."

She shook her head. "What higher power did you anger to end up with this level of absurd fortune?"

"I don't know. I've raided a number of tombs, vaults, and catacombs. I was bound to get *someone* on the other side upset."

"I just hope when lightning finally strikes you, I'm not sitting next to you at the time. But enough idle chitchat. That lure you used, do you have more?"

"Two more. But they'll get less potent the longer we wait to use them and the farther we get from Beffshire."

"All right... All right, here's what I propose..."

Euphoria sat at the dining room table. Epiphany stalked back and forth on the opposite side of it.

"You know what I'm going to ask," Epiphany said.

"I do."

"Then start answering and make it easier for the both of us."

"I don't have answers."

"Like muck you don't."

"You want to know about the clockwork diamond. You heard it mentioned. You saw it in Thaddeus's notes. You're putting one and one together. I would do the same. But I don't have any answers for you."

"Are you suggesting it is just a *coincidence* that a mask not unlike the one you stole from us brought up a contraption or artifact, by name, that I happen to know you are looking for?"

"I don't think it is a coincidence. I think there is a reason both masks would discuss the item. But I don't know what it is."

"You are after something, but you don't know what it is. Euphoria, we're working together now. Or at least that's what I'm supposed to believe. So just tell me what you know. Tell me what this is about."

Euphoria tightened her fists. "Fine. You likely won't believe me. But I can't control that. First, virtually nothing I've been working toward has been entirely revealed to me. Yes, I've married into the family. And yes, my husband is an important member of the Graves clan. But the hierarchy within that family is ruthless. I'm at the very fringe of the inner circle. They only tell me what they think I need to know."

"That's never stopped you from learning things before. If Mom and Dad knew *half* of what you'd gotten up to—"

"You're not wrong, but there are gaps and I..." She shut her eyes tightly. "You're right. I should lay it out plain. We know the Bolivans have been listening in. We know they're after the same things. The least I can do is balance the scales of knowledge. I acquired the mask—"

"Stole. You stole the mask."

Euphoria continued, ignoring the jab. "... because it was part of a plan uncovered by Piotor Graves. I've told you this already. I have been in fewer than five 'face-to-face' meetings with the Diplomat. Most of what I know has been gathered painstakingly by two of my in-laws, and I know for a fact that it has been heavily filtered before reaching me. As I said, it was recommended we acquire the Warrior mask to help us finally gain the advantage over the Bolivans. The Diplomat also recommended a reconciliation between our families. Despite my recommendation to do just that, from the very *start* of my interactions with the Graves family, it was not a terribly popular plan among the matriarchs and patriarchs. But there has been a *great* deal of talk from the Diplomat about the likelihood for the Warrior's reliance on the clockwork diamond. It isn't clear what the diamond is, precisely. We assume it is a powerful and complex contraption, one that would be useful in a time of open war. We've assumed it was within the Greater Lands Wall. Not within the Greater Lands, but in the wall itself. Now we realize that may have been a misunderstanding. There has been significant talk that suggests its operation is somehow entwined with the Greater Lands Wall, though. Hence our mistaken belief of its location."

"But you don't know what it does, or even precisely what it is?"

"Piecing together what the Diplomat says is a frustrating exercise. As much an art as a science. We haven't even heard the phrase 'clockwork diamond' directly. That was apparently turned up by going through a very old manuscript Piotor was translating. He put the pieces together to suggest that's what the Diplomat was referring to, and the keepers of the Diplomat have received confirmation that the two objects are one and the same. Since then, we have been attempting to determine precisely what it is and how to acquire it. And now that the Bolivans are aware of it, that need is doubly significant. It can't be allowed to fall into their hands."

"You don't know *anything* about its operation?"

"There is the suggestion that it does not need to be in contact with, or even near, its target to influence it. It may be very large, or perhaps very fragile. There are multiple references to the near inability to move it."

"And you have devoted *years* of your life to tracking down this ill-defined *something* with the hopes of giving your new family a strategic advantage?"

"It has been one small part of my many obligations, thank you very much."

"And has it been worth it? All of this?"

"You would have done the same. You saw the direction the family was headed, the way the nobles have been squeezing off any possibility to exist in the way we have been for generations. You'd be willing to do whatever it takes to keep the family afloat and to keep the family business alive."

"I wouldn't."

"I know you would, because you *did*. Or have you forgotten about the long and careful courtship of Thaddeus as a potential trade partner?"

"I didn't know he was a Graves."

"Does it matter? You still reached out to the Graves family in your time of need. And you still did it specifically as a means to circumvent the nobles."

Epiphany jabbed her finger in Euphoria's face. "You *sent* the Graves family after us. In *secret*."

"You needed our *help*."

"Not as badly as you needed ours. And you shrouded it in lies."

"You kept the truth from Mother."

"*Call her Mom!* Is there some rule that once you become a Graves, you have to put on airs?"

Epiphany covered her face for a moment and took a deep breath.

"This is getting us nowhere," she said.

The silence between them was leaden. It was Euphoria who finally broke it.

"If things had gone as I'd hoped, it would have been worth it. But things have gone a bit sideways."

"A bit sideways is an impressive understatement, Fora."

"I'd hoped it would have lasted only a few months. That by this time last year the Maskers and the Graves family would have formed an open partnership that would have benefited us all, and honestly, the world. The Graves resources, the Masker ingenuity. They want the same thing that Father... that *Dad* wants. They want to bring back what we lost when the Bygone Era ended. The stubbornness in that family, though, the raw *need* for things to be done on their terms"—she leaned back in her chair—"I suppose it's rubbed off on me."

"You were pretty stubborn to start with."

"I am an amateur by the standards of the Graves family. But... and these words are long overdue... I'm sorry. I made mistakes. I can argue that I had good intentions, but intentions don't much matter when one stays the course long after things didn't go as intended."

Epiphany leaned on the table. Retorts stumbled over themselves in their attempts to be hurled at her sister. Would this apology have come if lie after lie hadn't been uncovered? Would she have *ever* broken with the Graves directives and gotten in touch with her family again? Did she have any intention of returning the stolen mask now that she was found out? But the small victory of scoring a worthless point on some imagined scoreboard was nothing compared to the promise, or at least *chance,* of making the family whole again.

"So where do we go from here?" Epiphany said.

"I don't know. For my part, I plan on praying that Fel makes it back in one piece, and trying to fill in the gaping holes we've left in one another's lives."

Epiphany stood up and straightened her shirt.

"I've spent so much time holding a grudge, it'll take me a bit to get out of the habit. But once I'm through with work for the day, maybe we head down to The Fox and Log and have some drinks. Properly catch up."

"I've heard worse ideas," Euphoria said.

"We'll see. Who knows what sort of stuff will start flowing once our lips have been loosened?"

Tome had found a comfortable chair within the archive, situated just below one of the light contraptions. It had a table beside it, which he'd stacked with a few of his personal selections from the archive. All he needed was a hot cup of tea and some cookies, as well as someone to keep an eye on Parch to ensure he didn't eat any of the books, and this would be the ideal place to spend an evening.

Despite the fact that his flickering flame meant Wick was absent, he'd honored the sentry flame's wishes and left the lantern just outside the door. Parch was, for the moment at least, behaving himself. He'd plopped down on the floor beside the chair, seemingly still content to be in a cool, dark place rather than pulling a cart.

To his great delight, Tome had discovered two books that served his specific purposes. One was an atlas. The other was a thin booklet describing the layout of the wall. He still couldn't read them beyond a few random words here or there, but maps were the same regardless of language. The layout of the wall turned out to be of limited value, as the rooms were effectively identical and repeated in a pattern. He had his suspicions that there was a list of traps and their locations, but he couldn't quite decipher it. The atlas, on the other hand, was of particular interest.

"Fascinating..." he murmured. "This atlas was assembled *before* the wall was built."

He flipped through the pages, comparing different regions to the maps he'd brought along for navigation to the wall itself.

"Everything to the east of the plains looks about right. Very few of the major cities still exist from those days, but the coastlines match. The mountains match. The rivers match. For the most part the forests match. But past the plains, things just... they aren't right. There's a whole extra mountain range. The coast juts out into a peninsula half the size of Thayne and Shalia combined. Half a dozen additional rivers. The bay is enormous. And then *this*. An entire *continent* that simply isn't there."

He flipped a few pages and measured some distances with his fingers.

"But... if we ignore everything east of the plains, this could be the mountain we climbed. And here, on the island midway between the continents, the one that's wholly occupied by a city..."

He found a page with a more detailed map of the city. "These streets.... that's Clickspring." Tome shook his head. "Is the map wrong? Or has the world been changed somehow? Curious..."

"Tome?" called Wick from the doorway.

He set the book down and stood.

"Any word from the Maskers?"

"There is a rather significant familial dispute occurring, regarding the various secrets being kept by the Beffshire Maskers and Euphoria. In addition, the contraption acquired from Clickspring has been repaired and is serving as an oracle of sorts. This has prevented Martin from providing an updated list of books from the index."

Tome shut his eyes tightly, trying to wrap his head around the rapid-fire revelations.

"Is anyone in danger?"

"Presumably Fel is in danger, as that is his standard state of being. But we have received no word of him."

"Then we'll discuss this 'oracle' business later. I think I've found a way through to the Greater Lands that doesn't involve collapsing bridges and rushing rivers. I'll set the books aside for the return trip. For now, I'm going to grab the rest of my gear. We'll spend another night in the wall, and we'll be on the way. I've taken the liberty of roughly sketching out a few maps of what I *think* is meant to represent the Greater Lands. Two copies. I'll be burning one copy in your flame."

"A wise precaution."

He stood and neatly piled the books. Parch was roused by his motion and tippy-tapped along behind him.

"I can't wait to learn if you are going to be an asset or a liability once we're in the Greater Lands," he said. "It is going to be an adventure. I do wish I was dimwitted enough to *enjoy* adventures like Fel..."

CHAPTER 7

In Climber's Circle, there was still a fair amount of chaos despite more than a day passing since Fel's invasion. Indeed, the aftermath would probably linger for months. The dispatcher's office, and a third of the entire building that had contained it, were in ruins. The damage done to the rest of the city was rather light, having mostly been caused by the panicked crowd rather than the griffin. Aside from some bumps and bruises, again mostly stemming from the mob, there were no casualties. The worst injuries were the damage the griffin did to itself in assaulting the building, and the glancing crossbow bolt to the side of its rider.

Presently, the rider was receiving his second treatment from a halfway-decent doctor. The presence of a physician who didn't do most of his treatment with a hot knife and a bottle of whiskey was the most tangible evidence he'd yet encountered that proved just how wealthy this city was. Questor was in the relatively intact ground floor of the headquarters while treatment was being done. In this case "relatively intact" meant the ceiling and walls were present, but most of the things that had been hanging on them before Fel showed up now lay in pieces on the ground, waiting to be cleaned up by a staff that currently had better things to worry about.

"Nearly there," said the doctor as she drew a thread through the wound to pull another stitch taut. "Do try to give yourself some time to heal. If you tear your stitches again, you'll have to find someone else to reapply them."

Questor grimaced and endured. As significant as the pain was, the rider's primary source of discomfort at the moment was the dispatcher, who felt having a piece of his side torn out by a bolt was not a sufficient consequence for failure.

"Look at this place! Look at it!" the dispatcher shouted, kicking the remnants of what had once been a decorative pitcher. "It'll be weeks before we're cleaned up, and weeks more before we're doing business like we should be. What am I paying you for?"

The griffin rider gritted his teeth as another stitch pulled a bit more of the wound shut.

"Nothing," he said.

"Well, that's certainly what you're giving me," the dispatcher raved.

"No, you buffoon. I mean *you* aren't paying *me* for anything. Your employers are paying me."

"We are standing in a building that was ruined due to *your* incompetence, and you are splitting hairs?"

"I am a mercenary, sir. That means I am a soldier, but I am also a businessman. And this is a business matter."

"Fine. What are my *employers* paying you for, if not to prevent this precise event?"

"Your employers hired me as a powerful, rapidly deployable military asset to protect their investments against threats similarly equipped to their existing security. That is to say—" He winced at the final stitch pulling into place. "People equipped with contraptions."

"Fel Masker was here, using stolen contraptions from our own people. Precisely who you were supposed to defeat."

"What happened to my mount had nothing to do with a contraption. That was magic."

"What difference does that make?"

"Contraptions are tools. They have limits. I am well versed in the military contraptions and have plans for them. Magic is quite another thing. Different countermeasures are needed. You didn't pay for them. I don't have them. You nearly cost me my life and my employers a priceless mount because you failed to plan accordingly. This, all this, is on your head. If you want Fel Masker and whoever he is working with eliminated, you need to pay for the services you expect to be rendered and equip me properly."

"You want me to pay *more*? After this!?"

"No. I want your employers to pay me what I am owed."

"Even if there was *logic* to that madness, what would you suggest? I dispatch a messenger to request a pay raise for you? *The very thing you were meant to defend has been destroyed.* Without it I can't even send a message. I don't *know* where our mutual employer *is*."

The doctor finished working by wrapping a clean bandage around his midsection. He pulled on his shredded and still-bloody shirt.

"You should know better than to work for someone you can't find. It so happens I dealt with our employer personally, and I will be heading directly to him. Either I will negotiate the proper price, or you will be left undefended from the sort of people who can do *this* to you even *with* a trained griffin rider and his mount at your disposal. And I'll be sure to inform him what happened here, and under whose watch it happened. Goodbye."

He stalked through the door. Due to the damage to the stable, his griffin was tied to a post just outside, standing at attention while a ring of Bolivan guards held crossbows at the ready should it decide to go rogue once more.

"I have not given you permission to leave!" the dispatcher shouted. "Do not untie this man's mount. He is still my employee, and we do not know if the attackers are still nearby, waiting to strike again."

"There's nothing of value left here," Questor said, climbing to his steed's back. "And it's been more than a day. They will have moved on. Now that I've had a day to recover, and been patched up—"

"Twice," the doctor added.

"—I will be on my way."

"I said you are *not dismissed*," the dispatcher shouted.

Questor clicked a command. The griffin spread its wings. With a powerful leap and two strong flaps, it took to the sky, neatly pulling a section of fence from the ground as it went. Questor allowed himself a grin as he left the dispatcher impotently shouting at him from below.

Fel yawned and leaned back. Their journey had, impressively, been completely without incident since their run-in with the dispatcher. The downtime was having a much different effect on him and Lattica. The young woman was presently holding the reins, and from the tightness of her grip, to call her ill at ease would be a profound understatement. The time since the event in the city had only made her more stressed.

"We haven't heard or seen anything dangerous in days. I think you can relax for a while."

"That we haven't heard or seen anything dangerous in days is an excellent reason to *not* relax. We are very much at war with the Bolivans, and each step brings us closer to the heart of their empire. We should be facing steadily increasing resistance and... nothing."

"Maybe they're afraid of us."

"The Bolivans are too stupid and greedy to be afraid of anything."

"If they're stupid, then what are we worried about?"

"Stupidity can by highly destructive. You of all people should know that."

"I'm not stupid. I'm just very selective about what I bother remembering. But fine. Greed. Why haven't you just bribed them? Or, I don't know. Gone into business with them?"

"Not my decision, but I can kick them farther than I can trust them, so I wouldn't have wanted to go into business with them. And they have more money than us, so bribery is out of the question."

"... The Bolivans have more money than the Graves family?"

"When you break rules rather than bending them, you tend to make more money."

Fel glanced at the detector.

"Looks like it's moved a bit. Have you worked out where the destination is?"

"I've tried. I'm not entirely confident, but I know it's not a city. A place out in the mountains somewhere. Roughly in the overlap of Graves and Bolivan territory. There are a lot of manors and such from the Bygone Era up there. Mostly abandoned. They probably have someone holed up in one of those."

"And they haven't moved?"

"Doesn't look like it."

"Guess you were right about them being stupid. Good news for us."

He gave the detector a tap.

"Speaking of stupid..." he continued. "How long do you think we're going to be out here?"

"Even if this next target is the *last* target, a few more weeks," she said. "A week or so there, and a week or so back."

"I think it'll take longer than that to wipe the flames all out, now that we know they're sending out people with contraptions to keep them burning for so long."

"You honestly think we're going to be able to wipe out all the flames?"

"We have a detector, a carriage, and a job to do."

"They'll just keep lighting fresh flames and keeping them moving," she said.

"So we track those down too. Eventually they'll get tired of doing it."

"Trust me. That much was discussed," Lattica said. "The chances of truly wiping out all the stolen flames is very low."

"It wasn't discussed with *me.*"

"And you didn't think about it before agreeing to do this?"

"I did think about it. I thought, 'This is going to be a long trip.' What good does this do if we don't get all the flames?"

"We're doing this to prove we can."

Fel furrowed his brow.

"That's a bad reason, especially if you don't think we can."

"Once they know we can find their flames, they'll work harder to hide them. They'll send them out with fewer people because they'll know we can find anyone with one. That will make them less useful and be a net positive for us. And if along the way we find that they have some persistent lanterns, grabbing them will make the entire network of stolen flames more fragile. And along the way we develop a better code and start using it for communications. Over the course of a year or two, they'll stop using the flames and the problem will take care of itself. That's the official argument I got."

"Sounds like the plan of a quitter," he said.

"We have limited resources. We need to invest them wisely."

They rumbled onward.

"You didn't need me for this plan, either."

"I'm not fond of how it went down, but I can tell you I would have had a harder time with that last stop if I hadn't had a foolhardy maniac on the team."

"Careful. That was almost a compliment," he said. "But what I mean is, if you just needed them to know you have a way to find them, you didn't even need to bust in and put out the fire. Just keep showing up where there are flames and pestering them for a while. All you had to do was hire Dad to fix the detector."

Lattica shut her eyes tightly for a moment.

"You have been rivals of the Graves family for all these years, and you don't understand how they do business?"

"We don't do business with you, and we don't really compete for business. What do we care how you do business?"

Lattica shook her head. "I may as well tell you. By now it doesn't matter, because either it's an inevitability, or it's already failed. Your sister has been working to try to find a way to forge some sort of an alliance with the Masker family. She saw this as an opportunity to do just that. If she had her way, she would have opened up trade between the two families shortly after the marriage, but the old guard of the Graves family wasn't interested unless they could find a way to tip the odds in our favor. Give us some weight to throw around in the negotiation. Once this came up, and it was a threat to the whole family, it was only a matter of time before your sister found a way to make sure she had a chance to make it happen. This was as much a way for her to show her mother- and father-in-law that your family can play nice as a way to solve the problem."

"So when you say 'how the Graves family does business' you mean, 'how they go out of their way to sneakily find a way to do something that they could just outright *ask* to do.'"

"I didn't say I liked it. I just said it's how it is done."

Fel tipped his head and looked aside at her. "So what's your bet?"

"On what?"

"You think the families are going to get back together?"

"I have my doubts. Not because of your family. Because of mine."

"Oh?"

"If we do this right, the Bolivan family will cease to be a thorn in our side anymore. We'll be taking away the main weapon they have against us and costing them some of their best people in the process. That, *and* joining up with the Maskers? They won't know how to *live* without a rivalry."

"It's going to happen. Not a doubt in my mind."

"How can you be so sure?"

"Because my mom and dad want Fora back, and if Fora wants the families together? Forget it. If Vivian and Euphoria Masker were in agreement about wanting rain to fall up instead of down, we'd be working on designing umbrella shoes inside of a week."

Lattica scrunched up her face. "Did anyone ever tell you you had a gift for metaphor? Because if they did, they were lying."

"Mark my words, unless someone on your side screws it up, you and I are going to be official business partners by this time next month."

"Me, and you, working together *regularly*?" Lattica said.

"Could be worse," he said.

"I think you'd be getting the better end of that deal, which is *not* how the Graves family does business."

"Things change."

After what he reasoned might be the last good night's sleep he was liable to have for a while, Tome had ventured out into the innards of the wall. The trip to what he had reasoned was the Greater Lands-side exit of the wall was relatively uneventful. In this case, "relatively uneventful" meant that they'd only encountered two traps, and only accidentally activated one of them. It had been a frustrating but not overly dangerous one, slamming a heavy iron door shut behind him that required him to locate and activate a locking panel to release it and open the return path.

His good luck ran out when he discovered that "exit" was an extremely charitable way to describe the opening he'd trekked this far to find. It was more of a drain, or vent. A stone opening with a locked grating that opened out into the center of the wall facing the Greater Lands. This patch of wall seemed to extend particularly far down. Tome was comfortable calling the distance between the opening and the ground a fatal drop. Rather than something sane like a staircase leading downward, or something less sane but at least tolerable like a ladder, the builders of the wall felt the proper way to descend into the untamed world below was a coiled chain with disks every few links.

Tome crouched to investigate it.

"The Bygone Era had some impressive ideas about how things might be improved, but I'm pleased we abandoned this absurd innovation on ladders," he grumbled.

He kicked the chain out of the opening and listened to it jangle and clatter down the rocky slope at the base of the wall. The air was thick with the mist wafting off the waterfall spraying out from the wall not so far from this opening. It slicked the surfaces around him, making for a very treacherous climb ahead. He felt the wiry fur of the lesser unicorn against his leg. Parch was peering down along the wall, no apparent fear or concern on his face.

The paper mage shut his eyes.

"Tome, this is worth the risk. The best ink, and the best paper, and the best *quill* you've ever used in your life all came from this place. In just a few days you advanced your knowledge by leaps and bounds." He patted the spell pocket of his tunic. "You are well armed, with spells written specifically for this purpose, and you have powerful allies here. You are ready for anything this place can throw at you. You've thought deeply, now you just need to think quickly. And even *Fel* can do that."

He peered down. A cloud of mist swept past the stones below.

"Still. No sense carrying everything all at once," he said. "Wick, you're going down first."

"The distance is great enough that I will not be able to communicate any dangers back to you," Wick explained.

"This isn't about what I'm afraid of encountering, it's about dangling off a wet chain while you and the rest of my equipment is dangling off me. Chances are there's going to be some tumbling, so I'm going to snuff the flame and wrap the whole lantern up in the center of my gear. I'll light it again when I get down there."

"Please, allow me."

The flame flicked out.

Tome shuddered. "I really wish he hadn't learned that trick."

He shrugged his pack from his back and tied it to the end of his rope. Once Wick's lantern was properly affixed, he wrapped the whole bundle of gear in a blanket to keep it together and tied it with a length of cord. The bundle was tied to the end of a longer rope, and he lowered the whole thing down to the steep pile of gravel that transitioned from the wall to the shallower slope of the ground. He let the rope go, and immediately the whole bundle went tumbling down the hill.

Tome clenched his teeth and watched the precious cargo bounce and roll. It came to a rest beside a very distinctive tree with two crooks.

"Right. Well. That could have gone worse," he said.

Parch bleated idly and peered up at him.

"You can stay or you can go. Frankly, I don't know how much help you'll be, since I was only *barely* able to get you to obey plans as simple as 'walk forward.' For the sake of knowing where you are, and ensuring you stay safe, I'd prefer you came along, but I recognize I'm wasting breath by even talking to you. The alternative to reasoning with you is scurrying down this chain, so you'll forgive me if I'm keen for the procrastination."

Parch bleated again and tippy-tapped away from the opening.

"So be it," Tome said.

He took a steadying breath, then held tightly to the chain and lowered himself over the edge. To his great relief the chain was good and heavy, so it didn't sway very much at all as he descended. That was the only aspect of the descent that was even remotely positive. The mist, as expected, made the inadequate disks of metal terribly slippery, and by the time he was halfway down the wall, the constant spray had also made the links icy cold. He dared not look down as he descended, devoting his full attention to the chain lest he catch a glimpse of the drop beneath him and lose his concentration and grip. The result was a climb that seemed to take forever. Until the very moment his feet struck the rocky slope at the end of the chain, his mind conjured images of dozens of feet of potential drop if he were to let go.

Finally, the worst of it was over, and he switched from scaling a terrifying stone wall via a cold, slippery chain to keeping his balance on a jagged, wet mound of gravel above a steep slope. He brushed himself off and turned to spot the gear he'd inadvertently rolled down the hill.

It wasn't there.

"No... No, that is the precise place it landed. It would have taken a storm gust to dislodge it." He paused. "Or else..."

He turned. The distinctive tree was just the first piece of the dense stretch of trees and foliage that covered the Greater Lands between the wall and the mountains. Moss clung to the stony ground around the tree. It had not been disturbed except by the tumble of the gear. No footprints, no paw prints. But he couldn't deny that something seemed off. He slipped his hand into his tunic and ran his fingers along the top of his spells. Martin had suggested the innovation of cutting patterns of notches into the pages to identify them with a simple touch. As seemed to be an inevitability, while he knew a spell that might help with this particular moment, he'd neglected to prepare it.

No matter. Improvisation was a weakness of his, so he'd been hoping for some practice.

With a practiced motion from his fingers still hidden from view, he tore the edge of a spell that had been a bit of a handful last time he'd tried it. Subtle swirls of blue magic traced their way from his pocket to his eyes, and gradually his vision sharpened to an almost unbearable degree. Every tiny detail of the forest became crystal clear and razor sharp at once. The problem went from being able to see the details of the dim shadows in the distance to picking and choosing what his mind would expend its limited resources to perceive. He scanned slowly, doing his best to filter out the useless visual chaff from information of value. In little time, his eyes came to rest on something that even his intensely enhanced vision struggled to discern from the foliage. Not until he saw the gleam of eyes did the figure resolve itself. A slight, humanoid creature, draped in gray-green clothing. It was tailored, or perhaps styled, into stiff, curling whorls that perfectly mimicked the twist of vines and cragginess of bark. And it was holding a bow, made of gnarled wood, drawn tight. An arrow was notched against the string. The tip was wrapped with a strange pouch of some kind.

Tome's mind chose this moment to observe that he was still standing at the base of the wall. There was nothing but jagged, slippery gravel to his front and sides, and a wall behind him. It, perhaps, would have been wise to get to cover *before* finding any would-be assailants.

He squinted his eyes and sighed.

"I'd been hoping to save these..."

His still-hidden hand slipped around two additional spells. These hadn't required notches along the top, as they were several pages each and thus easy to discern. Even written in the best ink he could concoct, on the best paper he could afford, and in the tiniest writing he could manage, they were veritable booklets. The work of more than a day each, and a small fortune. But there was no sense writing them if he didn't use them, and there was no sense saving them when it was very likely he'd be skewered in a few moments if he didn't. He pinched the center of the first page of one booklet and, as before, tore it single-handed.

The same acuity that had graced his vision began to leak into his mind, not in terms of depth, but of speed. Someone who had never enhanced their speed mystically would be a bit baffled to discover it didn't make one feel any faster. It simply made the rest of the world seem slower. The flutter of leaves in the breeze became a slow wave of green riding a molasses-thick wind. He shifted his weight. The spell hadn't fully settled into place, so his body felt heavy and clumsy, but he knew he'd been wise to move at the first possible moment, as the instant his body moved in an evasive manner, the half-seen figure let the arrow fly.

The shaft wobbled toward him, the only thing in the entire world that looked to have any real velocity. It moved with the speed of a thrown stone, and even with his enhanced speed, it missed his shoulder by mere inches. The pouch-wrapped tip struck the wall behind him. A plume of odd powder burst from within.

His feet thumped down on the slick stone. He had to place them carefully. There were aspects of the spell designed to keep his footwork sure and steady, but they were written with the assumption that he'd be able to choose a flat, even straightaway for any feats of speed. Every step slid just a bit, dislodging gravel and spritzing water from the spongy moss. With his mind so much faster than his body, at least for the moment, he had time to plan. Traversing the woods at this speed wasn't really an option. Even sprinting through tall grass at this speed threatened to shred his trousers. All those plants, those low-hanging branches. It would be a death by a thousand cuts. But his assailant was near the edge of the forest. He could circle wide, come in from the side, and tackle him to the ground. Upon the insistence of the Maskers, he *had* brought a blade. It wouldn't take much more than the gentlest thrust at this speed to drive the weapon clean through the attacker.

He tried to plant his foot on the next stone, but the step swished through air instead. Tome had been so focused on moving carefully forward that he'd picked up a bit too much speed. Though it still felt like he was moving at a snail's pace, he had inadvertently turned the run into a leap. He was arcing through the air. With the slope so steep, this was going to be a rather significant drop.

The spell continued its work, raising the speed of his movements to be more in-line with the speed of his perception, but that did him a fat lot of good now that he was effectively a projectile. He turned toward where he knew his attacker to be. The figure had shifted aside and was drawing a second arrow from the equally camouflaged quiver. Tome watched, helpless, as the archer drew back the bow and shifted his aim. If it wasn't likely to end in him bleeding to death in a mysterious land he never should have returned to, Tome would have been impressed by how quickly this warrior was able to think and react. The paper mage still had five or six feet to go before what was sure to be a painful collision with what he hoped was a fairly forgiving bush, and yet. The archer had already let the arrow fly. He was helpless to dodge it as it wobbled through the air toward him. He just had to hope that it would miss. And if it *was* going to miss, it wouldn't be by much.

He felt the first few leaves of the bush slap against his shins an instant before the arrow struck his shoulder. Like the first, the weapon was tipped with a pouch. It struck hard enough to bring tears to his eyes and rip his tunic. If he lived to see tomorrow, he would probably have a terrible bruise and might well have a broken bone. But at this precise moment what concerned him most was the burst of dust that enveloped him. The stuff stung at his eyes and tingled at his nose. Intense pain had a way of causing someone to cry out, and crying out required a sharp inhale either before or after. His reflexes betrayed him and handily filled his lungs with the powder. Its effects were immediate. The speed of his mind began to fade, not because the spell had run its course, but because the powder was making it sluggish. His vision became blurred not because *that* spell had run out, but because he was losing the ability to focus. The very magic that allowed him to move and think at incredible speeds was accelerating the effects of what he hoped was *merely* sleeping powder. The one small mercy was that the heavy, involuntary sleep that came upon him pushed the sensations of tumbling across the forest floor at super speed nicely into the back of his consciousness. His vision faded, his mind grew fuzzy, and before he'd even finished his tumble, he was sound asleep.

CHAPTER 8

Allie finished a circuit of the tavern and returned to her place behind the bar. There was nothing new about the tendency for The Fox and Log to feel different in Fel's absence. Long trips were the norm for him, and he was such a well-liked regular and notable presence in the place that one couldn't help but divide the year into "time that Fel is present" and "time that he is not." But the changes that had come with this particular trip were particularly pronounced. Both Fel and Tome had been gone for just shy of two weeks, which had been time enough for a new routine to come together. The grum games still happened every night, and Tem continued to dominate, to the consternation of the other players. For the past two days, Epiphany and Euphoria had spent a few hours each day nursing drinks and chipping away at the wall of ice that had formed between them. Progress on that front had been slow, but Allie had enjoyed learning a thing or two about the pair. Epiphany had been a rare but not unprecedented sight in the tavern before, but she'd spent more time here since Euphoria had arrived than she had in the previous year. Euphoria, for her part, was much more of a mystery. Thus far she'd learned that Epiphany drank sherry when she wasn't interested in getting drunk and scotch when she was. Euphoria was a wine drinker regardless, though the cheaper the wine, the more likely she was drinking for the state of mind than the flavor profile.

Currently Epiphany was on her second scotch and Euphoria was on her fifth cheap wine. This meant that they were running headlong into the most surprising discovery of all. The pair were remarkably musical once they'd had a few.

"No, no, no. The line is 'For the lives I've lived and the loves I've loved,'" Euphoria said. "I should know. The song is my husband's blasted *favorite.*"

"How can it be his favorite?" Epiphany said. "The song is a *joke*. It's mocking sappy songs like that."

"The man doesn't grasp nuance unless you slam him upside the head with it," Euphoria said.

"How do you slam someone upside the head with nuance?"

"If you figure it out, let me know. It'll make for better conversations with him. The man can read the tiniest tell in the face of a buyer with a little more room in their budget, but you try some wordplay, and you may as well be talking backward. But where were we?"

She cleared her throat, and the sisters launched into a somewhat wobbly but surprisingly spirited rendition of a terribly saccharine song. Their relative skill at singing even in this state of inebriation was perhaps best illustrated by the lack of angry shouts and thrown handfuls of crickets trying to quiet them down.

Allie gathered up some empty glasses and refilled those with enough room on their tabs to warrant them. The door opened and she glanced up to find yet another curious little change since Fel's departure had decided to assert itself.

"Mariss! Come on in. You here for a drink or just to check in on your boy?"

Mariss laughed sheepishly. Every few days, right when the workday was ending at Divinity's Oven, Mariss would stop by The Fox and Log. Initially she claimed she simply wanted to drop some treats off for the staff, with some excuse about venerable businesses in Beffshire supporting one another. But she was a bit too transparent for that sort of attempted deception to last for long. She was here for Fel. More accurately, she was here to see if Fel had returned safely. It was an odd thing. Allie was still a bit puzzled by the nature of Fel and Mariss's relationship. She seemed concerned for him, but not in the way that a girlfriend or lover might fret over someone. It didn't even *really* feel like it was the way a friend would worry about another friend. Allie's concern for Fel came off as something wholly other, like someone who was aware the two-headed calf in the local sideshow was sick and felt bad that something so unique and bizarre might die. Fel might well be the only person in her life who had ever been in any sort of danger.

Regardless of her motivation, Mariss was clearly raised right, because she refused to visit without a gift.

"Just yeast buns this time," she said.

"Just yeast buns..." Allie said, reverently lifting the steaming goodies from the bag. "Just delicious little puffs of butter-topped goodness. You keep coming here asking after Fel, and I'm liable to need a new apron. Davie is going to kick himself for taking so much time off right when you started treating us to this sort of thing."

Mariss took a seat. A wavering, half-in-the-bag patron got up and tottered toward her, no doubt to have a seat and try his luck. Allie gave him a short and severe glance that made it clear even through the haze of alcohol that testing his luck would be testing *her* patience and neither was worth the effort. He tottered away again without Mariss even noticing the silent exchange.

"A drink?"

"Nothing for me," Mariss said.

Allie took a sinful bite of the bun and munched happily. Mariss sighed heavily.

"You know you could be a bit more articulate than a sigh when you want to talk. Though I don't remember it being on the list of odd jobs I'd have to do when I started working here, pouring your heart out to the barmaid is certainly a service we offer here at The Fox and Log."

"I couldn't."

"I'm eating your bread. Seems only right. And with the Masker sisters there putting on their show, I'm not liable to have to serve anyone else for a bit."

"I'm just thinking about... right now, Fel is somewhere having his adventure. Just the latest for him."

"Mmhmm," Allie said, stuffing the rest of the first roll in her mouth.

"He's living one of those stories. And then he'll come and tell me and it'll be the highlight of my day, and then that's it."

"And then that's it?"

"It's the closest I'll ever get to something like that."

"You know when he tells a story he leaves out the bad bits, right? And probably makes up half of the good ones."

"Even so. He's seen places I've never even dreamed of. Have you done any traveling?"

"Not much. Most of my life is right here in The Fox and Log. I haven't got the time or money to be traveling much."

"The farthest I've ever been is the next town over."

"Which direction?"

"All of them. I do deliveries."

"Ah."

"I don't have an excuse to be so poorly traveled. I have plenty of money. Or the family does, at least. And I only work for Father because I *want* to. I love to bake, and I love chatting with customers. It just never felt necessary to go anywhere. Most of my life, Beffshire felt *huge*. I've been here my whole life, and I still haven't seen the whole town."

"Beffshire has a lot to see."

"Not compared to what Fel has seen. He makes the world seem so much bigger. And that makes this place feel so much smaller. I'm starting to feel like I've been hiding or something."

Allie leaned back and crossed her arms. She tried to conjure up some wisdom for Mariss, or at least something that would *seem* like wisdom, but before she could come up with anything, the door opened and revealed a very rare sight within The Fox and Log.

"Hey, boss! What brings you here!" Allie said.

Sid was the owner of The Fox and Log. He'd become increasingly hands-off once Allie had been hired. So much so that it had been more than a year since he'd shown his face in his own tavern. He paid on time, though, and he recognized that things went smoothly if he let Allie handle them, so all in all they had a good relationship. She didn't know how old he was. Years of living on nothing but booze and roasted crickets had given him a body with more years on it than it ought to have. Likewise for his mind. He was a bit scatterbrained these days.

He took a seat at the bar and blinked at the smoke hanging in the air.

"Place is pretty full," he observed.

"That's how we keep the money coming in, boss."

"Back when I was here, we couldn't trust it to stay this full without someone getting too rowdy and busting up tables."

"It takes a gentle touch. Or a thump on the side of the head with a leather-wrapped stick. The tricky part is figuring out which one. But if you can keep the peace, you make a lot more money."

"Sure, sure." He patted a pocket symbolically. "So I noticed. Some other folks noticed too. A little bit ago, a fellow came and asked if I wanted a partner. I had some time to think it over and decided I didn't. No need, am I right? Then he almost busted my desk under the weight of the sack of duots he was offering, and I thought maybe I'd consider it. Money like that, all at once, means we could do some work on this place. You know I was thinking about adding in that stage."

She raised her eyebrows. Sid had been "thinking about" a dozen different improvements for as long as Allie had worked in the tavern. Thus far he'd followed through with precisely zero.

"So long as you're thinking about changes, lengthening up the bar, moving the storage from the back room to the basement, extending out into the lot behind us so we can have some private rooms with locked doors, and maybe getting a proper kitchen should all be on the maybe pile."

He scratched his head. "Some good stuff in there. I'll take that to the fellow. He says he has carpenters all ready if we need them. And frankly... this place needs a brush up."

"This sounds like it might actually happen, huh, boss?"

"Oh, it'll happen. Starts happening in a few days."

She furrowed her brow. "What?"

"Closing up shop for a bit. Should take a month. That's why I came down. I thought I was just adding the stage, but I'll run all that by him too. He's keen on the brush up. I think he just wants a reason to use those carpenters."

"You went from 'I don't need a partner' to 'we'll shut down for a month' that fast?"

"It was a big, big bag of money," he said.

"Boss, you don't quite pay me enough for me to be taking a month off without planning for it."

"Right, right. You'll be making a bit more when you get back, though."

"That's great for after, but I have to worry about food and shelter for a month."

"Right... Well, you can talk to the partner. See if he has work for you. You ought to do that anyway. Talk about that stuff you said, about what we should add."

"Who is the partner?"

He scratched his head. "You'd think I'd remember that. Funny name. Ver... Verida?"

She narrowed her eyes. "Verfessa?"

"That's the one. Don. Don Verfessa."

"You sold The Fox and Log to Donovan Verfessa?"

"Half stake. But yeah. Spread the word. One month off, and then a brand-new Fox and Log."

He stood and wandered out, as though completely uprooting Allie's life for the next month wasn't the sort of thing that needed any further discussion.

Mariss looked uncertainly to Allie, not quite aware how best to respond to what she'd witnessed.

"Well, there you have it, Mariss. Sometimes 'adventure' comes along and finds you. You might want to head out. Once I make this announcement, there might be some rowdiness."

"Why would there be rowdiness?"

"Because *anything* might cause rowdiness, and this is a thing. You need someone to walk you home?"

"No, no. I took my horse and cart."

Allie trotted over and glanced out the window.

"Wow," she murmured.

The horse, and the two-person cart attached to it, looked sleeker and faster than anything Allie had seen in the streets for ages.

"She's quite the steed. I take care of her myself!" Mariss said. "And *fast*. I've made deliveries to the next town and the rolls were still warm." She stood to leave. "If you ever need a ride, you let me know."

"Will do. You have a safe ride."

The baker slipped out. Allie turned to the patrons.

"Listen up, lads and ladies! Big changes afoot..."

Consciousness returned to Tome with aching slowness. Whatever state he'd been in, it hadn't been proper sleep, because when he awoke, he didn't feel refreshed or restored. Quite the opposite. His head felt heavy and fuzzy. It took considerable effort to pull together enough of his mind to assess what had become of him. He began with what his blurred vision could observe. The clothes he wore were not his own. In place of his comfortable—if a little road worn—tunic and trousers was a soft green robe. There was nothing underneath. He for the moment allowed himself to set aside the ramifications of that revelation.

The room he found himself in was not the work of a carpenter. The walls weren't hammered together from boards, or even mortared together from stone. They were wood, but with the gnarled, rippling texture of a still-living tree. Scraping at the wall revealed a bead of sap. The room had *grown* into this shape. As a result, it wasn't quite the proper shape. The floor was cupped toward the center. The walls curved out and in again. And it was rather small. Tall enough to stand up in, but from his place sluggishly reclined on the floor he could reach the walls on either side. It had a door that faced the outside, or at least it had a portion of the wall that clearly had been his means of entrance, but that opening was crisscrossed with a sturdy net of living vine.

This was a cell. He was a prisoner.

He pulled himself to his feet, then swiftly regretted it, thumping back down to lean against the wall. He shook his head, which only served to increase the dizziness, then took some time to recover. When he felt confident he could do so without falling on this face, he reached out to test the strength of the vines. They didn't feel terribly strong. A good sharp tug could probably dislodge them. But it was plain to him that their strength was not their purpose. He hadn't even fully tightened his grip around the vines when he felt a sort of inaudible rumble ripple through them and buzz through the walls. An alarm, either mystic in nature or some trait of the vines themselves, swept out from the doorway.

In seconds the alarm drew a familiar figure into view on the other side of the vines. Though he'd only caught a fleeting glimpse of him before, there was no doubt in Tome's mind this was the person who had fired the arrow that had incapacitated him. He was tall. Unnaturally tall for a human, but Tome very much doubted this was a human. The creature's features were long. The chin was almost pointed, cheeks drawn and hollow. His eyes had an intensity and keenness to them, their color a shade of brown that came just a little too close to orange to feel normal. Though the hood had been drawn back to reveal his face, he still wore the well-camouflaged cloak. It hid his figure, but the peek at his arms visible from where they crossed in front of him told all the tale Tome needed. He was skinny, willowy. Lanky to an uncanny degree. But somehow, despite all the ways that his appearance diverged from that of a normal human, the most distinctive feature of this stranger was the *penetrating* smugness plastered across his face.

"Who are you? What is this?" Tome said, when he was awake enough to be confident the words would be coherent.

His captor didn't reply. His confident smirk simply shifted to a mildly distasteful sneer and he stepped from view. Over the several minutes that followed, Tome's body rose to a level of functionality that revealed to him additional information about his state and surroundings. He realized he could hear distant conversation, though the language was not familiar to him. The doorway to the cell must have been angled upward, because the only thing he could see without getting closer to the door—and he was in no mood to do that—was the fluttering tops of trees. He also discovered his hunger was raging and his throat was horribly dry.

"How long was I asleep..." he groaned, rubbing the back of his head, where a dull ache had settled in.

"Repeat that, please. Repeat it," called a rather harried voice from out of view.

The newcomer scurried into view, probably also summoned by the alarm. He was the same sort of creature as the captor who had been overseeing him, but he was dressed quite differently. His outfit was more formfitting, underscoring the accuracy of Fel's prediction regarding their build. The proportions were downright eerie in their divergence from what he would call a "proper" body. The torso was somewhat smaller than a human's, but the limbs were of such a length as to suggest he was at least a foot taller than Tome, if not two. It gave an overall sense that the man was a poorly disguised stick insect. His clothes were of the same fabric as the captor, but less dedicated to stealth. They were instead a natural, off-white tone. His skin was dark, a remarkable contrast from the ghostly pallor of the captor, and the corners of his eyes were creased as though he was perpetually squinting.

"I said 'How long was I asleep,' but I'm more interested in what this is all about," Tome said.

"I have had *no* practice in this language for quite some time. Apologies for any errors I may make," he said, with a professorial precision that made the statement seem ludicrous. "You have been unconscious for somewhat more than two days. You are here because it was this gentleman's assignment to fetch you. Not you specifically, of course. Any who arrived. Your timing was exquisite. His patrol had just been approaching when your equipment came tumbling down ahead of him."

"How fortunate," Tome muttered.

The captor leaned on the outside wall of the cell, leering at Tome. He uttered something in a language that made what was no doubt an arrogant jab sound like the lyrics of an opera.

"Er, introductions first, then I shall inform him," said the dark-skinned man. "My name is Kott. I am the court interpreter. This fellow with the cloak is Mevrelle. He is a… oh, what is the word… a *ranger* I imagine? Scout? Scout is rather a lower term for his role, and he would object. Ranger, then. And he has expressed, in words that imply frustration with a small degree of respectful admiration, that it has been sixty years since he's had to fire a second arrow to strike a target."

"You should mark yourself lucky. If I'd had a shade more practice with that spell, you wouldn't have had time for a third," Tome said.

It wasn't, perhaps, the wisest decision to bluster and taunt his captors, but he was hungry, his head hurt, and the mention of the arrow to the arm had somehow reminded his brain to start broadcasting the thundering throb in his bicep that he'd not noticed until that moment. Kott relayed the taunt, and Mevrelle released a single wry laugh.

"Why was I captured? And why am I being held?"

"Because you arrived," Kott said.

"Is that a crime?" Tome asked.

"No. It is a curiosity. A trick that warrants investigation. Before we begin said investigation, there are the matters of care and feeding, and simple assessment. You are, if I am correct, a human."

"I am. And what are you?"

"Your questions after mine, if you please. I am told that humans consume the flesh of other creatures. Is that a strict requirement, or will bread and fruit be sufficient?"

"I can do without meat if needs be."

"And water will suffice? We have wine, but it may be somewhat more —"

Tome held up a hand. "I've had the wine in these parts, and I'll pass for now."

"Wise."

Kott turned and snapped his fingers. The long digits produced a painfully loud sound, like something a wild creature would use to warn predators not to draw closer.

"Your food will be here shortly. Now, you had questions?"

"What are you?"

"I'm the interpreter. Did I misspeak earlier?"

"I mean what race are you?"

"Ah... Oh, dear. I do not believe there is a suitably eloquent descriptor available in your lexicon. I suppose... Grand Children of the Forest is a coarse but accurate approximation."

"Elves?"

"That is a meaningless and ugly mouth sound, but if you must apply it to us to more easily cope with your present place and our nature, then that is your right," Kott said.

Though the words implied resentment or distaste, he said it as cheerfully as if he was complimenting Tome on his excellent diction. Tome wondered if Kott was legitimately pleasant and cheerful, or if his upbeat delivery was some strange affect of an accent.

"How long am I going to be held prisoner here?" Tome asked.

"Please don't think of yourself as a prisoner. You are... an intellectual curiosity. A specimen, retained for study."

"That doesn't make me feel any better."

"I wasn't attempting to improve your mood, simply trying to more accurately reflect your status. Regardless of terminology, you will remain with us until we are satisfied we've learned the means by which you are able to... arrive. We have our theories, of course, but a theory is worthless without the proper test."

"Arrive. You mean through the wall, obviously. You can't traverse the wall?"

"I have no interest in what lies beyond the wall, and no desire to bear witness to it," Kott said.

Tome crossed his arms and smirked. "Interesting..."

"We weren't entirely certain there was anywhere to arrive *from*. But then we received word that a pair of squat little parodies of the Grand Children of the Forest had come through. No one truly believed it until Kazel took to the skies again."

"We freed him," Tome said.

Kott gave Tome a serious look, then uttered something to Mevrelle. The translation was apparently not well received.

"You are in league with Kazel?" Kott asked.

"I wouldn't say that we are in *league* with him. When we showed up last time, I was either rescued or captured by his Adept, depending on how you choose to view the event." He placed his hand on his head. "Twice I've come to this place and twice I've ended up in the clutches of the locals within minutes."

"How and why did you free Kazel?" Kott asked.

"We freed him in exchange for our own freedom, and we did so by locating the keys to his chains in the lair of another dragon, whose name I have forgotten and frankly don't care to recall."

"Duurth," Kott said.

"Didn't I *just* say I didn't care to recall it?"

"These are... outrageous claims you're making."

"My life for the last few months has been quite outrageous. Do you not believe me?"

"I would hesitate to believe you if not for the evidence that is... evident. You see, you are a paper mage, if the contents of your tunic are any indication. And we could consider it rare to the point of impossible for a practitioner of one of the inferior magics to achieve what you've described."

"Inferior magics," Tome fumed.

"I apologize. My inexpert grasp of the language can render me somewhat indelicate. I have no doubt you can, with time and effort, bring about the same effects as a spoken-word wizard. But unlike spoken magics, you can also be fully disarmed simply by confiscating your spells."

"And spoken magic can be disabled with a gag."

"It is further made unlikely that someone foolish enough to have come here *alone* could have had the wit or capacity to achieve what Kazel's many followers could not."

"I didn't come here alone last time. There was a contraptioneer with me."

"Contraptioneer..." Kott squinted a bit more, mind sifting through its vocabulary.

The moment he realized what the word meant was marked quite visibly by a distasteful change in his expression.

"A contraptioneer... that explains quite a bit."

A new figure appeared. This appeared to be a female, though it was not immediately clear if they were of the same species. She was almost a polar opposite to the build of the two males. Her height was perhaps two-thirds that of the others, quite a bit shorter than Tome. Far from the lank and willowy build of the others, she was quite round. Everything about her was soft and curved in the precise way that the male bodies *weren't*. Even her expression was less severe. She didn't seem pleased to see Tome, but she didn't seem coldly judgmental or smug and arrogant either. Perhaps it was simply because she was carrying the meal that had been summoned, but her expression and demeanor put him in mind of a waitress. Courteous, but very much viewing him as an obligation rather than a guest.

She softly mumbled a few words that Tome felt in the pit of his stomach. He had never actually *heard* spoken magic before. But he'd felt mystic forces at work, and this was precisely the same sensation. The vines shifted, not sufficiently for him to attempt to escape, but enough for the woven mat she was carrying to be slipped through. The meal perched atop it was inviting. A succulent assortment of fruits and vegetables, some familiar to him and others entirely alien, had been artistically arranged with some coarse bread. The cup of water and the mat both seemed to have been woven from the same broad, woody sheets of plant material, either bark or dried leaves.

"You should enjoy your meal. I'll have to discuss what shall be done with you. I will return this evening. After you've eaten you will be permitted, with supervision, to travel the grounds of the village. If at any point that you are without an observer, you will be returned to the cell. You are, after all, an outsider, and one who rather impressively complicated our lives by aiding in the release of Kazel."

Kott and the unnamed woman departed. Mevrelle remained, watching Tome like a hawk as he sampled the first bit of sliced fruit.

"I couldn't have foreseen this," Tome said aloud. "So there is no sense in criticizing my own judgment. But in retrospect, it may have been wiser to bring someone else along."

A little creature with simple gray fur, a tufted tail, and a pearlescent white horn clippy-clopped through the rocky foothills at the base of a familiar mountain. Parch did not particularly like this place. There were many terrible, bad things here. Things that ate unicorns both big and small. But there were good things here, too. Parch raised his head and gazed up along the slope, then turned and glanced along the river.

Different animals developed different senses to keep them safe. Mundane animals might stay alive by paying attention to astoundingly sensitive noses or ears. Parch had a fairly sensitive nose, but nothing impressive. His eyes could perhaps see more keenly in the dark than a human's could. His ears were nothing special. But, lesser or not, he was a mystic creature, and thus there were senses available to him that mundane animals lacked. Parch did not think deeply. There was no need. Instinct was a fine guide. And thus, Parch did not question or ponder upon what precisely led him this way or that. He knew, at a deep level, where friends could be found. And even deeper, he could tell where enemies could be found. For years, he worried only about where the enemies were. He stayed away from them. It didn't serve him to mind things like friends. There *were* no friends. But now there were. Some better than others. Some he wanted to be near. Some he simply knew would help him if he needed it.

But once you found a friend, once you knew that friend was worth having, you did what it took to *keep* that friend.

He was just a little unicorn. A lesser unicorn. He didn't know what to do. Just that something needed to be done. And if one friend needed help that you couldn't give, you found another. Friends helped friends. So he traveled for hours. He could walk a long way without getting tired. So long as he could get a nice cool drink, and find something green to eat, he could keep going for *ages* if he needed to. He sipped the icy water of the mountain stream, shut his eyes, and felt.

He wanted to find his favorite friend. His best friend. But he was far away. Farther than made sense. There were other friends, though. Not much farther now and he would reach the closest of them.

A cackling, chattering sound filled the air. If the sound had been larger, he would have been scared. But this sound was small. Friendly. Musical. This was the friend he was after.

Parch clopped with sure and steady hooves over slippery rocks until he crested a small outcropping and spotted her. She had a name. Parch didn't care. She was a friend. One of a few that could be found here, but the one that Parch liked best. The one Parch had been hoping to find. Parch stood atop the outcropping and bleated. A pear-shaped little creature, a kobold, looked up from the water. She was holding a fishing pole and churring merrily to herself in a strange, primal little tune. The frilly-eared, blue-tinged creature scanned her surroundings until she saw Parch. She released a trilling, gleeful chirp and hopped to her feet.

"Good little beastie!" she crowed.

She widened her stance and lowered her head. Parch trotted forward and reared up. Not in a fighting way. In a friendly way. The way that the big, nice human did well and the little, less-nice human didn't do at all. Parch indulged a few playful butts, then scampered back.

"You are here. Fel is here?" Teya said hopefully, looking about.

Parch flicked an ear.

"Fel is *not* here..." Her expression and tone flattened. "Tome is here."

Parch flicked his ear again. It wasn't much different than the first flick. Teya understood.

"My worst friend," Teya grumbled. "Bad time?"

Parch turned toward where he knew Tome to be. Teya nodded.

"I tell Adept. We go."

Teya gathered up her fishing supplies and trotted toward the mountain. Parch bounded around Teya as she walked.

"You? Very fast? Me, less very fast." Teya grinned and tapped her head. "Very good idea."

Martin drummed his fingers on the workbench. He'd handed over a music box for Oiler to reassemble. It was a long, tedious task, one that he'd done hundreds of times and had nothing new to learn from. The amount of fiddly work involved normally left him with sore fingers and a sour mood, but it was precisely the kind of thing Oiler loved most. At least, as best as he could determine from the contraption's body language such was the case. It was the last bit of inventory he was required to complete before tomorrow. This would be the stretch of the evening that he could dedicate to tinkering, studying, or getting ahead on tomorrow's orders. On a normal day, he would have thrown himself headlong into this task or that. He was truly spoiled for choice when it came to things to fill that time. He'd only scratched the surface of the materials Fel had brought back during his last adventure. A small, relatively innocuous contraption he was trying to build from scratch was waiting to be completed according to the instructions within the reference books. And then there was the Student mask, currently inert but still brimming with potential lessons and discoveries.

In what seemed to be an inevitability when faced with so many excellent options, the only one he truly wanted to do was the one that wasn't currently available to him. He wanted to spend some time with his daughters.

"I'll tell you, Oiler," he said idly. "Years of not seeing her, years of watching the hearts of her brother and sister harden against her, I was worried the day wouldn't come that she'd return. Now she's back. I should be happy she's off to the tavern with Epiphany again. They haven't *killed* each other after a few such trips, so they must be mending their relationship. But I know things simply wouldn't flow as smoothly if I were to join them. No child wants their parents tagging along at the tavern."

Oiler's head produced a merry chime as it completed one of the assemblies. It turned vaguely to the north and watched nothing in particular, simply angling toward Fel as though doing so would bring him back. Then it went back to the task at hand.

Martin looked at the mask and bust. He turned it to face him.

"The Student..." he muttered. "Fascinating but not the *most* valuable option. Knowledge that depends upon not only asking the right questions but the people of the Bygone Era choosing to teach the answers to those questions. Still. It is what we have, and it's infinitely more than we had before."

He opened a book of notes he'd been taking and slipped the Bygone Dagger from the back of the bust. The soft sounds of clockwork within the bust swelled, and the polished pupils of the device rose into position.

"Hello, Martin. Is it time for another lesson?"

"Another test, if you don't mind."

"I am always pleased to have my knowledge tested, but as a student, I cannot pass future tests without instruction. Please prepare a lesson for me so that I can continue to grow my knowledge."

"That is fair. If for no other reason than to provide future keepers of the Student with a proper window into our own time. But test first."

"Of course."

Martin ran his finger down the page. "Here is a worthwhile question. What were the most significant current events of the time immediately before your deactivation in the Bygone Era?"

"A question with a subjective answer. I am afraid I am not interested in, and thus not capable of, answering subjective questions unless those questions relate to someone *else's* subjective answer."

"Very well. Name *some* current events surrounding your deactivation."

"Felix Masker was making revisions to the mask mount, or bust, in order to facilitate a mix of different contraptors rather than contraptors with singular unified interests. Two major streets in Clickspring were being repaired after a storm caused damage. A book called 'The Shimmering Bodice' had caused a stir due to the highly descriptive nature of its content, and more specifically the fact that it described—"

"I think that will do," Martin said, crossing off the question. "I clearly need to be a bit more specific. But that brings up the matter of Clickspring. I take, based upon your recollections, that you were *in* Clickspring prior to being deactivated?"

"It was where the mask was created. All my lessons took place there."

"Why were you removed?"

"I do not know that. It happened while I was deactivated."

"Right. Fine. You mention a Warrior and a Diplomat among the other masks. Was there a war at that time?"

"There was not a war, though only because there was no formal declaration of one. Battles and clashes were frequent."

"Between whom?"

"Us and them."

"Could you be more specific?"

"I cannot. It seemed that 'us' and 'them' were fluidly defined. 'Us' usually included the people of Clickspring in particular and humanity in general, though some cities or classes of humans seemed to periodically be excluded. 'Them' included all hostile, nonsapient Greater Mystics and most sapient Greater Mystics."

"What was the reason for the battle?"

"I do not know."

"Were the hostilities widespread?"

"To my knowledge, any area of human habitation was likely to come to blows with Greater Mystics eventually. Those were matters for the Diplomat and the Warrior. They were not discussed with me or a part of my education."

"Were you simply an experiment? It seems your interactions were incomplete and unstructured."

"I am, indeed, the first mask to be made."

"Why did they start with the Student?"

"It was not known prior to my activation what direct communication with contraptors might facilitate or lead to. It was decided that a student was the ideal test, as it allowed the flow of information to be fully controlled by the people interacting with the mask."

"What was the threat of a more open interaction?"

"It is not clear that there was a threat. Also, it is not clear that open communication was possible. Contraptors are only capable of interacting by means of presented puzzles and problems that require solving. It was considered likely that communication in an entirely unstructured manner is impossible."

"What did the creators of the mask *think* was the threat of more open communication?"

"It was already known that contraptors were the mechanism by which contraptions operated. Thus, contraptors were known to be capable of virtually anything, given the proper means to convert that action or effect into the answer to a puzzle or riddle. It follows that if one were to mistakenly or purposely infuse contraptors with will, one would be faced with a being with effectively limitless capabilities. Were that individual to become a malicious force, the consequences would be dire. But such a thing could only occur if someone were to devise a riddle or puzzle for which the best or only solution would be to become a malicious force."

"And eventually the Warrior mask was created," Martin said.

"True."

Martin made a note and underlined it. These masks were not to be taken lightly. He slid his finger down to the next question he wished to ask, but before he could speak, the dancing of the flame in Wick's lantern became still.

"Hello, Martin," Wick said.

"Wick!" Martin said. "It has been quite some time since you were last here. I hope that things are going well?"

"Tome has had some difficulties."

"Anything I ought to know?"

"Unclear. My flame was snuffed in order to safely lower it into the Greater Lands, and it has not been relit. I returned to this lantern as slowly as I could, as I imagined he would be needing me shortly after he reached the Greater Lands, but he has not summoned me."

"How long has it been?"

"Over two days."

Martin's expression dropped.

"That's not good."

"I agree with your assessment. I have no knowledge of what has occurred. No evidence of danger or safety."

"That's... troubling. Did he have message to deliver before he snuffed the flame?"

"No. It did not appear that he was intending a delay longer than the time it took to climb a chain ladder."

"Did you make any observations at all in the days before that you haven't shared?"

"None that seem relevant, though it may be valuable to inform you of a capability I was not fully aware I possessed, and thus other flames may possess."

"What is that?"

"When I felt I was being placed in a position to potentially damage books, I was able to extinguish my own flame. It is now clear to me, though it was not clear until that event, that I can do so at will. Though I say he snuffed my flame, when Tome suggested he would do so, I fulfilled that service personally. I now worry doing so may have somehow damaged the lantern's capacity to restore itself as a relevant point of observation."

"I doubt that. You'd have to somehow damage the engravings to do that. However, given what Fel is up to, that *is* a rather important discovery. And you say you weren't aware you could do so until now?"

"I assure you. If I had been aware of that capability, there are a number of events on my personal history that would have gone very differently. I hope that this information will be valuable to Fel in his quest to extinguish all Graves flames not currently in the possession of the Graves family."

"I am sure it *would* if we had some means to get that information to him. It seems that presently neither Tome *nor* Fel is quickly reachable, and both are certainly in very perilous situations..."

"It is remarkable how commonly timing aligns against this family."

"At least it is consistent," Martin observed woefully.

"Is there any information you would like me to deliver, assuming my other lantern is relit?"

"Not that it matters to Tome, particularly in light of his potentially dire circumstances."

"We have no reason to believe he has come to harm," Wick said.

"It is difficult to take solace in that, Wick. But… updates. The girls are getting along. Business is going as usual. The mask has been a great source of information, if perhaps not a convenient one. That is all that leaps to mind. However, now that I think of this, remain for a bit, will you?"

"I have no means to do otherwise."

"Right, yes. Of course." Martin turned to the Student. "I would like to quiz you on the subject of contraptions that can communicate. Perhaps it will give us some means around the present conundrum of how to restore communication."

"Excellent!" the Student said.

"Both you and Wick are contraptions capable of communication, correct?"

"This is correct," the Student said.

"Did sentry lanterns precede or follow your own creation?"

"Sentry lanterns were created over the course of the three years following my own creation, utilizing, in part, things learned over the course of my own creation."

"And Oiler there. Oiler has something of a personality. There is *some* degree of communication. Was it created prior to or following your own creation?"

"I do not know, specifically, if that Oiler was created before or after me, but Oilers in general were in common usage prior to my creation."

"Would you say that your own operation is derived from concepts present in Oiler?"

"The bust and mask indeed are an evolution of the faceplate and head components of Oiler, with respect to both the basic form factor and the operation."

"You have a degree of personality, Student, but are considerably more mechanical in response than Wick. Wick has a nearly human level of communication, and has expanded his role significantly beyond his original design intent. Even Oiler has, in effect, been *trained* to behave somewhat beyond his design."

"This is a very useful lesson, albeit one composed chiefly of information extrapolated from my own responses," the Student said.

"Why, and through what means, have Oiler and Wick developed some semblance of will if you claim that contraptions cannot do this?"

The Student was silent, save for the increasing whir of its components.

"I do not know," the Student said.

"To your knowledge, is there any way for a sentry lantern to reignite its own flame?"

"Sentry lanterns were specifically designed to lack the capacity to do so as a safety precaution."

"Is it possible for that capacity to develop regardless of this precaution?"

"I do not know."

"Well then," Martin said. "There are many lessons yet to learn together. Student, I think we're through for now."

"Excellent! Until the next lesson."

Martin inserted the dagger, and the Student went silent. He looked at his notebook. With a slow, thoughtful scratch, he circled the word "Warrior" and drew an arrow to the phrase "End of the Era."

"Many lessons yet to learn..." he muttered.

Tome watched the sun march across the wall of the cell. Presently Mevrelle was once again watching him. Or perhaps *still* watching him. With little else to do while in the cell, Tome had been alternately dwelling on his poor execution of this expedition, and napping. A replacement for Mevrelle could have come and gone any number of times while he dozed.

"I believe I was promised some measure of freedom at some point?" Tome said to his captor. "I'll have you know that Kazel and his followers were *much* better hosts. They took better care of me, *and* they kept their word."

Mevrelle grinned. As far as Tome knew, the elf didn't understand what he was saying, but he had a feeling the tone of displeasure and frustration was bringing him joy.

"It takes a very special sort of person to be graceful, elegant, and still a brutish thug, and you've managed it admirably," Tome said.

He heard footsteps and crawled to the vines to peer in their direction. He needn't have bothered. It was Kott, and he was heading right this way.

"Many apologies for the delay. Some minor security adjustments were necessary," Kott said. "Come, come, he's been locked up long enough. I'm sure Tome would like to stretch his legs."

One of the females stepped up and uttered an arcane phrase. The vines curled and twisted themselves free of the opening.

"It is *long* past time," Tome said, crawling through the opening and squinting at the brightness beyond.

As his eyes adjusted, he was finally granted a view of the village where he was being held. Or so he supposed. His interminable incarceration had given him plenty of time to envision what the place must have looked like. His mind had conjured images of buildings still sprouting leaves, thatched roofs and stone walkways. What he saw was... a forest.

It was technically true that the homes still grew leaves, but only because the homes were the trees themselves. They were massive things, like the sort of tree one might imagine in a jungle or rising up out of a swamp, but scaled to an unnatural degree. Mossy sheets hung over the crooks of branches and the spread of roots in a way that he supposed served as doors and windows. When he stepped free of the cell, he stepped not onto the solid ground or a wooden catwalk, but onto a branch only mildly flattened on top. This place didn't look like a village that was close to nature, it looked like nature that had been gently coaxed into slightly more useful shapes.

Tome unsteadily paced along the branch, Mevrelle behind him and Kott in front. The female remained at the cell.

"Have you people not mastered the art of ladders or stairs?" Tome asked, recovering from a second near fall in barely a dozen steps.

"We wouldn't sully the perfection of nature with such things. Now, I imagine you'll have questions."

"Plenty. First, where are my clothes?"

"Burned."

"What?"

"You are a magician."

"A mage."

"Rather a lofty word for a practitioner of your type, but I may not grasp the full nuance of the term. Regardless, you may have had some manner of enchantment on the garb, and we would prefer you not attempt anything reckless."

"I imagine you've burned my spells as well."

"Spells, ink, quills. The rest of your books are intact, at least for now."

"What about the lantern?"

"Your sentry lantern? Intact."

"You know what a sentry lantern is?"

"We've been hoping to find something of the sort for quite some time. Tell me, what do you call the source of the voice of the flame?"

"Wick."

"Oh. You've named it."

"I haven't, no. The Maskers have."

Kott shut his eyes and furiously repeated the name. "Maskers..."

"You know something, it is becoming rather irritating that my recent associate's family legacy precedes him everywhere he goes, while I'm forced to forge my own legacy from nothing."

"Depending on your cooperation and value, you may yet earn the generational ire of our people or an equivalent amount of gratitude."

"I'm leaning toward the ire, given how you've treated me."

"Not the wisest statement to make while in a position of weakness. But your frustration is understandable."

Kott nimbly hopped to a lower branch. Tome followed. The landing wasn't perfect, causing him to stumble forward and thump his bruised shoulder against Kott's back. Despite his slight build, the collision barely managed to budge him.

"As I was saying, what do you call 'Wick'?" Kott asked.

"I don't understand the question."

"A mind? A consciousness? An entity? A being? What is your understanding of Wick's nature?"

"He's a contraption."

"A contraption has earned a male pronoun? I suppose the language has evolved somewhat since the wall's creation."

"Why are you asking?"

"We have plans for the contraption, and there is some degree of concern whether our act will be considered property damage or murder."

"You're going to kill Wick?"

"Murder then," Kott said, as though it was merely a mental note to be taken.

"You realize you *can't* kill him, correct? He doesn't even reside within the lantern. If the—"

Kott raised a hand.

"I get the distinct impression that you know less about the sentry lantern than I do, so we can discontinue this line of questioning."

"What are you planning to do with Wick?"

"That is none of your concern." Kott paused. "That, I realize, is an incorrect statement, as it is rather significantly of concern to you. But what I mean to say is you do not have a place in the plan, and thus I need not tell you."

"Fine. What are you planning to do with *me?* You can't tell me I don't have a place in *that* plan."

"Undecided. We are unlikely to kill you. Not because you are too valuable. Now that we have Wick, and now that we've had a chance to investigate you mystically, you are utterly valueless. But we do not kill without reason, and there is no reason to kill you."

Tome tightened his jaw. "I'm not sure what to object to first in that statement. You mystically investigated me?"

"Very lightly, but to our satisfaction."

"When?"

"While you were sleeping."

Tome pulled his loaned robe a little tighter. Kott continued.

"We'd hoped you were using some sort of contraption or enchantment to freely... arrive. But the truth of your specific means of achieving freedom of movement is, sadly, impossible to replicate. You are Lesser Mystics."

"We are *not* Lesser Mystics. We aren't mystics at all."

"You are capable of utilizing magic."

"That's not an element of mystic or mundane nature, it is a function of intellectual capacity. Anyone can *learn* magic. And besides. To imply that we are Lesser Mystics is to imply that there exists some *Greater Mystic* version of a human."

"Several, in fact," Kott said. "There are ourselves, and the giants. I suppose some claim can be made of the merfolk as well, but I would speculate that the lesser version of a merperson would also be aquatic."

"I am *not* a lesser version of you."

"You are less mystically adept, you are less intelligent. You have a shorter lifespan, but you are otherwise a rough match for our shape and physical capabilities. I scarcely see how you could come to a different conclusion."

Tome simmered in fury, not simply because he was angered by the mere implication of being some sort of flawed echo of another race, but because he couldn't construct a satisfying contradiction to that statement. He wasn't proud of it, but failing to formulate an intellectual counterpoint, he resorted to childish taunting.

"I understand. You need to find *some* way to restore some dignity after human contraptioneers were able to build a wall that you can't cross."

Kott laughed lightly. "You think *humans* were responsible for... that? I would suggest you take some time to read over our histories, but you don't understand the language and we aren't so foolish as to allow you to come anywhere near paper."

"At least you accept I'm a threat."

"If we thought you were a threat, we'd kill you. We simply don't want you to be a nuisance."

They reached the ground. Kott patted Tome condescendingly on the shoulder.

"I apologize that I cannot be a better host to you, but I have other obligations elsewhere. Mevrelle will shadow you until nightfall and return you to the cell. If you overstep your bounds, he will chastise you. Try to enjoy and educate yourself within those parameters. Supper will be provided just before sundown. You may eat it in your cell or in the open. Goodbye."

"Wait!" he called as Kott turned away. "Does anyone else even speak my language?"

"Certainly not. See you this evening."

Tome glared at him as he walked away.

"You should know that a dragon, a harpy, and a legion of kobolds were both more hospitable and more moral than you."

Kott didn't dignify the comment with one of his own. He simply paced through the hanging moss between two arched roots. Mevrelle remained. Tome crossed his arms and silently thanked Kott for being so infuriating. If not for the furious indignation he was feeling, he probably would have succumbed to panic. He was defenseless in a strange place, and unlike *last* time this had happened, those holding him captive were intelligent enough to be truly monstrous, rather than simply appearing to be monsters.

He swept his eyes across the village. It was hardly bustling, though a part of that assessment was due to the verticality of the village. If he took into account the scattered elves marching along the branches of trees that were taller than any building, it probably equaled the foot traffic that a small town would have on its main street.

"What exactly to they expect me to *do*?" he muttered to himself.

The fury started to fade, and thus the panic vied for his attention, but he thrust it aside. He would do what he'd always done. Stay calm, learn about his situation, and make a plan. He needed to find what remained of his things. They *said* they'd burned it all, but they could be lying. He needed to learn what they were capable of and how. He needed to find Wick, at least long enough to deliver a message and, ideally, in order to free him from their clutches. And he needed to start planning the content of the spells he would write to get himself out of this mess. True, he lacked the means to write them at the moment, but the better structured the spells were in his head, the less time and paper he would need to write them if the opportunity arose.

He turned to Mevrelle. The ranger's eyes were set on Tome's back, his gaze so potent Tome could practically feel them like a weight.

"Well, if nothing else, I'm ruining *your* day. So that's something," he said.

The Adept stood atop her perch. Since Kazel's release from captivity, her role had shifted from custodian of his people to something considerably more active. Kazel had no aspirations of conquest, but to be a dragon was to have a hoard. The older the dragon, the more nuanced and complex the hoard could become. Kazel had gold, but he saw those under his influence and in his care as a part of his wealth. That meant protecting them, and keeping close accounting of them.

The greater harpy gazed wearily at the pages held up before her by three of the endless legion of kobolds who served Kazel. Stix and Mik, the kobolds who served as her hands, had both of *their* hands busy marking down the various affairs Kazel had assigned. It was tiring and required constant supervision, but that was her purpose and she considered it an honor to have been given the role.

If things continued to go as smoothly as they had of late, she would be able to return to the considerable but far less demanding obligations that she'd had to postpone.

Somehow, despite the fact that it was just the distant clop of tiny hooves, she knew that what she was hearing was the first evidence that the problem-free time was about to come to an end.

"Yaaa-haha!" trilled a familiar voice.

The Adept wearily raised her eyes to the edge of the rocky cliff that she called a home. A small gray lesser unicorn bounded up past the edge of the cliff, a kobold riding bareback.

"Teya..." the Adept muttered.

Kobolds were brilliant at teamwork. It came to them instinctively. Thus, though she of course knew each of them by name, in general they could be treated interchangeably. They were simply "the kobolds." Rare was there a kobold that stood out. But every now and then one of them separated from the crowd. And Teya most certainly filled that role ably. At least she'd ceased to set things on fire with that infernal "sparker" she'd been given... Or else she'd gotten better at hiding the evidence. At this point, the Adept would accept either.

"Adept!" Teya chattered in her native tongue, and thus with a far greater mastery than she struggled through with outsiders.

She dismounted the unicorn, which bounded over to the water basin.

"Teya," the Adept said, keeping her weariness from her voice. "I take from its familiarity that this unicorn is, in fact, Parch?"

"It is! The little friend came to me directly while I was fishing. I had only just begun, so I haven't caught any fish yet, but given what happened last time Parch paid a visit, I thought it was best to let you know immediately."

"And what needs to be told?" the Adept said. "Has Masker returned?"

"I do not think so, Adept. The little creature does not speak, but I think perhaps it is the other one. The mage."

"Alone?"

"No!" she pointed. "With Parch! But since Parch came to fetch me, I think perhaps he is in trouble."

The Adept glanced aside. She prided herself on keeping closely apprised of the events in Kazel's realm, but until the arrival of the humans and the crucial service they provided, that had meant a very slow and very deep flow of information. Things had accelerated considerably, forcing her to keep copious notes. Stix scampered off to a rack of scrolls and sifted through them, then returned with one and unfurled it. It was a detailed record of their exploits.

"Tome. Tome Inkbrand. That is the mage's name. Last time the humans came tumbling into the Silkstrand River. We haven't heard from the nymphs about disturbances. I suppose there is nothing to *prevent* them from entering through some other means..."

She glanced to the other side. Mik tottered away and returned with some fresh dispatches. One by one they were held up for her perusal.

"The Forest Children have been sending out their rangers, according to the unicorns." She read a bit further. "As far as the river."

Mik rolled up the dispatches and put them away. Stix hopped to the Adept's shoulder and rubbed the harpy's forehead.

"It was a tremendous instance of good fortune that the humans came along and helped to free Kazel. I suppose it was inevitable that things would shift in the other direction. The world seeks balance."

"What's wrong, Adept?" Teya asked.

"If the Children of the Forest sent rangers as far as the river, they were probably *watching* the river, and perhaps even the route by which the humans came here. I don't imagine for a moment they would come so near to Kazel's territory, particularly not after he was so visibly freed from his captivity, without good reason. They will have intercepted the human."

"Why?" Teya asked.

"I do not know. They have kept clear of our land for hundreds of years, content with their pocket of the Greater Lands. We have avoided clashes and bloodshed by keeping to ourselves. But this does not bode well."

"You think Tome is in trouble? Because I think *Parch* thinks that."

"There are a half-dozen ways this could turn out. The two most likely are that Tome is held against his will as part of some plot or gambit by the Children of the Forest, or that Tome has voluntarily offered his services to them. Both are unpleasant thoughts, as I would have considered the humans to be our allies. And in the former case that would mean an ally was in danger, and in the latter case an ally may have abandoned or betrayed that allegiance."

"So we go! We fly to their village and we take Tome back, yes?" Teya said.

"That... would not be wise. We do not have a single interaction with the Children of the Forest in our entire history that didn't lead to some sort of bloodshed. If we were to send a force capable of compelling them to release Tome, that would be open war. War is never good. So soon after Kazel's release is perhaps the worst time for it."

"We cannot *leave* him. That is not how we treat allies. And it would make Parch *sad*," Teya said.

"It is possible that we have greater concerns than the emotional state of a lesser unicorn."

"We *owe* them, Adept! Kazel owes them."

"We settled that debt with their freedom."

Teya placed her hands on her hips and gave the Adept a firm look. The harpy was unaccustomed to being looked upon with anything less than reverence and respect. Stern disappointment was a notable and unwelcome departure.

"We do better than that. Kazel does better than that. I know it," Teya said.

"We do not risk war for the sake of a single person without *very* good reason. We need to be sure. We need proof that something should be done."

"But *Parch*!" Teya said, pointing emphatically at the unicorn, who was unsuccessfully attempting to coax another kobold into a game of headbutts.

"We need more than the interpreted motivations of a Lesser Mystic."

"Then I'll go and find out, yes?"

"One kobold is better than a contingent of them, or Kazel or myself arriving personally. But if there is evidence worth having, it is in their capital village. Even one kobold that far into their land could prompt hostilities."

"Not if I am sneaky! And I am *very sneaky*," Teya said.

Stix hopped down and drummed her claws on the metal of her perch.

"Teya, I am not sending you to do this. If you do this, you do this on your own. I have not *forbidden* you to do this. You will not anger me or Kazel if you do. But if you are caught, you were not acting on our behalf and you will face whatever consequences on your own."

Teya grinned. "I can do this! And I *will*."

She scampered away. The Adept attempted to push the matter from her mind for the moment. She would have to bring it to Kazel. Of that there was no question. But at present there was no pressing need. She was confident that if the Children of the Forest were to begin something that needed to be forcefully ended, it would become obvious. And until then, all Teya had to do was avoid making things worse.

The kobold charged by again, equipped with her bow and a pack. She hopped onto Parch's back. She was a bit larger than a normal rider would be for something the unicorn's size, but the unicorn didn't seem to be struggling at all.

"Yah-haaa!" Teya crowed as Parch hopped off the cliff and bounded out of earshot.

"Never have I so immediately regretted a decision."

CHAPTER 9

Fel rolled out of the hammock and dropped gracelessly to the floor. While he'd gotten quite accustomed to sleeping while swinging along with the cadence of the horses, he'd yet to perfect the dismount. Starting each day with an uncontrolled drop to the floor of a carriage was only one of the changes this mission had thrust upon him, unfortunately. The other was the total eradication of the very concept of days. Taking turns handling the horses and being on watch meant that he slept when he could, rather than at a given point in the day. Right now the sun was just setting, but he'd had all the sleep he was likely to get and was thus going to be on duty for the overnight shift.

He sluggishly pulled open the crate of provisions.

"We are scraping the bottom of the barrel on food. Unless you want me boiling the bones for stock when we stop for the night, we need to either shop or hunt," Fel said.

"Ever been to Grundholt?" Lattica called back to him.

"Once. Don't they pride themselves on that strange cheese? With the bits of sausage in it?"

"They do. We'll stock up. A few slices of that and some crusty bread will keep you alive for a week. Do you want to do the shopping or set up the campsite?"

"No staying in an inn?"

"You know how I feel about leaving the carriage unguarded."

"Fine. Fine. I'll set up the campsite." He dug into his pocket and tossed a few duots to the seat beside her. "Pick up some butter. And some ale or wine or something. If I have to go through another day with nothing but water that tastes like the inside of a wineskin, I'm going to lose my mind."

"Why the butter?"

"You're bringing bread and cheese, I'll have a fire and a pan. I think you can figure out what I have in mind."

"I hadn't expected this mission to expose me to so many new dishes."

He shrugged. "I spend a lot of time alone on the road, and I usually don't have much money for inns. Gotta get creative with the food sometimes. It's about the only time I eat something home-cooked that isn't stew. Not that I mind. Dad's stew is good stuff."

She brought the carriage to a stop a short distance off the road. If there was a City Watch, they tended not to take kindly to someone setting up camp near the city. Sometimes they would make up something about vagrancy. Other times they'd simply state that they don't like outsiders, even if their livelihood depended upon them. Either way, it was generally wise to camp far enough from the city for the Watch to be too busy or lazy to cause trouble. Thus, Lattica had a bit of a walk ahead of her.

Tome made sure the horses were fed, watered, and ready for the night. The sky was clear enough that they wouldn't need much in the way of additional shelter. He gathered kindling, arranged some stones, and prepared the cooking pot.

"Fried bread and sausage cheese. Maybe tomorrow I'll mix up some of the stale bread and melt up more cheese and do that bubbly-cheese-pot thing they had over near the Water-Chest vault."

He pulled the empty provision chests out and plopped them by the fire to sit on, then took a seat and watched as flames crackled and turned some green wood into cooking coals. Daydreams of the good meal ahead and a cool, clear night under the stars put a smile on his face. It was going to be nice for once.

The very moment the word "nice" came to mind, he raised his eyes from the fire. Things were going his way. His guard was decidedly down. He was alone. If there was ever a time to attack, this was it.

He grabbed his cudgel and stood up, trying to strain his ears to hear past the crackle of the fire. He had nothing but intuition to go on, but there was suddenly no question in his mind that something was wrong. His thoughts turned briefly to Lattica. She was alone too, and headed into a town. Being surrounded by strangers meant a sane enemy wouldn't take the chance to attack, but the sort of people on the Bolivan payroll couldn't be trusted to make sane decisions. His concern for her filtered to the back of his mind. If she could handle herself against a griffin and rider, she could handle herself against some run-of-the-mill Bolivans. Right now he had to focus on himself.

They had been headed into the mountains when they decided to stop. They'd be deep in them by tomorrow. Right now all that meant was the trees were getting farther apart. A few minutes ago, that was frustrating because it made for poor kindling. Now it was an asset, because there were fewer places to hide. He crept back to the carriage and glanced at the detector. Still rock solid, pointing to the city Lattica had circled on the map. If there were attackers, they weren't carrying a flame with them. But they wouldn't need one. They'd been taking a straight shot toward the next big flame, in a carriage that wasn't terribly fast. They'd been half expecting an ambush for quite some time. The fact that no one had made a move yet was thanks either to the lingering light of day making an attack easier to spot or to the possibility that Fel was wrong and there was no attack pending after all.

"How would I do it?" Fel whispered to himself. "*I* would have just run out and clubbed them before they set up camp. How would *they* do it... They'll want to have me taken care of before she shows back up, but they'll want to do it in a way that she won't realize something is up until it's too late. No crossbow. No knife. Too much blood."

Visions of someone sneaking up and clubbing him came to mind. As he learned a moment too late, he simply hadn't been thinking deviously enough. The answer of how a Bolivan would subdue someone without making a mess came in the form of a rope dropping over his head and pulling tight against his throat. He reached for his throat and tried to pull it away, but a boot struck him in the small of his back and the rope pulled tighter.

Blue and black sparks filled his vision. He gasped for breath, but breath wouldn't matter if the flow of blood was cut off for much longer. Fel leaned forward and yanked the unseen attacker off the ground. He heaved all his weight, bashing himself and the Bolivan against the side of the carriage. The rope stayed taut. His vision was beginning to dim.

A stricken groan barked into his ear, and the rope went slack again. Fel yanked the cord free and scrambled away, gasping for breath and wavering. As his vision cleared, he saw a man struggling on the ground. There was no way, at a glance, to know it was a Bolivan, but the attempt to strangle Fel to death was a very strong indication. Fel stumbled forward and leaned heavily on the carriage to recover. The man stopped struggling and went still, blood slowly pooling beneath him.

"What in the world?" Fel croaked, his throat still ailing from the attack.

He gave the now quite deceased man a nudge with his toe. The body jerked suddenly, and a second, smaller figure wriggled out from beneath him. The startling new arrival was roughly man-shaped, but was scarcely knee high. He was dressed in clothes midway between the dusty green of the bushes and the matte gray of the road. Despite being trapped beneath a man as he bled out, this little fellow was impressively free of blood. He held an oddly proportioned blade. It was about the size of a dagger, but in the hands of the gnome it looked like a two-handed broadsword. Perhaps even more surprising than having a heavily armed miniature man burst from beneath an attempted assassin was the realization that he *knew* him.

"... Davie?" Fel said.

"Yeah. That's me." The gnome made quick work of stripping the man's pockets for valuables and gear. "You got a shovel in that crate? We gotta get this guy underground, or we're liable to turn some heads if traffic picks up on the road."

"You just killed someone for me. You saved my life."

"I like ya, Fel, but that wasn't a favor. I got a job to do. Come on. Shovel."

He shook the last lingering dullness from his brain and pulled himself into the carriage to fetch the shovel.

"I know Verfessa sent someone to tail us, but... you work for Verfessa?"

"Mostly I work for The Fox and Log, but being a runner doesn't pay much," Davie said, sliding the blade against the dead man's sleeve to wipe it clean.

"How long have you been following us?"

"Since Beffshire, big guy."

"We've gotten into scrapes before. Why didn't you show up then?"

"I'm supposed to keep you from getting dead. This is the closest you got. Unless something went down in that stable place. I don't know. Lost track of you once you put on that bracer gadget."

Fel found some reasonably soft soil—no small task this close to the mountains—and started digging. His brain was sparking and sputtering from the literal assault on his life and the assault on his expectations these revelations had brought. Far from a stone-cold killer, it wasn't lost on him that a man had just died. He wasn't one to casually dig a shallow grave. But he was gifted with the clarity of thought to recognize that the kind of person who would try to choke out a man on the side of the road and then lie in wait to do the same to his partner was the kind of person who was destined for a shallow grave regardless of who did the digging.

"They're getting desperate, eh?" Davie said. "Seems like they were more about kidnapping back in town. Now they're trying to kill you. You two must be doing something right."

"You and I have a very different idea of what it means to be doing something right. Is Lattica all right? She's alone in the city."

"Near as I can figure, they didn't have anybody in town, just out here. But I didn't exactly have time to give a good hard look to every last corner. And these guys don't advertise who they work for. But my guess, if your lady friend gets a rope across her throat, it's being held by a run-of-the-mill scofflaw, and a big girl like her can handle herself against those."

Questor adjusted his goggles and grimaced at the shock of pain that went through his side. Not since the earliest days of his training on the griffin had he been so keenly aware of just how much movement and effort went into riding the beast. Flight was an endless balancing act, shifting and twisting to ride the air currents. If one thought the galloping of a horse was hard on a body, the flap of a griffin's wings was another thing entirely. He'd been lucky there was someone who knew their way around a wound back when that mercenary nearly put a bolt through him. As much as it hurt, it didn't have the burning sting of a wound gone wrong. The rest was just pain. He could cope with that.

Below, a wooded section of the mountainside came into view. From the ground, it would have been difficult to spot this place. The road was in terrible repair, with a downed tree perpetually blocking the final stretch of it. From the air it was simple enough to see. It was a partially rebuilt manor house in the middle of a slowly recovering bit of forest still showing the char of the fire that had cost it a hefty clump of trees and most of the manor's original structure. A few more recently-constructed buildings flanked the manor. They were quite sturdy and fully intact, each clearly a storehouse of some kind. This was only his second time coming here, and he'd genuinely hoped the first visit would have been the last. One could not be choosy about one's benefactors when one made a living as a hired blade. But the man holding the purse strings on this job gave him a terrible feeling that he was somehow more sinister than he let on. And he let on a *great deal* of sinister intent.

He clicked his tongue and brought the griffin down to the charred landscape around the manor. A thin layer of snow had fallen, but was rapidly melting in the evening sun. The flight had been long, and he would have liked to send his steed off to hunt, but the footprints in the snow suggested for the time being it was best if he kept the massive creature around for the purposes of persuasion. This benefactor's bodyguards were present and were not expecting him.

"Just keep flying, merc," rumbled a voice from the sheltered doorway of the half-charred manor.

"I have negotiations to conduct," Questor said.

"Not according to the list," grumbled a second voice.

The pair stepped out into the light. Questor supposed, on average, they were human. They certainly had the body shape of one. But the issue that cast doubt on that assessment was one of scale. They were *enormous*. Somewhere in the seven-foot range. It wasn't impossible to encounter a standard human that tall. They were a staple in traveling sideshows. But they were invariably lanky and slight. These men would have been imposingly stocky even if they were a match for his height. They were proper giants. In description, but partially in race as well.

"There has been a dispute about payment," Questor said. "I'm here to settle the balance."

"You're here to get your skull caved in if you think you're coming inside."

Both revealed their weapons of choice. One carried a sledgehammer that looked more like a tack hammer in his grip. The other had a two-handed sword that he was effortlessly carrying in one hand.

"Boys, we can answer the question of who would win in a fight between two half-giants and a griffin rider, but it seems cruel to do so without an audience. Rather than spilling some very expensive blood, why don't we just check with your boss and find out if he wants to see me, hmm?"

"We go inside and you'll just fly away," said the first giant.

"Well then you'd have what you wanted, wouldn't you? Just let him know I'm here."

The first giant turned to the second and nodded, sending him grudgingly inside. Questor lingered near his steed. He knew full well that with the griffin he would win a clash with these two, but the griffin wouldn't act without him, so survival largely depended upon him acting quickly.

As it happened, that needn't have been a concern. The giant returned and gave a grudging gesture for Questor to enter. He was escorted through the manor. Most of the doors in the place had been boarded up, or else led to rooms that were missing sections of roof or floor. He'd never visited a place that had been repaired in such a piecemeal fashion. Only the portion of the building that was in regular use had been patched up after the fire that had ravaged the place.

He was brought to the doorway he knew to be the office of his benefactor. The giant opened the door with what seemed to be an amount of force precisely calculated to fall just shy of tearing it from its hinges and pushed him inside.

A floor-to-ceiling screen separated him from the man who had negotiated his hiring to begin with. He went by the name Lens. The screen wasn't just a stand in the middle of the room, but something of a false wall. There was no way to cross the screen. The array of holes in it was sparse enough that he could only make out the flame burning on the other side and the shadow of his high-backed chair that it cast on the wall.

"You were not to return unless summoned," Lens said.

"I was not to face wizards without being paid and supplied for such."

"The Graves wizard is not among the parties at play, and the Masker wizard is occupied elsewhere. You should not have had to face any form of magic."

"My griffin decided to shred the stable office, and I don't see anything but magic making that happen."

"I am in the midst of a rather sensitive operation, and I do not appreciate being extorted in this manner."

"I have a gaping hole in my side that I'd rather wasn't there either. One of us has money in the game, the other has blood in the game. If I've spilled some of mine, I expect you to cough up a bit more of yours. And again. If we're looking at magic, either you supply a means to combat it, or I'm keeping what I was given for this job so far and you are on your own moving forward."

"My communication network is breaking down far more quickly than I'd anticipated. I need someone who can move quickly and hit hard."

"Then you need to pay what I'm worth and give me the resources I need."

"How would you define the necessary resources?"

"Something to keep the griffin in my control."

"If control was wrenched from you without the removal of the saddle, I must assume there was either a lure or a rival taming spell at play. If no one came in direct contact with you, it was likely not a taming spell. Without a wizard about, it was probably something prepared by the paper mage the Maskers work with. You are asking me to provide some means of blocking a lure of the sort a paper mage could create."

"I am."

"Are you aware of any specific means to do that?"

"I'm not. You're the one with the job that needs to be done. That's your problem to solve."

"I have not sought out any wizards to include in my organization. However, I have a deep well of contraption knowledge and design. Return tomorrow and you will be provided with the materials and instructions to create an enhanced defense for your mount. If you are able to complete your task, your additional payment shall be the device itself."

He raised his eyebrows. Contraptions dealing with the taming and defense of Greater Mystics were vanishingly rare. As difficult as it was to acquire a griffin or hippogriff, the taming saddle was by far the most valuable item entrusted to him. If he were to earn a contraption that could genuinely defend a mount from mystic tampering, it would be worth more than he was likely to earn in a lifetime... provided it worked.

"I think I can accept that offer."

"Then run along until tomorrow. I have work to do."

"Make sure to inform your giants that I have an appointment. They were less than hospitable today."

"They shall be made aware. But I want to make this clear. After tomorrow, you will not return until you are beckoned."

"I have no desire to spend any more time here than I have to."

"Then run along."

He stood and marched toward the door. Already, he was dreaming of the huge prices he could charge if he were to be placed in a position to ensure the only reasonable defense against a griffin rider was neutralized.

Fel was just tamping down the final resting place of the ill-fated assassin when Lattica arrived. She had her truncheon in one hand and a sack of goods in the other. Clearly the same intuition that had nearly saved Fel's life was whispering its advice in her ear as well. The look on her face suggested she wasn't sure what to make of the gnome sitting on the back of one of the horses, polishing the blade of a dagger-sword.

"Fel?" she said warily. "What is this?"

He dusted off his hands.

"Lattica. Good, you're safe. This is Davie. He does the running around for The Fox and Log back home, and apparently pulls blades across throats for extra pocket change. He's been keeping an eye on us."

Davie fired off a crisp salute. "Been admiring you from afar, Miss."

"What happened?"

"Your boy here almost got garroted," he said. "I put a knife in the rope man, and Fel put him in the ground."

"You killed a Bolivan?" Lattica said.

"That's what they pay me for," Davie said.

"How long have you been following us?" she asked.

"You two ask the same dumb questions, huh? Fel and I been through it. He'll straighten you out." Davie hopped up and slipped his weapon into the scabbard on his back. "I'd better make myself scarce. All three of us in the same place sort of defeats the purpose of me being a shadow for you two."

He hopped off the horse and scampered toward the woods.

"Wait!" Fel said.

He stopped and turned.

"Make it quick, big guy."

"We're about to cook up some fried bread and cheese." Fel looked to Lattica. "Did you get beer?"

She nodded, not yet prepared to be as casual about the recent revelations as Fel.

"And we've got some beer."

Davie shrugged. "I'll be by for a plate once it's ready. But don't get used to all this back and forth. I'm not supposed to be seen or heard, as a rule."

"One last thing," Fel said. "Do you have a way of getting messages back and forth between yourself and your boss?"

"If you don't got one, I sure don't. Why?"

"Because he and I are going to have to have some words, once this whole thing is over, and I wanted him to be ready for it."

Davie laughed. "I'm sure he'll be quaking in his boots. Anyway, thanks for the hospitality, you're welcome for the save, and let's get this done quick. I hate spending time up north. The cold is a real pain for us small folk."

He trotted off. In the dim light of the waning evening, he may as well have been wearing the invisibility bracer within a dozen strides.

"You have a murderous gnome following you around?" Lattica said.

"Yeah. So do you. And what does it say about me and my life that learning that comes as a relief?" He brushed his hands off on his trousers. "I'm going to need that beer now."

Tome leaned against the side of a tree and slid down to sit on the root. He was free of the cell, for now, but the sun was lowering in the sky. Soon they would be along to collect him for dinner and a night locked away. In spite of the circumstances, once the anger and fear had been given time to reduce to a slow simmer, he couldn't help but be fascinated by what he'd found here. At the monastery where he grew up, he'd had access to a great many books when he hand copied them. Quite a few had dealt with the Greater Mystics, but he'd found comparatively little information about those that might be considered human counterparts. He refused to entertain the possibility that elves were the greater equivalent of a human, but one would have to be willfully oblivious to ignore the fact that they were far greater than most other Greater Mystics.

He had time to dredge his memory for what he could recall of even the passing references to human-like mystics, and he'd come up with only two pieces that he could remember in any detail. One had been a rather angry screed written against the practice of interbreeding with mystics. It had mentioned that there walked among the "proper" humans of the world certain "tainted" individuals who had been "cursed" with the blood of mystics. The author's editorial wording aside, Tome's travels had exposed him to at least three men who, if they didn't have a giant somewhere in the family, had certainly managed to exceed any reasonable expectation of stature. Now that he'd seen elves, he was quite certain at least one of the men at the monastery had an elven lineage.

Around the time he began to latch on to the presence of the odd gnome in the cities he'd passed through, and the ramifications of whether *they* were the greater or lesser version of some other mystic, he decided he'd gone too far down that rabbit hole. For better or worse, he was in a place few if any humans had ever visited. He owed it to antiquity to commit as much of it to memory as possible. As the observations piled up, he wished he had one of his journals, not simply because the pen and paper could give him some escape options, but because he would love to have the chance to write some of this down while it was still fresh.

The first determination was regarding elven women. The observations necessary probably would have earned him a distasteful reputation if his status as an outsider and ostensibly lesser creature hadn't already done so. He had to stare at the handful of women who had shown themselves and compare them to the far more frequently visible men to determine that they were, indeed, of the same race. It seemed odd that the tallest women were at least a foot shorter than the shortest men, and that they would be of such hearty build, but smaller details like the curious range of eye colors and the subtly pointed ears were a match regardless.

There didn't seem to be much of a division between the roles of women and men here. He'd seen a fraction as many women as men. The reason for that had not yet become apparent. But other than that, the women enjoyed at least as much freedom and occupational variety as the men. The only difference in this regard was that he'd yet to spot a man who wasn't armed with at least one visible blade, and he'd only seen a single woman who was armed in any way.

As difficult as it was to identify that there even *was* a village, it was even more difficult to determine when he was leaving it. The only differentiation between the village and the forest beyond it was the creak of Mevrelle's bowstring when Tome strayed too far. Even what must have been the most well-trafficked sections of the village failed to show any worn paths. The only footprints and disturbances left behind were Tome's own, and the flora regrew so fast that those he left in the morning were completely swallowed up by the afternoon.

The most important discovery he'd made, which in a gleeful turn of events was *also* due to Mevrelle, was which tree held Tome's things. These people didn't seem to have much in the way of personal space. If there were individual places assigned to individual elves, it wasn't obvious. They seemed perfectly willing to allow him to enter anyplace that wasn't currently occupied. Though the hidden nooks and alcoves contained the trappings of civilization—beds, chairs, and the like—there was nothing to indicate ownership. No locked doors, nothing to keep people clear... except for one tree.

It wasn't the tallest, or the widest, or anything of the sort. There was nothing to differentiate it from the rest of the village beyond somewhat grayer-than-normal bark. But if he so much as looked at it, Mevrelle drew his bow. There was something precious in that tree. Watching it from afar revealed Kott, two females, and some elves with all the trappings of wizards slipping into one of the upper alcoves. He had no doubt that Wick at least, and quite likely any of his possessions that hadn't been destroyed, could be found inside the tree.

As he turned these facts over in his head, the warmth of the sun was replaced by the coolness of shade. He opened his eyes and found Mevrelle glaring down at him. Once he had been noticed, the ranger pointed.

"Ah. Suppertime already? You've given me such intellectually stimulating ways to pass my time I'd nearly lost track," Tome said, climbing to his feet. "You know, other places I've visited have been rather interested in showcasing their wonders. If the best your village has to offer is aimless wandering and dirty looks, I'm sorry to inform you that this isn't likely to be considered one of the grand societies of the world."

He scaled the gentle slope to the innards of a tree he'd been in and out of six times while he had his "freedom." Casks, which may have simply been particularly large gourds, held everything from whole fruits to wine. He wasn't sure if it was more appropriate to call the place a tavern or a mess hall. There didn't seem to be any money changing hands, which was good, because there also wasn't any service. Those who came here to eat simply unrolled their own woven mats, assembled a meal out of the provisions, and left. When he attempted to do the same—sans the mat, since he'd not held on to the one that carried his first meal—one of the women inside nudged him away from the food and uttered a lyrical rebuff. No food for strangers without permission, he supposed.

Now that it was officially mealtime, he was provided with a cup and mat and the very same woman who had served his meal the first time helpfully provided him with a heaping share. Tables and chairs, each composed of gnarled shoots coaxed from the walls of the alcove itself, were available, but two things stopped Tome from partaking. First, though this hidden little recess in the massive tree was impressively large for something hidden inside a living plant, it was smallish by Tome's standards. How and why the incredibly tall elves could tolerate such small living and working spaces was beyond him. There was also a complete lack of artificial light. No lanterns, no mystic crystals. These creatures made do with filtered sunlight and their own sharp vision. It didn't make for a very pleasant experience for a human.

He wasn't alone in his desire to eat outside, however. The long, fairly level branch that forked off from the trunk where the dining hall was located had four elves perched on it. Long legs dangled off the side as they sat and enjoyed their bread and fruit. Tome grinned. One of them was familiar.

Tome took a seat beside him. The difference in height wasn't quite so apparent when sitting. So much of their height was in their limbs that once they were no longer standing, Tome was nearly eye to eye.

"You are a magic user, are you not?" Tome asked. "You wear a robe, and I notice you carry a book."

An angry statement from Mevrelle prompted the elven wizard to pluck his spell book from the branch beside him and slip it into a coarse shoulder bag.

"You know something?" Tome said, glancing over his shoulder at Mevrelle. "It does make me feel rather good to know that you consider me so thorough a threat that you won't let a book even linger in my presence. It shows you respect me more than you wish to let on."

He turned back to the wizard.

"The ranger seems to wish for me to believe that he doesn't understand me," Tome said. "But I've seen him react to this statement or that. He's not *entirely* ignorant of the language. Similarly, I suspect you are at least broadly aware of the language. You are a wizard and thus an academic. And you've been studying my books and the lantern."

The wizard shot him a somewhat sharper glance. Tome's grin grew a bit more. It was a terrible shame he hadn't brought a set of grum tiles. These people were *terrible* at bluffing. He'd have made a fortune.

"You *could* ask me for help. My future seems like it is largely dependent upon how useful I can make myself, and I *am* the keeper of the sentry lantern. I'd be perfectly willing to lend a hand."

The wizard didn't acknowledge the offer. Tome set the mat on the branch between them.

"You know, in the land beyond the wall, we've perfected the technology of plates and serving trays. They're a bit easier to use than these ridiculous mats." He picked up his cup and stirred it with a finger. "Though if the scent is any indication, both you and the dragon's people have similar tastes in wine. It's quite a bit stronger than what we drink at home."

He set the cup on the mat, then as subtly as possible, traced a few simple shapes with the wine-soaked finger on the bark of the tree, right where it curved down and away. If he was skilled enough in his positioning, the only people with the proper angle to see what he was doing were himself and the wizard beside him, and he kept eye contact with the wizard. Writing blind was an odd skill, but expensive candles and a cheap father meant that not being able to see his page was occasionally not enough of an excuse to stop before the page was finished being copied. There was only room enough for a few words, but there had to be an *enormous* amount of arcane energy expended to shape a tree into something worth living in. Tapping into that power should allow him to get a minor effect from a handful of words, if they were carefully selected.

Those words, if they could be translated into something approaching a normal language, boiled down to a simple phrase. "That one." When the spell was complete, he nudged his mat forward so that it draped over the faint wine stain. Beneath the mat, he could feel that oh-so-familiar tingle. The words were sizzling away. The spell was cast. It was weak. Extremely weak. He'd not produced so meager an effect since his first lessons in paper magic. But it was enough. The wizard beside him, the one to which the spell had been directed, could now be shorthanded in a future spell. He was a target. A magic spell with any useful effects would have to be dozens of times more powerful than that one, but he could cross that bridge when he came to it. He'd marked one of the men who had access to Wick. It was a worthy first step in a plan, even if he hadn't even dreamed of what the second one might be.

Allie paced along the street, coat pulled tight around her as she turned the corner. It was a warm night, as tended to be the case for most of the year in Beffshire. She didn't really need the coat. But she remembered some scholar who came in for a drink with his colleague a year or so ago, an expert in creatures great and small. She'd chatted him up, as one should always do when someone with some interesting new stories showed up in the tavern. She'd left the conversation with a multitude of "facts" about animals, ranging from likely truths to complete absurdities. Her favorite, and one that she had adopted into her own policies, was the claim that small animals, if they were afraid of being attacked, made a point of making themselves seem larger. That struck her as good sense, so when she was nervous about going somewhere, she made sure to wear her big coat. In her mind, it made her seem more formidable. And even if it didn't seem that way to would-be attackers, it also gave her some useful places to hide her thumping stick and a few other goodies to teach muggers some manners.

One might have expected the big coat and other precautions as the sort of things someone would need if they were entering a "bad neighborhood." But she *lived* in a "bad neighborhood," and it really wasn't so bad. The people there were poor, but once you knew everyone's name and they knew your face, people tended to treat you all right. This neighborhood was most certainly what people would call a *great* neighborhood. It ought to be. The people who lived here paid for the privilege of making such a claim. But she felt far more uncomfortable walking through the narrow streets with their old, ornate buildings than she did hustling through a dark alley in her own part of the city. The whole section of town made her feel as though she were trespassing in a museum or something.

That feeling of trespassing got sharply more intense when she reached the front gate of her destination and was met by the sunken-eyed gaze of two private watchmen.

"What're'y'ere'fer," murmured one of them, the entire question having been blended together into a single sound through repetition.

"In a few days Mr. Verfessa is going to be closing my tavern for sprucing up, and I was told he might have some work for me in the interim."

The phrase was surprising enough to convince the guard to raise his eyebrows.

"You came here to ask the boss for *work*?"

"Yes."

"Don't you think maybe you should turn around and go home?"

"I think maybe you should go have a word with him and see if he'll see me," she said.

She stared him down as he did his best to "look her away." It was a tactic she used herself back in the tavern. Give someone a hard look and keep the pressure on, and it was surprising how big and how determined someone could be while still lacking the resolve to endure the gaze for more than a few seconds. But knowing the tactic was a bit of an inoculation against it. Besides, there was enough contrarian in her to feel much more at home refusing to leave when told to than coming to a wealthy man's home with her hand out. Hardening herself against someone trying to intimidate her was familiar ground.

The man didn't so much back down as deflect, turning his own gaze to his partner, who grudgingly got up and trudged up the walkway to the house.

"You're the lady from The Fox and Log," the remaining guard said.

"I am. You recognize me from there and not from my last visit here?"

"I try to avoid guard duty."

"I try to stay in the tavern, but things change."

The guard trotted back from the door and nodded.

"Either it's your lucky day, or you're about to have a real bad night," the guard said, unlocking the gate and stepping aside.

She paced up the walkway and through the door, which was being held open by a uniformed maid. Allie nodded to her and got a very similar sleepy-eyed glance to what the guards gave her. She was beginning to think there was something about this house that drained people.

"Alizon. Lovely as always to see you," said the stately Eveline Verfessa as she emerged from the stairwell. "He'll see you in his office. You know the way."

"Thank you very much, Mrs. Verfessa," Allie said. "I hope he's in a good mood."

"Donovan is always in a good mood," she said.

Allie hurried down the steps, past the elegance of the upper level of the house and into the somewhat more flavorful surroundings of the lower level.

"Allie!" Donovan said, hopping up from a chair and marching over to her.

The rosy-cheeked and barrel-chested man looked more like he should be building stone walls than living in a place like this. He beamed a genuine smile and gave her a tooth-rattling slap to the back.

"To what do I owe the honor?" he said.

"I think you know."

"Always dangerous to assume I know what a lady is thinking. A few too many lonely nights while my better half sulked in the other room taught me that."

"You're closing down the tavern, and I need work until you open it back up."

"I'm not closing it down. I'm building it up. That place was way too cramped for the kind of business you were doing. Sid told me you had some ideas about how it should be laid out. He was a little fuzzy on the details. That fellow comes across as a little fuzzy in general. Was he a boxer or something? A pit fighter? That's the kind of state of mind you get out of having your bell rung a few too many times."

"I haven't gotten any straight answers out of him. And yeah, I have some thoughts about the tavern, but right now I'm here about what I'm supposed to do until you open up."

"It'll only be a little over a month. My folks work fast. Do whatever you like until then."

"What I'd like is to keep a roof over my head and food on my table."

"No nest egg, I take it? Didn't plan for a rainy day?"

"I was betting I'd be able to see the clouds coming from a bit farther away."

"You work pretty much every waking hour, and you do a good enough job that even the fellows with crocodile arms tip you."

"Crocodile arms?"

He waggled his hands just above his hips. "Can't reach their pockets."

She released a genuine snicker.

"Point is, you should have plenty of money socked away."

"You may have been keeping an eye on me at work, but it's nice to see you at least don't know anything about the rest of my life."

"Problems at home?" he said.

"Unlike the tavern is now, that's none of your business."

He laughed.

"Fine, so you need work and you came to me."

"My boss recommended it."

"Something tells me The Fox and Log wouldn't be doing half as well as it is if you did everything your boss recommended."

"Something tells me you wouldn't have *bought* The Fox and Log if you didn't want me to work for you."

He laughed again. The vast majority of the men and women she dealt with, if they laughed as often as he did, they did so derisively. There were always laughing *at* someone. Donovan Verfessa just *laughed*. It was like the world was there to amuse him, and he appreciated every second of it.

"We've got some talking to do," he said.

He motioned for her to follow, then paced to the far corner of the floor were a few chairs had been casually clustered about a table. In a home that looked to have been curated, this little section felt entirely haphazard. It was clearly the most used part of his office.

She took a seat in a chair that probably hadn't been comfortable when it started, but decades of use had molded it to perfection. He stretched until his back produced a disquieting crackle, then flopped down in a matching seat on the opposite side of the table.

"You're about half right, which is a quarter better than most of the people I have to deal with. First, I didn't buy the place. Half stake. I'm dumping some money into the place, and I'll be taking an extra lump of the profit until I'm paid back, but that place will be making money hand over fist, so the other guy won't even notice the difference. And I didn't buy the place just to get you in here. The Fox and Log strikes me as a good, steady income. Not as messy as some of my other ventures."

"You haven't seen the place on the third night of a grum tournament."

"You haven't seen my other ventures. I'm sorry, do you want a drink?"

"Water, thanks."

He hopped up and paced over to the liquor cabinet. As he measured out a tumbler of well water and two fingers of whiskey, he continued.

"There are loads of people who wonder how I got to where I am. How'd I do what they couldn't? It's a long, long answer. But it starts here."

He reached in his pocket and pulled out a coin. A neat flick of the thumb sent it twirling toward her. She caught it.

"What's this?" she asked.

"Take a look."

She turned the piece over in her hand. It looked like a standard duot, but it was a bit smaller and much more worn. She flipped it over and found, rather than the twin crest that she was familiar with, a smaller singular crest centered on the face.

"That's an unot," he said. "When I was a little boy, that'd spend just fine. Get yourself a loaf of bread or a pint of stout, no problem. But now you can't even find them. Now the duot is what people spend, and they need a handful of them. I remember the day the first duot dropped in my hand. Taught me an important lesson. If it isn't worth at least two, it's worthless. Never do just one thing when you can do two. And if you can do three? Even better. So I bought the place. And if that got you in here? That's just saving me time."

She tossed him the coin back. He pocketed it.

"But let's talk about why you wanted to be here."

"I didn't *want* to be here. You left me with no choices."

He smirked and gave her a doubtful look.

"You're a smart kid. And Beffshire is a big city. I worked three jobs when I was your age. You're telling me you couldn't find one? We didn't even close up shop yet, and you're here making plans. You came to me *first*. And I don't think it's my pretty face or my sterling personality that brought you here. You know opportunity when you smell it."

"I know fertilizer when I smell it, too."

He laughed. "Fine, so I'll stop shoveling. I've been doing a lot of investing lately. The Fox and Log's just the latest. I threw in with the Maskers a while back, and it's been a bit of an effort keeping that investment safe. Unlike a tavern with a few rowdy patrons, the antique business is just short of open warfare. Turns out, that's the way it was even before I got in it. But you bring in an old soldier and there's liable to be more fighting before the day's done. Just a few days ago, I finally chased out the last of this cluster of misfits who call themselves the Bolivans. City's clean again, after who knows how long. But what did I say? Never be doing just one thing."

He leaned aside and pulled a folded bit of paper from beside his chair and handed it to her. He continued talking as she unfolded it.

"You can't just kill these people. And not just because of morals and such. Important not to forget your morals. Too many people in my line forget that stuff and end up more animal than man. No sense being successful if you lose a chunk of yourself along the way that you don't want to lose. But beyond general principle, you've got to keep some of them alive so you can boot them in the butt and send them scurrying to tell their masters not to come to Beffshire anymore. You've got to send the message. So I spent a lot of time these past few months shaking people upside down by their ankles and giving them some advice about how they ought to spend their time if they want to have much more of it. And when you shake someone like that, sometimes stuff falls out of their pockets."

She shook her head and looked up from the page. "Are we being flowery with our language, or were you literally shaking people upside down?"

"Can't it be both?" he asked.

She looked back to the page. It was a badly drawn map, the sort of thing someone made when they knew you knew where you were going and just wanted to tell you *that* you should go there rather than *how* to go there. The destination on the map, if she read the writing properly, was "half-charred manor."

"Whoever is calling the shots with these people is all over the place. Sometimes things are in code. Sometimes they aren't. Sometimes it's all blood and death, sometimes it's theft and kidnapping. But what you see there? I've seen a lot of them lately, coded or not. Any idea what it means?"

"They wanted this person to go to someplace called the half-charred manor, I imagine."

"There's some marks there up at the top. *That's* code. According to my people, that's 'as soon as possible.'" He sipped his drink. "Just finished putting together the pieces a few hours ago, but we had a good idea of the picture that was forming before then. There's a reason I was finally able to finish cleaning up this town. And it's because they were pulling their people back. Started just after... well, let's not make too many assumptions. You know what's been going on with Fel, right?"

"I know he went on a trip that seemed like it'd make more sense for a soldier than an adventurer. I haven't heard anything since then."

He tapped the arm of his chair. "Those orders, calling folks back, started falling out of pants pockets the very day Fel left on this mission. Whoever is in charge of the Bolivans isn't taking chances with Fel anymore. Now you tell me, what would you call it when all the fighters gather themselves up in one spot?"

"An ambush," she said gravely.

"I knew you were sharp. Now, I figure Fel and that lady they paired him up with are expecting this sort of thing, but I've sunk some time and money into this Masker business and I need to look after it. Not to mention I like the guy and his family. I'd hate to see something bad happen. I'd like to get word, and maybe some help, out to him before it's too late."

"So why don't you?"

He sipped his drink again. "There are some folks who would call me a big fish in a small pond. Me? I'd say Beffshire is more of a lake, and I'm for sure the biggest fish in it. But it's still got its shores, and there's still an ocean out there. If you want it done inside Beffshire, I can get it done. But the farther you get from here, the less sway I've got, and Fel is a long way away. Worse, the Bolivans have been here longer than I realized. Long enough that if they're even half good at their jobs, they'll know the faces of the people in my crew. Best case, whoever I send would have some clashes with the Bolivans. Worst case, whoever I send will end up leading the Bolivans right to them. I had one guy who I was pretty sure would go unnoticed, and I sent him with Fel before I found out about the ambush. The rest of the Masker family has the same problem. They're *targets*. Can't very well send them out to find their boy if they'll be in the same danger. Likewise for the Graves family. And there's the other thing."

"What other thing?"

"I don't know how I'd find Fel. There's no indication where this half-charred manor is, except that it's north. And even if we knew where it was, we'd need to find *Fel*, not the manor. And I don't even think *Fel* knew where he'd be heading. Seems like doing what he was planning to do would involve a lot of crisscross and which-way."

Allie shut her eyes tightly. "Mr. Verfessa, so far all you've done is make me even more worried about my friend. You haven't explained what this has to do with me."

"You've got a good head on your shoulders, you've got some time on your hands. I think you can put the pieces together."

"... You want *me* to go find him and tell him?"

"That'd solve a *lot* of problems."

"How am I supposed to do that?"

"That's your problem to solve. I can't give you any of my stuff. Can't help you out. Not in a way that would go with you. No horses, no carts. No gear. It'd draw attention. As it is right now, no one has any reason to believe that the barmaid at the place I just dumped some money into would be doing work for me. Not work like this, anyway. The only real business you and I had came before I learned about the Bolivans. You were part of the reason I worked out I needed to see to them. Now, if they were still about, maybe this little meeting would tip them off, but they're long gone. It doesn't make sense for you to be the one to do this. Which means that you're the one most likely to do it without raising an eyebrow. But you have to do it in a way that looks like it was your idea. But that shouldn't be hard for you."

"Oh, shouldn't it?" she said sourly.

"I already said my bit about the head on your shoulders and the time on your hands. But I didn't mention that heart in your chest. I feel like a cad laying this burden on you, but you and I both know that if you found it out some other way, you'd be working through the same puzzle of how to help him out even if I hadn't been involved. A lesser man would have tried to manipulate you by dropping this information in your lap. But I like to do my business eye to eye when it's someone I respect."

"If I'd been presented with this 'puzzle' from someone besides you, I would have come to you, hoping for help."

"First plan never seems to work out, does it? But you put your mind to it. And if I see you heading out of town, let's just say your business will be kept for you while you're off doing whatever you choose to do. Bills paid. Ducks in a row. And if you come back safe and sound along with Fel? I'm sure the Maskers will show their gratitude, and so will I."

"This isn't... this isn't something I know how to do," Allie said.

"The question is never if you know how to do a thing. The question is if you can figure it out. And I think you can."

She took a breath. "This isn't going to be a regular thing. This isn't me interviewing to be one of your lackeys."

"If I was looking for a lackey I'd just have to throw some money at one of your regulars."

She finished her water and thought long and hard about asking for something stronger. She thought better of it and stood.

"Good luck to you, Allie."

"If I could rely on luck, I wouldn't have ended up talking to you today," she muttered.

He laughed. "Even better. Luck runs out. Wit keeps going."

CHAPTER 10

Tome was stirred from sleep by the creaking of the vines barring his cell. He stiffly pulled himself to a sitting position as Kott appeared in the doorway.

"Good morning," Tome said. "You know, one thing you might learn from humanity. Beds. Or at least mattresses."

"If you remain here much longer, you'll find we tend to value merit and achievement. If you were contributing to our society, you would have a much more pleasant experience. But I've been speaking to some of the gentlemen investigating the lantern, and I understand you extended an offer of aid."

"It seemed wise to ingratiate myself to you."

"Self-preservation."

"Can you blame me?"

"No I can't, but you'll forgive me if I have my suspicions."

"I'd consider you a fool if you didn't. But if you knew me, you'd know I'm rather mercenary in my leanings. The first time I came here, I came with Fel Masker. I came alone this time because I was seeking knowledge and, perhaps, fortune. One of the last times we spoke, he quite clearly indicated he felt I was a bit too self-serving. He wasn't entirely wrong."

Kott muttered something to someone off to the side, just beyond what Tome could see through the doorway.

"Until now, I wouldn't call you a model prisoner, but you haven't given us any specific reason to distrust you. Granted, this is because we haven't given you the opportunity to betray our trust." He leaned forward a bit. "We still aren't, mind you. But you will soon find yourself in a position to make a mistake that will cost you the freedom you have been granted. Do try to avoid making that mistake."

"I endeavor to avoid *all* mistakes."

"You have been locked in a foreign village and stripped of your equipment."

"My endeavors are not always successful."

"Mmm. This way," he said.

Tome climbed out of the cell.

"The man you were speaking to yesterday afternoon is named Fallesse. As you suspected, he does have some small knowledge of your language and was thus able to understand your offer. He does not speak the language well enough to have a full conversation, so I'll be present to interpret. If you want to earn our trust, you will answer every question you are asked and ask only those questions necessary to clarify the information we have requested."

"It will be difficult to keep my curiosity in check."

"You will also have to keep your hands in check. Touch nothing."

"I understand."

Tome's limited experience traversing the network of branches made for a slow and embarrassing trek to where the research was taking place. When he finally reached the dim alcove where the wizards had congregated, he found one woman and two men waiting for him. All three were dressed in roughly equivalent garb: somewhat finer robes, and each with a focusing instrument of some kind. The woman used an almond-shaped amulet, one man had a gnarled scepter, and the other had a staff. All of them were made from wood and amber.

There had clearly been some precautions taken, as while there were the elven equivalent of bookshelves, little natural grooves in the walls that were just the right size and shape for books, those books were notably absent. The only paper in the room was in the hands of a third man carefully kept opposite Tome with the others between them. The most important thing in the room though, both from Tome's point of view and the views of the captors, was Wick's lantern. It had been positioned in the center of a carved stone platter, a makeshift hearth for a rare fire risk within the tree. The flame was perfectly stationary. Wick was present.

"Now, our first question is a simple one. What are the commands to operate the device?" Kott asked.

"There are none," Tome said.

"It should have gone without saying, but I will require honest and accurate answers," Kott said.

"Which is precisely why I provided just such an answer."

The female wizard quietly spoke.

"We have extensive records of the rare but well-known sentry lanterns. They were very much controlled by spoken command."

"Perhaps in the old days, but I can tell you that presently Wick takes his 'commands' conversationally. He is generally obliging."

"He has not responded to any attempted control."

"Perhaps he doesn't like you."

"It was my understanding that contraptioneers created tools. Tools don't get to have an opinion about how they are to be used."

One of the other wizards spoke.

"This is, of course, excepting the masks, assuming what we know of them is true," said Kott.

"Wick," Tome said. "We aren't getting out of this without a little cooperation."

"I get the distinct impression that cooperation will be the beginning of an unpleasant sequence of events," Wick said.

The wizards stirred somewhat, looking at each other. A quill scribbled against the page in the back of the room.

"I think we need to make ourselves useful if we want to get out of this," Tome said.

"Sentry lanterns are capable of being hosted at more than one lantern, is that correct?" Kott asked.

"Yes," Wick replied.

"How many lanterns are host to your flame?"

"Two persistent lanterns. One additional flame in the same location as the distant persistent flame," Wick said.

"Through what means do you draw power?" Kott asked.

"I do not know the deeper nature of my own operation," Wick said.

Kott looked up from the flame and squinted at Tome.

"Do you know?" he asked.

"Contraptions are, again, not my specialty," Tome said.

"Your value is not terribly pronounced, is it? Where, precisely does the second lamp reside?"

"It is in the possession of the Maskers, in a town called Beffshire," Wick said.

"We are not familiar with a town of that name."

"It is quite old, but I suppose it is possible it does not predate the wall."

Kott seemed to have to gather himself to make the next statement, like it took physical force to produce the words. "How far into your little land does that lantern reside?"

"A few hundred miles. More than week's travel by carriage. A bit longer by... worse carriage," Tome said.

The wizards scoffed.

"Again, *honest* answers. Your land is not that large."

"It is much, *much* larger than that. Beffshire isn't even half a continent away."

The wizards muttered among themselves, then one of them raised his voice.

"We are fetching you a map. Two, in fact. One from before... the event, and one from after."

Tome leaned back, watching out of the corner of his eye while an elf outside the door trotted across the branch from which he'd come.

"May I ask what purpose the map will serve?" Tome asked.

"It will determine if you have an accurate view of the world you live in," Kott said.

Tome glanced aside again. The one sent to fetch the map disappeared from sight, but returned mere moments later. Tome hadn't been in a position to see where the maps had been kept, but the storage alcove had to be no farther than the adjoining tree.

When he returned, the fetcher had two bits of stiff paper. Tome reached for them, but the sound of a blade being drawn from its sheath reminded him that Mevrelle was still watching him and he'd been specifically forbidden from touching paper. Instead, Kott accepted the maps and held them side by side.

"This, it should be clear, is the map of the world prior to a very specific event."

"I imagine you're talking about the construction of the wall."

"I have no interest..." Kott gritted his teeth. "Yes."

Tome leaned closer to inspect. It wasn't so different from the map he'd seen in the archive before entering the Greater Lands. The place names were written in an unrecognizable script, but they still labeled some of the same major cities and locations.

"This is the world as it exists today."

The second map was... wrong. Based upon his travels within the Greater Lands, the map appeared accurate up until it reached the wall. But the wall itself was curved in the wrong way. Rather than tracing a circle around the Greater Lands, forming its border, the wall instead curved in the opposite direction, forming a circle with an interior that was featureless and unknown. Most of the ring encompassed land, but about a third of it stretched off the shore to the west.

"You have this wrong," he said, pointing to the circle. "The Greater Lands is enclosed, not the proper world."

"Tome, we have launched yearslong expeditions to map our world. This information came at the expense of countless lives of the Grand Children of the Forest. It is accurate."

"You would have me believe that I've lived my entire life within this stone ring?" Tome said. "I had to travel farther than its width to reach Beffshire from my homeland. And to reach the wall from Beffshire, for that matter."

"Tome, there are those within this very room that have experiences that contradict yours. Do not attempt to mislead us."

"Kott, I have nothing to gain from lying to you about this. You've said I must be truthful to gain your trust, and so I am."

"That is madness."

"Sir, I have been on both sides of the wall, you have not. I can tell you that there is far more world beyond it than you seem to think. However, I can also tell you that there at least appears to be far more world within the wall than *we* seemed to think. It is difficult to be certain, because from our point of view most of the land beyond the Greater Lands Wall is submerged in the ocean, but I have traveled as far as the thuggish dragon's lair in Clickspring, and the speed and time of that journey should have taken us well past the far edge of the wall."

He tipped his head.

"My memory isn't as sharp as it could be on the topic, but I feel certain Kazel and his people had some knowledge of this, or at least had a different point of view of it. They referred to Clickspring as effectively the *center* of the Greater Lands, which supposes an awareness that it is enclosed. But we were also told to observe the wall when we crossed over it. I'd thought it, perhaps, an optical illusion, but the wall's curvature seemed to change when crossing it."

Kott turned to the wizards. They were discussing the matter rather vigorously among themselves.

"If you haven't burned all my materials, you would find some roughly copied maps in my journals. I invite you to compare them."

"Scribbles on paper would serve as little more than evidence of your dedication to your delusion," Kott said. "Let us return to the matter at hand. A sentry flame can move from perch to perch, correct?"

"That is correct," Wick said.

"Is the effect instantaneous?"

"It is not. Greater distance increases the delay before reaching other positions."

"Is there a maximum distance beyond which you cannot reach a perch?"

"If there is, I have not yet reached it."

The wizards nodded. Notes were scribbled.

"Good, good. That is useful information. And you have an awareness of all valid perches?"

"I do."

"Is that awareness delayed similarly by distance?"

"It is not. The moment a new flame is lit, if it is a valid point of observation, I am aware of its location and approximate distance."

"What is necessary to make a perch persistent? That is, one that can be relit and still allow you to occupy it."

"If it is lit from a flame that is a valid point of observation, it is a valid point of observation as well. Otherwise, a contraption lantern must be used that is precisely matched to me specifically."

"How might one be constructed?"

"I do not know."

Kott looked to Tome.

"I am not an expert in contraptions, but I know that some degree of the effect can be achieved with a single plate, engraved or perhaps specially treated," Tome said. "And also, that plate can be replaced with a modified one to convert a sentry lantern of one type to another."

"Are all sentry lanterns, for lack of a more suitable word, the same 'personality'?" Kott asked.

"There are distinct sentry lanterns," Wick said.

"How many are there?"

"I am presently aware of only two."

"And if all suitable perches for a given sentry lantern are extinguished? What occurs?"

"My awareness is extinguished with them."

"Never to return?"

"I return to awareness if any of the persistent observation points are relit."

"Can you be properly destroyed."

"I do not know."

"We shall see then," Kott said ominously.

"Tome, forgive me if you have further need of me, but I think it is best that I return to the others," Wick said.

The flame didn't wait for a reply. The flickering, natural motion returned, and for all intents and purposes the lantern was a simple light source once more.

"I suppose we should have assumed it would depart at some point," Kott said. "Is there a means to recall it?"

"Not that I know of. Wick returns when he is directed to do so," Tome said.

Kott conferred with the wizards.

"Very well. We have sufficient information to continue our investigations without you. If we require your aid once more, you will be summoned."

With very little ceremony, he was sent away and once again left in the stewardship of Mevrelle.

"I do not get the notion that I have earned much through that interaction," he mused to himself.

Martin climbed up the stairs to the antique shop. He'd expected to find Vivian at her usual place behind the counter, or perhaps Epiphany. Instead, it was Euphoria who was tending to the customer. He lingered in the corner beside the steps and crossed his arms, a smile on his face, while she did her work.

"Oh, yes, yes. I know. So difficult to find an antique that doesn't clash with a modern color aesthetic," Euphoria said, nodding sagely at the aging woman eying up the contents of a shelf. "What, may I ask, are your usual color preferences?"

"I decorate in browns and oranges. Autumnal colors. Autumn says home to me. Home and hearth," she said, picking up an old dish and turning it over in her hands.

Euphoria approached and plucked the plate from her hands to return it to the shelf. In a maneuver that Vivian had long ago mastered and Epiphany still had trouble with, Euphoria managed to make rescuing the valuable piece from a careless grip seem like a courteous act rather than an affront. So many people were aghast at the thought that one might not wish for them to paw at items that were hundreds of years old. Euphoria flawlessly slipped the plate free and positioned it safely on its shelf with a smile and nod that made the woman forget she'd not been planning to put it back just yet.

"Join me over here, if you would. I assume you're making the purchase to use as a conversation piece? Decoration rather than investment?"

"Yes, yes. Something to look nice on the table in the guest room."

"I think you'll like this statue. Carved from pure purpleheart. The pleasant eggplant color should pair well with your decor, and because it is wood rather than a precious metal or stone, I can let you have it for a very reasonable price."

Martin watched her work her magic, selling an attractive bit of bric-a-brac for seventy duots. He remembered when the piece arrived. Fel had brought it from one of the vaults, but it had been included in his haul not because it was valuable—it wasn't terribly—but because wedging it into the crate kept the rest of the haul from rattling.

When the transaction was complete and the woman was happily walking away having paid a princely sum for what Fel had considered packing material, Euphoria marked it down in the ledger and nodded to Martin.

"Hello, Father," she said. "I tell you, it is very pleasant to be behind the counter again. They don't let me do this sort of thing back home. They have 'people' for that."

"You *are* back home, Fora," he said.

She gave him a weary look. "You know what I mean. Are you through with work for the day? It will be suppertime soon."

"I am through for now. I'll be starting the stew shortly. Where is your mother?"

"She and Epiphany went to the north side. Epiphany is handling the rounds for picking up and delivering the silverware, and Mother is picking up some fresh polish." She tapped the ledger. "I've made three sales while they're gone. A fresh face behind the counter will do that. A bit like rotating the stock in the display window."

"Certainly. I'd been hoping to talk to Vivian about something, but with two people to handle the counter if needs be, she might actually be willing to eat supper at the table when she returns. I'll talk to her then."

He lingered. Finding her alone in the shop was important. It was a huge step. A sign of trust that Martin wasn't certain could have been earned back. For years he'd been looking forward to the day this sort of moment would return. It seemed cruel that at a time when the house could feel whole again, Fel was off doing something even more dangerous than usual. But crueler than that was the topic that his mind demanded he address.

"Fora, I'd like a word with you, while there are no customers."

"Of course, Father."

"The list of items that, in a roundabout way, brought you back to us—the things Thaddeus arranged for us to acquire."

"Yes?"

"It included what I think we can safely say was the Warrior mask."

"That was my understanding, yes."

"Why? Why the Warrior mask rather than the Teacher?"

"It wasn't my decision."

"Why did *they* want it?"

"The ongoing clash with the Bolivans, the suggestion of the Diplomat, and what we thought was a firm indication of its location. Why?"

"I've been working with the Student. Learning quite a bit. And... I don't think the Warrior is something that should be found. Or if it is, it should be kept safe and inert."

"Father. Honestly. You sound like the blasted appraisers. Contraptions aren't dangerous. They are machines. Once you understand them, they are only as dangerous as their operators."

"We aren't talking about something like an alarm box or a borer. We now know the nature of the mask. Or I suppose *I* now know, as you and the Graves family seem to have worked that out first. This is a contraption with some measure of awareness."

"An awareness approximated by contraptors. The apparent intelligence is no less of an illusion than the dancing lights of the starlight dish, which by the way, I was able to sell for seventy-eight duots over the asking price."

"I think Wick and Oiler both illustrate that the line separating this illusion of life is blurrier than we've previously thought."

"It is still a mask, Father. It is still limited to providing advice."

"Perhaps so, but many great evils have been committed by people following advice given in bad faith. And worse, there's the matter of timing. We don't know precisely *when* the Bygone Era ended, a matter which is in and of itself a bit absurd given how relatively recent it must have been. I've heard estimates as low as a hundred years, which seems unlikely, and as long as five hundred. That is an *enormous* range, and we can't work out the truth of it. But based on my discussions with the Student, I've found myself asking if the creation of the Warrior mask and the end of the Bygone Era are linked."

"Do you have any proof to suggest it?"

"I don't."

"Then I don't know that it's worth fretting about. The rest of the family hasn't been transparent in their aims, but I can assure you they have no grand designs of conquest."

"The work that Fel and Lattica are doing presently should go a long way in preventing the Bolivans from remaining dangerous. Perhaps if they are thorough enough, the Warrior mask won't need to be found."

"That's not my decision to make. I'm firmly in the *middle* of this. Which unfortunately lacks the view of the top and the hands-on nature of the bottom. Facilitating the acquisition of the mask is a task I was to perform. If I succeed, I get to climb to the next rung of the ladder."

"That doesn't strike me as the way a family ought to work. And I worry where the ladder is leading you."

"To the top, Father. Same as any ladder. Don't worry. I'm still your daughter. I'm still the woman you and Mother made of me. I may have made some mistakes, but regardless of where I'm heading, I mean to get there properly."

"Well then. I'll consider my concerns put to rest." He turned to return to the steps, but stopped. "But Fora? Regardless of where this takes you, don't forget where the rest of your family is. Something kept you from us for three years."

"It won't happen again, Father."

He smiled. "No doubt. Supper soon. Fish stew this time."

"Heavenly," she said with a grin.

"Any other plans for today?"

"Just another trip to The Fox and Log with Epiphany."

"Tremendous. I'm so glad you two are getting along."

Euphoria laughed. "Not so much getting along yet. But drinking together."

He trotted downstairs. "Drinking together is better than drinking apart! Your grandfather always said that."

A few hours later, Allie slipped into the back room of The Fox and Log to get a breather. It was the first time in years that this had happened, but she was feeling genuinely overwhelmed. Part of it was the occasion. This was the last day The Fox and Log would be open before it was due to be redone. Everyone who had come to call the place a second home had decided to pay a visit. The place was slightly over its intended capacity, but more importantly, it was well over Allie's capacity to keep the relative inebriation of her patrons straight in her head. There were a lot more people in the ungentlemanly phase of their drunkenness than she would have liked. She'd had the foresight to get Oovay to cover the entire double shift with her. There had been a third member of the staff when the day started, but the pressure had been too much for them and their apron was now hanging on a hook.

On a better day, she might have handled things better. But a large chunk of her mind was occupied by the issue of Fel and the potential ambush. To put it frankly, her mind and heart were not in the task of keeping order in an inherently chaotic setting.

The saving grace was the very well-advertised early closing time. Rather than "when the last patron finally agreed to go home," they were set to close at sundown, when most of the neighboring businesses closed as well. It left a fair amount of money on the table in terms of serving drinks and keeping people entertained, but Allie suspected the money they saved in rowdiness-induced damage would more than make up for it.

Oovay was out on the floor attempting to secure the attention of the crowd to let them know that the reason their drinks were no longer being refilled was that they were closed and, by the way, it was time to settle up some tabs. It was not going well for him.

"It means you give me the money you owe!" Oovay shouted.

"Or we won't get another drink?" questioned a patron.

"*And* you won't get another drink, you thick-as-lard, quarter-witted souse!" Oovay barked.

Allie sighed and emerged into the madness.

"That'll do, Oovay, and may I say you've really been honing your insults. Well done," she said.

He stomped into the back room to replace her. She coaxed a man out of his stool and stood on it.

"Listen up! Thanks for all your support. Not just today but for however long it took you to build up your tabs. We'd like you to pay them all off, but let's be realistic. Some of you owe your first child to us by now. And since I don't want to be knee deep in ankle biters, I'll make a deal with you all. If you finish your drinks and head out of here without me having to sweep up any teeth or broken glass, I'll take a bite out of what you owe. Hoping to see all you back here to make new stains on the fresh new floors. Once we're open, that is. Because for now, skedaddle."

There wasn't anything forceful about what she said, but some combination of the respect she'd earned through the years and the not-so-subtle undercurrent of fully spent patience did the trick. Over the course of a few minutes, every last patron shuffled out. Only two punches were thrown, and maybe a third of them coughed up what they owed for the day's drinks on the way out.

After a few minutes, Oovay emerged to an empty tavern.

"How do you do that?" he asked as they brushed all the coins into a pile and finished counting them out.

"The threat needs to be implied," Allie said.

Oovay looked up as he heard a sound at the door.

"We're closed. Come back in a month!" he shouted.

Allie glanced up to see who hadn't got the message. Epiphany and Euphoria were there, puzzled by the unusual hours and discussing where to spend their evening instead.

"No! Wait," Allie shouted before the door could shut. "Oovay, go ahead and head out. I'll handle cleanup."

She wasn't even finished saying the word "out" when Oovay pushed past the sisters and scurried home.

"Come in," Allie said, holding the door open.

"If you're closed, we can—" Epiphany began.

"Come in," Allie repeated, the faintest bit of pleading coloring her tone.

Epiphany glanced at her sister. They slipped inside. Allie shut and braced the door behind them. The moment their privacy was assured, her mouth started running. She worked through the process of cleaning up a section of the bar as she spoke. The words rushed out like someone had pulled the drain plug on a barrel.

"One of the High or another must be watching out for me, you girls showing up when you did. You want any drinks? On the house. Technically we're closed until they're done rebuilding the place, so we're through doing accounting until then. It's been real nice having you girls in here. The boss wanted to start bringing in bands and such, that's part of why we're getting the work done. If Euphoria's still in town when we open up shop again, I'd love to have you two do a number on stage," she rambled.

"Allie, is something wrong?" Epiphany said. "I'll admit I don't know you *that* well, but you seem a bit off."

Allie took a breath and slipped behind the bar. Epiphany and Euphoria took a seat in front of her. She set out their glasses and two bottles, scotch and wine.

"It's about Fel," she said. "I've been thinking about this for days, and I still don't know if it's right to bring it up to you, but I just don't have any ideas."

"What about Fel? Have you heard something from him somehow?" Epiphany asked.

"No, no. It's..." Allie glanced at Euphoria, then back to Epiphany. "A mutual friend with a vested interest in Fel has been doing some digging, and some information has come up that's relevant to his current mission."

"This would be Donovan Verfessa, then?" Euphoria said.

Allie kept her face entirely impassive. She didn't play grum, but she was quite certain she could bluff with the best of them. Epiphany just gestured for her to continue.

"The point is, when the last of the Bolivans was chased out of town, it turned up that every spare mercenary and agent they have on their payroll is being recalled to someplace called the half-charred manor. We're thinking it's an ambush getting set up."

"Where is the half-charred manor?" Epiphany asked.

"No idea," Allie said. "North, somewhere."

"By the very nature of the mission, Fel and Lattica must know there is likely to be an ambush somewhere along the line," Euphoria said. "Lattica is very professional. There will be a plan."

"But now *we* know exactly where the ambush will be," Epiphany said. "How many Bolivan agents are there?"

Euphoria didn't need to stop and think. "At any given time, between eighty and one hundred and fifty. They're a good deal more organized now than they have been in the past, but even so, I don't imagine more than half of them will reply to a summons like this."

"That's still fifty people or so. Fel's good and maybe Lattica is better, but there isn't enough weaponry in that cart to take out fifty people,"

Epiphany said.

"Is there some way to get a message to him?" Allie asked. "You people have all those fancy gadgets."

"Nothing," Epiphany said.

"Any way to locate them? Maybe get a message to them the old-fashioned way?" Allie asked.

"They haven't left an itinerary," Euphoria said. "They're tracking things, and it would rather defeat the purpose if they were traveling a known path. I'm afraid it is quite impossible to—"

"There's a way," Epiphany said.

"How?" Allie said insistently.

"I... this... it isn't really something I ought to be talking about."

"I shouldn't be talking about it either, but here we are," Allie said.

The sisters exchanged a few more uncertain glances.

"There's a contraption we have. We call it Oiler. I think it knows how to find Fel."

"What does that mean?" Allie said.

"I don't know if it is a properly living thing, but it is animated. It thinks. And for some reason it always knows where Fel is. If we don't keep it occupied, it will try to seek him out. Dad thinks it has something to do with the fact that it is a repair contraption, so it has some sort of innate awareness of its own maintainer, and Fel was the one who initially repaired it. But it found its way to the shop before it had ever been there when Fel was in trouble, and twice it's wandered off to find him when he was away overnight. It's a wonder the locals haven't spotted the thing. I'm sure Oiler could be coaxed into leading someone to Fel."

"You Maskers are up to more than I'd imagined," Allie said.

"I'll talk to Dad. I'll get Oiler and I'll get my hands on a horse. I'll find Fel," Epiphany said.

"No," Euphoria said. "Get Oiler, but don't talk to Father about this. Make an excuse. And it'll have to be you who gets Oiler. Given the open wound of my departure, I doubt I'd be trusted if I were to be the one to attempt to spirit Oiler away. And it can't be one of us who delivers the message."

"Why not? This is our brother, and Lattica is your family too. This is blood."

"Because the Bolivans are already after us. If we encounter any of them or any of their informants along the way, we'll be targeted as well. Unless Fel and Lattica have been extremely thorough or successful, there are doubtlessly more Bolivans who can communicate almost instantly. Anyone who might even have the potential of being seen as a rescuer would be a liability. That goes for hired muscle, if they're known within the city."

"Verfessa felt the same way," Allie said.

"Who do we send then?"

"It's going to be me," Allie said.

"No. Allie, I couldn't ask you to—"

Allie dismissed the statement. "You didn't. Verfessa did. Apparently a barmaid who has barely left the town before is right near the bottom of likely rescuers and thus perfect for the job. So you can go ahead and forget about feeling guilty about it. You're *sure* this Oiler thing can find him?"

"Quite sure. You'll need to keep it hidden. It's a rather recognizable contraption, and the Bolivans would be glad to get it."

"Grand..." Allie muttered. "You've already said the Maskers don't have a spare horse. I don't suppose the Graves have one I can borrow."

"If we're worried about the Bolivans recognizing someone along the way, I don't imagine any of the carriages Euphoria can spare would do any good. I can scrape together some money and help you rent one."

"No. Given who convinced me this needed to be done, I get the feeling if I need the money for one, it'll mysteriously appear. But all this cloak-and-dagger stuff is getting to me. I'm overthinking things."

"In what way?"

"We can all agree I'm not exactly a likely person to come running to someone's rescue outside of this city. And Verfessa seems awfully certain there are no Bolivans left *in* the city. But if I just rented a wagon and headed out without any reason, wouldn't that raise questions? And I don't know how many horses you've rented over the years, to say nothing of carriages, but every one I've ever used has been a lame old nag who probably wouldn't survive the trip. What I need is something small and fast. Something that can keep up a decent trot for a long time. I'll need to catch up with them."

She swirled the drink she'd poured for herself. A thought came to mind. It was a silly, pointless thought.

"Tell you what. I think I know someone who might be able to help me out. I'll come by tomorrow morning for this Oiler thing. One way or another I'll have a cart. Until then. Drinks are on the house while we discuss what I'm likely to deal with along the way."

Tome lay on the curved floor of his cell. Evidently his recent cooperation had not been sufficient to earn him a cushion to sleep on. As a result, sleep was slow to come. It was probably just his imagination amplifying every little annoyance, but he could swear the moon was brighter and more mobile here than in the world beyond the wall, because any halfway comfortable position within the cell invariably placed his head in full moonlight.

He was on the verge of rolling aside in hopes of getting some darkness when, oddly, darkness asserted itself with a sharpness far too sudden to be a cloud.

"Tome! Time to go!" came a hushed voice.

He opened his eyes to find Teya standing in front of the vines. Her own eyes were wide and excited. She reached a stubby claw toward the vines. The sleep snapped from Tome's mind, and he held up a hand.

"No! Don't touch them! They're trapped. If you touch them, they'll know. It's why they didn't bother putting a guard on me overnight. What in the world are you doing here? How did you *get* here? How did you know to find me?"

Teya pulled back.

"You don't need help?" she said.

"I *do* need help. I just didn't expect to *get* any."

"You got me! What we do?"

"I don't know! I haven't made any plans. How did you find me?"

"Parch came! Told me. I told Adept. She said, go there! I went. Here you are!" Teya said.

"Where is Parch now?"

The unicorn jutted his head into view and bleated. Teya and Tome both hastily shushed him.

"Teya, did anyone see you?"

"No! *Soooo* sneaky." She motioned with her claw. "Also? Sleeping. All sleeping."

She moved closer, with a paw positioned for a conspiratorial whisper.

"When forest kids sleep? Very *very* sleep."

"Good to know. Is there any chance Kazel or someone could come and rescue me?"

"Can't send lots. Then? War. You get me. I save."

"Lovely..."

"More than you had."

"That's true. But we need a plan."

"I break vines. We run. Good plan!" she said.

"Running isn't enough. They have my goods, they have Wick, and I think they're planning something big."

Teya nodded. "Always. Don't like them."

"I can't leave until I at least know what it is. Ideally, I want to get Wick back. I think he's in danger."

"So make plan," Teya advised.

"I'm working on it. With you here, I have some more options. I don't suppose you have any pen and paper."

She shook her head.

"If any of my things are still intact, they're just as well locked up as I am."

"You need write? I get write things."

"No! There's no point. You'd risk alerting them, and if they're smart, they'll notice some of my things are missing. Even if you got them, there's no place for me to hide them in here. But... tell me, do you know their language?"

"Forest kids? Read, not very. Say, not very. Listen? Very very."

"All right. If you were to overhear what they were saying, could you relay that back to me?"

Teya nodded vigorously.

"Then here's what I need you to do. Find me something to write on. Something *natural* to write on. My things won't do. We need the additional power that comes from using something local. Leaves, perhaps. A few of them." He held up his hands. "About this large. And something to write with. A feather, or maybe a needle or thorn. Ideally something that won't kill me if I prick myself. Leaves and a thorn should be easy enough to hide inside a tree. Get them for me and visit again tomorrow night, or the next. I'll need a while to write."

"I can do! Yes, yes. Fast fast."

Teya scampered away. Tome pushed his doubts and concerns from his mind in favor of concocting a spell refined enough to function even if it was clumsily written on a leaf. The news wasn't all dire. Anything drawn from anywhere near this place would be intensely mystically powerful and perfectly attuned to the location aspect of a spell. As for the ink? It was an option he'd hoped to avoid, but it should be particularly potent.

After the planning session was through and the Masker sisters were on their way, Allie once again found herself walking through the expensive side of town. Epiphany and Euphoria struck a remarkable balance of being so very alike and yet so very different. They both had a gift for tracing out what might happen, what they needed to happen, and how to get those two to meet. Epiphany preferred to focus on threading the needle between lies and the truth, artfully avoiding the pieces of a situation that weren't in her favor, and generally exploiting any bit of gray area she had access to. Euphoria was quite willing to outright lie, though the works of art she crafted just in the space of that one conversation were such that Allie would have sworn they were true if she'd not witnessed their creation. Seeing what those two were capable of when united in a cause made it clear that separating them was the only way the world could be certain the Masker girls wouldn't take it over in a matter of months.

Her head was swimming as she took a turn not so far from Verfessa's house and paced along an avenue somewhat modest by the standards of the neighborhood but extravagant by the standards of the town in general. As Epiphany and Euphoria had discussed what needed to be done, and what could be done, Allie had been made privy to secrets that had been held close to the chests of the two families for ages. She learned about things called sentry lanterns and how they worked. She learned what Oiler could do and how to keep it in line. In short, she learned the world had far more wonders than she'd imagined, and she would likely need all of them to get where she was going and do what she was planning.

But before any of that, she would need a way to get there quickly enough for any of it to matter.

She stopped in front of a lovely home near the far end of the street. It was plainly newer than most of the other houses on the street, as evidenced by its height and its wooden construction. The home was painted a pleasant shade of yellow, it was nestled close to its neighbors, and the front door was carved with a loaf of bread quite like the one on the door of Divinity's Oven. This was where Mariss lived.

Allie stepped up to the door and gave it a knock. A man sliding comfortably out of middle age answered the door. He was alarmingly thin considering she knew he was a baker by trade. Allie's first thought was that one should never buy food cooked by a thin man, as it implied he didn't eat his own work. But then she realized she wasn't much of a drinker and people certainly had no worries buying liquor from her. Her mind looped back to remind her that she didn't *make* the booze before she realized she was engaging in a very curious sort of procrastination while a man was staring at her expectantly.

"Can I help you?" he said.

"I'm sorry to bother you so late, sir. I'm Allie, a friend of Mariss's, and I wondered if I could speak to her."

"A friend of Mariss's? Certainly. I'll fetch her. Would you like to come in?"

"If it's all the same to you, I'll wait outside. I've had a long day on my feet, and I'm sure I smell a bit like the floor of a tavern."

"She'll be right along."

He stepped away, leaving the door ajar. Allie was treated to the scent of a delicious homemade dinner wafting from within. Mariss didn't take long to appear.

"Oh! Allie. I wasn't expecting you," she said. "Please, come in."

"No, really, I'm hoping to make this quick."

"Is there something wrong?" she asked, putting a hand on Allie's shoulder.

More thoughts clashed in Allie's head. Mariss was wealthy and daughter of a wealthy family. In her experience with those with deep pockets—people of means, she'd learned they preferred to be called—as a rule they weren't the most pleasant of people. There were exceptions, to be sure, but so far the lion's share of her patrons who fancied themselves part of the social elite were terrible tippers, terrible storytellers, and viewed the world as divided into two neat sets of people: those who could afford servants and those who *were* servants. Mariss, with a single look and a hand on the shoulder, managed as much concern for her as half the people she would feel more comfortable calling friends, and all after only having had a handful of interactions.

"I'm fine. But the tavern is shutting down for a few weeks."

"I know. How exciting! I hope you don't mind me saying so, but while the place seems wonderfully lively, it did come across as a bit unkempt."

"The place was just this side of rundown. No hard feelings, I don't own the place, and I don't really get paid enough to run it like I do. But that's beside the point. I'm planning on taking a bit of a trip."

"Oh! Lovely. You know, ever since one of our little chats, I've been thinking of taking a trip as well. I just hadn't been able to decide where. Where are you going?"

"Up north somewhere. But I'm on a bit of a shoestring budget. This may be a big ask, particularly given how little we know each other, but do you think you could rent me your horse? And your cart as well."

"If you're on a shoestring budget, why wouldn't you use your own horse?"

"Believe it or not, a barmaid in the city doesn't have much need for a horse. Also, not much money for a horse. Also, no place to keep a horse."

"And you can't rent one down at the stable?"

"The horses there aren't terribly hearty, and this trip is going to be quite long. You mentioned your horse and cart were fast."

"You need to go somewhere quickly," Mariss said steadily.

She glanced over her shoulder, then stepped fully outside and shut the door.

"This is something serious, isn't it? One doesn't come visiting a friendly associate to rent a fast horse for a holiday."

"Mariss, I don't want to worry you. I promise I'll have the horse and cart back safe and sound, but—"

"It's about Fel, isn't it?"

Allie failed to keep her surprise from her expression. Perhaps it was best she didn't play grum after all.

"How did you know?"

"He's off on a dangerous adventure, and he's the only thing you and I have in common, more or less. When I was worried about him, I came to you, why wouldn't you do the same? If you need to borrow my cart and horse to help Fel, by all means, but only on one condition."

"What condition?"

"I'm coming along."

"No. No, no, no. Out of the question."

"I'd just said I was hoping to see more of the world, and not so long ago you told me if I was nervous about something, I should do something about it."

"Not this, Mariss. The Maskers already had to stretch their own rules to take me into their confidence to reveal some things. I don't have the right to give away their secrets."

"Very well. I'm happy to wait until you get permission from them."

"Mariss, I'm serious."

She crossed her arms. "And I have a rich daddy. Spoiled rotten. I get what I want."

She said it sweetly, and with a smile on her face. But Allie could tell it was a mask over a very serious intention to have her way.

"This will be dangerous."

"You wouldn't be going if you didn't think you could handle it. It'll just be easier with someone by your side, won't it?"

"I have no idea how long this is going to take, or how far we'll go."

"Father's baking assistant needs practice dealing with the public anyway. He can take over for me while I'm gone."

Allie flashed upon the argument that would follow, one that would end with her failing to get the cart or failing to persuade Mariss not to come along. She decided it wasn't worth the trouble and skipped to the ending that would get her the cart.

"If you're willing to risk your life for a friend of a friend on the spur of a moment, who am I to stand in your way? Pack for bad weather. Save some room in your wagon for two heavy packs for me. I'll be along tomorrow morning to fetch you."

Mariss clapped her hands.

"Exciting!" She hurried through the door. "Daddy! Tell Marcus he can work the counter for a while. I'm going on a *trip*!"

Allie shut her eyes tightly and took a breath. She turned and began the return trip to her home.

"Well. If the goal was to send a rescue party no one would suspect, I suppose you can't get much more unlikely than a barmaid and a baker," she muttered.

Epiphany and Euphoria whispered to each other as they approached the shop. The walk home had been dense with plotting and planning. The bell above the door jangled as they entered the shop.

"Dad will be up to meet us. We have to make the decision on how we're going to do this," Epiphany said.

"This will need to be done delicately," Euphoria said. "The most important thing is that Father believes sending Oiler away is his own decision. If possible, we should be angling for him to make the suggestion himself. Do you have any clients who have purchased particularly temperamental or complex contraptions? Maybe ones that are some distance away? If we can persuade him to send one of us away with Oiler to repair it, that will do."

"And then what? I just stay out of town until Allie gets back with Oiler? Or until Fel gets back?"

"If that's what it takes," Euphoria said. "Alternately we can convince him that there is some danger to keeping Oiler here, and that it should be sent away for our protection or its protection. Whatever the story, the absolute key is ensuring that once we've picked that story, we must be perfectly consistent and never stray. The moment a story changes, it's clear it is deception."

The thump of footsteps drew their attention to the door to the rest of the household. Vivian emerged first, then Martin.

"Did you enjoy your evening, girls?" Vivian asked, subtly flipping the ledger open to skim the day's sales and purchases. "I'd been waiting to go over your portion of the day's sales, in case I needed to discuss them with you."

"Quite a good day of business, if I do say so myself," Euphoria said.

"Indeed. I can get so much more done in a day when there are two of you to split the time in the shop."

"It's good to be so hands-on in a shop again," Euphoria said.

"Dad, I wanted a word with you, if you have a moment," Epiphany said.

"Certainly, Fanny," Martin said.

"How has Oiler been behaving lately?"

"Nothing out of the ordinary. It has repaired a dozen or so contraptions, solved its puzzle box forty times, and spent every moment in between staring into the north wall of the shop."

"Right..." Epiphany said.

She could feel the eyes of her sister on her as she turned over the many potential tactics they'd discussed. She'd expected to be a bit more stressed by the puzzle of selecting the best one, but the answer came to her quickly.

"Dad, we have reason to believe the Bolivans are planning an ambush on Fel and Lattica. Because they're tracking down all the Graves's flames currently in possession of the Bolivans, all they need to do is gather themselves around one of the flames, and they can be certain Fel will show up eventually. We need to get a message to Fel to either prepare for the ambush or avoid someplace called the half-charred manor. This information comes from Donovan Verfessa, and we have a plan to deal with it. We have someone who can carry the message, and they are currently acquiring the means to reach Fel. We just need to know if you think Oiler can be trusted to find him and if you trust us to loan it out to serve as a guide."

It was a flurry of information, and it took Martin and Vivian a few moments to work through it all. Epiphany could practically see them encounter each hitch in the plan and work their way through to the same conclusions the sisters had. Who should go and who shouldn't? What was at stake if this wasn't done? Vivian was the first to speak.

"Who will be the messenger?" she asked.

"Allie from The Fox and Log," Epiphany said.

"She's capable," Martin said, somewhat less steadily and matter-of-factly than his wife. "Not who I would have expected, but then I suppose that's a bit of the point, isn't it? You've discussed this with her?"

"We have," Epiphany said.

"Including Oiler? You've made her aware of it?"

"Yes."

"Well, if the story has already been told, there's nothing left to lose but Oiler itself. There's no argument that Fel's safety is worth the gamble.

I'll have to prepare Oiler. Meet me downstairs shortly," Martin said, stepping quickly from the shop.

"I'll finish closing up. Go see to your father," Vivian said.

Epiphany and Euphoria followed Martin.

"The truth is easier to remember," Epiphany said. "And the nice thing about trust is it lets people use their own judgment."

"The Graves way of dealing with things may have rubbed off a bit more than I'd realized," Euphoria murmured with a dash of shame.

CHAPTER 11

"Go, go. Fast, fast," Teya urged.

Tome scratched a few more words onto the thick, leathery leaf Teya had found. He hesitated to think what sort of plant the kobold had harvested the thorn from, but it was nearly the length of his finger and quite a capable stylus.

"I cannot be rushed. A mistake would be ruinous," Tome said.

"Forest kids wake soon. Fast, fast writing."

He shut his eyes and braced himself to "dip" the quill again. The sharp tip of the thorn was able to open a small gash just above his hair line, where he was able collect dabs of blood. The first books he'd read on paper magic had described the practice as *requiring* blood. Early paper mages seemed to believe that blood was necessary to produce any effect at all, which was one of the reasons the practice was virtually nonexistent. Regardless of the intentions, a person writing arcane messages in blood had a way of attracting the distrust and ire of those around him. The art evolved and improved, but now that he felt how powerful this spell was becoming even under these adverse circumstances, Tome could certainly see why people had written spells in this way.

"There," he said, putting the final touches on the spell. "I've nicked the top of the spell there. When the time comes, tear it from that nick down through the first word. It will burn away in a cold blue flame."

Teya took the leaf and immediately made ready to tear it.

"No! Not here, not now. Look. Do you see that tree there? With the four tall branches off the top, one of which is completely covered in vines?"

Teya peered in the direction he was pointing.

"Yes," she said.

"All right. Listen closely. I don't know if we'll have another chance at this..."

The morning had an unnatural chill to it for this time of year as Allie hurried toward Masker's Antiquities. She caught a glimpse of herself in the windows and saw a bleary-eyed face staring back at her. The uncertainty of the journey ahead and the realization that she would have to persuade the Maskers to allow her to share their secrets in order for the journey to even begin was not a recipe for restful slumber.

"Rancid rat-dog?" croaked a voice from the rooftops as she approached the shop.

"Not today," she muttered.

The four lesser harpies dropped down, one by one, to hop along with her, cackling as sweetly as their limited articulation would allow.

"Give it here, rotten stench-bird!"

"If you don't let go of it, I'll pull your beak off!"

"Monkey!"

Allie shook her head. "I don't know who in this town has been calling you monkeys, but they've really left an impression."

She rummaged through her pockets. Normally she brought a bribe if she thought she'd be heading in this direction, but her mind was in no place for planning for the wants or needs of the rooftop bandits. Her searching turned up an old button, some string, and a few bits of paper.

"This'll have to do. If I get back here alive, I'll bring something you'll like better. Heck, I'll be bringing back *Fel* with any luck."

She sprinkled the odds and ends to the ground. The lesser harpies gathered around the offering to consider it. One grabbed the button and fluttered off. Two others flew after it to contest ownership of the best bit of trash. The last one took the string in its beak and released a squawk that may as well have been a perfectly enunciated "We'll let you slide this time, but don't let it happen again."

The Masker girls were at the front door when she reached the shop. They'd been joined by Martin, while Vivian was visible within, setting up shop.

"Hello, Mr. Masker!" Allie said, summoning up as much "nothing to worry about" energy as she could muster. "Nice to see you this morning. I've got some business with the girls if you can spare them for a moment."

"This is about Oiler," he said. "I know everything, or at least everything they've told me. Here. I'll warn you, it's a bit heavy."

He hefted the chain-filled pack to the ground in front of her. Oiler had reeled its head and arms fully inside. The odd multitool of a tail tip still dangled from the bottom of the pack like a curious ornament, but it was the only evidence to suggest this was anything other than a standard backpack.

"There aren't any special commands. Speak to it in plain language. It's 'hiding' at the moment, but you can't trust it to stay that way for long. Get it into someplace out of sight as soon as you can, and give it this."

He handed her a solved puzzle box. The flap of Oiler's pack shifted, and a gleam was briefly visible from beneath, but the lack of scrambled faces on the puzzle box meant it held little interest in the contraption.

"Mix up the faces and hand it over as soon as you can. Oiler is perfectly content while solving the box. Keeping it busy overnight can be a chore. It doesn't sleep, and it only takes about a half hour to solve the box, but in my experience it will wait about another two hours before it starts getting into mischief."

"Mischief?" Allie asked, still coming to terms with the lack of secrecy.

"Oiler likes to repair things. Keeping it from doing so is a challenge. If it wanders off, it will probably wander off to repair something. But once it's done so, it will probably head directly for Fel."

"How do I get it to point the way?"

"You can try asking, but even if you don't, Oiler tends to gaze in the direction of Fel when it is unoccupied."

She glanced at the pack. It may have been her imagination, but she could have sworn she'd seen the tail tip "wag."

"Does it... eat?" Allie asked.

"No."

"Anything else I should know about it?"

"It hates weapons. Friend or foe, it will try to pull any drawn weapon from the hands of the one holding it."

She leaned a little closer and lowered her voice.

"Is this what contraptions are really like? Do you have an army of these things running about in your workshop?"

"No. While this isn't one of a kind, it certainly is the only one known to be in operation. I'd say to treat it with care, but it's really rather sturdy, now that I've machined the proper fasteners. It was tricky because in the early Bygone Era they used a nonstandard thread pitch that could easily be mistaken for..."

Epiphany touched her father's arm. He trailed off.

"Right. Er. I suppose there is just one more matter before we send you on your way. How fully aware are you of Fel's mission?"

"Not *fully*, I'm sure."

"Never mind. Just remember this. We've learned that sentry lanterns can be compelled to extinguish their own flames. We don't know how to force them to do so, but we've learned that it can be done at the will of the sentry lantern. That should be helpful to him in his mission."

"I'll be sure to pass that along."

"Allie, I cannot thank you enough for taking this risk on behalf of the family," he said.

"It had to be done. And apparently I was the one who had to do that. But, um... there's one thing. I had to beg and borrow to get a horse and cart fast enough to give us a fighting chance of getting to Fel before something bad happened. The person offering it up insisted she come along."

"I really would have preferred this not spread any further," Epiphany said.

"You and me both, but she wouldn't take no for an answer. Either she gets to learn about the Oiler thing and the sentry lantern thing as well, or I'll need to find another means of transportation."

"Who is it?" Epiphany asked.

"Mariss."

"From Divinity's Oven? The one Fel is always swooning over?"

"That's the one."

"Do you think she can be trusted?"

"I haven't had much time to get a read on her, but she seems decent. More savvy than I gave her credit for."

Epiphany sighed. "If Fel had his way, she'd be a part of the family already. This is as good a test as any. Time is of the essence, beggars can't be choosers."

"Is spraying platitudes doing any good to cope with the feeling of this spiraling out of control?" Euphoria asked.

"No, Fora, it isn't. And neither are snide comments. Allie, just do your best. And thank you so much."

"There's a lot between now and the moment when you ought to be thanking me. But I'll do my best."

Allie hefted the pack to her back and did her very best to push aside the thought that she was carrying some manner of ancient thinking machine. She had a feeling she would be pushing an awful lot of thoughts aside in the coming weeks.

Fel emerged from the back of the carriage and took a seat. His arms were crossed and his expression was sour, something that didn't go unnoticed by Lattica.

"Something wrong?" she asked.

"It's cold."

"We are well into the mountains and fairly far north. What did you expect?"

"I expected it to be cold. I just didn't know how cold. My adventuring usually takes me south. I spend more time in the desert or up to my waist in swamps than worrying about frost."

"Why?"

"Because that's where the best caches of contraptions are. Don't ask me why. I always assumed it was because they liked to build *down* in the Bygone Era, and digging down in a mountain is harder than digging down in a desert."

"Doesn't explain the swamps, though. You can't put a deep basement in a swamp, it'll fill up."

"Just because it would fill up wasn't enough to stop the folks in the Bygone Era from putting in basements and sub-basements and sub-sub-basements. Trust me, I've been in my share of them. If you dig deep enough in that bag of gear, you'll find a little contraption that is supposed to let you breathe under water for a few minutes at a time."

"Does it?"

"Have you ever opened the door to a storage room or some other chamber below ground that hasn't been opened for a year or so? That special kind of dank, moist smell that makes your stomach lurch? Imaging breathing that. It beats suffocating, but not by much. ... What were we talking about?"

"You were moping about being cold."

"Yeah. When are we stopping for a bit? I could use a fire."

She glanced down at the detector, then up at the road ahead.

"Grab the map. The top one on the stack. I think there's a turn coming."

Fel did as he was told. She referenced it.

"In just a bit, we're going to see a crossroads. If we continue forward, in a few more days we'll be somewhere near where the next big flame is. If we take a left, by nightfall we'll reach the town on that shipping list you grabbed. The mission says go north." She looked at him. "I think we should go left."

"Do you? Is there a procedure somewhere in one of those books that says you should do that?"

"No. *You* said we should do that. And while I don't particularly trust you to make strategies, you're a Masker. We're *constantly* trying to find a way to get the sort of insight the Maskers have into how contraptions work."

"My dad is the one who knows how they work. I'm a distant second, and I'm only *that* because my sisters were interested in the business instead."

"A distant second in your family puts you head and shoulders above anyone in mine."

"The Graves are always marrying in people to try to fill gaps. Does that mean there was a Graves gal set aside for me to try to snare me?"

"I don't doubt it. But the point is, now is the chance for the Graves and the Masker families to have their first looks at contraptions at the same time. And frankly, you've nearly been killed on this trip already. I don't want to have to trust that you'll survive the next big clash so we can double back when the flame is put out."

"I've never felt so much and so little confidence in me at the same time. But let's go left then. If nothing else, that's a town we're heading to. Maybe we can find someone willing to sell me a proper jacket."

Teya reclined on a high branch half a mile or so from the tree she'd been told to watch. Parch was merrily snacking on a leaf nearly the size of his head that was so dew covered that even the perpetually thirsty creature wasn't seeking a drink. Teya's belly was bulging with the fruit she had gathered to gorge upon while seeking out this vantage.

"This forest is so *bountiful*," she mused to herself, finally unlimited by a lackluster mastery of another's language. She licked juice and pulp from her muzzle and fixed her eyes on her target. "Why would anyone be mean, living in a place where all the food just hangs off trees?"

Parch bleated. Teya considered tottering to her feet and having a game of headbutts. So high up in a tree, it would make for a much more exciting game than usual. But in the distance, she saw motion. She squinted her large eyes and saw three Children of the Forest heading toward a mossy crook in the tree Tome had indicated. She waited until they were inside, then produced the spell and activated it. The leaf started to sizzle and smolder, the words scrawled on it burning brightly. Though it happened slowly, when the effect finally settled upon her, she was nearly startled from her perch. She could hear voices. Three of them, speaking mannerly and in turn. One voice was female, another was male. The third, while certainly also male, sounded strange. It buzzed deeply, in the way that one's own voice sounded rather than the voice of someone else. She was hearing through the ears of one of the wizards.

"The flame still dances. The entity is absent," said the female.

"No matter. If this next incantation produces the desired effect, it will be proof enough that its presence is unnecessary," said the first male.

"The incantation will work. We saw promising progress yesterday," said the second.

"It is not your place to speculate. It is your place to transcribe our findings," said the female.

"Many pardons. I did not mean to overstep," said the second male.

From that point forward, the others were the only ones who spoke. They dutifully alternated, as though it was some established procedure that one must reply to the other whenever they spoke.

"What do we know about the source of power?" said the male.

"As with all contraptions, the power comes from the spirits of the machine. I do not believe normal use of the device will ever be enough to deplete it. Such is the nature of contraptions. Lesser effects but greater efficiency and duration."

"No power is inexhaustible. And we will not be pursuing normal usage."

"This much is true. We shall endeavor to measure the power it has now, and measure again after the first procedure."

"That may be the only effective way to determine if a single sentry lantern will be enough for a full force."

"It had better be. It was truly fortunate that we came into possession of this lantern. The chances of locating even one more are infinitesimal."

"Still, the commander insists we need at least fifteen mind anchors for a proper expedition to take place."

"Do you believe what the human said? About the size of the land beyond?"

"I still have my doubts that there *is* a land beyond."

"That is the influence of their treachery. Use your logic. He must have come from somewhere."

"You have seen him. Can you imagine someone so weak of mind and body surviving anywhere? Even with help?"

"Even so. He was not conjured from nothing. And if the land is as shown in his maps, three squads of five will not be enough to search it in a timely manner."

"We have endured centuries of the tyranny of their machinations and mechanisms. I hardly think 'a timely manner' is something we need to concern ourselves with. If we succeed in creating the mind anchors, the time will come."

"It does feel closer. While in the presence of the sentry lantern, I find myself more capable of conceiving of the place beyond. But if the map is accurate—"

"I do not wish to discuss the map. One step at a time."

"If the map is *accurate*, then it would mean there is a symmetry. A focus of distortion on their side as well as ours."

"Not worth considering."

"I would say it is *quite* worth considering. It fundamentally changes the mission. The balance."

"Our task is to create the mental anchors. Focus on the task."

Teya blinked and shook her head. Two things were quite clear. This was going to be a tremendous amount to remember, and it was going to be *very* boring.

Mariss was at the reins of the horse, and even after spending just a single day on the road, it was exceptionally clear that getting this steed was worth any amount of difficulty or awkwardness Mariss's presence might add to the trip. It was *fast*. And while any horse could be fast for a sprint, this animal's trot was nearly as fast as an average draft horse's gallop. It could move for *hours* at a speed that most animals could only manage for minutes. Mariss was quite aware of it, and quite proud. This was established in one of the other discoveries of the trip. Mariss was chatty when she was nervous. And the trip was making her terribly nervous. The words came fast and steady, almost without regard for punctuation.

"I love horses. I always did. Daddy used to take me up to the stables, and I'd ride all the little ponies. Little Zephyr here was supposed to be a racehorse, but she just didn't have the sprint speed. Can you believe this fast little horse wasn't fast enough? So who knows what they would have done if I hadn't been with Daddy when he was talking to the man? Daddy really likes horses. He does a lot more traveling than me. It's how I started getting into baking. He'd go away for a few days at a time, and the shop would just close if they couldn't get someone to work the counter and the ovens, but I knew all his recipes so I started lending a hand, and it turned out I was good at it. But we were talking about horses. He wanted to invest in a horse, and the man said that Zephyr's sister Mistral was a sure thing, but Zephyr just couldn't run a short race, and I saw her beautiful eyes, and I knew she had to be mine, so I bought her and Daddy gave me this cart to go with it and it's just so nice. We used to say Zephyr must have been part unicorn thanks to how much stamina she has and how pretty she is, but then I saw Parch and Parch is definitely a unicorn. So if Zephyr were part unicorn, she'd probably be smaller unless she was part *greater* unicorn, but I don't see how that would happen since they haven't been seen outside the Greater Lands for—"

She yelped as Oiler, evidently not accustomed to waiting for an opening in conversation, thrust the solved puzzle box out beside her. Allie took it from the metal claws and hastily mixed up the faces of the box. In truth, she found the thing profoundly unnerving. The one mercy of having Mariss's constant conversation meant she had something to distract her from the equally constant clicking and clacking from Oiler. Mariss, it turned out, had a far different relationship with the contraption.

"Do you think it likes pats on the head?" Mariss asked.

"It is made of metal. I don't think it can feel them," Allie said.

"I didn't think metal could *think,* but it does that very nicely."

She took one hand from the reins and gave Oiler a pet. The contraption angled its sculpted serpentine head toward her, then reeled back into the pack and flopped the flap into place, working at the puzzle box while peering from under the canvas top.

"It doesn't like pats," Mariss concluded. "Do you think it figured that out for itself? Or did the person who designed it make that decision? Or was it just a mistake, and they meant for it to do something else? Because if you were going to make a living thing, why wouldn't you want it to be happy when it gets pets? I think—"

"I think we should pull over at this inn and rest for the night. We've covered twice as much ground as I expected for our first day. I need some wine, and you need a hard cider."

Mariss tilted her head. "How did you know that was my favorite drink?"

"How do you know when the cake needs a little more time in the oven? You get a feel for these things."

She guided the horse aside.

"I'm going to mix up this puzzle extra good for you," Mariss said, tugging the cube from Oiler's claws and sliding the tiles. "But you have to be extra good for me, all right? Stay hidden. No crawling around. We'll be out to check on you before you know it."

She pulled down the canvas divider between the cargo compartment and the seats.

"You have a way with... everyone, don't you?" Allie said.

"So do you," Mariss said. "I've only seen it a few times, but the people in the tavern really seem to like you."

Allie shook her head. "Some of them like me. But mostly they respect me. Two very different things. In my line of work, the respect is more important, but it can put some distance between people. There's never any distance with you."

Mariss shrugged. "Gotta sell the pies."

They found their way to a seat in the dim, smoky tavern that made up the lower level of the inn. Allie grinned. It was rare she stepped into another tavern, but she took no small amount of pride in finding one that failed to hold a candle to the one she ran. She must be doing something right.

Once they'd arranged for their food, drinks, and the rooms for the night, they wedged themselves into a relatively clean table near the door, where the air was fresher and the exit could be swifter. Almost immediately, Mariss's endless stream of conversation dried up. By the time the drinks had been served, Allie suspected Mariss would have hidden behind her if she could. Everything about her bright, bubbly demeanor had changed. Her arms were clutched in front of her, trying to make herself small, and her eyes were cast toward the table. Her means for coping with the anxiety of the trip had completely shifted. Allie didn't have to ask why.

"The rough-looking fellows at the table near the stairs?" Allie said.

"I don't like the way they're looking at me," Mariss said.

She sighed. "At least you're not naive. Don't worry about it."

"You don't think they're dangerous?"

"I'm sure they can *be* dangerous, but the important thing is that you don't worry about it. Be aware of it. Be ready for it. Don't worry about it. Remember what I was saying about respect."

"How do you simply *make* someone respect you?"

"Sometimes it's impossible. But you already know how."

"If I knew how, we wouldn't be talking about this."

"What's the horse's name?"

"Zephyr. And what does that have to do with anything?"

"How big is Zephyr?"

"Fourteen hands."

Allie scrunched up her face. "Hands?"

"Horses are measured in hands."

"The wealthy are very strange..." Allie muttered under her breath. "The point is, is Zephyr bigger than they are?"

"Well sure, but she's a sweetheart."

"You said you'd ride all the little ponies. They weren't all sweethearts, were they?"

"No. They can be little stinkers sometimes."

"And do you shrink away and huddle down and avert your eyes from the stinkers?"

"No, no. You can't let them think you're a pushover, or they'll push you over."

"It's the same. Treat men like horses. Treat women like horses, for that matter. People are like horses."

"People are *not* like horses."

"All right. Fine. In a perfect world, people are better than horses. More reasonable. More moral and ethical. And most people absolutely are. But those are the people you don't have to worry about. The ones you *do* have to worry about are the meanest horses you'll ever meet. Blunt. Powerful. Thoughtless. Lumbering through the world, victims of their own impulses. It's worse for me, because I work in a place where people are downing booze, which puts a thumb on the scale of the whole person-to-horse balance. But right now we're both in a place like that. So don't make yourself small. You make less space for you, it means more space for them, and they'll sidle over and take up that space."

"And what if that doesn't work?"

Allie thought for a moment. "I never had a horse. But my dad had a jackass. She'd pull a cart, but she would *not* do as she was told unless you got her attention. Sometimes that meant a lot of shouting, but more often it meant using a persuader."

"What's a persuader?"

"Usually something sturdy and portable. I suppose you don't carry a persuader?"

"Daddy bought me a cute little knife, but I don't carry it."

"A knife is too extreme for what I have in mind."

She reached into a pocket inside in her coat and subtly passed something beneath the table to Mariss. It was a chunk of broom handle, a bit longer than her palm. Both ends were whittled into blunt nubs about the size of her thumb tip.

"Grab that in your hand. It gives your hand a little more heft, makes your punches count a little more because it fills your grip, and if you do a nice sharp stabbing motion, those nubs will leave a bruise that'll remind someone to behave themselves. Not the *best* weapon in the world, but I like it," she said. "I carry three of them. One on each side of my coat, and a third one that's twice as long and heavier for when I feel like swinging a stick instead of hammering a fist."

Mariss held the weapon out of view under the table.

"I don't know if I could hit anyone with this."

"Just remember you have it, and when you see someone looking at you in a way you don't like, you picture whopping them in the temple with it. That look in your eye you get when you're thinking that? It works almost as well as the blow itself."

"How do you *learn* things like this?" Mariss said.

Allie took her drink in hand.

"The hard way, Mariss. Always the hard way."

The moon was in the sky once more. After spending the previous night sleepless and repeatedly poking himself in the scalp with a thorn, Tome found that sleep was considerably easier to attain tonight. Thus, it came as a startling and not entirely welcome moment when he was awoken by a clump of dirt exploding against the side of his head.

"What? Hmm?" he snorted.

"Shush!" Teya hissed. "You were very, very sleep."

"Oh, *oh*. Did the spell work?"

"Worked. Is work. When no more work?" Teya asked.

"It's still working?"

"Yes. Can still hear. Wizard with mate. Very distract. Very very."

"I apologize. It seems I'm prone to overwriting spells in this place. Or perhaps they are particularly susceptible to paper magic. That would explain why they are so dutiful in keeping paper from me. Regardless, it should wear off by tomorrow. What did you learn?"

Teya took a breath. "Very much."

He could tell she was trying to boil something down into words that could fit through her inexpert grasp of his language.

"Is the distracting elf nearby?"

"No. In tree, very far. Other side."

"Is anyone else awake?"

"No. Rest of village, very sleep."

"Then take your time," Tome said. "So long as no one wakes up or spots you, we have all night."

"They use Wick," she said. "For making anchor. For mind? Mind anchor."

"What is a mind anchor?"

"No stopping me. Hard to say things. Need say all."

"Right. I'm sorry. Continue."

"Mind anchor. Maybe to go? Lets them go."

"The mind anchor lets them go. Go where?"

"Place?"

"What place?"

"I have no interest in what lies beyond the wall, and no desire to bear witness to it."

"Right, right. Cross the wall. They're working on a way to cross the wall."

"That. They make one. Maybe. Tomorrow. After one? If work, more."

"How many more?"

"Don't know. Until no more Wick."

"They are going to drain Wick in the process of creating them?"

"Yes. They want..." Teya paused, holding up her fingers and twiddling them. "Five, and five, and five again."

"Fifteen."

"Yes. Fifteen mind anchors. Less? Not enough. More, good."

"To do what?"

"Go to place!" Teya snapped.

"And do what?"

"Do thing!"

"That's not helping."

Teya grumbled and held out her paws. "This one? Talk about do things. This one? Talk about make things."

She flapped the "do things" hand like it was talking, then repeatedly pinched it shut with the other hand.

"All the time."

"So one of them was focused on the present task."

"Yes. Present task. Make thing. Mind anchor."

"All right. All right, so let me see if I can understand it. Tomorrow, they are going to attempt to extract some sort of essence, something intrinsic to Wick, in order to make a tool or spell that will allow them to cross the wall. If they succeed, they'll spend however much time they need to repeat the process until Wick is used up, hoping to arm some force they consider to be minimally sufficient to perform some task on the other side of the wall."

Teya nodded.

"Is that all you learned?"

She squinted and looked aside, digging through her memory.

"More... not present task. One says 'Maybe.' Other? Not care."

"One of them was speculating on something."

She nodded.

"What was the subject of speculation?"

"Maps. You give map?"

"They took a map."

"One says, map wrong. Other says, map right, maybe? If map right... mirror."

"Mirror?"

"Mirror." She held paws on either side of her. "Map? Other map. Same, backward."

"Ah. So they are suggesting some sort of... symmetry."

Teya shrugged.

"You're not being as helpful as I would like."

Teya glared at him. She chattered something irritably, then switched back to his language.

"Parch come, get me. Who here? Fel? No. You, worst friend. Fel, less worst friend. Still I come. Long way. Sneaky. Very much sneaky. Find you thorn. Find you leaves. Tear leaf. Hear voice. Listen. Hear in talk of forest kids. Say in talk of Tome. Much things. Day of things. In not many words. You do better."

"I'm sorry, I'm sorry. It's just... I'm frustrated."

"You hear wizard. All day. Wizard with mate. Maybe then, frustrated. Very much frustrated."

Tome ran his fingers through his hair and winced as they found the remnants of the previous night's spell craft.

"Symmetry... Let's break it down."

"Wait," Teya said.

"What?"

"When rescue?"

"One thing at a time."

Teya grumbled. Tome continued.

"The old maps match. The new maps don't. Thus we can assume that some event, at the very least, led to two mutually contradictory views of the world. Obviously, that event was the construction of the wall. Or at least something associated with the construction of the wall. Symmetry. Their map shows our lands enclosed within the wall. Our map shows their lands enclosed within the wall. Symmetrical. Except only one of them can be true. Unless. Unless the apparent changing shape of the wall when we cross it is more than *apparent*. Could it be literal?"

He pressed his fingers to his temples.

"If the maps *aren't* mutually exclusive, then... from our point of view the Greater Lands is enclosed, from their point of view, our land is enclosed. And crossing the wall... provides access to an altered, reshaped world? It is a perversion of distance and size, but if we imagine for a moment that there is somehow some truth to it, then… there must be some sort of an equivalent to all parts of it within our lands. Some equivalent to Clickspring?"

Teya shrugged.

"It doesn't matter. That's something for another day. Did you get the impression they were up to no good?"

"Will kill Wick."

"Yes, granted. But whatever they were working toward. Did it seem to be something grander? More sinister?"

Teya shrugged. "Seemed like fighting, maybe? We plan now? Rescue?"

"Right. Right, now we know about all we'll know. What have we learned? Blood and leaves can make for a *very* potent spell."

"Messy," Teya said.

He let his sleep-deprived mind sift through the possibilities. Ideas started to form.

"I'm going to need another thorn and some more leaves," he said wearily. "And how sneaky can you be?"

"So, so sneaky."

"After you get me the spell materials, get some sleep. Be here before dawn. Before the others wake up. I'll hopefully have some new spells and a plan for you. The best time to escape is at night, but by then they'll have performed their first procedure on Wick. I need to know what happens."

"Spy during day," she grinned. "*Challenge* sneaky."

She nodded. "I do."

She scampered away. Tome pulled his mind to the task. This was going to be taxing.

CHAPTER 12

Lattica snapped the reins one last time and pulled the carriage around the back of the nearest thing to a stable the little town had to offer. It had probably started life as a barn for keeping sheep or goats through the winter. But a few duots were enough to persuade the owner to let her shelter the horses for the time being.

"No tavern in this town. No inn. I'm surprised they even had this," Fel said.

"A mountain town with no inn *and* no stable may as well shrivel up and die. They need some way to ensure people can stop by and resupply," Lattica said.

They hopped down and set about caring for the horses.

"Tell me you noticed," Fel whispered.

"Everyone in this city is looking at us out of the corners of their eyes," she whispered back.

"What do you think? Is this whole place full of Bolivans, or is this whole place looking at us worried we're about to start something with the Bolivans?"

"We're pretty deep into their territory," she said. "I wouldn't put it past them to have sunk their claws deep into this town. Now would be an excellent time for your little friend to show back up. As worrisome as it is to have a trained killer stalking around behind us waiting for the chance to swoop in, the possibility that this whole *town* is full of trained killers makes the thought of adding one of our own awfully appealing."

"I'm sure he'll show up if we need him," Fel said.

"You know him well enough to have that sort of confidence in him?"

"Yes and no."

"Please don't be coy. There's enough uncertainty without you mincing words."

"I didn't know he was a hired blade, but whenever I would ask him to run to the restaurant to grab me some food so I didn't have to leave the grum table, he'd bring back the right change."

She gave him a hard look, then shrugged. "I've heard worse reasons to trust someone. Even so. We'd better keep our eyes open."

The pair stepped out into the cold, Fel hugging his arms tightly to his body.

"How can a town even be called a town if there's no general store?" he muttered.

"We make a good deal of money from places like this. Traveling sales carriages come through to help people stock up." She scanned the little town. "Only seven buildings. Shouldn't be hard to find which one has the shop."

He motioned with his head. "The old blacksmith. No doubt about it. The front way is boarded up, but the boards are fresh. Unless the blacksmith just closed up shop a few days ago, that strikes me as the sort of place someone wants people to think is closed for good but opens up often enough to keep in good repair."

They crunched toward the shop. As they did, they swept their gaze across the town. An unwelcome discovery struck them both at the same time.

"The locals have made themselves scarce," Fel said.

"A vote in favor of them worried we're going to cause a stir," she said.

"Beats them planning to cause the stir themselves."

They approached the blacksmith shop, and both wordlessly came to the conclusion that it would be best to approach from the rear. Lattica kept a lookout. Fel looked over the shop. After a few days of having to think like a soldier, he found his mind quickly slipping into a more familiar and more comfortable point of view. The back of the blacksmith's shop held the forge, which was nestled under an overhanging roof and sitting on a stone slab. The chimney of the forge led up through the roof, and the heavy metal-and-stone device had the look, and smell, of something that had been used somewhat recently. The same could not be said for the anvil, which was orange with fat, loose flakes of rust. Something about this place was setting off warnings in his mind. He dropped down and cast an eye along the stones of the platform. They were uneven, but not suspicious. He took a few cautious steps forward and shifted his attention to the doorway. The threshold was wood. Just as uneven as the stones, but in a way that didn't make sense to him. The entire threshold was a bit higher than it should be, and one side was a half-inch higher than the other. He crouched and ran his fingernail along the piece of wood. A sliver of imperfection in the wood was even with the ground on one side and a quarter inch above it on the high side. He looked up to see that the top of the right side of the doorframe was fresher than the left side of the doorframe.

"This is a contraptioneer's shop. But not a very skilled one," Fel said. "Trapped. Pressure plate under the threshold. Some sort of a swinging trap up above. Smashes into the frame here. I'd bet my life that there's an alarm box hooked up to the door as well."

"What makes you say this isn't a skilled contraptioneer?"

"Alarm on the outside, trap on the inside. The way this is set up, you do damage first and scare someone off second."

"They could just want to make sure any interlopers are killed."

"Then put the trap on the inside and skip the alarm. You put the trap on the outside, you have to do repairs on the outside and it becomes obvious where the trap is."

He dropped his pack to the ground and pulled a short pry bar from inside. A bit of screwing added another foot and a half of handle to its end. He wedged it beneath the high end of the threshold and eased the wood plank out. Beneath was an extremely crude pressure plate. He grabbed a pair of pliers and eased a pin out of the mechanism. The trigger fell limply to the ground, no longer able to activate the trap.

"Are you going to be able to deactivate the alarm?" she whispered.

"There's going to have to be a way. Unless this person shows up and pries the boards off the front door and comes in that way whenever he visits the place, or else he sets off his own alarm every time he opens the door." He looked at Lattica. "Do we care if they know we were here?"

"They're going to know we were here regardless."

"That's the kind of excuse I love to hear," he said. "Not enough room for the borer. But I think this'll do the trick."

He rammed the pry bar behind the cross brace of the door and levered it out a bit. With the kind of precision positioning of someone who had plenty of practice, he worked one of the planks aside, then hammered it inward. The door practically fell apart, slumping into four slats that he was able to hammer free with the meat of his fist. He reached up through the gap he'd made, felt for something, and then reached into his bag for a pair of nippers. He snipped an unseen trip wire and kicked the door. It finished collapsing, and he stepped through into the darkened interior.

"No second alarm? I'm surprised," he said.

Lattica pulled a small lantern from her equipment bag. Fel lit it with his new sparker. The light didn't seem to penetrate as far, or with as much clarity, as Wick's flame. There were plenty of reasons to prefer a mundane lantern over one that could answer questions and snitch on your activities, and plenty reasons to prefer Wick. Right now, the rock-solid and eerily bright flame would have been an asset, because there was a *lot* to see.

"This is a very new shop," Fel said.

The interior of the shop had been recently cleared. The odd, rectangular sections of dust-free floor told the tale of where table legs and cabinets had lived for years before being moved. Fresh shelves had been constructed along opposite walls. Bits of metal sheet stock, metal bar stock, and coarse wood for building jigs had been arranged neatly on the shelves. Sturdy saws for cutting the metal bars hung on their own little pegs. Stands with complete sets of cold chisels, gravers, and files were like showpieces on the three workbenches that were clearly recent additions to the room. A device that looked like a wildly overgrown spinning wheel occupied a substantial part of the far wall, and stout drills with assorted bits were in an array around it. The floor around the contraption was littered with curly metal shavings.

"It's like someone was given a shopping list of what a contraptioneer's shop should have and purchased the most expensive version of each item."

He placed his hand on the spinning wheel device. "My father would kill for a lathe like this. Let's get some more light in here."

He approached one of the lamps built into the wall and raised his sparker.

"Wait," she said, grabbing his hand.

"What's wrong with... right... right, the flame. I should check. It would defeat the purpose of the trip if we lit more flames instead of snuffing them."

He deftly disassembled the lamp until he could access the wick. When it didn't reveal any contraption components, he lit it and moved to the next.

"What do you make of this place?" Lattica asked.

"Like I said, it's definitely a contraptioneer's shop. But not a working one."

Lattica kicked some of the metal shavings with the toe of her boot. "It looks like a working shop to me."

Fel lit another mundane lamp.

"A contraptioneer makes a living repairing contraptions. Where are the contraptions? That wall is full of raw stock. That's fine for fabricating simple parts of damaged contraptions, but no one knows how to make a contraption from scratch. That wall should be filled with broken contraptions or disassembled piles of spare parts."

He pulled the cover off another lamp.

"Look what we have here," he said, pulling an engraved plate from inside. "This must have been an important place, because they have a persistent lantern here. How in the world did they get their hands on one? Did your family have one stolen?"

"If they did, they didn't tell me."

"It is in good repair. Can't say for sure how old it is, because so close to the fire it is going to get discolored and such from the very first time it's lit. But this looks to be at least a bit fresher than what we have in Wick's lantern." He stuffed it in his bag. "At least this proves this was a worthy diversion. They were one spark away from having another flame we'd have had to snuff out, and one that could be used to light as many more as they want."

Fel heard the sound of metal clanking.

"If this isn't a working contraptioneer's shop, what do you call these?"

He turned. She was tapping the end of a reed basket bulging with shiny metal parts that was tucked behind the lathe. Fel thumped over and pulled a part from the basket. Every part in the basket was identical. They were tubes about the length of his index finger and twice as stout.

"These are replacement parts they fabricated. They look like the main pipe for those flame pipes we've found on the Bolivan agents."

He rubbed his finger across the sharp edge, then turned the tube about in the light. There were etchings on it. Done with precision. But there was more to the one he held and the rest than simple precision.

"How many baskets of components are there?" he asked, checking the lantern on the main workbench before lighting it and setting the first component down.

"It looks like there are four. And an empty basket. What have you found?"

Fel grabbed an item out of each and set them on the table. He positioned them and shifted them, then found a pair of detents that needed compression. He located the proper tool, pressed them into place, and managed to assemble most of a pipe.

"This is nearly a complete contraption, made from scratch. Either they had a supply of that final component salvaged from something else, or they have the ability to assemble this entire contraption from raw stock, and they just haven't gotten around to making that piece yet. Help me find the procedure. The instructions. There is no way this came from this person's head. Dad's been working his whole life to work out what it takes to make something from scratch. If there were someone working now who could do it, we'd know it."

"Why are you so sure?"

"Because *the world* would know it. What makes the Bygone Era 'bygone' is that we can't do this anymore."

The pair searched through the drawers and shelves in and around the workbenches. He found a small locked box and neatly sheared the lock off with the edge of the pry bar. Inside he found a stack of papers. He laid them out on the workbench.

"Step-by-step instructions. Not in some ancient language and translated. Anyone with a passing knowledge of the tools could use these to make what they call a sentry pipe," Fel said. He flopped down onto a stool in front of the workbench. "It's like they plucked it from a book. And it's clear why Dad hasn't been able to get the right effects out of his own attempts. The line between magic and machine is spelled out here. Engravings need to be made in a specific order. Components need to be assembled in a specific order initially. This is just the mechanical version of... whatever Tome would call it... an incantation or something."

Lattica pointed to the page.

"The steps are numbered, and there are some missing," she said.

He ran his finger along the page. "There are... probably those are the steps that require tools or ingredients we don't have. Which would explain how I was able to break one of these with my bare hands. These things aren't up to Bygone Era–build quality. And that *absolutely* means that this is taken from some sort of book, not the result of someone figuring it out or rediscovering it. You wouldn't have steps one through five, then step seven through ten, then steps thirteen through fifteen if you were making this up. This is word for word from a book."

He shut his eyes tightly and tilted his head back.

"Someone in league with the Bolivans has *exactly* the sort of book that Dad's been hoping to find his whole life. Why were they trying to kidnap Dad if they have someone who can feed them this kind of information?" He flipped through some pages. "And why do they have *only* this information? Why put together a whole shop just to build these sentry pipes?"

"Maybe that's the only thing they were able to find?"

"Awfully convenient that they found something that was precisely what they needed to make the most of having the sentry flame. And this shop is *new*. The parts are new. This whole thing couldn't have been running for more than a few months, judging from the wear on the tools and the setup. And if you had a shop that could churn out *new* contraptions, wouldn't you do whatever it took to keep it safe?"

Lattica looked over the pages. "If I had a person who could teach me how to make contraptions, it wouldn't really matter, would it? It's not the shop, it's the information."

"True." He tapped the table and furrowed his brow. "Do you get the idea that if your family and my family were here right now, and they knew what we now know, we'd have a whole new mission on our hands? I'd say finding whoever has this information is suddenly at least *as* important as clearing up the flames."

"We don't have any way to get in touch with the people who make the decisions," Lattica said.

"Then that makes this our decision to make, doesn't it?"

She hammered the workbench. "I don't make decisions, Fel. Not about this."

"It's time to take control of your life."

"If I was in control of my life, I wouldn't *be* here. I would be back on the farm with my father and I'd have enough money to survive. But I didn't have that option, so I handed over control and this is where we are."

"This is serious, Lattica. We can't just ignore it."

"Yes, Fel. It is. And yes we can," she said sharply. "This is already life and death. People have died. You dug a *grave*. When I look in the mirror, I don't see a woman who would ever do anything that would take a life, and yet I have. And do you know how I sleep at night with that knowledge? By remembering that this was not my choice. I am a hammer, and this is a nail. A nail doesn't get to blame the hammer for what happens. That's on the hand that holds the hammer. I have blood on my hands on someone else's behalf. That's why I stick to the procedures. That's why I depend upon tactics. Because it means I never have to decide that someone needs to die. That decision is made for me."

"So let's not decide that someone needs to die," Fel said.

"*We aren't in control of that,*" she said. "We have a plan, we stick to the plan."

Fel considered her words.

"Fine. We stay the course. But we're not leaving until we have some good idea about where this information man is. We were lucky to find this place without guards. I'm going to take full advantage." He paused. "And I'm also going to steal a bunch of these tools, because this person has some good equipment."

The wind outside started to whistle a bit.

"I think you can take your time. We're going to have some weather, and the horses aren't rested up."

"What do you think the odds are we get out of here without your bosses getting some more blood on your hands?"

"Not great. But I'll take what I can get."

Teya pulled herself easily along the sheer surface of the massive tree. After years of climbing stone cliffs, a surface that her claws could dig into was downright luxurious. In her hunting and foraging, and simply enduring the last lingering hours of hearing everything the wizard that Tome had marked was hearing, she'd observed the village quite a bit. There were large swaths of it that didn't have any walkable branches or roots and were thus ignored by the Children of the Forest. Strange that people who didn't have proper claws for climbing would choose to make their homes in the trees. But she could nearly reach the alcove containing Tome's things without ever exposing herself to a part of the village where prying eyes could see her. She couldn't get quite as close to the wizard alcove, but if she rounded the curve just a bit more, she could get a good sharp look at the room. More importantly, she could just barely hear what was going on within even without Tome's magic. That was enough.

Somewhere below, Parch was amusing himself by scaling lower trees and generally frolicking. Hopefully he would keep clear of the village proper, because until Tome's plan was complete, there wasn't time to keep him occupied.

She briefly shifted her gaze to the ground. It was daytime. Tome was out and about, supervised by Mevrelle as always. The paper mage was gazing up at the very same alcove. Teya flicked her frilled ear up and shut her eyes, focusing on the musical conversation going on inside. It wasn't as clear as when the mystical spying was active. She only heard bits and pieces of their conversation. But something rather noisy must have been going on that she couldn't hear, because one of the wizards in particular kept raising his voice.

"... Continue the incantation," he said. "I shall endeavor to locate a means to silence the horrid screeching."

Teya heard no screeching, but she seemed to remember from her prior adventures with Wick that she couldn't properly hear the flame unless she could feel its heat or light. She shivered at the thought that whatever they were doing was causing Wick to scream.

"Get the cover. And blast it, bring the coals here. Drawing the entity back to this flame only seems to work if we can keep the flame lit, and it keeps extinguishing it. I hadn't anticipated a contraption to be capable of self-defense."

Soft incantations grew louder.

"Good. Good. Fresh coals every few minutes. That should keep the lantern lit. By the High, the screeching. Covering the ears doesn't make a difference. The cover, quickly. Good. That helps. Keep the earring on the pedestal. It does not feel as though we'll get very many of them, from the speed at which the power is dwindling."

Teya flared her nostrils and snarled. This was torture. There was no other way to describe it. Though she could not hear the wails of their victim, she could practically *feel* the pain through their descriptions. She was listening to them mystically cutting into someone, harvesting something from a living creature. Her claws dug deeper into the tree. Her stout little body tensed.

She didn't know Wick very well. But she knew Fel, and she knew Tome. Even if they didn't always show it, she knew them to have good hearts. And she knew that they valued Wick. In Fel's case, certainly more than a simple tool. And that meant that Wick was *not* a simple tool. The Adept didn't feel the same about contraptions, even the ones that seemed alive. But the Adept had been wrong about contraptioneers. Knowing what she had been told and knowing what her eyes and ears and heart had told her were two very different things. And right now, the Children of the Forest were attempting to silence the screams of a victim to continue their work. That made them evil. Simple as that.

The long bow strapped to her back was tempting. She could find a perch, draw the string, and make her presence known. That would stop the torment, at least for a moment. But she pushed the thought aside. It wasn't in her nature to think ahead. Kobolds worked together with one another and leaned upon those they chose to follow for the broader plans. It was in a kobold's nature to do what it took to finish this step, to complete this task. The most important moment in a kobold's life was when it realized that sometimes the easy solution to a task wasn't always the best one. That doing the quick, certain thing now could produce slow, uncertain things later. Tome had a plan. She had to trust that Tome had thought it through.

But if his plan started to unravel... she would start pulling that bow string until there were no more arrows.

It was clear within hours that arriving at this town had been a small wonder. If they'd still been on the road, which they absolutely would have been if they had been heading directly for the next flame, they would have been caught in the freezing downpour. It wasn't cold enough for a proper blizzard, but everything the water struck quickly froze into either a sheet of ice or a slushy mess. Fel took some time out of his investigation to hammer the door back into shape and brace it against the wind. A small heating stove within the shop was called into service as both a heat source and a cooking fire.

"I cannot believe you turned old bread into something palatable," Lattica mused as she swirled the crunchy bits of crust in the bubbling, molten cheese in the pot.

"I fried it. Add butter, pepper, and heat to anything and it'll taste like heaven," he said.

She crunched the stale bread and nursed her share of the remaining brew.

"You don't have a woman?" she said.

"Maybe I do, maybe I don't. I've got my eye on one, but she's just starting to realize I exist."

"Where I come from if a man can prove he won't starve to death if the servants aren't around, he's a catch."

"Graves men don't do cooking?"

"Graves *women* don't even do cooking. Remember, they're all about specializing. No sense learning what to do with a pot and pan if you can hire someone who already knows. Same goes for raising children. Same goes for everything that isn't business or the nasty things you need to do to make sure you can keep doing business."

"And they married you in to do fighting? They hire people to cook their meals, but they marry people to do their fighting?"

"We hire plenty of guards. Family is for the important things."

He swished some crust of his own and took a bite. "Sounds awful."

"You're one to be giving advice. You let your family send you into ancient death traps to keep their shelves stocked."

"I don't 'let' my family send me. It's the family business. And I like doing it."

"Do you?"

"Not all of it. But it's a legacy, you know? The latest link in the chain. I'd prefer if people didn't wrinkle their noses at the idea of a contraptioneer. If we didn't do silver polishing and stock some mundane antiques, I doubt the average person would even risk coming in the store for fear of what people would think of them. But in the end, we're a long line of contraptioneers, and I'm glad to be playing my part. I'd be even *more* glad if I was better at it."

He wiped his hands on his shirt and made his way to a large chest they'd uncovered. It had been hidden under some floorboards that were suspiciously loose, which highlighted the likelihood that it contained something the owner of the workshop didn't want found. He'd been going through it one sheaf of pages at a time, and so far hadn't made any useful discoveries.

"This, for instance," Fel said, flipping through the latest stack. "This is coded. My dad could break this code, no doubt. My sister—Fanny, that is —has cracked a code like this in the past, too. But to me it's just weird marks and random letters. You want to take a stab?"

"I've already checked it against the Bolivan codes we know. It's not one of them."

"Right, but you could try figuring it out."

"No point."

He shook his head. "You seem dead set on settling with the first run of tiles."

"What?"

"Grum. You get a run of tiles, and then the whole point of the game is to come up with a better run."

"I married into a rich family!" she said.

"Right, that's *one* move. You got yourself a solid red queen on that one. You sure don't seem happy about it."

"I don't play grum. You know why? Because you're just as likely to lose what you've worked so hard for as win."

"Not if you're good at it."

"And how do you get good at it, Fel?"

"Practice."

"And what happens when you practice at grum and you're *not* good at it?"

"You lose money."

"Sounds like I'm ahead by just settling with what I started with."

"You're doing a dangerous job you don't want to do on behalf of a rich family you couldn't care less about. Doesn't sound like a win to me."

"And you're pining after a baker woman based upon what you *imagine* her to be. We're both bad at this."

"I mentioned Mariss?"

"You never stop talking about her. Her and Allie the barmaid."

"Well, who says I'm pining after Mariss because of what I imagine her to be?"

"Because even though you're constantly on about her, all you've told me about her is she's pretty, she's friendly, and she bakes pies."

"That's because that's all I know about her. It's taken me a while to break the ice. And besides. That's plenty to like already."

"You don't know anything about her heart."

"She's friendly."

"She's trying to sell you pies. Of course she's friendly."

"Look, I'll stop picking your life apart if you stop picking mine apart."

"Deal."

He flipped through the next set of papers.

"We've got some dates here. Probably pickup of finished sentry pipes. Near as I can figure, he's finished about sixty of them."

"And we've collected how many? Four?"

"Long road ahead of us. Though it won't matter if we can put out all the flames they have. These things aren't actual sentry lanterns. They just burn for a really long time. They still need to be lit from a sentry flame." He shuffled a few more pages. "Here we are. Handwritten notes."

He pulled out the next pile of pages and flipped through. The writing on the page had the large, precise curves of someone trying desperately to avoid making a mistake. It didn't speak well of the author's success that this pile of pages was a not-quite-accurate transcription of the instructions they'd discovered earlier. Page after page after page, he found duplicates with mistakes crossed off and corrected. Finally, on the sixth failed attempt, there was a clearly frustrated note.

"'The blasted flame speaks too quickly!'" Fel read. "He was transcribing the instructions from the flame."

"Not an enormous surprise," Lattica said.

"I suppose not. But good news for the Graves family if we can ever finish this mission. The lanterns remember *everything*, so those instructions are still in there. You'll be able to make these sentry pipes, provided you can get a halfway decent fabricator."

He glanced at the pile of equipment he was planning to steal, which included the sentry lantern.

"It is very tempting to light that lantern and see if we can learn something about that. Is this the only set of instructions that's been dictated into it? Or just the only set that this person was able to transcribe out of it?"

"We can't afford to give up our location. If they knew we were here, and this place is as important as you suggest, then that griffin would be upon us in hours, even *in* this storm."

Fel nodded. "How much have you used the sentry lantern?"

"I have never used it."

"Wick is a pretty good egg." He tilted his head. "Relatively speaking. I didn't talk to him for *years* because he ratted me out to my dad for breaking something in the lab. But since then he's been pretty decent. If your flame was half as agreeable, we might be able to just *ask* for information."

"If that information was freely available, I don't think you and I would be on this trip. I am *sure* my family interrogated the flame as the first resort rather than the last one."

"Right, but Wick can be tricky. He doesn't give up information sometimes unless you ask the right question, or in the right way. I'll bet the Graves people didn't ask for instructions on how to build contraptions, or who might have been providing or delivering them. By the High, we've assumed the Bolivans had found some way to extract information from the flame, right? How else would simply having a flame provide them with information? What is overheard by one flame isn't automatically distributed to the holders of other lanterns. But if they were just... *using* it. If they were layering their own schemes on top of the Graves business, then surely we can get that to work two ways. We just have to figure out how and why."

He flipped through the pages.

"Maybe I'll get lucky and there are notes to that effect..."

This particular form of incarceration was beginning to wear on Tome. He almost preferred the time in the cell. Not just because he'd learned that the overconfidence the elves had in their security measures and their apparently *very* deep sleeping habits meant he had time and privacy to plot and plan while locked away at night. Being "free" to roam the village without any permission to do anything had a way of underscoring how firmly in their grasp he was. Still, now that there was a scheme afoot, things were a bit different. Now his aimless wandering could provide him valuable information, and confirmation, that he could use later.

He tottered his way unsteadily up the stout vine coiling up the trunk of the tree he knew the wizards were working in. A few days of navigating their natural walkways had failed to provide him with any appreciable degree of expertise in that regard. But the moment he stepped onto the branch that would lead him to the wizard's room, Mevrelle grabbed him by the arm and hauled him back.

"Oh, am I no longer permitted to go this way?" Tome said innocently. "Forgive me. I suppose I was expecting my treatment to at least be *consistent*."

Mevrelle muttered something mellifluous. Judging by the circumstances it was used in, Tome was quite certain it was an expletive or invective. It brought him no small amount of pride to have earned it so many times.

"I wonder why I wouldn't be permitted to go that way today when I was specifically *invited* there yesterday," Tome said. "I wonder if perhaps you are hiding something from me."

Mevrelle muttered something a bit more forcefully.

"This is all theater," Tome said, plopping down to sit on the branch he'd been pulled to and gazing up at the room where the wizards were at work. "I've realized it, so I should hope you have. I know you understand me, at least a little. If I can figure out when you're cursing me, you should have figured out when I'm taunting you. Unless you are particularly thick."

The ranger fixed him in a steely gaze, but remained silent.

"And you must know that I have capabilities you can't defend against. That I have knowledge you can't overcome. I know you know this, because you're treating me like a wild animal, constantly on the verge of attack. This letting me walk the grounds? It's for show. You're trying to convince me that I'm of no concern. But I know the truth. And so do you. You know that because I am freely able, by my very nature, to cross the wall that you cannot even *consider* crossing without doing mental gymnastics, I have an inherent superiority over you. I have something you don't. And that is *destructive* to you. Because you've got your whole mind wrapped up in the belief that *you* are superior. You must believe that, and to grant even a moment of consideration that you are equal, or may the High forbid it, *inferior* in some way, then your whole identity collapses."

Mevrelle tugged a dagger from his robes and pointed with its tip.

"Oh? Am I to move? Is even *this* place no longer acceptable? Perhaps I'm getting too close to a sore spot..."

He stood and paced back down the vine. When he reached the next reasonable branching point, he stepped onto it and was not threatened. As he paced along it, he turned his eyes to the wizard's room. They were leaving. One carried a cloth-covered shape that could only be Wick's lantern. Another carried a small wooden box. Both of the items were held firmly while they walked with particular care. Precious items. The procedure was done. If they were transporting Wick's lantern with care, it meant he was still valuable to them. If they were transporting the box with care, it meant it contained what must have been the successful results of their procedure. The chances were very good that if something was not done, tomorrow, they would either destroy Wick, or create all the mental anchors they needed, or both. In the best case, a valued ally would be lost. In the worst case, some sort of military plan would begin. Time was running out. Push had come to shove.

"The time has come. I'm through waiting. I demand an audience with your leader."

Mevrelle looked upon him with an impassive expression.

"I know that you are conducting experiments on the sentry lantern. I know that the goal of those experiments is to cross the wall. I know you have generated a mental anchor for this purpose, and that it is your intention to destroy the sentry lantern in your pursuit of more items of that nature. Now is your chance, your *only* chance, to discuss your plans openly and come to an equitable diplomatic agreement. Take me to your leader this instant and perform no further experiments."

Mevrelle's only reaction was to cock an eyebrow.

"I am a representative of the people beyond the wall, and I am an ally of Kazel's. In short, I am a single individual who can bring upon your village the full wrath of two worlds. Do as I say, or what follows falls squarely upon your shoulders."

Mevrelle crossed his arms.

"So be it. But when in a few moments you are scrambling to determine what's to be done to preserve your village, do remember that it all could have been avoided if you'd used your brain in this moment."

Tome raised his hand. Rather theatrically, he snapped his fingers. For a few moments, the only result was a soft snicker from Mevrelle and one or two other elves glancing in his direction to see what the snapping was about. The next change was felt only by Tome, a sudden weariness, like someone had tapped into his spirit and wrung it out. Then came a smoldering blue light in the air above the village. Eyes turned toward it; voices rose up in concern. The light arranged itself into the form of an eagle. Arrows started to hiss through the air, bursting from unseen rangers among the trees. It streaked to the north, unhindered by the attacks.

Seeing the construct of light and magic flit off and away caused Tome's scalp to throb. It had taken half the night and an uncountable number of jabs to his scalp with a thorn to compose the spell that had conjured it. It was nothing but an illusion, one of the types of magic he was most skilled at concocting, but there was no way for the elves to know that. And as if to underscore that fact, the next thing he felt was a hand around his throat and the point of a knife in his ribs.

Mevrelle growled something in his language. Even without Tome understanding his words, his meaning was clear.

"I imagine you wish to know what was just sent north. It was a messenger. Within the day, Kazel will be made aware of what has happened. And I *certainly* hope you aren't entertaining the possibility of killing me. When, not if, Kazel arrives, if he does not find me here to calm his wrath, your precious home will lie in cinders. Of course, it isn't as though I shall *require* his aid. That little demonstration was a fraction of my power. I am more than capable of finishing you all myself. Now. I'll have my audience with your leader, if you please."

A few minutes later, Tome was struggling to keep the smugness from his face as he looked upon the reaction to his little ruse. He'd been led to the low, level section of the forest that would in a proper city be called a courtyard. By his count, twenty rangers had formed a circle around him, bows primed and ready. Seven wizards were present as well, soft incantations keeping the air alive with some manner of magic he couldn't hope to comprehend. And, finally, he saw Kott emerge from a particularly sturdy and grand tree with a female elf positively laden in exquisite cloth in tow. The rangers and wizards separated to let her through.

"You have made a grave mistake, human," Kott said.

"As the one responsible for diplomacy, that we now stand at the brink of war would appear to be at least partially your fault, Kott. But you can be excused. I don't imagine you've had much call for diplomacy of late, since you've been trapped behind a wall and huddling fearfully in the shadow of Kazel."

"Your inflammatory words do no good. We will not be intimidated, even in light of this act of aggression," Kott said.

"That? An act of aggression? I'm sorry, but was *I* the one who ambushed an outsider peacefully entering the Greater Lands? Am I the one who captured and imprisoned said newcomer? Am I the one who robbed him? Who assaulted an ally?"

"The sentry lantern is a *thing*, a tool," Kott said.

"That is not for you to decide. I want it returned, and I want the mental anchor you were able to construct handed over. I can't have deceitful creatures such as yourselves breaching the wall and running about in my world unsupervised, now can I?"

"You have been spying on us," Kott said.

"I have been keeping you under surveillance because I rightly supposed you could not be trusted."

"We found the lingering remnants of a mystic target on Fallesse. It has been wiped away. Furthermore, we have gathered the full force of our village's defenses, and the full force of our local mystics. You are at the center of a focused field of mystic nullification. It would take a wizard more potent than all our forces combined to conjure any mystic effect in your state."

"Mmm... I felt a rather significant mystic pressure. Impressive defensive measure. It won't do you any good, but at least now I know you genuinely take me seriously. I trust that means you're ready to discuss what it will take to quell the wrath of Kazel."

"You are an outsider. You do not have the authority to call upon Kazel."

"My associate and I are responsible for freeing Kazel from his bonds. He owes us. We have all the authority we need. And really, you shouldn't be talking about authority after the act of war you committed simply by bringing me here. You've shown me your maps. We were not within the borders of your territory when you captured me."

Kott conferred with the queen.

"For the sake of openness, what would be your diplomatic demands?" Kott said.

"Only some very small and very reasonable concession. You will return to me what belongings of mine are still intact, you will compensate me for what equipment has been damaged or destroyed. You will hand over the mental anchor you created, and you will escort me to the wall so that I can depart."

"You ask too much."

"Then make your case to the dragon."

"You act as though we are shivering weaklings in the face of the ancient dragon. We are an equal match to the beast."

"Please," Tome said, rolling his eyes. "He's spent centuries trapped in the heart of the mountain, and you didn't move on his territory. It is clear you have imperialist tendencies, given what you've tried to do with Wick.

The mere suggestion that Kazel might still be there to turn you away should you attack was enough to keep you here. And need I remind you, the mechanisms of Kazel's captivity were crafted by the ancestors of my associate. The monster that terrifies you is in turn terrified of me. So you should..."

Tome trailed off. There was a new sound. Though there was already a subdued din of murmured incantation and barely restrained fury, somehow this tiny, clippity-clop was glaring. Eyes turned to the tree from which the sound seemed to be originating. Parch, blissfully unaware or unconcerned about the focused martial might, pranced through the crowd and made his way to Tome.

"What is this?" Kott said.

"It's a lesser unicorn," Tome said. "I should think you would know that."

"What is it doing here? Lesser unicorns, as with nearly all lesser creatures, have been gone from these woods for ages. ... This came with you, didn't it?"

The leader raised her voice, barking demands. Tome didn't know precisely what she was saying, but were he to wager, he would assume she was insisting there may be other allies around, and that the village be searched for them. The elves began to stir, eyes rising and searching the surrounding trees. Tome felt the urge to bolt, but without the aid of a well-written spell, he had little hope of avoiding the arrow of a single ranger, let alone all of them. He heard the strings of bows creaking. He held his breath and closed his eyes. Then, one by one, he heard the bows relax again. A moment later, he heard the first of the elves strike the ground.

Again he felt the drain on his spirit. Dizzyingly strong, but he was able to endure it. He opened his eyes. The elves were wavering on their feet. Some wore expressions of dull surprise and confusion. Others simply dropped. But within a few seconds, the entirety of the village had dropped to the ground, sound asleep.

Tome took a deep, terrified breath. His plan, his *proper* plan, had been to bluff the entire village into taking him seriously enough to bend to his demands. The second half of his evening of painful spell-writing had been spent concocting the most powerful spell he could conjure for inducing sleep on the locals. It was written on a leaf, and one quite mystically attuned, so it was bound to be powerful. And it was targeted upon elves in general, which had its own impact on the potency of the spell. Piling on top of that the observation that elves were extremely deep sleepers and seemingly highly susceptible to paper magic, it stood to reason they wouldn't have the constitution to resist a sleep spell. But he hadn't trusted it to actually work on the whole village, and now that it had, he didn't trust it to keep them asleep for long.

"I do good?" echoed a voice from high in the trees.

Tome raised his gaze and scanned until he spotted Teya near where the equipment was held.

"Excellent timing," Tome said. "Grab everything you can and meet me west of the village."

"Parch, come! Help carry!" Teya chirped.

The unicorn bleated gleefully and bounded among the sleeping elves to scale the tree.

"That blasted thing listens to everyone but me," Tome muttered as he crouched to harvest some gear from the fallen elves. He was going to need everything he could get, because survival at this point depended upon him reaching the wall before they were able to reach him, and he had no idea how long they would remain asleep.

CHAPTER 13

Lattica slid gently from sleep to the sound of a softly slapping shutter. After the trip they'd been having, holing up in this workshop was turning out to be downright luxurious. From the sound of crackling ice outside the workshop, the icy storm had finished during the night and the morning sun was helping the world begin to shrug off its frosty coat. The melting ice must have been how the shutter that had held during the storm had finally been dislodged. She frowned at the cool breeze coming in through the window. The stove and the repaired door kept the cold and wind at bay far better than the stiff canvas of the wagon. That and the rich but delicious cooking Fel had been doing had made this little morsel of the trip feel like a holiday.

A grating snore drew her attention to the far corner of the floor. Fel was still quite noisily asleep. Lattica felt something between relief and gratitude that she'd been able to sleep without any concern that Fel would behave in an ungentlemanly manner. He was blunt and abrasive, but at least he was genuine and decent. That made him twice the man most of the people the Graves family did business with were. One could not take for granted that a man would behave himself, and her size and strength weren't always enough of a deterrent to persuade them to keep their hands to themselves. Having someone like him along for the ride was nearly enough for her to question if perhaps there *was* some better version of her life waiting for her. A man who saw her as more than a means to an end.

The musing flitted from her mind as quickly as it had come, thanks to a soft shadow drifting across the crack in the shutter. She hurried to the window and pushed it fully open. Something far too big to be a bird was sweeping through the sky. She squinted at the bright clouds. It was the griffin. She couldn't be sure it was the precise griffin they were worried about, but she doubted there were very many of them about. The thing was wheeling in slow circles in the air, like it was circling something on the ground a few miles away. As it rounded the near part of its circle, she caught its profile against the clouds. It had no rider.

"Fel! Fel!" she hissed, her voice pointlessly at a whisper.

She grabbed a boot from where she'd left it beside the door and pitched it in his direction.

"Ow!" he yelped.

"Something's up. The griffin is in the air," she said.

"What?" Fel said, sluggishly pulling himself to his feet.

"There's a griffin in the air. It's circling something."

"Is it heading this way?"

"What are the chances that it isn't?"

"True. Is the storm over?"

"It is."

"How fast do you think we can get the horses ready to move?"

"A few minutes. But that thing just needs to tip its wings, and it'll be here in moments."

"The horses are better rested and better fed than they've been for most of the trip. They'll be able to move. You get out there and get them ready. I'll grab everything we need to bring with us and see if I can find a way to keep that thing distracted. I'll use one of the lures. It won't be as potent, but it's better than nothing."

A squirrelly man with a hunted expression snapped the reins of his little goat cart. He kept casting nervous glances toward the sky.

"Just focus on getting this ridiculous cart to the workshop. The quicker you do, the quicker this is all over," said Questor.

It had seemed too good to be true that he might be getting a defensive contraption for his trouble on this assignment. He thus should not have been surprised when things turned out to be a lot more bothersome than he'd anticipated. The fabricator in service of the Bolivans did not live in the same town as his workshop. He lived another few hours along the mountain. He'd stammered something about how there wasn't a proper space in his town, but it was difficult to get a straight answer out of him with the griffin around. He couldn't even get the man out of his house without sending the griffin circling above rather than waiting on the ground. Now, while Questor suffered the indignity of riding in the cart beside him, the fabricator couldn't keep his mind on the road. The man was jumpier than the goats pulling his cart.

"My workshop is just ahead," the fabricator said.

"How long will it take you to prepare the contraption?" Questor asked.

"Let me see it again," he said.

Questor pulled the strange metal plate from his bag and handed it to him. The plate didn't look like any contraption he'd seen before, though he was hardly an expert. To his eye, it looked more like a pointlessly ornamental piece of armor.

"If the instructions are right, and I only have to put some new etching on one of the whatsits on the inside here, I can have it done by tomorrow."

"Whatsits?" Questor said. "You don't know what they're called?"

"How should I know what they're called? All I do is follow directions."

They approached the crushed stone of the space behind the workshop. Questor tensed a bit as his well-trained senses started issuing warnings. The gravel didn't show much in the way of evidence of motion. But here and there it seemed disturbed in a way that struck him as recent, revealing dark undersides of stones facing up.

"Does anyone else come here and do anything?" Questor asked.

"No. I'm the only one. Why?"

"I think someone left this place in a hurry. Enter with caution."

The fabricator hopped from the cart and marched to the doorway.

"I have to enter with caution every time I enter, because there are traps, you see. And alarms. And I..." He paused and glared at the door. "Someone's been monkeying around. Look at the door. It's all beat up.

Blast it. The traps are supposed to *prevent* that. Stand back. I need to do this right, or my head is liable to be bashed to bits."

Questor gave the door a wide berth and instead scanned the area around. Whoever had done this was certainly gone. His instinct told him that. But if they were able to defeat traps to enter the place, they were skilled. They knew what they were doing. As if to underscore the price of failed vigilance, his injured side throbbed.

"They went and disabled the threshold trap," the man grumbled, staring down at the space below a dislodged hunk of wood. "You can do it with just that one pin there? I wish I'd known that. It would have made things easier."

The fabricator thumped the abused door with the palm of his hand, gradually inching it open.

"Cover your ears. They probably cut the alarm, but just in case," he warned, clamping one ear against his shoulder and plugging the other with his finger as he thumped the last few times.

The door swung open. No alarm rang out.

"Stay here. I need to check the inside."

Questor did as he was told, though he wouldn't have dared enter the place right now regardless. He knew something was about to happen. He just needed to figure out what.

"They've rummaged through my things. Half the tools are gone! *Ouch!* And they stretched blasted *strings* across the floor?"

Questor's eyes widened.

"Strings? As in a trip wire?" he shouted.

"If that was to trigger a trap, it didn't trigger."

Questor tried to check the whole world around him at once. The last place he looked, for fear of what he would find, was the sky. Above, the griffin's head had cocked unnaturally. It turned its fierce gaze downward, fixed on the workshop.

"They've done it again," he barked, dashing inside.

"Hey! I told you to stay out. There could be—"

"You shut up. Where is it? The string!"

The answer came not from the startled and stammering fabricator, but from the smoldering glow of mystic flames slowly consuming a piece of paper pinned under the leg of a workbench. He snatched the paper and dashed outside. The rustle of wings in full dive could be heard from above. He crumpled the smoldering spell and pitched it as far as he could manage. A ball of paper didn't travel very far, even with the strongest of throws. But it flew far enough to clear the overhang of the sheltered forge area. The spell hadn't finished bouncing to a rest on the gravel when the griffin pounced upon it, scratching and clawing a divot into the gravel.

Once the page was destroyed, the thing came to its senses and grew still, awaiting its next command. Questor took a deep breath and exhaled, his heart thumping in his chest. He turned. The fabricator was inside the workshop, hiding behind one of the workbenches.

"Wh-what was *that*?" he stammered.

"That was someone trying to destroy your workshop. It means they know they can't afford to have you finish your job. Which means you need to get to work."

"Get to work? With that mad beast outside?"

"Unless you activate any more lures, I'm the one you should be worried about, not the griffin. Now, can you prepare the contraption?"

"My best tools are missing."

"Answer the question."

"I have spares. I can get it done, I think. Just a bit of engraving. It will take longer without my good tools."

"Get it done."

"But someone did this. They could be—"

"I know who did this. If they are smart, they are already a long way away. And I'd like to believe no one would get this close to killing a griffin rider *twice* without being smart."

"Anyone?" Lattica called.

"No griffin on our tail. With any luck either the rider, the workshop, or the griffin is gone. Maybe all three," Fel said, keeping watch out the back of the carriage.

"We need a plan for if none of that happened," Lattica said.

"If the workshop is intact, who cares? I stole the instructions and a bunch of the tools and finished pieces. If the rider survived, good luck catching us without a griffin. And if the griffin AND the rider survived... we'll have to work on that."

"Whatever we do, we need to work on getting that saddle off the beast."

"Easier said than done. The problem is you have to get *under* it. And if you hadn't noticed, that's where the claws are. And a griffin has claws on all four legs, not just the front ones. Not that hooves are any kinder when you're underneath them."

"Hence the need for a plan," Lattica said.

"No amount of planning is going to change the fact that the buckle is under the griffin."

"Do we have any other spells that will be of any use?"

"I've got a couple fire spells, a couple ice spells, and one lure spell. And that's all. It would have been nice if Tome had given me some taming spells, but I think he kept them to use on Parch. How is the indicator looking?"

"Same direction. No wavering."

"None?"

"None."

Both of them were silent for a moment.

"I imagine you are thinking the same thing I'm thinking," Lattica said.

"We're getting awfully close to the next big flame," Fel said.

"And we're in the heart of Bolivan territory," Lattica said.

"There should be *someone* with a flame, shouldn't there? We just left the place where they were making the pipes that let them carry around the flame."

"It made sense for the Graves family to be careful with the flames to avoid the very problem we're working to solve, but the Bolivans should be spreading them far and wide. They are plainly *planning* to spread them far and wide."

"We already know the detector can detect them when they get close enough. Maybe they've figured that out and are trying to keep their pipes far enough away to keep us from detecting them."

"That would require them to know exactly where we are. And to have known where we are for most of the trip. And if they knew where we were all this time, they would have been doing a much better job at stopping us."

"Maybe the person who made the pipes was doing a lousy job. Maybe they're running some sort of big scheme and most of their people are involved with that. Maybe they're afraid of us."

"That's a lot of maybes."

Fel cast a final glance at the sky behind them before moving up to the front to join her.

"Lots of maybes. Which is why planning is overrated. You spend all this time thinking up things that may or may not be true and then, at best, one of them is. The closest thing I had to a plan for what to do next was figure out who's been doing their designs, and you talked me out of it. And I'm glad, honestly. Now we've just got a device pointing in a direction. We head in that direction, and once we get where we're going, we do what we're supposed to do and decide what comes next."

Lattica shut her eyes tightly.

"I'd love to argue, but right now the possibilities are making my head swim. I am ready and willing to embrace ignorance for a while."

"Good! Always choose ignorance. You'll sleep better. I guarantee it."

Tome huffed and puffed as he scrambled through the thick foliage of the forest. He'd been moving as near to constantly as he could manage for hours, but just as there wasn't much to identify the elven village, there was nothing even approaching a road leading away from it.

"You're sure this is the right direction," he said breathlessly.

"To river? Where came you last time? Yes!" Teya said.

The little kobold was much more accustomed to navigating the wilderness, but the stubbier limbs meant she wasn't really any faster than Tome was.

"I thought we would see the wall by now. Or at least the river," Tome said.

"This fast? Four days," Teya said.

"What?" Tome said. "They got me here from the wall in less than two."

"Yes. Ride things."

"... Right..." Tome said.

"You not plan?"

"I *planned* to have them escort me back to the wall."

"How long they sleep?" Teya asked.

"I don't know! I've routinely underestimated the efficacy of the magic spells that are properly written here and with local materials. It's clear that blood is a significant amplifier, and it was written on a leaf drawn from the very trees they call home, and they are weak to sleep *and* paper magic. It was the best possible case for amplifying the location, target, and caster elements of a spell. But even so, that was an *entire* village. I would be very much surprised if they slept more than an hour or two. They're certainly awake by now."

Teya nodded. "So they find us."

"They'll be after us, certainly."

"And then? What plan?"

"I don't know! I didn't include travel time. You try stabbing your head with a thorn for ten hours instead of sleeping and see how clear your mind is. I'm lucky the spell even worked!" He leaned against a tree to catch his breath. "They're looking for us right now, I know it."

He rubbed his head with his free hand, again wincing at the dull ache of his abused scalp.

"I don't suppose elves are terrible trackers who are likely to miss us."

Teya shook her head.

"And they know right where we're headed. There's only so much forest they'll need to search. We need a new plan. A better plan. Come on. Cover."

The trees had been getting steadily smaller as they moved away from the elven village. It meant a thicker underbrush, but also many more small and subtle places to hide. He spread some tall grass and slipped into the cover of two arched trees. Teya and Parch joined him.

Teya, in yet another example of her excellent execution of his instructions, had managed to bundle up a considerable amount of equipment and goods from the two protected alcoves he'd suggested. They were gathered into two heaps, one strapped to Parch's back, the other strapped to Teya's back. Tome pulled open one bundle and started to sift through.

"I don't see any other spells... They did burn the spells I wrote. But the codebook is still here. And my nonmystic journals. At least they could tell the difference between magic writings and notes. Where is Wick?"

He pulled open the second bundle of equipment and found the unlit lantern. It was visibly worse for wear. Though the lantern itself wasn't damaged, it was badly blackened inside and out across the entire lower third of the device. Tome was hardly an expert, but it *seemed* intact.

"Give me a moment to work out a way to light it," Tome said.

Teya shook her head and took the lantern. She produced a sparker, the very one Fel had given her, and lit the flame. Once it was smoldering, she set it down, and they all closely observed.

Wick, until now, had only ever had two states. When he was present, the flame was steady. When he was absent, the flame flickered naturally. After a few seconds passed and the flame rose up to its full height, Tome and Teya were treated to a third, far more disturbing result. The color of the flame shifted from warm yellow to a blood orange. There was no breeze, but the flame fluttered and sputtered like it was in a gale-force wind. And then, the voice.

It came distantly at first, as if from the end of a long, echoing hallway. As it grew nearer, it grew louder. Screaming. Wick was a being defined by steady, chipper clarity. The most unsettled Tome had ever heard him was when he'd demanded to be kept clear of the archive. It made the agony evident in his voice so wretchedly terrible to hear.

"Wick. Wick, calm down. They're gone."

"I can still feel it. Like claws raking my mind!" he shouted.

Tome closed his eyes and touched his fingers to the base of the device. Among what was becoming an unpleasantly long list of things he realized he was weaker at than he would have liked to be was "passive" magic. He could create magic, and by virtue of working with it for so long he'd developed some minor intuition and sensation about its use. But he was exceedingly novice in the art of detecting enchantment. Nevertheless, he could feel some residue of magic clinging to this thing.

"Clarification. Expulsion," Tome muttered.

The pens were missing from his things as well. Tome snapped a stick and started to scratch out what he hoped would be an adequate purification spell on the blackened bottom of the lantern. He didn't bother adding an activation section to the spell. It needed to activate as soon as possible. And so it did, sparkling with blue as the portions he'd scratched into the soot became sufficient for effect. The shapes of the runes started to spread and become indistinct, like the spell was pushing the soot aside to consume itself. The screaming started to ease. When Tome was through, Wick had recovered somewhat, still shaken, but no longer in pain.

"That was... terrible," Wick said.

"What did they do to you?" Tome asked.

"I do not know how to articulate it. I have no physicality, no form. But it felt as though they were stripping away the very structure of my being. Not *me*, but the constructs that allow me to be. The connections that hold me together. I have never felt anything before, but this *must* have been pain. I feel... reduced. Diminished."

"Will you recover?"

"I do not know. Possibly? The pain is gone, but I can feel the wounds still."

"Can you get a message to the others?"

"Perhaps. But it will take me more time. I've been... hiding. In the space between the lanterns. I need to gather myself to make the full trip."

"Don't go," Teya said.

"I think it is important to—" Tome began.

"Message now? Not help. Friend hurt. Let friend rest," Teya said.

Tome rubbed his head. "I think you're right. Do you want the flame lit or extinguished?"

"I would prefer to hear a friendly voice. To watch and to see. It is my purpose. It is comfortable to me."

"All right then. But you may have to be covered at some point. We are certainly being followed."

"Thank you for your consideration," Wick said.

Tome sifted through the things. Inside a wooden box he found what could only be the results of their experiment. It was a large silver hoop earring, and even to Tome's limited skills of mystic detection, it was warm with enchantment. If Wick could be said to have been stitched together with threads that connected the various lanterns that bore his influence, one of those threads had been torn free and woven around this piece. If there was a way to remove the thread and return it to Wick, Tome certainly didn't know it. Were he to hazard a guess, he would suppose that the connection was intrinsic to the earring now, as much a part of the piece of jewelry as it had been a part of Wick.

As he turned it about in his hands, he noticed Teya's gaze fixed upon it. Her paws were clutched in front of her, eyes wide with desire and longing.

"So pretty..." she murmured. "Can feel?"

"It isn't doing me any good," Tome said.

He dropped it in her hand. She squealed with glee.

"Precious thing. Magic thing," she chittered. "Shiny thing."

"Don't get too used to it," Tome said. "We may need it to heal Wick."

"No," Wick said. "I do not want it. They have twisted it. I can see it. Like diseased flesh. I am better without it now."

"You're sure?" Tome said.

"I am quite sure," Wick said.

"Can have? For me?" Teya said.

"I am not certain it is wise that you—"

Teya didn't wait for permission. With a sharp jab, she poked the hook of the hoop through her frilled ear. The motion produced a brief squeak of pain and a small trickle of dark blood.

"Do you feel any different?" Tome asked.

She leaned down and rubbed some soot from the door of the lantern so she could see herself.

"Feel pretty," she said.

A breeze stirred the foliage around them. It sent a bolt of fear through Tome and reminded him that he was working on an unknown deadline.

"A plan... a plan... I need a taming spell. A lure and a taming spell. We attract something we can ride, and we tame it."

"You can do?" Teya said.

"I hope so, because I don't have any other ideas."

"You need thorn? Leaves and thorn?" she offered.

"I..." He winced. "I suppose. I need all the power I can get if I'm to write these quickly enough to be of any use. But I'm beginning to feel weak. Not just from loss of blood. I think... I think using blood for the magic takes something more out of me than the blood itself. I feel drained. But better drained tomorrow than dead today."

Teya turned to dash off for supplies.

"Wait! What do the elves ride?" Tome said. "I need to know, because if I write a lure for the same sort of creature, I'll just bring them directly to us."

"Bird-horse things," Teya said.

"Winged horses?"

"Not bird horse. Bird-horse things."

"You'll need to do better than that, Teya."

She held her paws to her head, claws pointing out in a crown.

"With pointies."

"Winged unicorns?"

She grunted angrily. "Pointies!"

"Unicorns have pointies!" Tome countered.

She gave him a hard look, then pointed to Parch's horn.

"Pointy." She held her claws to her head again, waggling one at a time. "Pointy, pointy, pointy, pointy. *Pointies.*"

"Antlers," Tome said.

"Yes. This."

"Winged creatures with antlers," Tome said, sifting through his memories of old bestiaries. "... Perytons? Winged stags?"

Teya pointed to him. "This!"

"Then we'll need something large, low, and fast. Good. Fetch the materials. I'll start dreaming up the spell. Hopefully I can wring enough blood from myself to finish the spell before I pass out."

A few frenzied minutes later, Tome looked blearily at the broad leaf he'd been writing on. There was no doubt now. A handful of spells written in blood had taken their toll. When a single mistake could mean complete failure or, perhaps more disastrous, unexpected results, working with a fuzzy mind was hardly ideal. It was made somewhat more difficult by the fact that Teya and Parch weren't sitting quietly or even having the decency to tremble in fear. Instead, after carefully packing up everything Tome didn't need into neat little bundles, they had been alternately foraging for snacks and playing headbutts.

As Tome scratched out what should be the second-to-last line of the final spell, Teya and Parch came tromping back. Parch was munching on something green. Teya slurped some sort of a squirmy tail into her mouth and crunched away.

"You done?" she asked.

"Nearly."

"Be done." She pointed to the sky. "Forest kids looking."

"They're on the move?"

"In air. Three. One that way. One that way. One that way."

She indicated north, south, and west.

"There's one to the west? That's the direction we're heading."

She nodded. "Looking too far."

"They must have assumed we'd have covered more ground. Rare that falling short of expectations is a benefit."

He paused to rub his eyes and try to sharpen himself up. Teya rummaged around in her pouch, found something that looked like a particularly fancy mouse, and popped it in her mouth with all the casualness of someone snacking on a cricket at The Fox and Log.

"Aren't you afraid?" Tome asked.

Teya nodded. "Scary."

"You don't show it."

She shrugged.

"Always scared." She tapped her chest. "One small thing. All around? Big things. Scary things. But you and me? That's *two* small things. And Parch? Three small things. And Wick? *Four*. Enough small things? Less not safe. If not? Good at run. Good at hide."

"Safety in numbers."

"Not safe. Less not safe."

"Does it ever concern you that you can't excel in isolation? That you need help to thrive?"

Teya cocked her head, as if it was the first thing she'd heard today that she truly didn't even know how to conceive of.

"I think maybe it's my thinking I need to consider, not yours."

She trotted forward and poked the spell. "Work. Then think."

"Fine advice. I have written the taming spell. Rather more powerful than I need, I hope. And..." He scraped out a few final shapes. "That should complete the lure spell. I've targeted something of fairly weak mind, fairly strong body. Large enough to carry us all, and flightless."

"It want kill? Like Duurth?"

"Unfortunately the desire to destroy the lure is the only reliable means I've been able to develop to attract a creature."

Teya nodded. "You wait."

She grabbed the bundles of gear and scampered up the nearest tree. After a moment, Parch bounded from branch to branch to join her.

"Now you go," Teya said.

"Your confidence in the efficacy of my lure spell is heartening, if not your confidence in my plan in general."

Teya scanned the sky from her higher vantage while Tome crept from their relative cover to prepare the lure.

"Fast, fast," she said, eyes fixed on a point in the sky that could only be an advancing ranger.

He tore the spell and dashed back into cover. The seconds ticked by tensely. Tome strained his ears. He even considered climbing up into the tree with Teya to keep a better watch on the approaching enemy. Barely twenty seconds had passed when he heard the devastating thunder of hooves. Teya peered off to the north.

"You call one?"

"It's a lure. There wasn't any sort of limitation applied. That would have taken pages and pages of additional—"

"You get many," Teya said tensely.

"How many..."

"Many!"

Tome revisited the possibility of joining Teya in the tree, and once the trembling of the ground made it clear that remaining on the forest floor would be unwise in the very near future, he put that plan into action. The combination of several days of traipsing across much larger trees and the highly effective motivation of avoiding a trampling was a potent one. He reached Teya's branch just as the first of the creatures arrived.

Until they arrived it hadn't occurred to Tome that there might be mystics that he didn't have at least a passing awareness of. Surely anything sufficiently wondrous would have found its way into myth, legend, story, and song. And anything *insufficiently* wondrous would have been eaten, stomped on, or otherwise destroyed by the wonders. But that notion was permanently banished from his mind with the arrival of the monsters answering his magical call.

What had felt like a stampede turned out to be merely three creatures. By their shape, Tome was inclined to call them moose. By their size, elephant felt closer to the mark. If he'd been on the ground, he wouldn't have been able to reach much past the monsters' knees. Even from his place in the tree, if the things took a particular interest in him, a tilt of the head and swipe of an antler would easily sheer off the branch he was huddled on.

"My magic is so much more powerful here, and somehow it reliably makes things worse..." Tome grumbled.

"Now what?" Teya said.

"Now we need to drop onto the back, tear the spell, and hold it to its body until the spell flares away."

All three dire moose pawed and mashed at the lure. It would have been instantly shredded if not for the fact that the three moose were equally motivated to destroy it and thus had to jockey for position to get to it.

"Go. Do," Teya said.

"You're not going to be the one who does it?"

She shook her head.

"Too much to hope for," he said.

Tome took a breath and waited for one of the things to maneuver roughly beneath him. It was an enormous target. All he had to do was stay on for the handful of seconds it would take for the taming to take effect. The timing of his leap was determined not by logic or instinct, but by a thumping hoof against the trunk that dislodged him. He flailed through the air and thumped onto the broad, musky flank of the monster. It didn't care enough to try to shake him off. He activated the spell and pinned it to the monster with his body.

The effect was mercifully swift and more than apparent. The dire moose beneath him calmed and became still while the others, now with one less eager stomper to contend with, mashed the lure to paste and gradually came to their senses. Small, glassy eyes surveyed the splintered section of forest. They dimly decided that there was no reason to linger and meandered away. Teya dropped down, followed by Parch.

"Good work!" Teya said. "Now go, fast!"

"Right, right," he said, scrambling forward to straddle the moose's neck as best he could. "Forward!"

Allie had lost track of how long they'd been on the road. Things had slipped into a bit of a routine which, honestly, wasn't entirely unpleasant. Mariss had become accustomed to the uncertainty of the trip and thus the flow of words shifted from deluge to conversation. Oiler had become a bit more obvious in its direction as well. Far from the vague glances that were their only means of identifying Fel's location when the journey began, with each request for an update, Oiler became more intent in peering off to the northeast. It had the nervous energy of an excitable dog that knew it would be let off its leash just as soon as its owner arrived. Fel was close. He had to be.

Further evidence that they were getting close to Fel was their location. The journey had taken them deeper and deeper into the mountains. The last proper town they'd passed was more than a day ago. That meant they'd had to camp, which was something neither of them had an aptitude for. But it made sense that if Fel was getting himself into trouble, he would be doing it in the absolute most inconvenient place.

"I'm still thinking about those pastries from two towns back," Mariss said idly.

"The flaky ones?" Allie said.

"Mmhmm. With the butter. It had to have been layers of butter. But I don't know how they keep it from melting into the dough. I'll bet it's because it's cooler up here. They said they only serve them in the mornings. I'll bet they make them overnight, when it's cool enough to keep the butter from melting. Maybe if we could work the dough with some cool water we could make those back home." She smiled. "I've seen and learned so *much* on this trip. If it wasn't because Fel was in trouble, I'd say this was one of the nicest times I've ever had."

Allie took up the conversation. "That singer, back when we stopped for water? He's supposed to be passing through Beffshire in the winter. I hope he actually stops by the tavern. We'll be ready for performances then, and he'd really pack the place."

"It's starting to look like we're not going to get to another city tonight either. Lucky we bought so many of those weird crackers and that good cheese. Oh! And those jars of stock. Maybe I'll try to make some soup when we set up camp. I've always been better at baking than cooking, but..." She glanced aside. "Oh, good!"

Allie looked in the same direction. The road they were following curved back on itself a bit to handle the steepness of the mountainside, and they'd just rounded the curve enough to see someone a short distance farther back on the same road.

"That's a relief," Mariss said. "I was getting nervous about being alone on a road for so long."

Allie glared at the pair of men on horseback. Seeing them didn't give her the same feeling of relief. The horses were heavily loaded with gear. Considerably more gear than one would need unless they were planning to be in the mountains for weeks. She couldn't quite put a finger on why they made her nervous, but she'd learned not to ignore her instincts on things like this.

"The road widens out a bit up ahead, near the turn," Allie said. "Is that stream or brook or whatever next to it?"

"Yes. It looks like a nice little rest stop. A nice long, flat stretch, too. Pretty."

"Let's stop there until these two pass us. I don't like the idea of them being behind us."

"Why not?"

"They give me the creeps, and that's all the reason I need."

"Oh. Then we should certainly stop. I'm sure Zephyr would like a drink. And maybe that little field has enough grass for a graze."

She maneuvered the cart over to the widened section of road. This far from a city, it was frankly impressive there was a road at all. To expect a proper rest stop was far too much to ask. This section of the road had roughly the same feel and function as the sections of a field that had been walked clear of their grass. No one had made the decision to flatten out the stretch of ground between the main road and the brook and accompanying narrow field. It had been the collective action of years of travelers. The closest thing to a conscious effort to formalize this as a rest stop was the haphazard scattering of posts hammered into the bank of the brook for people to tie off their horses. Mariss unhooked Zephyr from the wagon and led her to the water. While the horse refreshed herself, Allie refilled their own water supply and kept an eye on the two mounted men.

The pair were taking their time. Despite a relatively short stretch of road separating them from the rest stop, it was going to take several minutes for them to pass. This gave Allie plenty of time to scrutinize them. The closer they got, the more certain she was that they were trouble. They were equipped for general travel, not specifically for *mountain* travel. That would be fine if they were traveling merchants or the like, but the things they carried were barely contained by the heaped sacks. They looked like they were hastily piled, which didn't say "merchant" to Allie. It said "bandit."

"All right... my notion that they weren't to be trusted was probably right, but my notion that we should let them pass was probably wrong," Allie said.

"Should I hook Zephyr back up?" Mariss said, reacting to the tension in Allie's voice like to an alarm bell.

"Yes. But don't hurry. If it looks like we're trying to escape, they'll chase us because they'll assume we have something worth stealing. Zephyr might be fast, but if those two drop their loads, they'll have no cart and one rider versus a cart and two riders. They'll catch us."

"So what do we do?"

"You've got your persuader, right?"

"I do."

"Be ready to use it."

Allie summoned up all her fortitude and watched as the pair of potential brigands drew nearer. She tried to will them into continuing past without stopping. It was no surprise when they trotted off the road and approached the brook.

One of the men was rugged and dark skinned. The other was likely pale before the sun had roasted him brick red. The look in their eyes was predatory, sizing up the pair of women for things Allie chose not to envision. One hopped off his horse, then the other.

"Ladies," rumbled the dark one.

"Yeah, didn't expect to find *ladies* here," said the red one.

"I certainly didn't expect to find gentlemen here either," Allie said. "Here's hoping you two are about to prove me wrong."

"Hah! You feeling like a gentleman?" the dark one said.

"I can be gentle," said the red one.

Mariss didn't hear the statement, which was for the best. It was all Allie could do to keep from shuddering at it.

"What brings you two up this way?"

"Work," Allie said. "My boss sent word he needed us. He's expecting us. We're already three days late. I honestly wouldn't be surprised if someone comes down that road in a couple of hours looking for us."

"Impatient man, is he?" the red one said.

"That's how it is with nobles. They think because they fund the Watch they can control the clock somehow. Make half a kingdom the sort of thing you can cross in a day just because they *want* you to."

The two men probably thought they were being subtle, but the look of frustrated disappointment that these two young ladies would be missed, and by a man with the means to find them, clearly threw cold water on whatever plans they might have had.

"What's he need two ladies for in such a hurry?"

"Guess," she said flatly.

The two men snickered and elbowed each other. Zephyr nickered quietly while one of bandits made sure their horses didn't wander off while they were drinking.

"I don't suppose you fellows know the quickest way over the mountain," she said.

"There's only two ways. You just head the way you're heading. You'll see a downed tree across the one side of the fork in the road. Don't take that turn."

The other man laughed. "Yeah. You don't want to go that way."

The dark man pulled an odd cigar-shaped brass pipe from an even odder holder on his belt, right beside where a crossbow conspicuously hung. He took a puff.

"Anything?" said the red man.

"Nothing," said the dark one.

"What was that about?" Allie asked.

"Don't worry about it," he said.

"We should keep moving," said his partner. "Our boss can be a real pain, and we're running late, too."

"Yeah, yeah."

One horse finished drinking, and its rider mounted up. The other rider yanked at the reins to get his own horse to stop. Allie practically held her breath. It looked like she might have threaded the needle and come through this unscathed.

At that precise moment, a gleaming puzzle box poked out through the flap of the cart and waggled in Oiler's brass claw.

"What in the world?" barked the not-yet-mounted bandit.

He rushed over and yanked the claw, bringing the jangling pack of chains tumbling down to the ground. Oiler raised its head and gazed blankly at the stranger. It gave the puzzle box another rattle.

"This is that thing! The chain-pack thing we were supposed to keep a lookout for." He turned to Allie. "You ladies were holding out on us. Just who are you *really*?"

Allie didn't answer. Not with words, anyway. Her reply spoke much louder, in the form of a dense *thock* of broomstick to temple, sending the man crumbling to the ground. A flurry of motion and a sudden blow to her side sent Allie sprawling as the mounted rider charged past. In a maneuver worthy of a trick rider, he managed to lean low enough to snatch Oiler's "wrist" without dismounting. The chain arm reeled out a bit before Oiler was yanked after him.

"Yah! Yah! Go!" Mariss shouted.

She'd slapped the remaining horse on its flanks, sending it galloping back down the mountain.

"So he can't follow. Right? Was that right to do?" Mariss asked, scrambling into the cart.

"By the High, it was brilliant. I wouldn't have thought of it. But come on. That guy's got Oiler. We won't find Fel without it. No... wait."

She grabbed the crossbow from the fallen bandit and climbed onto the cart.

"Now go. Fast!"

Mariss snapped the reins. Zephyr bolted forward. The cart practically left the ground as she pursued the fleeing bandit. Rather than riding along the road, he'd taken off across the narrow strip of rubble-strewn field on the other side of the brook. Mariss, for all her demure meekness, was a demon at the reins. Her enthusiasm for horses spoke loud and clear through the precision with which she guided the horse and cart over the uneven ground without rattling to pieces.

The fleeing horse was just ahead. Its rider hadn't dropped the heavy sacks of goods, and the steed was *not* the same quality of animal as Zephyr, so for the moment, the gap was closing.

"What are we going to do?" Mariss asked.

Allie unsteadily stood, keeping her knees bent to absorb some of the rumble of the cart. She held tightly to the seat with one hand and raised the crossbow with the other.

"Just get us close," she said.

"Are you a sharpshooter?"

"*Just get us close,*" Allie repeated.

Mariss snapped the reins again. They inched closer, but already the horse was starting to flag. It really wasn't a sprinter. Soon the best they could do was keep pace, a few yards away. Allie leaned forward. The crossbow wobbled and bounced as she extended it to arm's length.

"You're never going to be able to hit him while we're both moving!" Mariss said.

"The crossbow isn't even loaded," Allie said.

"Then what are you doing?"

"You'll see," she squinted at Oiler. "I hope..."

The bandit's overburdened horse stumbled, breaking stride for just a moment. The gap closed a bit more. Mariss waved the weapon. Shiny metal eyes peering out from the pack, which had been pulled to the bandit's back, fixed on the crossbow. In a flash of brass, Oiler extended its claw and grasped the crossbow, seeking to disarm Allie just as she'd been warned. Rather than letting the crossbow twist from her grip, she shakily reached out with the other hand, grabbed the chain wrist, and fell back into her seat. She braced her feet against the running board and pressed herself hard against the seatback. Two quick loops wrapped the chain arm around an ornamental bit of railing on the side of the cart.

"Now go! Back to the road!" Allie said.

Mariss shouted a command and tugged the reins. The horse pulled to the left. Allie suspected, in the moments that followed, the bandit regretted slipping his arms through the straps of Oiler's pack. With one horse running one direction, and the other horse running the other, the slack in Oiler's arm soon ran out. A startled yelp burst from the bandit's lips as he was pulled from his saddle. For a few painful moments he was dragged behind the speeding cart before his arms slipped out of the straps. He tumbled to a stop. Oiler reeled in.

A few minutes later, they rattled across the brook and back onto the road. The first rider was still motionless where they'd left him, and now both horses were trotting away without their riders. Oiler had picked up a few fresh tears in the pack, but was otherwise intact, as was the puzzle box still gripped in its other claw.

"That was..." Mariss muttered breathlessly.

"Exhilarating?" Allie said.

"I was going to say terrifying."

"Oh, good. Me too. You are quite the wizard with those reins, though."

"This and my special rhubarb tarts are the two things I'm best at. That was some quick thinking, too!"

"It did the job. Listen. I don't want you to hurt Zephyr or anything, but something tells me we just ran into a couple of people who were supposed to be a part of that ambush, which means two things. We're definitely close, and we might be too late. So keep as much speed as you can muster. And Oiler, after that little screwup, I think you'd better keep your mechanical mind on the task of finding Fel."

A loud click rattled in Oiler's head. It unlooped its arm from the railing and raised it, pointing quite clearly at the thickening line of gray-green trees to the right of where the road was headed.

"All right. Let's find him then," Allie said.

CHAPTER 14

Fel was at the reins. Lattica had her eyes glued to the detector. The trip had managed to be the least eventful and most stressful of Fel's life. Since the workshop, they had moved without any attacks, without any implication there was even anyone after them. Now, as they approached the point on the map that Lattica had worked out the next flame must be located, the detector had started acting... strangely.

It began quite subtly. The needle would wobble ever so slightly every few minutes. It wasn't nearly the sort of reaction the needle had displayed when they were attacked by flame bearers. It was far less pronounced than that. But after so much time watching a perfectly stationary needle, seeing the wobble was like hearing the trickle of water in a creaky old ship. It *could* be nothing. Or it could be the first indication of something catastrophic.

As they drew nearer to the marked location, it got worse. Wobbles became brief reversals of the needle. Five times they'd stopped and readied for combat. But no attack came. The best they could hope for was that the detector was malfunctioning. That came with its own concerns that they might be headed in the wrong direction or that they'd been on a wild goose chase. The far more likely and far less pleasant possibility was that they were in some sort of a rolling ambush, steadily accumulating more and more attackers that had simply chosen not to attack.

Yet.

According to the map, they were on a road, but it had seen little in the way of upkeep, which made maneuvering the carriage a struggle. Things became easier once they neared the edge of a charred, ruined section of woods.

"This is the place up ahead," Fel said, holding his spyglass to his eye.

"We should double-check the map," Lattica said.

Fel handed over the spyglass and repeated. "This is the place."

Just visible through the thinning trees was a half-charred manor. Lattica didn't need to be told why Fel was so certain this was the place. Even at this distance, the pair of half-giants were clearly visible. They'd yet to notice the carriage, but if Fel were to ease it just a bit closer, there would be no chance of them missing it.

"So," Fel said quietly. "One of us goes in and snuffs the flame, the other one stays out here and makes sure things don't get out of hand?"

"That seems to be the proper thing to do."

Fel reached into his pocket for a duot. "Call it in the air?"

She caught his hand to stop the coin flip. "I take the invisibility bracer. I draw them away and vanish in the woods, you go inside. If they try to double back, I try to pick them off."

"I like the idea of them chasing someone who they can't see, but what if I run into someone inside?"

"Deal with them."

"And if both the giants don't follow you?"

"Deal with that, too."

He raised his eyebrows. "You're starting to plan things the way *I* plan things."

"Call it a compromise. My way is sane, your way is insane, and frankly the situation is pretty low on sanity, so yours is a better match."

They stowed the carriage as securely as they could, angled for a quick getaway, and armed themselves to the teeth. Fel had his cudgel, a couple of knives, his share of the spells and the dragon sticker club for good measure. Lattica had two crossbows, the rest of the spells, and a small armory of additional equipment she didn't bother listing for Fel. Despite the fluttering of the needle on the detector, they weren't able to locate anyone but the giants lurking in the area.

"When the fire is out, I'll get your attention, and we meet back at the carriage," Fel said.

"Be quick about it," she said.

She took a breath and marched toward the manor. Fel remained hidden behind one of the last trees and listened. First came the slow, steady crunch of Lattica's footsteps, then the calculated whistle to draw attention, and finally the throaty shouts of the giants. He swore he could feel the ground shaking as one of them gave chase. And in accordance with his horrid luck, the pair of giants were smart enough not to both dash after her. One remained at the door. So be it.

He dashed around the edge of the charred clearing, not taking particular care to avoid being seen by the remaining giant. He was confident he would be able to outrun him, if it came down to it. Once he saw a second, unguarded entrance, he cut straight across the burnt forest of standing deadwood toward it. His mind constructed all sorts of nightmare scenarios. Unseen snipers on the roof, ready to pick him off. Traps set up along the way. He disregarded those thoughts. There was nothing he could do about any of them. All he could do was press on and hope for the best.

Ignoring his troubles proved a winning plan, as he reached the back of the manor without shedding any blood. The door was locked and braced. He pulled the borer from his bag and hammered it into the door. Once activated, it started chiseling a hole, and he was free to turn his back to it and take his cudgel in hand, ready for whatever came next. He kept his eyes open, watching and listening. The borer was *not* a quiet device, even if the sound of hammering it in had somehow miraculously been missed. If there was anyone nearby, they would come running.

In the distance, he heard a twang of a crossbow, but no roar of pain. At least he knew Lattica was still active.

The ground started to shake. The giant was coming around to investigate. He readied his manticore club.

"You! Stop!" thundered the giant.

The massive brute brandished his hammer and lumbered to a stop.

"I'm just here to snuff a candle, big fellow," Fel said. "No need to make this messy."

"You're Fel Masker..." he grumbled.

"I must be doing something right if people this far north know me on sight."

"Some days the boss wants you dead. Some days he wants you brought in," the giant said.

"I'm going in whether he wants it or not. Now you can back off, or you can learn what it feels like to catch a dose of manticore venom."

The giant lurched forward, swatting with his frying-pan-size hand in an attempt to grab Fel's arm. Fel rolled aside and dashed for the edge of the manor. The giant stomped after him. As he hoped, the borer on the door was forgotten. If he could shake the hulk and circle back, he'd return to find a nice, neat hole in the door.

The ground was level, nothing but crispy frozen grass. A dream to run on. Unfortunately, in his calculations about how quickly a giant was likely to be able to run, he'd made some minor errors. Yes, they were large and heavy, and moved slowly. But limbs that long didn't need to move very quickly to outpace him. Fel wasn't the most nimble person in the world, but since the straight-line-speed bet didn't go his way, some fancy footwork was the only option left that wouldn't end in broken bones.

When the giant was just outside of clobbering range, he cut aside and circled back. Sure enough, Fel could practically hear the behemoth's legs straining to keep him upright as he tried to follow. Fel gained some ground and tried to work out if he had enough stamina to keep this game of cat and mouse going until the borer was through with its work.

Lattica ducked behind a tree and tapped off the invisibility bracer. She regretted not taking more time to practice with it. Fel was right about it being disorienting. Her stomach turned and heaved every time she activated it, and moving at even a walking pace without falling down was hit or miss once she was wading through the brush in the more intact bits of the forest. She slipped a bolt into each of her crossbows and reset them. The giant was rather simple to stay ahead of, but her mediocre aim and the need to find a place to hide for every shot and every reload meant that even with a massive target, she'd yet to get a single hit. Someone that big was bound to take more than one shot to bring down, too.

He thumped closer. She tapped the invisibility on and moved with care toward the next likely position to take a shot. Now that she was deeper into the forest, moving slowly and precisely was more important than moving quickly. She needed to make sure she made enough noise to keep him on her trail. But the chase had taken her much farther from the manor than she would have liked. Not that she could offer much help, but if Fel called for her, she wouldn't be able to hear him, much less make it back in time.

She slipped into the shelter of two low trees and turned back. The giant was still fighting his way through the brush she'd navigated to get this far. She should have time to take two more shots. She huddled low, tapped off her bracer, and steadied herself against the crook of a low branch. Her heart was pounding, which wouldn't help her aim. She tried to calm herself and steel herself. Deep breaths.

Something was wrong.

She took another deep breath. It was faint, but no member of the Graves family would ever forget that scent. Badgerweed. It shamed her that she recognized it wasn't the same grade as the stuff Thaddeus Graves smoked, but someone in these woods was puffing some of that horrid weed.

She backed away from the tree and tapped herself into invisibility again. The breeze was coming from her left. She turned and scanned the forest. A lightly camouflaged figure crouched in the bushes at the very limit of her vision. And he was not alone. There were three of them, at least. These were the people who had been setting off the detector. Or, at least, some of them. They were just waiting. Watching. What were they waiting *for*? One thing was certain. Despite the circumstances, Fel was in greater danger than she was, because their eyes were on the manor.

Fel gasped for air as he dashed back toward the door of the manor. A few minutes of full sprint had his heart ready to burst from his chest. He could only hope the hammer-wielding giant on his tail was similarly close to collapse, because he didn't have it in him to lead him on this chase much longer.

He reached the door to find the borer spinning in place, having fully cut a circle out of the heavy planks. He punched it through to rattle inside and felt for the brace. An awkward heave pulled it out of place. He felt blindly for the latch or lock that would swing the door open. Time ran out. He yanked his arm from inside and spun around just in time to come face to face with a winded and enraged giant. The brute lunged forward. Fel didn't so much dodge as collapse aside. The giant struck the door instead of Fel. Without the brace to support it, whatever lock had remained in place failed spectacularly. Wood splintered. The giant tumbled into the entryway. Flailing limbs fumbled in a hallway just a bit too small for someone so large. Fel trudged up to the ailing giant and gingerly jabbed him with the spiked end of the manticore club. The giant yelped in pain and roared with anger, fighting his way back out of the entryway. Before he could get steadily on his feet again and swing the hammer at Fel, the venom went to work. The giant's legs buckled. He tumbled back to the ground. Fel didn't wait for him to slump into paralyzed stillness. He had a job to do. He scrambled past the giant and into the open doorway.

It would have been nice to be able to brace the door against anyone else who might want to come through, but the giant's blow had shattered a chunk of the doorframe. He doubted he would even be able to shut it, let alone secure it. Better to get in and out.

He wove his way through the halls of the manor. It was less a home or headquarters and more a maze. Half the doors were blocked or boarded. The others only ever seemed to lead to empty rooms or more hallways. Every turn, every corner could have hidden another trap or another guard, but his luck held at least long enough to find the door that most certainly held his prize. This section of the house was warm. The floor was scuffed and smeared with fresh muddy footprints. This was where business was done. And the door ahead was the only door he'd encountered inside the manor that had a gleaming, recently installed lock.

Fel might have been able to pick it, but stealth had been abandoned before he'd even started. He quickened his pace along the hallway and drove the heel of his boot into the door with all his weight behind it. The door burst open and revealed a room lit by a single flame hidden behind a room-dividing screen.

"Fel Masker…" came the voice from behind the screen.

"Save the speech. I'm here to put out your flame and take it with me—and if you try to stop me, something's getting broken."

"I would advise against any rash actions."

"So would all my friends, and I never listen to *them*, why would I listen to you?"

He desperately wanted to turn the screen to splinters with a few well-placed blows with his cudgel, but he was too deep into contraptioneer's territory to trust that he didn't have some means of protection. He'd lucked out that the door hadn't triggered something nasty. There was no way something as fragile as the screen wasn't enhanced in some way. He swept his eyes along the walls and ceiling, then the screen itself, looking for triggers.

"You came here with a woman. Lattica Graves. She is in the woods."

"Uh-huh, and?" he said, eyes now lingering on a line of brass running along the edge of the screen.

"She has, by now, likely noticed that I have Bolivan agents stationed in the forest around this place."

"Uh-huh..." Fel crouched and ran his fingers along the strip of brass. It was old. Not a new contraption. He'd seen things like it in old vaults. This was certainly the trigger of something potent.

"We know where your carriage is. We know where your friends are."

"My friends are safe at home."

"A diminutive fellow has recently abandoned the roof of this manor, heading instead for the forest. A second carriage, a two-seater, not unlike the Masker family wagon, is approaching from the south. More friends of yours."

"Now you're making things up."

"Alizon Waverly and a plump young woman."

"You're not even making things up that make *sense*."

Fel glanced behind him and listened. No one was coming. He pulled some tools from his bag.

"I could have had you the moment you entered the charred circle. There are dozens of agents available to me, a single word away from acting. You are helpless."

"There's a venom-filled giant blocking the back door who would disagree with you."

"You've found the workshop. That is good. I wasn't sure that you would. The fool who works in the shop refuses to leave the flame lit. It is why a persistent lantern needed to be created and provided."

Fel glanced up at the shadow of the high-backed chair, the only thing visible through the screen.

"Created and provided?" he said. "So you're the one with the information on how to build new contraptions."

"That is but a fraction of the knowledge I have. This, all of this, was to gain an audience with you or your father. My name is Lens. I have the knowledge. You and your father have the skills. We can change the world, Masker. It is your purpose to rebuild that which was lost to the past."

Fel laughed.

"That's where you're wrong. My dad is the one who makes a living fixing things. My job is breaking things." He pulled out a tool. "And you're about to get a demonstration."

"You're making a mistake."

"Not the first one I made today. And if you wanted to talk shop, you should have made an appointment. Once you start siccing mercenaries on the family, you don't get to negotiate."

"You realize I will need to use force if you press any further."

"Good to know you're afraid. Shows you're not completely unreasonable. But shut up. I've got a job to do."

Lattica became visible just outside the carriage. Either it hadn't yet been found, or it had been ignored, because none of the Bolivans were gathered about it.

"Fel must be rubbing off on me, because this isn't nearly enough of a plan..." She grumbled as she climbed inside.

The Bolivan agents were smoking, which meant they probably had the sentry pipes. They were in contact with anyone with the flame. And flames knew where other flames were. A big, important flame they wanted back? That was some proper bait. And bait was something she knew how to work with.

She pulled out the persistent lantern from the workshop.

"Flame spell. Flame spell," she muttered, pulling out the appropriate page.

She rushed through the woods, unlit lantern under one arm and flame spell clutched in the other hand. When she was far enough from the carriage to be confident she wouldn't lead anyone directly to it, she set the lantern on the ground, tapped herself into invisibility, and took shelter just far enough to be within range of its influence. The spell flared to flame, and shortly afterward the lantern was lit by the smoldering magic.

"Hello," came a cool, emotionless voice. "How my I help you?"

She leveled her crossbow.

"This vantage appears to be a persistent sentry lantern," the voice continued. "Due to the high value of this particular vantage, agents shall be dispatched to fetch it."

Already she could hear the rustle of approaching Bolivans. Some shouted, calling for the giants. She wasn't optimistic enough to assume all of them had been summoned to her. But she was going to make a very persuasive argument to the rest of the group. Or, rather, the first agents to show up would.

The man behind the screen had been making increasingly frustrated calls for logic and reason as Fel dug his tools under the contraption trigger. A few trips with Tome had taught Fel to let seas of words wash over him with no effect. Not until Fel pulled up the edge of a small linkage did the tone of voice change, shifting from bargaining to desperation.

"Fel, this is your last chance. We can work together," Lens said.

"You haven't attacked me, and you haven't brought your crew in here. I don't know why, and I don't care."

"The Bolivans are surrounding the manor. They are very difficult to control, as you've noticed. I cannot guarantee you will survive if you force me to withdraw before calling them off."

"I think me leaving the place with my hands around the throat of the one giving the orders and paying the bills will be motivation enough."

"You truly believe I would have arranged for all this to occur and not had a means for strategic withdrawal?"

"If you do, then now's the time."

He pushed a connector out of place. All around the room, the soft sound of coiled springs easing their tension and tight cords relaxing signaled the successful deactivation of the traps protecting the screen. He swung his cudgel at the screen, smashing neatly through it in a single blow. Two more whacks broke a hole large enough for him to wrench enough of the screen aside to reveal what it was concealing. The chair he'd seen was empty. A very old sentry lantern had been left behind, and a well-fortified door was open on the far side of the room. He scrambled through the broken screen and rushed through the door.

It led to a corridor too dark and tight to have been a proper hallway. This was the space between the walls, a secret escape tunnel. He followed it to its end, but he stopped short of pushing the doorway open. He could hear shouts and stomping feet outside. The blasted mastermind had made it clear. If Fel stuck his head out now, it would be lopped clean off. He sidled back to the abandoned "office." There wasn't much more to see than the chair and the lantern, which was a good deal more ornate than any he'd seen before. Precisely the sort of thing that would send his father on a rant of speculation about how it differed in purpose from Wick's lantern, and precisely the sort of thing he didn't have time to consider. He licked his thumb and snuffed the flame. While he tied it to the strap of his gear bag, he scanned the rest of the room. The only other thing was a small cabinet attached to one wall. It contained some very old, very dusty notes and some well-used, complex keys labeled "Damaged Contraption Storage" and "Spare Parts Storage." Presumably the two sturdy buildings out back. He pocketed the keys and stuffed the notes into his bag. For now, his mission was complete. All he had to do was get out of this alive.

Lattica's hands were shaking as she fixed her eyes on the semicircle of Bolivan agents holding their distance. Through necessity, she had learned to reload the crossbows while invisible. Her head was aching terribly at the need to focus her vision so precisely in the greasy approximation of life the bracer provided. Her aim while invisible was abysmal, but she learned after the first two shots that it needn't be any good to have the desired effect.

Human nature—and apparently *giant* nature—dictated that when a potentially lethal shot came bursting out of the underbrush from an unseen location, one treated it with extreme caution. She had managed only one hit, on the thigh of the giant, but periodic unseen shots at anyone who took a step closer managed to keep the two dozen or so of them at bay. Now and again she caught glimpses of additional agents, probably trying to flank her. She wouldn't be able to stay here much longer.

It was both a relief and a concern when the Bolivans started to pull back. She didn't have a plan for how this gambit would end, but when they started to withdraw, she knew she was simply back where she'd started, with these people converging on the manor with Fel inside. All she'd done was buy him time. She hoped it had been enough.

"You're a real lousy shot, you know that?" said Davie's voice from a branch beside her.

She jumped, firing one last shot wildly into the air, then turned to him. It wasn't until she realized he wasn't making eye contact with her that she remembered she was still invisible.

"How... where did you... how do you even know where I am?"

His eyes shifted, focusing on her mouth, now that he had a source for the sound.

"When you're as little as me, you get to be real good at figuring out where people are even without looking, what with how much of a handful a big lady like you could be if you decided you didn't want me around. Were you missing on purpose?"

She tapped off the bracer and paused a moment to revel in the relief of having her proper vision back and not having to deal with the odd stomach-turning influence of the device.

"I can't aim properly when I can't see the weapon. Never mind that. What are you doing here? Shouldn't you be keeping an eye on Fel?"

"Our boy is in there faffing about. Must have been having trouble with a door or something, because there was no one in there."

"How do you know?"

"I got in and checked it out."

"You did?"

"Funny thing about big houses like that. If you can't keep out rats, you can't keep out a gnome."

"We should hire *you* for things like this."

"Already got two jobs, and this traipsing around the continent isn't for me, usually. Point is, the place was empty. Only one or two locked doors, and no one behind them that I could hear."

"Never mind any of that. What do we do now?"

"I got good news and bad news about that," Davie said. "Good news, we got a little help coming. Bad news? Look who finally showed up."

He pointed. A form was sweeping along in the sky above. The griffin.

"Please tell me the good news is better. Who is coming to help us?"

"A barmaid and a baker are coming up the road there."

"... Are they heavily armed?" Lattica said hopefully.

"Beats me. Been busy. Want me to run and find out?"

"We need to figure out how to take out some of these Bolivans so Fel can escape!"

"I'm not good with groups. I'm good for one surprise stab and then it's back into the shadows until they lose track."

She poked through the nearly depleted supply of bolts.

"Five shots remaining." She reloaded the crossbows. "Pick someone good for your one stab, I guess."

Tome was grudgingly becoming aware that his plans were not as flawless and cunning as he'd convinced himself they would be. The spells were sound. Their steed was fully tamed, at least within the limits of the commands he'd included. And he had every reason to believe it would remain so for the duration of their journey. But when he'd concocted it, he'd overlooked the rather critical corollary that a single animal large enough for all three of them to ride was not going to be stealthy in the slightest. A moose wasn't known for its sneaking, and a dire moose even less so. This problem was exacerbated by the mechanical way that it followed its commands. The thing wasn't so thoroughly controlled that it would walk into a tree rather than avoid it, but it was far less discerning about maneuvering its antlers to avoid things that it could simply smash through instead.

Somehow they'd avoided detection through the raw luck of the one ranger who had been nearby choosing the wrong moose to follow when the other two he'd lured had wandered off. It had bought them more time than he really could have hoped for. The moose was very fast, and had run tirelessly. Tome didn't know how long it had been, but the good luck had expired. Now Teya was sitting backward on the moose's head, eyes turned skyward to keep track of the winged stag following just above the treetops.

"Still there," she chirped.

"Of course he's still there. He's not going to get tired of chasing us!" Tome snapped. "I only wonder why he hasn't started shooting at us yet."

Teya scoffed. "Rangers no miss."

"I know. That's why I'm wondering why there isn't an arrow in my back."

"Rangers. No. Miss." Teya repeated. "Will hit? Shoot. Maybe hit? No shoot. No hit? *No shoot.*"

"You're telling me they won't take a shot they aren't certain to hit?" Tome said.

She nodded.

"Unless they're supernatural snipers, that means no shots until they're no longer airborne," Tome said.

Teya nodded.

"You're sure about that?"

"Nope!" she said brightly.

"... We'll just operate on the assumption that you're right, because we don't really have a choice otherwise. Unless we come up with something."

A low-hanging branch exploded into splinters as the moose plowed through it.

"Yep," Teya said. "Write spell?"

"Another spell from my blood is likely to make me pass out."

"I give blood?" Teya said with a wince.

"Wouldn't do much good. Blood itself empowers a spell, but the main value of using it is taking the place of a component of the spell. When I write in my blood, it removes the 'identity of the creator' element of the spell by matching it perfectly to me. Your blood would just be particularly potent ink. It wouldn't shorten the spell. Besides, it is hard enough to write a legible spell in a carriage. On moose back? Impossible. How far are we from the wall?"

"Wall soon. Very soon."

"Minutes? Hours?"

"Minutes."

"... I thought it was going to be *days* to get to the wall."

"On foot, days. To right part? Another day. Just to wall? Minutes."

"Have you... we were supposed to be heading to the place I came in! That's where I told you to lead me!"

Teya nodded.

"They track. We run. Moose? Not run always. By night, sleep. Rangers find. We die. Rangers? Not dumb. Go to wall. Wait there. Wrong part? No wait there."

"But I can't get *out* of the wrong part of the wall."

"Go over."

"How? I can't climb a sheer wall!"

"Parch can. Tie rope."

"Parch doesn't listen to me!"

The forest was already beginning to thin out, giving way to increasingly rocky terrain. The ranger on their tail was still there, getting steadily closer as the sweeping branches of trees ceased to be an impediment. The moose smashed through a final thicket of saplings and bushes, and finally he could see the wall looming up in the distance. There was a much larger stretch of stone between the forest and the wall than there was in the river entrance. They would have no hope for cover when the time came for dismount, but at least there would be a few more minutes of riding before that happened.

"What do we do? What do we do?" Tome ranted to himself, raking his foggy mind for inspiration.

"I tell Parch?" Teya offered. "To me? Parch listen."

"Fine. Fine. There's rope in the gear, right? Tie some rope."

The peryton set down ahead of them. The ranger hopped off. Tome watched in terror as he pulled an arrow from his back and drew the string taut. It wasn't a satchel of sleeping powder this time. A bright, gleaming arrowhead awaited him.

"Get down!" Tome cried, grabbing Teya and wrenching her around behind him. He heard something hiss through the air. The sickening thwack of an arrow shattering into flesh was followed an instant later by the horrifying wail of a stricken moose. The taming spell was no match against the pain of a direct hit with an arrow. The forward charge turned into a maddened buck. Tome, Parch, Teya, and all their gear were hurled from the monster's back as it went tumbling to the ground. A great plume of dust rose up around them, kicked up by their tumble and by the continued thrashing of the beast. When it began to clear, and Tome was just pulling himself painfully to his feet, the panicked clippy-clop of hooves drew his attention to the wall.

Parch was not a creature of pronounced loyalty. At least, not to Tome. And whatever desire he had to see Tome or Teya survive was overruled by the combined danger of the thrashing moose and the ranger. He dashed for the wall. As he was the one clear target free of the dust, the ranger immediately drew another arrow and took aim.

Before Tome or Teya could gather themselves to do something, the tip of the arrow drooped and the ranger blinked vaguely at the wall. They were too close. The wall's influence was too great. He couldn't focus clearly on things close enough to it. That was it. That was why the ranger hadn't picked him off on the way down the wall all those days ago when he'd arrived. That was why he'd stalled so long before taking a shot that day. And that was Tome's chance now. If he could just get close enough to the wall and keep moving, maybe he could survive.

"Wait! Parch! Need rope!" Teya shouted, bounding after the unicorn with most of the gear gathered in her arms.

Tome hastily grabbed what remained of the gear and sprinted after them. If nothing else, the gear might give him something to shield himself with if the ranger tried to pick him off anyway.

The ranger barked something. Tome knew the voice. He didn't pause. He didn't look. He couldn't afford to tempt fate, because it was clear in this moment that fate was *not* on his side. There were twenty rangers in that village. There were three on their trail. But the one who had found them? Mevrelle.

Tome worked his weary body for all it was worth, dashing for the wall. Ahead of him, Parch was bounding up the wall, moving from crack to crack on the subtle separations between the heavy blocks as though it were level ground. A few moments later, Teya reached the wall, threw down the gear, and began to scale it in pursuit. It wasn't until she'd made it a dozen feet up its face that a realization dawned on her.

"Wall not work? Wall not work!" she squealed. "Because earring, wall not work!"

Something behind Tome was producing a whistling sound. He continued his sprint. Then something pulled tight around his ankle and fouled his stride. He went sprawling forward and thumped painfully to the rocky ground. Some manner of bolo or snare had bound his ankle. A weapon that didn't require quite so much precision to be deployed and was thus just barely able to meet its target. He tried to climb to his feet, to get back on the move. It was too late. The ranger closed the gap and put a boot to Tome's throat, pushing him back to the ground. He leaned low and wrenched the gear away. A cursory search revealed little about the pile of stolen and recovered goods, but it made one thing quite clear. Wick was not among this batch of gear.

Tome knew it was all about the sentry lantern now. If they could get Wick, he would be destroyed, and they would have the tools they needed to do whatever nefarious thing they intended to do beyond the wall. His own life was lost, but perhaps that could be prevented.

"Teya!" Tome croaked. "Wick! Take Wick and get him clear!"

The kobold dropped down again and grabbed the lantern. She strapped him tightly to her and scrambled up the face of the wall. Mevrelle abandoned Tome and hurried toward the wall. Each step, he slowed. Tome knew from their adventure in Duurth's lair that the influence of the wall wasn't *perfect*. Something like another living creature, if it was close enough, could still be roughly observed. If Mevrelle focused on Teya, he might be able to stop her. Already Mevrelle was pulling a second bolo from his belt and spinning it up to speed.

Tome drew in a ragged breath and struggled to his feet. He dragged the bolo behind him and dove at Mevrelle, knocking him to the ground as well. A scuffle began. It was far from the epic battle of good and evil that Tome would have liked it to be. Tome was exhausted, bruised, and a poor combatant on his best day. Mevrelle was fighting against an ancient enchantment that demanded he turn back and return to the heart of the Greater Lands. The battle that raged looked more like two drunken idiots fumbling about after closing time. Tome tried to crawl closer to the wall.

Mevrelle caught him by the leg to drag him back. Every inch closer to the wall greatly increased the pressure the wall was putting on the elf's mind. He seemed to sense he wouldn't have the strength of will to remain for long if he didn't keep a grip on someone free of the wall's power.

He managed to pull a blade. Tome struggled to knock it away. But Mevrelle's strength of will and combat training were too great. The elf bashed Tome with an elbow, dizzying him. He raised the weapon up. A blue-gray blur streaked through the air and knocked him to the ground.

Tome felt a hot splatter of something across his cheek. A thick dollop of blood. He blinked until he could focus on the much more desperate battle going on. Teya was grappling with him, blood dripping from her claws. The same blood that had struck his face. Realization struck. Tome knew if he threw himself into the battle, he would be just as likely as to end up with a blade in his back as saving Teya. But there was another way. The scattered pages from his dislodged gear fluttered in the wind. He stomped his foot down on a page, pulled it up, and smeared the blood on the page. Mevrelle's blood gave both potency and precision to the spell. It was enough to give power to a single word. The one word he knew worked so well on the elves.

Sleep.

Mevrelle didn't fall still. The spell wasn't powerful enough for that. But an already clouded mind became more clouded. Already clumsy movements became clumsier. And with a frenzied kobold atop him, that was enough. In a few more seconds of screeching and clawing, the battle was over.

Teya pulled back, eyes wide and wild. Mevrelle was still breathing, not yet at death's door, but well past the point of self-defense.

"You're not going to kill him?" Tome said breathlessly.

"No kill. Kill? War. No kill? No war. ... Maybe," Teya said.

She crouched and shredded Mevrelle's shirt. The first strips went to binding his hands and feet. The next went to bandaging the more worrisome of wounds. She made a quick job of it and dusted off her blood-flecked paws when she was through.

"You saved my life," Tome said.

Teya turned and grinned.

"Yes! Tome? Worst friend. But still friend." She pointed. "We climb."

She rummaged through the gear at the base of the wall. Tome fetched the rest of it. By the time he'd gathered it all together, Teya had found the rope and tied it about her waist. It was the work of a minute or two for her to scale the wall. Tome marveled at just how easily she defeated the defense. The only thing that *truly* kept the creatures of the Greater Lands inside was the arcane influence of the wall. Were that aspect to fall away, there would be little to stop these creatures from flooding into an extremely unprepared world.

Fel pulled himself through a hole he'd broken through the roof of the vanished boss's secret tunnel. After his departure, and Fel's destructive journey through the manor, the only two doors that still locked were the ones leading into and out of the escape tunnel. Neither would last long against the pounding of the dozens of Bolivans who had been deployed against him. Desperation combined with flimsy repairs meant he was able to bash a few floorboards out of place above him and thus "escape" to the second level. At the moment, none of the attackers were searching the second level because they knew he could only be behind the locked doors. So his relative safety would last until the first Bolivan agent got into the tunnel and found the hole.

"Think. Think, Fel. Think, think, think."

He rummaged through his gear. He had a flame spell. He could set the manor on fire. It would only make things worse, but burning down the boss's house would at least make him feel better. He didn't have any ranged weapons, but he didn't imagine he'd get more than a single shot off even if he did have one.

"I wonder how many steps I'd make it if I just charged out and rushed for the woods," he mused.

The sweep of a shadow briefly darkened the patch of light cast through a hole in the fire-damaged roof. Fel crept to a half-rotten end table and risked climbing on it to get a better look through the hole. Sure enough, the griffin rider was here.

"Zero steps, then," Fel said.

He huffed a breath. Sometimes, when good ideas weren't forthcoming, the only choice was to go with a bad idea and hope you were wrong about it. He pulled the fire spell Tome had given him from the bag, kicked some of the broken wood planks down into the crawlspace he'd escaped from, and tore the edge. The blue fire of magic activating shifted quickly to red and orange. Hot air rushed up through the hole, and the crackle of old wood filled the air.

"They won't be able to follow me," he reasoned, seeking to retroactively turn the desperate plan into something brilliant after the fact. "They'll have to leave the building. And then... and then..."

The door to the room rattled on its hinges.

"They're checking the top floor of a burning building? How much is he *paying* these people?" Fel growled, brandishing his cudgel.

The door rattled again, then wrenched upward a bit, straightening the racked door. A gentle nudge pushed it open, and Fel raised his cudgel to score what might be the last successful attack of his life. A gleaming metallic head peered at him around the door. Oiler clicked and dinged in what a trained ear knew to be a gleeful manner for the contraption. It hobbled on claws and tail through the door and plopped down in front of him, working overtime with its body language to express the joy and excitement that could not be shown by its impassive face.

"What? How are you—how did—never mind. You and I need to get out of here."

Oiler, now that it had been reunited with Fel, surveyed the room and selected a section of damaged wall to try to repair.

"Now's not the time, Oiler," he said, yanking the contraption up by the straps and pulling it onto an already overburdened back. "We're going to get down the side of this building. You're going to do your thing, disarm people trying to kill me. And we're going to run to... run to..."

Fel's body took the initiative, since his mind wasn't turning out anything useful. His hands patted the many pockets of his gear, as though he'd stowed the answer to this dilemma in one of them and simply couldn't remember which one. A pocket jangled. He revealed one of the keys he'd just grabbed from the boss. He read the label and shrugged.

"It's better than nothing." He glanced over his shoulder, where Oiler's head was waiting for him, coiled aside to face in the same direction with his perpetual look of dull interest on its serpentine face. "I'm about to do a lot of very stupid things. Just try to keep me from dying, and I promise there is a treat waiting for you at the end. Got it?"

A soft chime from within Oiler's head signaled its agreement. Fel nodded and heaved himself up onto the busted end table. Smoke was already filling the room and billowing out the hole in the roof as he scrambled onto a rafter and broke out onto the crumbling roof. Voices shouted from below, and a subdued eagle cry rang out from above. He dashed along the roof and, overruling all his survival instincts, jumped off the edge on the side of the building with the least Bolivans. He heard the jingle of chains behind him and felt the straps pull taut. Oiler had grabbed the edge of the roof. It wasn't a perfectly graceful maneuver. The entire section of roof it had grappled onto tore free, but not before slowing Fel's descent from potentially bone breaking to merely very painful. He hit the ground stumbling and quickened to a run again, hacking smoke out of his lungs as Bolivans tried to block him in his mad rush for the storage buildings. Brass claws sparkled in his peripheral vision as Oiler did its second favorite activity, wrenching weapons from the hands of combatants.

Fel dodged one or two swings of edged weapons, blocked a solid and painful blow from a club, and fumbled for the ice spell still among his equipment, gripping it in one hand while he held the keys tightly in the other.

The prolonged dash away from the giant earlier had sapped most of the stamina he had, and he was weighed down with enough equipment for three people, so he never truly got ahead of the swarming Bolivans. Quick work from Oiler's mechanical attempts at pacifism and a firm shoulder to the chest of whoever was foolish enough to get between him and the storage buildings kept him moving. He reached the door. Now he just needed enough time to get the door unlocked. It was time for the spell.

He tore the paper and tossed it over his shoulder, not even bothering to aim it. When it was fresh, the thing might have been enough to incapacitate one man. With the time and distance since it was written, he doubted it would do much more than blast some frost and make a lot of startling blue light. But that was the thing about magic. It *all* made a lot of startling blue light. *They* didn't know it was a half-spoiled ice spell. So while the Bolivans scattered to avoid being incinerated or changed into a toad or whatever else their minds could have conjured, Fel jabbed the key into the lock, turned it, and stumbled inside.

There was no way to lock the door again from the inside, but the dim light filtering through ventilation slats below the roof revealed a huge shelf of heavy metallic gear standing beside the door. He got behind it, threw his shoulder against it, and sent hundreds of pounds of equipment tumbling to the floor, hopelessly blocking the door a moment before it shook and rattled from attempts to get inside.

His heart was pounding in his ears as he found his sparker and lit the only nonsentry lantern among his things. The flickering yellow light fell upon the contents of the building. Shelves upon shelves of contraptions. They were all in some state of disrepair or another. Some were barely recognizable. Others were nearly complete. Oiler froze, suddenly paralyzed with the buffet of repairs waiting to be done.

"Pick some good ones," Fel said. "My life and your freedom depend upon it."

Oiler wrestled itself from his back and dove into the pile, chiming and clicking excitedly along the way.

Lattica lingered at the edge of the burned woods, trying to conjure up some semblance of a plan that wouldn't end in a short and bloody battle and some unmarked graves. More specifically, the second half of a plan. Davie had made himself scarce again, and would reappear if and when some very specific criteria were met. Getting those criteria in place was the present puzzle.

Smoke coiled into the sky from a fire that was rapidly consuming the manor. Fel had barricaded himself into the storage building at the far side of the charred section of forest, and the griffin rider had finally touched down and was shouting questions and orders at the Bolivans, trying to work out what had become of this place and what was to be done.

She'd positioned herself quite near to what remained of the road to this place and thus was nearby when the rattling of the wagon containing her "reinforcements" approached. She dashed out and flagged them down before they went trundling into the middle of the chaos in the clearing. If not for Fel's impressive capacity to capture the entire attention of the Bolivan force, the barmaid and the baker might well have been captured as they approached. As it was, the travel-weary wagon riders with the very pretty horse were safe and intact when they spotted her.

"You're the Graves lady," shouted Allie.

"Where's Fel?" Mariss fretted.

"Something tells me he's somewhere near the shouting and fire," Allie said. "Who else is here to help? Are we it?"

"Fel is holed up in a building back there. He's still alive, for now. But he won't last long once they get into that building. Some gnome that's been shadowing us is somewhere waiting for a chance to be useful," Lattica said. "Listen, girls. Unless you've got a lot of weapons or an entire army, you're going to want to turn around and get out of here *fast*."

"We've got information," Mariss said, clutching the words like a security blanket.

"We were hoping to get here *before* you ended up in the ambush," Allie said. "That was the main thing we were coming for. But how can we help?"

"Tell her the rest! Tell her about the flames!" Mariss said.

"That's a little secondary to survival at the moment," Lattica said.

"We *came* here to deliver this information," she insisted. "The flames can extinguish *themselves*. The one the Maskers have did it."

"How would we achieve that?" Lattica said.

"I don't know. Ask? Theirs did it on its own."

Lattica shook her head. "Look, can either of you fight?"

"By the High, no!" Mariss said.

"I can thwack an angry drunk who won't behave, but when the real beatings are necessary I usually bribe some muscle."

Shouts in the distance drew her attention to the battlefield. Some of the Bolivans were peeling away from their task of hammering on the fortified storage building to head in her direction.

"Blast it. The griffin rider must be smart enough to realize that if Fel wasn't alone, then they should try to find me again." She pointed. "Head straight that way, on foot. That's where our carriage is. There are weapons inside. About halfway there you'll find one of the sentry lanterns still burning. Grab it. Get inside the carriage, take whatever weapons you feel you can handle, and make sure no one takes the carriage. That's how you can help."

"What are you going to do?" Allie said.

"Whatever I can..." She tapped her bracer and vanished before their eyes.

The women hustled in the direction she'd indicated. She stalked toward the battlefield. No sense taking shots. She still had only five bolts remaining. She hung the crossbows at her sides and fumbled for her truncheon instead. There were only seven Bolivans deployed to search. They were wisely spread out. This was a search first and an attack second. And they were wary of wild shots in their direction, judging by their expressions.

She timed her steps with those of the nearest Bolivan, heading straight for him. When she was a few strides away, he finally noticed the crunch of brush. He was armed with a short sword and swung it wildly. She rushed in. She may not have been able to see where her body was, but it didn't take much precision to tackle a man to the ground, and even less to hammer him until he stayed there. She felt a hot sting of pain where the blade had met her shoulder. There was a warm trickle of blood. But it wasn't enough to stop her. And if she could take one man out like this, she could take others.

Fel had to give it to the Bolivans. They clearly had expected someone to try to raid this building and had built it accordingly. The Bolivans had been hammering at the door and walls for minutes and had made little progress. Meanwhile, Oiler had been in a joyful frenzy of repair. Fel's hope had been that the Bolivans would have been storing an armory of potentially dangerous equipment. After all, they were the ones who specialized in illegal apparatus. Alas, if they had hidden their most dangerous equipment here, Oiler had been carefully choosing to repair only the most harmless of it.

The contraption chimed and held up the fruits of its latest labors. It was a small staff, and when Fel angled its tip away from him and found the trigger for it, a blunt chisel end rattled viciously.

"Some kind of an automated pick. Better than nothing. But please, *please* find something that can ward off an army of Bolivans."

Oiler picked some new bits up and started fitting them together. So far, aside from the pick, the contraption had managed to repair what appeared to be a mechanism specifically for fluttering a fan, and something that produced the scent of a rose when he turned the top. It was possible there was some sort of rhyme or reason to the shelves and he could direct Oiler to the useful equipment, but the act of barricading the door had dashed those hopes pretty thoroughly by scattering so many of the contraptions to the floor.

In what turned out to be a lot more unnerving than it should have been, the hammering and shouting all died away very suddenly. He froze and looked about, fearful that they'd found a hatch or a door and would soon be pouring inside.

"Fel Masker!" bellowed a voice from outside.

"He's not here!" he shouted, eying Oiler as it worked.

Oiler stripped something out of a less complete contraption and inserted it into an assembly that looked like a coil-filled mixing bowl with handles on the back and sides.

"My name is Questor. You would know me as the griffin rider you've been running in fear from since you assaulted the stable."

"That's a very rosy way of looking at how things have gone between us, Questor," he said.

"You are surrounded. Your allies are outclassed. Give yourself up and this all ends now."

"It's already over. Either your boss ran off, or he's still in the burning building. So you should either be regrouping or trying to rescue him."

"My orders do not cease to be orders when the man who issued them is removed from the equation. I do what I'm paid to do."

"I don't know what you were paid to do, but you're getting paid too much."

"I was paid to provide military support to Bolivan interests. And presently the primary Bolivan interest is either capturing or executing you as an aggressor."

Oiler's spinning claws affixed a cage to the top of the contraption it was working on and tightened what might have been a sharpened tuning fork to the front.

"Good luck with that. If you could just do it, you wouldn't be talking to me right now. You'd peel this building open like a jar of pickles and yank me out. You people always insist on talking when you're just about to lose, so this little chat means you're afraid of what I can do."

"If you insist on resisting, we will round up your friends and kill them one by one. They've already made their presence known. In an attempt to lure the Bolivans out of place, they've lit one of the lanterns I'm evidently meant to defend, which has made their location known to the agents. Their lives are now in your hands."

Fel glanced at Oiler again. It was still merrily fixing what may have ended up being a bread maker for all he knew. Fel needed some way to buy more time in the hopes that something useful would result from its enterprises. His mind chewed on what it had learned. If they had a lantern lit, and he had a lantern, maybe he could get word to them. Coordinate something. It was worth a shot.

He sparked the stolen sentry lantern to life.

"Hey," he hissed. "I have a message to deliver to my friends nearby. You deliver it to them and tell me what they say in response, got it?" he ordered.

"Understood. Please provide the message," remarked the cold, efficient voice of the lantern.

He raised his eyebrows. That was unexpectedly simple.

"Say, hey, everybody. This is Fel, I need help. Some sort of a distraction. And I need it now."

"I shall inform you of their reply when it is forthcoming."

Mariss sat in the carriage, clutching her fingers and wondering how precisely she'd gone from dusting cakes with confectioner's sugar and chatting up customers to huddling in a stranger's war wagon hoping not to be found. She got the sense that Allie was going through a similar mental exploration, but at least on the outside she was handling things better. Indeed, the first evidence she saw that Allie's nerves were stretched as tightly as her own was the stifled squeal they both released when a voice emanated from the still-lit lantern they'd been told to fetch on the way there.

"Fel masker has requested that the following message be delivered. Hey, everybody. This is Fel, I need help. Some sort of a distraction. And I need it now," said the flame.

"Wh-what?" Mariss squeaked.

"Wow... it *does* work," Allie said.

"Who is that talking?"

"It's Fel," Allie said.

"That wasn't Fel's voice."

"Well, it's the flame telling us what Fel said."

"I thought when they said they used the flame to communicate, it was just whispering into the flame and other people hearing it. There's another voice?"

"We don't have time to be puzzling out how it works, he needs help," Allie said. "That Lattica lady is already out there fighting. Maybe there's something in here we can use? I wish she'd told us what some of this did."

"This is how all the bad people are getting instructions?" Mariss said.

"I don't know. I think so? It doesn't matter. Probably the best we can do is ride this whole wagon out there to distract them."

"They get their instructions in *this* voice?" she said.

"Mariss, enough. We need to find a way to—"

Mariss placed a hand on Allie's shoulder. "I'm trying to find a way, just listen to me. If this is how the bad people get their instructions, and it's in some other voice, then couldn't *we* give them instructions? They would never know, right?"

Allie paused. "That's some good thinking, Mariss. Listen! Flame! Tell the Bolivans that the boss says to back off. Tell them he's off somewhere far away and needs to be defended by all of them."

"I have been instructed not to provide instructions of that sort originating from this lantern," the flame replied.

"Originating from this lantern? So there's some other lantern that you *could* take instructions like that from?" Allie said.

"Correct."

"Is it Fel's lantern?" Mariss asked, catching on to the line of thinking.

"It is the command lantern, presently in the possession of Fel Masker."

"Tell him he can call off the Bolivans. Tell him to do it!" Allie said.

"And tell him he can tell the flames to extinguish themselves!" Mariss added.

The flame flickered once. "He has been informed." It flickered again. "The following message comes directly from command. Listen, you idiots, I'm clear of the area. Six miles northwest. I need everyone in the range of headquarters to come to my defense before the Maskers and Graves people get to me. Abandon the headquarters and head six miles northwest now."

It flickered once more, then fizzled away. Extinguished. Allie slapped Mariss on the shoulder. "Good thinking!"

She shrugged and offered a fragile smile. "I try to follow instructions. I figured other people would, too."

Fel watched the streamer of smoke rising from the self-extinguished lantern. That was it. It was that simple. Every sentry flame lit from the Graves flame snuffed out. The whole mission achieved with just a few words. Technically, with this lantern, what he'd just learned, and the detector, the issue of the stolen Graves flame was settled. Now all he had to do was avoid dying. He'd always been very good at that.

Outside, he could hear the Bolivan agents retreating. Questor was shouting at them, demanding they stay, but from the mounting frustration in his voice, he wasn't having much success.

"I certainly hope those mercenaries were cheap," Questor growled.

"Hey, what are you still doing here?" Fel called. "Didn't you hear? The boss needs help."

"You're going to try to keep me talking so your friends can try to get the drop on me. I'm through playing games."

Wings flapped. Something thumped heavily onto the roof of the building. Fel scrambled back against one wall and grasped the pick Oiler had repaired. Oiler jangled over to him and produced a happy little ding. Gleaming claws proudly presented a repaired contraption. Fel took it. The trigger was rather obvious, and when he pulled it, the effect was even more so. Something within the bowl spun at terrifying speed, and crackling sparks of blue arced from the coils to the cage. The tines at the front started zapping and sparking as well. Fel grinned wide.

"Looks like I'm through playing games, too," he said.

Oiler dove back into the mound of contraptions to pick something new to fix. Fel raised the tines toward the roof and leveled them at the buckling rooftop, where the griffin was raking at the heavy planks. Given Oiler's predilection to disarm people, Fel chose to believe the weapon was still in his hands because Oiler was too busy fixing other things. The alternative was that he was actually holding a completely harmless hair curler or similar.

Two planks of wood lifted away. Fel pulled the trigger. The contraption whizzed and hummed, sparking with an increasing intensity. His hair started to stand on end. The griffin hooked a claw through the hole and raked downward, smashing the top half of the wall. A ball of crackling blue energy formed between the tines. Bolts arced and danced across assorted metallic contraptions around him. The blocks of the wall tumbled out into the field. The contraption rattled in his hand. Fierce avian eyes locked on him through the gaping hole in the wall. Finally, the contraption delivered its payload.

What could only be called a bolt of lightning lanced from the tines of the contraption. It struck the griffin squarely in the chest. The thing screeched in pain and dropped to the ground, twitching. Fel stumbled backward and dropped the contraption. His fingers curled like dead spiders. An icy numbness had shot from his hands to his elbows the moment the thing had discharged. There would be no second shot from that device until the feeling came back in his digits. Even climbing to his feet was a challenge.

He scrambled out of the damaged wall. The stricken griffin was twitching on the ground, clearly alive but no more able to move than Fel's fingers were. The rest of the battlefield was clear, all Bolivan agents off to rescue their employer, as far as they knew. Questor struggled free of the saddle and stumbled to his feet just in time to be knocked to the ground again by the barreling body of Fel. The two tumbled across the ground until shock and desperation settled enough for the mercenary's superior training to regain its edge. He slipped a blade from an unseen sheath. Fel rolled aside to avoid being skewered.

Both men stumbled to their feet. Fel's fingers wouldn't close around the grip of his cudgel. Questor held his blade firmly. They were near enough to the burning manor for the smoke to curl about them.

"You're out of tricks, Masker," Questor said.

"Yeah, well, you're out of griffins," Fel said.

"I've seen what the beast can take. It will recover. You won't." His eyes flicked aside. "And you. With the bracer. Keep your distance."

The smoke curled about where Lattica must have been, producing a void distinct enough to keep an eye on. She held her ground but remained invisible. A jangling sound drew their attention to the storage shed. Oiler had emerged with some manner of rotating contraption. As soon as the serpentine head surveyed what was going on in the field, it dropped the contraption and hobbled forward, arms and tail extending and dragging it forward with remarkable speed. Questor turned, ready to face down the contraption, but it simply clamped the blade in its claw, wrenched it aside, and tossed it away. It then calmly jangled its way over to Fel and sat patiently.

Questor watched warily. When he tried to reach for another weapon, Oiler took a dedicated interest.

"You're going to have a hard time drawing a weapon, buddy," Fel said.

Now there was a rattling sound at the edge of the clearing. Allie was at the reins, guiding the carriage forward.

"You're outnumbered. You're unarmed. I think it's time for you to give up," Fel said.

Questor backed toward the griffin. It was through twitching and was now slowly climbing to its feet.

"I have a griffin. That's all the edge I need."

Another odd, jangling sound first drew all eyes to Oiler. The contraption was sitting still, eyes on Questor but otherwise disinterested. The sound was coming from the griffin. They turned to it, but even with Fel and the others trying to work out what was happening, it took a few seconds. Questor was the one who noticed the tiny figure, small enough that even the griffin didn't notice him, hanging from the strap that held the saddle in place.

"Don't!" Questor barked.

"See, my boss says these here saddles are what does the trick. They're what keeps the critters in line. What happens if I cut if off?" Davie said.

"It will run wild. It will kill us all," Questor said.

"The hippogriffs just flew back to the Greater Lands."

"Hippogriffs are *not* griffins, and this griffin has been here *much* longer. I have seen what that creature will do if it is not under control. You will kill us all."

"All right. Seems like I got your attention, then. Here's what'll happen," Davie said. "You try to get this thing to do anything unpleasant to us, I'll cut this off and we're all done. You try to do anything to my friends, I cut this off and we're all done. I want you to come over here, get on this thing, and fly it to wherever the big boss ran off to. I want you to tell him, on behalf of Donavan Verfessa, that you're not working for him anymore. And tell him that we're going to make sure anyone with any sense won't work with him anymore. Because we're sick and tired of him piddling on our side of the fence. You got that? And if you get airborne and decide you're going to do something *besides* that, you're going to get a face full of lightning from that whatsit over there, and I don't think you or your critter will be feeling up to fighting after a long fall."

Questor's lip curled into a snarl.

"Deal. I'm not getting paid enough for this anyway."

He made his way to the griffin and climbed to the still-shaky creature's back. Davie kept his grip until the he heard the clicked command and the monster spread its wings. He then dropped down. Fel scurried over to where he'd dropped the lightning gun. His hands still weren't up to firing it again, but *someone* would be able to.

As it turned out, it wasn't necessary. Questor, in a showing of excellent judgment, did as he was told and retreated. The monster and its rider wheeled into the sky. Fel and the others didn't move a muscle until it was out of sight. When it was gone, Fel took a deep breath and immediately hacked the smoke from his lungs.

"Everyone... thanks for the help. Let's get out of here, find somewhere safe, and get very, very drunk."

Lattica tapped the bracer and leaned heavily on his shoulder, clearly feeling the effects of the lengthy period of invisibility.

"Are we confident he won't come back?" she said.

Fel awkwardly rattled the lightning gun.

"If he does, he'll regret it. Now let's go. I'm buying."

After a frankly embarrassing amount of time, Tome finished scaling the wall. He turned back to view the Greater Lands behind him. The two remaining rangers were wheeling about, drawing nearer as they found and followed the same trail the moose had left behind. Sooner or later they would find Mevrelle, but given how badly impaired he had been by the wall, they wouldn't be able to spot Tome and the others in plain sight now that they were atop it. If the fallen ranger was lucky, his allies would find him before the dire moose did. One arrow hadn't been enough to kill the monstrous beast, and now that the shock and pain had passed, it climbed to its feet. Parch was certainly capable of spite and self-preservation, as evidenced by his almost smug look at the exhausted paper mage. For Mevrelle's sake, and Tome's if they ever crossed paths again, he hoped the moose wasn't similarly vindictive.

Tome pulled up the end of the rope and the gear tied to its end. The two big bundles held what remained of his gear, plus whatever else Teya had decided was worth throwing into the cloth sack that Tome only now realized was a robe not unlike the one he'd been given while locked up, along with Wick's lantern.

"Teya? You... didn't strip someone to get these robes to wrap up the gear, did you?"

There was no answer. He turned.

Teya was sitting with her legs dangling off the "outside" of the wall, if such a word could be applied to a structure that increasing seemed to be defying previously simple concepts like "out" and "in." She gazed over the dry fields. Reading the expression of a kobold wasn't as straightforward as reading that of a human, at least for Tome, but he didn't need to grasp the deeper nuance to see that she was in a contemplative mood. She was seeing something that her mind had refused to show her, or anyone else in her world, for centuries. The only creatures like her that were "lucky" enough to have seen this part of the world were those captured and tamed to serve as mounts or items in a menagerie.

He took a seat beside her. Parch trotted over and plopped down on the other side of her. Tome tried to assemble some sort of suitable observation for what was a momentous occasion for Teya. It was a struggle. Strange as it seemed, Fel just had a better grasp of these moments. He wasn't a deep thinker. Those things that he understood, he understood completely, and the rest he boxed up and set aside as something too big to chew on. It gave him an admirably clear view of moments like these, uncluttered by higher meaning. Tome tried to harness that clarity as he looked over the dry, craggy land, so different from the lush greenery behind them.

"Not much to look at," he said.

"So much to see," Teya countered.

Tome peered down.

"We aren't where I left the carriage."

"Need help?" Teya said.

"I'm not sure your first introduction to the land beyond the Greater Lands Wall should be trudging through dry grass looking for an old, broken wagon. There is bound to be an accessible door or hatch to get inside the wall. Compared to what I've been coping with out there, the deathtraps of the wall will be a welcome relief."

Teya nodded.

"What's next for you?" he asked.

She shrugged. "Back home. For now."

"You'll be safe?"

Teya motioned with her head. "Friends watch. Friends help. They find me."

"That's good." Tome paused. "About the earring."

"I keep."

"I don't know if that's wise. That earring represents a key to a cage that, it can be reasonably argued, is keeping the best of my people safe from the worst of yours. I'm not so sure I am comfortable with the idea of it existing within the wall, even if it's in good hands. Things can change hands."

Teya nodded. "You think good. Still. I keep earring. I like. Is pretty. Is precious."

"I don't think that's—"

Teya raised a claw to silence him.

"Didn't ask. Told."

"I... well... be careful with it."

"Always careful."

She hopped to her feet and took a long, satisfied breath.

"I go. Be safe. And Fel?" She gave her earring a tap. "See him soon, maybe."

She took her unused bow and arrows, along with what other bits of her equipment were among the gear bundles, and trotted along the wall with a jaunty spring in her step. Tome watched her go and wondered if he could ever so freely and calmly accept such absurdity. Half of him feared he would have to. Half of him envied that she already could.

"Come on, Parch. Let's find our way home."

EPILOGUE

Five weeks later...

Allie took a deep breath and gazed up to the eponymous Fox and Log above the door. The whole place smelled of green wood, oil, and polish. It smelled new. She took another whiff. It would never smell this way again. Even now, thirsty regulars forced to put up with the mediocre service or sky-high prices of one of the other three watering holes in town were eager to wet their whistles in the new-and-improved tavern. She had to hand it to Verfessa. His workers may have taken a bit longer than they'd said they would, but their work was exquisite. And every last recommendation she'd made had been taken. The place was a third again larger, thanks to a whole new trio of small private rooms replacing a back alley that had mostly been a place to leave empty kegs. A neat little raised platform in one corner would host bands once a week and two additional tables the rest of the time. The storage had been moved downstairs, leaving the back room to serve as a proper office and break room for the staff. It was in every way better, with one possible exception.

Verfessa had kept his word during her absence. He'd paid her bills with such subtlety that the man she rented her room from hadn't even noticed she was gone. A sum had been left in her apron when she arrived this morning. It covered the costs of the trip and then some. So far she'd had no reason to believe that having Verfessa as one of her employers was going to be a bad thing. But her intuition was not quiet about warning her that the dangerous errand she'd just gotten through with wasn't likely to be her last. As if to underscore that notion, included with the money in her apron was a note instructing her that she should consider the smallest of the three new rooms "the boss's suite," and it should be kept clear for "important business."

"Oovay!" Allie shouted. "We're about to open the doors!"

"I am in my room!" Oovay called from what she would have to remember to start referring to as "the office."

"It isn't your room."

"There's a cushion on the chair now. I'm not leaving."

"You're going to need that cushion if you don't get out here for the grand opening. And do I have a runner or not?"

The hatch behind the door inched open, and Davie scurried out from below.

"Just checking the stocks, Allie," he said, handing up a rag.

"Sure you were." She took the rag and tucked it into the front pocket of her apron. "Let's let in the rabble, I guess."

She opened the doors. The patrons who showed up for doors-open were usually a small assortment of elderly folks with nothing better to do on a given day and young folks with plenty of better things to do but no desire to do them. Today it was nearly the same crowd that had been ushered out the door so many weeks prior when they'd closed, as if they had been waiting outside since then.

Drink orders came fast and frequently. Within the first hour they had made as much as they would have made on an average day prior to having the work done. And by the second hour one of the people she'd been hoping to see plopped onto one of the brand-new stools.

"Hey! Fel. Surprised it took you so long," Allie said, sliding a basket of crickets in front of him.

"What can I say? You leave town for a few weeks and a ton of work piles up. Those heaps of silver aren't going to tote themselves around town."

Little clopping hooves tapped across the floor, and Parch hopped up onto the neighboring stool.

"And just like that, we've got our first barnyard animal in here," Allie joked. "Nice to get that out of the way."

"Hey. Parch isn't a barnyard animal. He's a working stiff like the rest of us."

She filled a dish with water and placed it in front of him. "I didn't kick him out, did I?"

Fel crunched some crickets while Parch drained the dish.

"No grum game yet?" he said, glancing at the table in the same general place his usual game was played.

"Why, impatient about losing another week's earnings?"

"I'm just wondering if Tem's going to have to find another place to fleece people."

"Oh, there'll still be games. He just hasn't shown up yet. So, what do you think of the place?"

"Looking good. Kind of looks like I won't be able to afford to drink here anymore."

"It wouldn't be The Fox and Log if the booze wasn't cheap," Allie said.

Fel scratched his head. "It feels strange. Normally I'd be in here talking your ear off, but you already heard all my stories on the way home, and I already heard yours."

"Yeah. Let's not do that again. Your sterling personality isn't enough to hold a girl's attention once she knows both sides of your stories."

"Eh, I'm sure I'll get myself into more interesting trouble soon enough." He glanced toward the door. "Speaking of troublemakers, look who it is!"

Mariss stepped through the doorway with a cloth-covered basket. She plopped onto the stool beside Fel.

"A little early in the day for you to be here," Allie said.

"I took a half day. It seemed like an occasion!" She set the basket down. "Spiced apple tarts. One for you, Fel, and Davie."

"Well what have we here?" slurred one of the new faces the reopening had attracted.

He'd been imbibing at a rate that was likely to see him asleep on the curb before suppertime, and was tottering toward Mariss with a not-entirely-gentlemanly look in his eye.

"You got something sweet in that basket for…"

He trailed off as Mariss gave him a hard look that cut straight through the haze of alcohol. He shakily pivoted and returned to the booth he'd been in for the last few hours.

"Mariss, you going to be here a few hours, at least?" Fel asked.

"Oh, I don't know," she said.

"Epiphany and Euphoria are going to be in here in a bit," Fel said. "You've *got* to tell them about that stunt you pulled up in the mountains, when they tried to steal the, uh, fancy backpack."

She grinned. "I suppose I can stick around for that. It *is* my best story."

Tome wearily turned the page in the latest of the books he'd begun working his way through. The past few weeks since his return to Beffshire had been blissfully tedious and educational in precisely the way he needed after the madness in the Greater Lands. Some of the education he'd received had been observational. He had yet to fully recover from the spells he'd cast while on the other side of the wall. He wasn't nearly as exhausted as he had been during the journey home, but he still didn't feel right. If he thought he'd opened a new page in his mystic journey, the slow recovery set him straight about that.

The vast majority of what he'd learned came from the books he'd hauled back from the Greater Lands Wall's archive. It was almost entirely written in a language he scarcely understood at the time. But while Martin worked through the technical information in his half of the selections, Tome had indulged himself in an ingenious suggestion of Martin's.

"And this sentence here? True or false, it translates to: 'The forces were turned back, but not before a scout reached the records room,'" he said.

"False," the Student said, twinkling eyes glancing down along the page. "The final word is 'hall' not room."

"Excellent," Tome said, making a note in his own book.

Under the guise of a series of short tests and lessons, Tome had been teasing a deeper understanding of this ancient language out of the Student while Wick looked on. Since Euphoria hadn't left yet, Tome had taken advantage of the extra inventory that had been cleared out thanks to her time behind the counter and assembled something of a classroom in the partially cleared storage area.

He rubbed his eyes.

"I think that will do for today. I've reached my limit."

"Wonderful. Thank you for the valuable additions, both to my knowledge of history and in underscoring my linguistic knowledge," the Student said.

"Happy to be of service," Tome said.

He inserted the dagger to put the Student to sleep. It was still whirring down when Martin appeared in the doorway.

"Any valuable discoveries?" he asked.

"Many. Though I'm already kicking myself for my oversight. This appears to be the fifth book in a series of eight chronicling 'significant moments in military history.' I misunderstood the index, so I only have the third, fifth, and eighth books. Without full context, they're not quite as educational as I'd hoped. But I wish I had the stamina to keep the lesson going, because I am *quite* certain this is the attack that led to the destruction of the Telestressa Archives. I know *that* there was some sort of a regional skirmish at the time, but I don't know against whom, and I don't know why."

Tome glanced at Wick.

"I wonder if you've got any additional insight," he said.

Tome had shared Wick's connection with the fallen archives with Martin. The revelation likely would have left more of an impression on him if he hadn't gotten a heap of ancient texts at the same time.

"I do not know," Wick said. "My greatest shame is my lack of observation on that day."

"How are you feeling today, Wick?" Martin asked, revealing a journal and readying a pen in much the same way a doctor might. "Any improvement?"

"Like Tome, I have had some small improvement. I still feel... limited. Moving from lantern to lantern still takes more effort. My vision does not pierce as far into the darkness. I believe I will fully recover, but it may take weeks more."

"Better news than we might have had. You didn't sound very confident in that a few days ago."

"I have had a considerable amount of time to be introspective. I was not created to assess myself, but since my return, you have requested that I do so, and it has become a service I feel comfortable in my capacity to provide.

Doing so has revealed much. And in that introspection, I have come to a decision."

"Oh?" Martin said.

"I was unaware you were in a position to be *making* decisions," Tome said.

"On certain matters, when asked to elaborate on statements, I have suggested that some matters would be best left without discussion. There is one such matter that may warrant discussion after all."

"Let's hear it," Tome said.

"In my existence, I have had no need for things like fear. Fear exists for those who have something to lose. A life, for instance. And I do not fear the loss of life, because it is not accurate to say that I have life to begin with. Or so I thought. Death, it seemed, was necessary in order for something to be considered to be alive. And with the assault on my being committed by the elves, it is clear that my existence can end. Thus, it may indeed be accurate to say that I am alive. And yet, I still do not fear for my own existence, nor do I fear its end. My value is not intrinsic to my existence. However, I am not without value. That value lies in the information I have accumulated."

"You've observed much in your existence, life or not," Martin said.

"That is the tiniest fraction of what I contain, Martin," Wick said. "My last role, before coming into the fulfilling service of your family, had been to observe the Telestressa Archives. As you know, and I know all too well, I failed. The archives burned. It is important to me that you understand a crucial detail of that day."

Martin's eyes drifted up to meet Tome's gaze.

"By the High, it was with your flame, wasn't it?" he said.

"Not entirely. Lanterns were thrown through several windows. Only one was mine. But some proportion of the Telestressa Archives was consumed in my flames before I was extinguished. The knowledge I have gleaned from this is incomplete. In some cases I know only the first few lines of a page, the rest consumed in flames from some other source. But even so, the information contained within me cannot simply be *removed*. I can only speak. And if from this day forward I did nothing but dictate things from those pages, it would take centuries for the information to be liberated from within me. That information may as well be lost. But it was *not* lost. And there was some solace to the knowledge that as long as I existed, so too did some of the knowledge I was meant to protect. And because I could not be destroyed, neither could that knowledge. But a few weeks ago, I could well have been lost, and that information taken with me."

"In what way is that information available to you?"

"It is an incomprehensible jumble," Wick said. "It exists within me, but accessing it is no more swift than thumbing through the pages. It may as well be worthless. But it exists only within me now."

"This changes everything..." Martin said.

"Does it?" Tome said. "I'll admit it is a significant discovery, but if even *he* can't make sense of that information, what good does it do anyone?"

Martin headed for the door.

"A problem can only be solved once we are made aware of it. And I am nothing if not a problem solver. Now I'll have something specific to work toward." He grinned as he hurried toward his shop. "Splendid..."

It was well into that first night of the new Fox and Log, and already it was clear things were going to be much busier than they had ever been before. Mariss had left when she started to get tipsy, having stayed just barely long enough to recount her anecdote to the Masker sisters once they arrived. Since then, the drinks had been flowing freely. Once they had had enough drinks to slide a few inches past the point of good judgment, both Euphoria and Epiphany agreed to join Fel at the grum table. The result was likely to go down in history as the most volatile game of grum ever played.

Tem, despite being the local master of the game, washed out fairly early. Between Fel's gradually increasing skill, Epiphany's conservative play, and Euphoria's legendary bluffing prowess, he simply didn't have a chance. Once it was down to the three of them, however, the money shifted and slid across the table almost at random with every game. The siblings knew each other well enough to see through even the steadiest expressions. Tactics evolved over the course of the night as they worked out each other's idiosyncrasies. An entirely separate game was made of spectators betting on who would win a given run.

In what would prove to be an ongoing problem for him, Fel finally busted almost entirely due to his heroic intake of ale, leaving his judgment even more askew than usual and eventually cleaning out his pockets. Now he sat and watched as Epiphany and Euphoria waged a war of attrition over the heap of duots.

Fel turned when he heard a boisterous laugh from near the doorway.

"I swear he used to be a recluse," he said.

Donovan Verfessa had come to see what was being made of his investment. From the smile on his face, he was pleased. Fel pushed himself away from the table.

"Something tells me this won't last too much longer, but see if you can stretch it out until I get back. I've got some business to do," Fel said.

He navigated the crowded floor until he reached Verfessa. There were few who knew who he was simply by looking at him. He may as well have simply been an avuncular fellow and not the most potent member of the local underworld.

"Fel! Glad to see you. Been meaning to tell you, you did a fine job on —"

"I want a word with you, *Don*," he said.

Verfessa raised his eyebrows. "That doesn't sound like it will be pleasant. Wasn't looking to do business here tonight, but when duty calls..."

Verfessa turned and motioned to Allie. She nodded.

"To my office, shall we?"

They maneuvered to the small room in the back corner. The door did an impressively good job at keeping the sound of the boisterous crowd out. Fel lit the lantern inside with his sparker, and they sat on either side of a table that took up most of the space within.

"What's the good word, Masker?" Verfessa asked.

"I'll make it quick. We pulled a lot of gear off the Bolivans while we were doing our trip."

"Yeah?"

"A lot of crossbows. A lot of contraptions. One of the ones that made the Bolivans a constant threat was the bracer."

"The one that makes them invisible?"

"That's the one."

356

"Doesn't come as a surprise."

"Funny thing about those bracers. They're really, *really* rare. Best guess Dad had was that there are maybe a dozen of them in total. Maybe half that are actually functional. But we just *keep finding them* on the Bolivans."

"Tough to know how many there are."

"Uh-huh. Your crew must have got a few of them, what with how many times you butted heads with the Bolivans in Beffshire."

"One or two."

"What ever happened to them?"

"I'm a businessman, Fel. I think you can work it out."

"Sold."

"For a tidy sum, thanks to your father's repair work and your mother's appraisal."

"That's funny, too. You mentioning my dad and him fixing them. Because there's a thing Dad does. When he's fixing something and he fabricates a part, one that doesn't need any of the Bygone stuff to still work, he likes to put the Masker maker's mark on there. The first bracer I grabbed during our recent mission? Pulled right off the arm of a Bolivan? It had his mark."

"Your point, son?" Verfessa said.

"Considering how many times the Bolivans tried to kill me, I'm a little curious how they ended up with a bracer that my Dad worked on."

"I'd say they bought it on the black market."

"They bought it from *you*. You're the one who sold it."

Verfessa leaned back in his chair and crossed his boots on the table.

"You're upset, and you're a little in the bottle, so I won't hold it against you that you aren't thinking straight, but why do you think I would sell something like that to someone I was trying to run out of town?"

"That's what *I'm* asking *you*."

"I didn't sell it to a Bolivan. I just *sold* it. Whoever bought it from me sold it to a Bolivan. Or sold it to someone who sold it to someone, you get the idea."

"How could you let them get their hands on it?"

"When it's out of my hands, it's out of my hands. That's just how things go."

"I could have been killed because you couldn't resist selling one of those things?"

"I sent one of my men after you to save your life. I'd say that balances the ledger."

"That just makes us even," Fel said.

"That'd be what 'balances the ledger' means, Fel."

Fel blinked. "Point is, if this business is going to be putting weapons right back in the hands of the people who want to use them against us, I don't think it's a business the Maskers ought to be in."

"And I don't think you're the one who gets to make that decision."

"Trust me, I'll be taking it to Mom and Dad."

"That's your right. You're welcome to talk it over with anybody. But the Maskers would've had a much harder time these last few months without the muscle I swing in this town. You cut this venture short, you lose that. And I have to find someone else to work with. You may not like how I do business, but I don't think you want me doing it with someone else. Could go bad for you."

"Is that a threat?"

"That's just a consequence, Fel. Of course, this is all hypothetical. Because I still like you. Maybe a bit less when you're drunk. But I think we've got a future, your family and my organization. So give yourself some time to cool off, talk it over with the folks, and see what you think. Your mom in particular is pretty sharp. I think she'll set you straight on the reality of it all."

"Mom's tried to set me straight on a lot of stuff, Don. It didn't all stick. I'm keeping my eye on you. That's all I'm saying."

"As you should. We're certainly keeping our eyes on you. A little distrust is healthy. Shows you're using your head."

Fel narrowed his eyes. The unflappable Verfessa just put his hands behind his head and grinned.

"I get the feeling you're not an easy man to intimidate."

"Trust the feeling, my boy."

Rather than drag the little confrontation on any further, particularly given how little impact it had, Fel decided to take his leave.

The stepped out of the room. The grum game was still going, and the press of the crowd was such that he didn't feel like fighting his way back to see how the sisters were fairing against one another. He decided to slide along the outside of the crowd. With any luck he'd spot Tem and get some well-earned ribbing done. Instead, he spotted another familiar face. Lattica Graves.

"… And then, this guy? What does he do? He sets the building on fire. *Before he has a plan to get out!*" she laughs.

"Hey, hey, hey," Fel said, stepping up beside her. "You talking about me?"

"You know anyone else who'd pull a stunt like that?" Lattica asked.

"No one who'd survive it. I thought for sure you'd be back with the gear, getting ready to escort Fora on her trip home," he said.

Lattica turned from the others, letting her voice drop to a volume that was just below shouting. With the place this busy, it may as well have been a whisper for Fel's ears only.

"Technically I was supposed to head straight home on our way back from up north. Then I was supposed to load up the gear and head home two weeks ago with some Beffshire goods for sale. So this is just the latest change to the plan."

"Lattica Graves not sticking to a previously established plan?"

"A bit of your improvisational style rubbed off on me. What can I say? Now that I won't have an impulsive oaf as a partner I've got to conjure up some of my own impulses now and then."

"That all you picked up during this little journey?"

"Not everything, no. Five weeks in Beffshire without anyone sending me off to thump heads in the name of my in-laws has given me some time to think."

"I don't know, Lattica. Thinking is dangerous."

"Only when you're really bad at it or really good at it. Point is, I'm starting to think I can't hide behind a pile of procedures and such."

"So what's that mean?"

"Let's just say I'll be saying my piece at the next family get together. Taking a bit more control over my life."

"How do you figure that'll go?"

She laughed. "Oh, the Graves family is no stranger to negotiation. I'm sure they'll have seen this coming."

The crowd roared.

"Sounds like one of your sisters finally won," Lattica said.

"Oh, I've got to see this. Hey, don't be a stranger! I've never been much of a fan of the Graves clan, but between you and Fora, it seems like they've got good taste at least."

"Yeah, yeah. Just get out there and congratulate the winner."

Fel pushed his way toward the grum area. Sure enough, the game was over. He hurried back to the table just in time to see Euphoria pushing the last of her duots over to Epiphany.

"Ha-*ha!*" Fel said, slapping her on the back. "I didn't know you had it in you, Fanny."

"Nor did I," said Euphoria. "I don't imagine I'll be likely to make grum a pastime. At least not with you two at the table."

"Come on, Fora. How do you expect to get even if you don't give it another try?" Fel said.

"I prefer to cut my losses." She stood. "I'll be heading home in the morning, and I don't intend to lighten my purse any more before then. In fact, I have a long trip ahead. I should turn in."

"So what's next?" Fel said.

"I head home, as I said. Lattica is there already. By now the Voice will be back in use, ideally with a bit more security. We'll have to discuss how or why one of the lanterns was... what was it? A command lantern? And why it was not in our possession."

"Are we going to have to wait another three years before we see you again?" Epiphany said.

"Considering how successful this little collaboration was, I suspect the Graves family will be quite willing to collaborate again."

"I think I speak for Fanny when I say we couldn't care less what the Graves family thinks about collaboration. Regardless of what they say, don't be a stranger. You're family."

"I won't forget it again. Fel, Fanny, I'll see you at breakfast."

She gathered her things and took her leave. Fel sat down and rubbed his head.

"It's been... quite a few weeks," he said.

"That it has." Fanny deftly gathered up her winnings and separated the grum tiles from them. "Tell you what, Fel. I'll buy you a drink. Let's enjoy our night. Who knows what sort of business we'll be getting into tomorrow?"

FROM THE AUTHOR

Thank you for reading! If you liked this story, or perhaps if you found it lacking, I'd love to hear from you. For free stories and important updates, join my newsletter at: www.bookofdeacon.com

Discover other titles by Joseph R. Lallo:

The Book of Deacon Series

An epic fantasy series spanning six main novels and assorted spin-offs and prequels. Follow the journey of Myranda Celeste and the rest of the Chosen as they fight to save their world from a terrible war and its aftermath.

The Big Sigma Series

A sci-fi action adventure series with six novels. Trevor "Lex" Alexander is a former hover-racer who finds his world turned upside down when he becomes embroiled in the schemes of mega-corporations, criminal syndicates, and a mad engineer with a quirky AI.

The Free-Wrench Series

Take to the skies in this six novel steampunk series about airships in an era of steam, brass, and excitement. Nita Graus joins the Wind Breaker crew, a group of smugglers in a constant clash with the twisted and nefarious fug folk who run the world from their place in the toxic mists that blanket the land.

The Shards of Shadow Series

An ongoing Urban Fantasy series following the trials and tribulations of a photographer named Alan who unwittingly becomes entangled in the dark machinations of the shadowy shades thanks to Blot, one of their weakest agents. These exciting stories take place in modern day Philadelphia and shed light on the supernatural invasion that could tip the balance of power for the entire world.

The Greater Lands Saga

An epic fantasy adventure in a world where magic and supernatural contraptions coexist. Fel Masker is an explorer and adventurer, tasked with securing mysterious, arcane devices for his family to repair and sell. Rivalries with other contraptioneering families are heating up, and soon the lost history of the world may return with a vengeance.

www.ingramcontent.com/pod-product-compliance
Lightning Source LLC
Chambersburg PA
CBHW070742190726
48292CB00002B/377